SALVATION—OR MADNESS

Avall felt a fist of fear clamp around his heart. This wasn't real, simply wasn't happening. These were his *friends,* yet they were trying to force him to do something he feared beyond all reasonable fear. He was King, too, and they his council. If he said no, his word had the force of Law.

And if there was civil war in Eron, it would be his fault.

There was not, he realized dully, any option that didn't result in pain. One way or another, he was doomed. It only remained to work out what form that doom would take. Trouble was, he wanted to *be* a good King, to be *remembered* as such.

He recalled how the last time he'd worked with the master gem it had sucked at him, though not quite as badly as on the previous occasion. And he also remembered what a short while that linkage had lasted. One could endure anything if one knew how long one must endure it.

"I'll do it," he announced. "But I'm not responsible for the consequences."

"Consequences?"—from Tyrill.

Avall regarded her levelly. "This could kill me or drive me mad," he informed her flatly. "I'd suggest you start considering my successor—if you aren't already."

SUMMERBLOOD

A TALE OF ERON

TOM DEITZ

BANTAM BOOKS
New York Toronto London Sydney Auckland

SUMMERBLOOD
A Bantam Spectra Book

PUBLISHING HISTORY
Bantam Spectra trade paperback edition / April 2001
Bantam Spectra mass market edition / March 2002

SPECTRA and the portrayal of a boxed "s" are trademarks of
Bantam Books, a division of Random House, Inc.

ISBN 0-553-58206-2

Published simultaneously in the United States and Canada

Bantam Books are published by Bantam Books, a division
of Random House, Inc. Its trademark, consisting of the words
"Bantam Books" and the portrayal of a rooster, is Registered in U.S.
Patent and Trademark Office and in other countries. Marca Registrada.
Bantam Books, 1540 Broadway, New York, New York 10036.

PRINTED IN THE UNITED STATES OF AMERICA

OPM 10 9 8 7 6 5 4 3 2 1

For Soren, Leif, Steve, and Janet
would that I had met you all sooner

Acknowledgments

John Butler
T. J. Cochran
Ashley Goodin
Anne Groell
Deena McKinney
Howard Morhaim
Lindsay Sagnette
Juliet Ulman

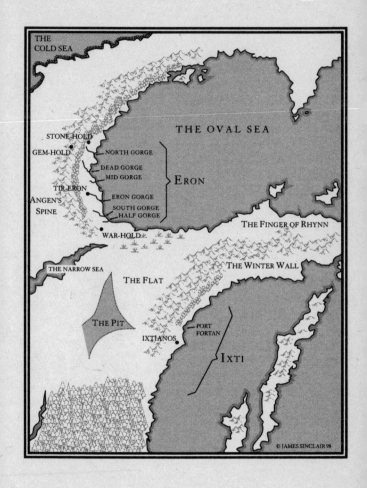

PART I

CHAPTER I:

TESTS AND TEMPERING

(ERON: TIR-ERON—HIGH SUMMER: DAY XL—MIDDAY)

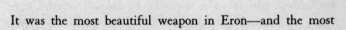

It was the most beautiful weapon in Eron—and the most deadly.

It was one of the three most beautiful *objects* in Eron, and had been made, in large part, by Eron's most beautiful woman. Who also happened to be its best bladesmith—and its third best smith of any kind.

Never mind that she was Avall syn Argen-a's wife, and thereby consort to the High King of all Eron.

None of which explained Avall's reluctance to touch that weapon now.

The Lightning Sword, some had begun to style it, though it wasn't lightning that blade brought from the Overworld, but something less easily defined—and more potent.

Avall's slim, callused hand hovered a finger's length above the gold-leafed ropework casting that comprised the hilt. A ruddy gem gleamed balefully midway along its length—a gem there was good reason to assume was what most of his countrymen would have called magic.

That was why he hesitated, swallowing apprehensively, as he let his gaze slide around the room.

It was the topmost chamber of the least-used tower in the lofty, rough-rock pile called the Citadel, which was the seat of Eron's High King—which title, for a quarter year, and much against his will, was now Avall's. The walls slanted slightly inward and were made of beige sandstone, smoothed to an even, grainy finish, but with no ornamentation save a band of interlace relief at waist level. The floor was stone as well, beneath vaults of a different stone, and the sturdy oak table-safe against the wall opposite the single door was likewise hewn from stone. Narrow windows marking three cardinal directions matched the door for height; and the warm light of summer afternoon lanced in through the western one, flooding the chamber with a cheery radiance at odds with Avall's anxious scowl.

His shadow brushed a pair of stone benches flanking the oak-barred entrance, the nearer of which was occupied by his two closest friends—who appeared by turns frustrated, nervous, and impatient, clutching, as they did, the rest of the royal regalia. The younger, his cousin, Lykkon syn Argen-a, would be twenty the upcoming autumn; the elder, Avall's bond-brother, Rann syn Eemon-arr, would be twenty-one at summer's end. Like Avall himself, they were middle-sized young men, tending toward slim, as did most of their countrymen, and with the near-ubiquitous dark blue eyes and handsome, angular faces of High Clan Eronese. At the moment, all three sported short-cropped black hair growing out from the close-clip they'd affected during the recent war with their southern neighbor, but shoulder length was far more typical.

They were even dressed alike, in soft indoor slippers, house-hose, and short-tunics that favored their slender bodies. Avall and Lykkon were in Argen's maroon; Rann, in Eemon's midnight-blue, quartered with Stone's black and silver. An incredibly beautiful shield spanned the space between the floor and Lykkon's knees. Kite-shaped, it was, though curved; made of alloys the working of which was denied to Avall's sept of Smithcraft; and ornamented with patterns that, while not quite traditional interlace, nevertheless evoked it.

Rann held the helm in his lap. A gem identical to that in the sword gleamed between the gilded-bronze browridges—a gem Avall had found himself, when the helm had merely been part of a commission for a now-incapacitated King, and he but an ordinary smith, newly raised to manhood. Were it not for the gleaming nasal between the gaping eye sockets, it would strongly resemble a skull; what with its gently domed crown, and the angular cheek guards to either side that mimicked jawbones.

Lykkon exhaled pointedly, drumming his fingers on the shield's upper rim. "It won't bite," he chided, when Avall's hand showed no sign of moving.

A deep breath, and Avall picked up the sword—by the scabbard, yet even so it nudged at him, like a pet demanding notice. Or a serpent poised to strike. Turning, he motioned his companions to their feet and unlocked the door one-handed, before following them out and to the left, up a curving stair that spat them out on the roof one level higher. Inward-curving merlons rose around them like stone fingers—though whether they shielded those within or the world without, Avall wasn't certain. Only two of the Citadel's towers rose higher, visible as shadows against the north face of the gorge in which Tir-Eron lay. Lore's tower was taller, too, but it was farther down the Ri-Eron and blocked from view by the stair turret. Not that height was needed in any case, as much as the privacy it afforded. For, in spite of being utterly exposed, no one else in Tir-Eron could see what transpired there.

"I'm trying to test some things," Avall told Rann, who stood nearest. "And while this isn't the best place for what I plan, it's the only one available without traveling for at least a hand."

Rann's reply was one of those absent, preoccupied nods that served him as conversation of late.

A shadow flickered across Avall's face, but he suppressed the urge to confront its cause. There'd be time for that later: time and more time. "Lyk," he continued pointedly, "I probably don't need to tell you this, but I want you to observe this *very* closely."

Lykkon likewise nodded, and stepped closer to the stone table that Avall had caused to be erected, with great secrecy, in the middle of the tower three days before.

Atop the polished granite lay a hand-thick slab of the strongest steel Eronese metalsmiths had yet contrived. That, in turn, was covered by a span-wide strip of white velvet, which shrouded an oblong mass raised another hand above the steel.

Avall whisked the fabric away, revealing a series of identically sized ingots of every major metal known in Eron, ranged from soft gold and tin to alloyed iron, all interspersed with lengths of oak, ash, pine, and maple, and four kinds of glass. The whole row was slightly shorter than the sword blade.

" 'Waiting proves nothing but patience,' " Avall informed Lykkon, to preempt his cousin quoting the ancient proverb. And with that, he retrieved the helm from Rann and set it upon his head, twisting his neck to ensure a proper seat, while Rann moved to buckle it beneath his chin. A metallic rustle to his left was Lykkon fitting the shield to his outstretched arm. Avall fumbled for the grip, careful not to trigger what a onetime rival had set there.

And then there was no more cause for delay. Waving his friends back to the relative safety of the turret, he slapped his free hand against the helm in a certain way, even as his other squeezed the shield's grip. Hidden studs triggered hidden barbs in helm and shield alike, and metal bit into his flesh, drawing blood, then feeding it by embedded lengths of rare bloodwire to the thumb-sized red stones gleaming between his eyes and within his fist. A deep breath, and he unsheathed the sword, fingers already seeking one final trigger.

Found—and then that hand, too, fed the gems blood.

And with that feeding, Avall was fed in turn.

Power ran up his arm from the sword, and met more rushing toward it from the shield, and the two collided in his brain, which was itself being empowered by the gem in the helm.

And so he stood there, poised and tense, as his mind sought to wrest those forces into balance.

A moment it took, while they warred within him, for the regalia had been made for the previous High King and suited the paths of his mind more precisely than Avall's. Then, abruptly, he was ready. Had he wanted to call down lightning to smash the surrounding stones or reduce his companions to chunks of charred meat, he could have done so with a twitch of a finger.

Yet when he closed his eyes and envisioned the Overworld, and the sword ripping a gateway through to that place, and gathering up matter there like jam scooped onto a knife, he tried to make the smallest rent possible and retrieve the merest mite of Overworldly matter he could manage.

Even so, the sword tingled in his hand.

And when he could wait no longer—when the sword was like his impassioned manhood desperate for release in the throes of lust—he slowly lowered it until the blade was a finger above the ingots.

And let it fall.

Metal rang, and the sky rang, and power flowed out of him like water from a broken jar. The world turned stark white for half a breath, and smelled of hot ores and scorched wood. Rather like a forge smelled, actually. But if this was a forge, Avall was Lord Craft himself—and it was blasphemy to claim so close an identity with The Eight.

He was vaguely aware of Lykkon easing nearer, and of Rann hanging back, before his vision cleared enough to witness what he had wrought.

The sword had sheared through the wood like a scythe through new grain, and the path of its passing showed clear down to the underlying steel, which had also begun to part. The other ingots had likewise been sundered. Which he'd expected. What he'd been curious about was how the damage would manifest beyond the point of impact—to determine whether it was heat or some *other* energy that accompanied the weapon's use.

"What do you think, Lyk?" he asked his kinsman.

Lykkon fanned smoke away and squinted closer. "As best I can tell, there's no correlation between melting points of metal and extent of damage. The steel shows signs of damage farther out than the lead, and the tin's just cut straight through, with no sign of melting at all."

Avall blinked within his helm. "And the glass?"

"Raise the sword."

Avall did—and found that the blade did not come away cleanly. Instead, one glass ingot rose with it, as though the sword were a log that had frozen in ice. Lykkon touched the ingot gingerly, then gave it an experimental tug. It resisted briefly, then came free—showing a narrow channel where the blade had been. But no sign of melting.

"Not the same effect," he mused. "Beyond that, I'll need to do some measuring. But my guess—" He paused and looked at Avall. "My guess is that some substances either go straight to smoke and vapor—or straight to the Overworld."

Avall could wait no longer. Resheathing the sword, he snaked his other arm free of the shield, then reached up to remove the helmet, grateful to taste clear air and see open sky. Setting the regalia aside as though it were any Common Clan soldier's gear, he inspected the ingot more closely. "You're right," he agreed. "Not much melting."

"Which means?"

A shrug. "You tell me."

Lykkon scowled. "I don't know *what* it means. But if we're right: If that thing draws matter from the Overworld, which manifests here as energy, like the shield sends energy from here to there, where it manifests as—well, we don't *know* how it manifests—I think what we have here is a case where you've sent *matter* to the Overworld. Otherwise, there'd be some sign of melting along all the relevant junctures, and there isn't."

"You said it could've vaporized," Rann reminded him.

Lykkon shrugged. "There's no way to tell at present. I'll have to think of some way to test that notion. For now—"

"For now," Avall finished for him, "I've had enough experimenting." Without waiting either comment or consent—he was, after all, King—he distributed the regalia among his comrades and shooed them back into the tower. A trickle of blood slid into one eye, from where the helm-gem's trigger had pricked him. He rubbed at it absently: the price one paid for knowledge.

They paused in the holding chamber only long enough to return the regalia to the table-safe and lock the door, before continuing down another level to a room that was far more opulent than the austere one above. These walls were covered with fine tapestries, the floors with luxurious carpet, and the furniture, though sparse, was comfortable. A small table by the door held a carafe of wine, chilling beside three golden goblets—which Lykkon filled without asking. Rann found a sofa and flopped down in it, looking listless. Avall settled beside him, closer than the sofa's size required. He stroked Rann's thigh absently, the familiar flesh hard and sleek beneath the thin sylk of summer hose. "So," he began, accepting a goblet from Lykkon with his free hand, "what am I going to do with what's upstairs? I've given myself two days to decide, and two days aren't sufficient."

"You've had two *eights*," Lykkon retorted. "You've also had opinions from everyone from Tyrill and Preedor down to my brother, Bingg. I can't tally the times you and I have hashed this out, or—I imagine—you and Strynn and Merryn. And Rann," he finished awkwardly, looking flustered.

Avall didn't know if he likewise looked flustered, but he certainly felt that way, given that Rann was paying them no mind at all. Not from spite or rudeness, he knew, but for another reason. Rann's Common Clan lover, Div, had departed Tir-Eron two eights ago as part of an escort for the royal harper, Kylin, who wanted to retrieve his chief-harp from Gem-Hold-Winter. Which was convenient, since Div also needed to secure a few things from the hold she'd appropriated in the Wild, before closing the place for good—so everyone assumed—and returning to Tir-Eron, where she had an appointment in the Royal Guard. Rann had been listless and distracted ever since, in spite of Avall's efforts to keep him occupied. Not for the first time did he wonder how Rann comported himself when the two of them were apart. Then again, he and Rann had a formal bond, with the security thereby implied. Rann had no guarantee Div would return, beyond her word. Given the difference between their ages and stations, there was reason to think she might not.

Rann patted Avall's hand. "I'm sorry, Vall," he murmured. "I just don't have anything to add."

Avall stood abruptly. Suddenly furious, he stomped to the window and leaned against its casement, glowering. "Dammit, dammit, dammit!" he spat. "You lads are no help at all. You're supposed to be my friends. More to the point, you're supposed to be royal advisers, you're supposed to—"

"We're *not* supposed to make decisions for you," Lykkon broke in harshly. "That's part of being King."

"Which I never wanted to be," Avall shot back. "Which you know perfectly well."

"Because you've told everyone in sight every time you've seen them since it happened," Rann muttered.

"And I still say," Lykkon added, "that if you'd try to like it, you might find you actually do. It can't be that bad, Vall. Anything you really can't manage, you can foist off on someone else. If you're clever, you can foist off nearly everything."

"Except the wretched regalia," Avall growled.

"Which isn't necessarily bad," Rann inserted. "It adds fear to the equation you've already got."

"Which would be?"

A resigned sigh. "Liking and respect—which are *not* the same. Those of us who know you, by and large like you. Those who don't know you—which includes everyone who was at the Battle of the Storms last spring—still respect you for what you can do."

"Story of my life," Avall snorted. "No one cares who I am, only what I can do, and more to the point these days, what I can do for them. I had no idea there were so many needy people in Eron—not in need of food or material goods, but for someone to *think* for them. I had no notion how badly the plague had gutted this country. How many whole clans have no one with passion enough to act quickly and accept change, yet who also have sufficient experience to distinguish between risk and foolhardiness."

Lykkon chuckled. "You sound like you're a thousand years old."

"I feel like it, too—sometimes. But the fact is, we're a nation of old people, who are mostly set in their ways, and those like ourselves, who are barely more than children and who get tired of running into a rule or a rite every time we turn around. We've *no* folk who are neither tired of making decisions, nor scared to make them. Look at us. None of us has either father or one-father. Lyk, you don't even have a mother."

"Which has nothing to do with why you can't decide what to do about the regalia," Lykkon observed quietly. "You also sounded like you had a second point—before you so conveniently distracted yourself into another whining session."

Avall felt another stir of anger, though he wasn't certain if it was his *self* that felt it, or his uncomfortable royal persona. He fought it down ruthlessly.

"What I was going to say," he continued with forced calm, "was that the mere existence of the regalia—especially the sword, which the lower clans seem to think is the key to everything, which it isn't—is a temptation to too many people. It represents too much power in too small a place."

Rann chuckled grimly. "I'm not sure about everyone else, but I'd be willing to bet Priest-Clan would give one of The Eight to know where you store it."

"Which is why I have the entire Citadel between it and the outer gates, and ten levels of well-guarded tower under the supervision of what's left of the Night Guard, and *that* under Veen, whom I trust as much as anyone who's martially inclined—besides Merryn, of course."

"Forgetting that your wife is also from War," Lykkon noted dryly.

"Forgetting."

"Speaking of forgetting," Rann took up, "one thing *you're* forgetting is that one reason you're so popular is that you command that which gave us victory over Ixti. People who've won something are generally happy people, even if it only restores the previous norm. People like heroes, and you've provided one. The fact that you're young doesn't hurt, either; nor the fact that few outside your clan and the Council had heard of you, which gives you an aura of mystery."

"Nor does it hurt," Lykkon went on eagerly, "that the new King of Ixti adores you."

"Speaking of whom," Rann put in, "what *about* Kraxxi? Do you think he'll be able to retain power, given that—"

"Given what?" Avall snapped. "He's the legitimate heir. He's been trained to be king since birth, which I certainly haven't. He's made the best peace we've ever had between our two countries."

"Some would say he's sold Ixti's independence," Lykkon challenged. "There are some—most of whom are beating a hasty retreat back to Ixti, fortunately—who would say that he's unable to decide anything without your permission—or Merryn's, even though we know he had exactly three private audiences with her before he and his army withdrew. But in any case, a big chunk of Ixti's army has now been to Eron. We're no longer rumor and myth to them. And they will have seen—or heard—how little resistance we gave them. For generations we relied on War-Hold to police the border, and the rumor of War-Hold's impregnability to forestall attack. The Eight know we've seen how much power rumor and reputation can manifest."

"Countering that," Avall replied, "is the fact that the people in Ixti are probably a lot like the people here. They'd rather be comfortable and happy than rich, powerful, and anxious—at least in their hearts. Most of them probably think that any move against Kraxxi will bring down the wrath of Eron upon them—in the form of the Lightning Sword. Which brings us back to that."

"So," Rann sighed, "has this conversation accomplished anything? Has it changed your thinking? Has it brought you closer to decision?"

"It's made me decide that I'm going to get everyone I even halfway trust together for one final meeting on the subject and *then* decide."

"And in the meantime?"

Avall shrugged. "Well, you know I'd *like* to get in some smithing, since that's what I've actually been trained to do."

Rann cleared his throat uncomfortably, exchanging glances with Lykkon. "While we're speaking of uncomfortable topics, we might as well bring up the other one."

"The gem," Lykkon added. "We've no choice, Vall. It's another wild card in the Kingdom."

Avall snorted. "A few more of those, and we can cheat for the rest of our lives."

Lykkon's eyes narrowed. "It *is* getting better—so you said. The last time—"

"I said that to make you leave me alone about it," Avall growled. "Clearly it didn't work."

Yet his hand was already fumbling for one of the two fine chains that hung around his neck, one silver, one gold. It was the gold he sought and reeled from the depths of his tunic. A sphere of thick glass depended from the end, within which something gleamed murky red. A metal band also encircled it, with a minute clasp to one side. Holding his breath, Avall touched the clasp. A tiny click, and the sphere parted, releasing its contents into his palm.

A gem.

Like the three gems that adorned the regalia. Like the gems that Rann and Strynn—and he himself, on the other chain—wore around their throats.

But this was the master gem. The first-found gem. The

gem that had awakened so many things in the last half year, many of which should have remained quiescent. It had been the only gem, too—for a while—and Avall felt a unique bond with it. Certainly it was he who had found it in the mines beneath Gem-Hold-Winter. He who'd awakened it with his own blood by purest accident, and who'd discovered—and was still discovering—the powers its like could confer on humankind.

Unfortunately, those powers were not easily concealed, and first Avall's cousin Eddyn, then the late King of Ixti himself, Barrax min Fortan, had coveted that gem. And when a careless accident on Avall's part had resulted in Eddyn seizing it and promptly disappearing, only to find himself hundreds of shots away—which had, in turn, resulted in the gem falling into Barrax's hands—why, then Avall had feared he'd lost it forever.

He'd been devastated, too—at first—for the link 'twixt gem and wielder was stronger than he'd known. Which hadn't stopped Barrax from trying to master the gem in his own right—a mistake that had cost him his life.

Which was why Avall feared to use the gem now.

Rann and Lykkon were watching him, too. And those two most cherished friends would show no mercy.

"Maybe it's changed," Rann murmured, barely audible.

Avall shot him a disgusted glare. "Maybe."

And closed the hand, still oozing blood from where it had held the sword, around the gleaming stone.

But where once it would have greeted him with something akin to gladness—with a rush of power, liking, and well-being, rather like a friendly dog, now he met a dark, shrieking madness like that same dog cursed with the foaming plague.

He'd expected as much, however; was even used to it, a little. The problem—and danger—came when he ventured deeper into what ravened there.

Barrax had been wearing the gem when he'd died, and his death had imprinted itself within it, so that beneath that surface gloss of madness, Barrax's death lay coiled and waiting, ever ready to tell its own tale of his horror and despair. Yet even the shell of madness that enclosed it had sense enough to warn him away, like burning guardsmen around a house engulfed in conflagration.

He touched it anyway, in case—

In case, he supposed, the terror within might, even slightly, have abated.

Yet no matter how gentle his mental probe, death felt him, grabbed him, and sucked him down.

It was like falling . . . forever.

Worse, it was like that first jolt of fear that falling engenders—repeated endlessly.

And with it came endless regret, and endless anger, and a waxing dread that what waited at the end would be more horrible than the journey there. But worst of all was the fact that he could feel his *self* dissolving, like the lights of the city winking out one by one. Except that every light was a memory, and he had no choice but to watch them die.

And that but for one brief moment.

Then it was gone—because someone had set fire to all of reality, and in that fire, his link to that waiting death was consumed.

He blinked, opened his eyes. And, caught up in that characteristic slowing-down of time that accompanied use of the gem, had ample occasion to note Lykkon standing before him, gaze shifting between Avall's face and his open—and empty—hand. A hand that was still stinging from where Lykkon had slapped it to knock the gem away.

Avall was on his feet at once, and on all fours as quickly, desperate to find the gem. For whatever it did, it was his and he would never abandon it again.

"It's here," Rann offered mildly, kneeling to reach under a chair. His voice sounded coarse and stretched—almost a growl: another residual effect of the gem on Avall's senses. He wore gloves, too, Avall noted. Thick ones he would not have brought by accident.

"Are you—?" Lykkon began hesitantly, concern adding years to his young face.

"I'm fine," Avall managed, through a series of deep breaths punctuated by the shivers working with the gems provoked. Time had almost shifted back to normal.

"If you're sure . . ."

He masked a shiver with a shrug. The others were shivering as well, he noted, with smug satisfaction.

Rann rose, pried the gem's locket from Avall's other hand, reinserted the stone, then closed it again and returned it. "Was there any change?"

Another shrug. "*Maybe* it wasn't as bad as the last time—the same way having one finger immersed in ice water while the rest of you is being burned alive wouldn't be as bad as all of you burning."

Lykkon—true to form—had filled mugs of hot cider, and thrust one into Avall's free hand. "Can you be more specific?"

Recalling the memory was like tearing the scab from a wound. "It was more or less the same," Avall conceded. "But the bad thing, Lyk, is that I know that beneath the madness and the warning and the memories of Barrax's death, the gem I remember still exists. It's like one of those stories where you have to win through all the traps around the enchanted palace to rescue the princess."

"Which means?" Rann prompted.

"Which means I'll *have* to try it again. And that I'll put it off as long as I can, and that I'll hate it just as much when I do."

"I'm sorry," Rann murmured. "For what it's worth. And I repeat what I've offered before. If you ever want to link with me, I'll go there with you. Strynn probably would as well."

"So would I," Lykkon chimed in, "if you'd let me use your other gem—as would Merryn and Bingg and several other folks. They—we—think that maybe sane gems might cure insane ones."

"It's not really insane," Avall spat. "It's just full of death. And it's terrible, and I would never, ever inflict that on anyone

I cared about. And when I say that, I'm very glad I *am* King and can forbid it. Which I hereby do."

Rann grunted and sat back down, looking glum. Lykkon merely looked thoughtful, and jotted something in the journal he always kept with him.

The room lapsed into silence, though troubled looks spoke loudly. Eventually Avall finished his drink and rose. "Well, lads," he said, with forced ebullience, "Kingship waits on no man—and I have an errand I *must* attend to. If either of you feel like braving a trip to Argen-Hall, I'd be glad of the company."

It was just as well Avall sought companions for his journey, and not merely Rann and Lykkon, but an eight of Royal Guard under the command of compact, square-faced Lady Veen, who was one of three new Guard-Chiefs he'd appointed after the war.

It was also a mistake to go on foot, even if uncrowned and uncloaked, since they had scarcely traveled half a shot along the wide riverside promenade that began at the Citadel before Avall was recognized by one of those clots of disgruntled Common Clan citizens who'd become much more prevalent since the war.

And while the strength of his reputation rested largely with Common Clan, so did one of his greatest threats.

He knew who they were the moment the first overripe fruit sailed past his face to land liquidly on the cobblestones a span to his left. More followed—and worse. He resisted the urge to hasten his step, even as the Guard moved off to quell that disturbance—with quarterstaves, since Avall had forbidden the use of blades for that purpose, save in self-defense.

Nor was it the offal that concerned him, but the words.

"The Eight belong to everyone," came the chant, low at first, but swelling in volume, with the odd extra comment thrown in. "The King serves The Eight, not The Eight the King." And "Heed The Eight or breed more wars."

The Commoners were backing away, however—but with challenge in their eyes that did not bode well for future altercations. Avall had already started to recall the Guard when the second heckler from the right suddenly broke ranks with his fellows and charged, brandishing what looked like an Ixtian sword—probably loot from the war. "Heretic!" he yelled as he pounded across the paving—so suddenly he pierced the line of Guards before they could recover.

War-Hold-trained reflexes set Avall at alert, while Rann and Lykkon moved to flank him on either side. Even so, the man was barely four spans away before Avall finally found the hilt of the sword ritual required he wear. Yet his blade had scarcely cleared the scabbard before the assailant froze in place then bolted—back to rejoin his fellows, who'd retreated to the wall beside the river. All defiance had vanished from their faces. Indeed, it looked as though they might all jump in if Avall pursued.

Veen looked to Avall for direction, reluctant to forsake her greater charge for a lesser. He motioned her to return, sick at heart at what the man's failure of nerve implied. They feared him; that was certain now. Worse, they feared the sword he did not even carry at his side. Their words remained, too: a legacy of doubt.

"They think we caused the war," Avall murmured to Lykkon. "They think that because Gynn and I were forced to use powers they assume came from The Eight, we're claiming that power for ourselves."

Lykkon shook his head. "They *think*, cousin, that you risked cutting them off from The Eight to serve your own ends. Priest-Clan makes a dangerous foe."

"Eellon risked much when he locked up their Chiefs," Rann added.

"Because they threatened to rebel in the middle of a war."

"We know that," Lykkon retorted. "Those others—"

"*Some* of them call me hero—for reasons for which they've no more proof."

"Cousin—"

"It's a knife edge," Avall sighed, and by then the Guard had closed ranks with him. Still, he didn't relax until he reached the rough trilithon gate that marked the entrance to Argen-Hall-Prime, the stronghold of Avall's birth-clan and -craft. Not that he paid much heed to the ancient splendor of truncated towers and round-arched arcades sprawling off to either side; rather, he made straight for the Clan-Chief's suite on the third level.

And almost quelled before the door for fear of what lay inside, whose domain he was suddenly very conscious of invading. Indeed, King or no, he might well have retreated down the hall, had the door warden not been someone he knew: a slight, narrow-faced youth named Myx, who was only a few years older than he. Originally from Stone, and distant kin to Rann, Myx's star had risen with Avall's by virtue of his simply being at the right place at one very crucial time, and swearing an oath so potent it still bound him.

And Myx, at least, would be honest with him concerning what he was about to face.

"Shall I announce—?" Myx asked carefully, a sad half smile of friendship overlying deeper pain.

"I'm not here as the King," Avall gave back. "But—how is he? Really?"

Myx merely shook his head. "Better you see for yourself, Majesty. Expect the worst, and you won't be disappointed."

Avall exchanged glances with his companions, squared his shoulders, took a deep breath, and motioned for Myx to open the door.

The chamber to the right of the entry vestibule was unlit, but someone had left the windows and doors open in the room beyond, so that the sweet air and bright light of summer still entered. The effect was unsettling, too, Avall's own brushes with death having been accompanied by cold. It seemed impossible someone should die on a warm, sunny day.

But Eellon syn Argen-a, who was still officially Chief of Clan Argen, which ruled Smithcraft, was dying.

Very quickly, it appeared.

Avall approached the sickbed with trepidation. In order to accommodate the large number of visitors come to pay their respects to the old Clan-Chief, and to better facilitate what little treatment was attempted anymore, the suite had been stripped almost bare. Eellon's bed lay with its head precisely placed between two archways that led into the sunlit room beyond. Low sofas lined the walls, but they looked uninviting—and probably were, to discourage lingering visitors.

As for the old man himself—Avall was glad he was swathed to the armpits in a sweep of glimmering golden fabric. Unfortunately, the color made Eellon's already sallow complexion look worse. As it was, his face looked like someone had draped wrinkled, yellow-white sylk across a skull on which a nose and lips had been hastily wrought from clay.

Yet he breathed—a reedy, raspy, rattle.

And, in spite of all efforts to the contrary, he stank: a too-sweet smell of sweat, rot, and pain that no amount of Ixtian incense could abate. Avall wished he'd brought a stick of imphor to chew—not only because the fumes could overpower most other odors, but for the false strength the drug imparted.

Myx was right. Eellon was worse than ever; indeed, he was only technically alive. It was a sad conclusion to ninety years, Avall reflected, most of them spent strong of mind and body, and more of them strong of mind alone. But then, last winter, a cough had become a fever in the lungs. Headaches and accelerated heartbeat followed, and then one day Eellon had grasped his head in Council and collapsed. Something had ruptured in his brain, his healer said. At least the old Chief wasn't like some men thus afflicted, who lolled half-awake, trying desperately to send words along the dead paths between a living brain and a useless tongue.

Avall didn't touch him or speak to him. That would provoke nothing but frustration for both of them, though he could hear Lykkon stifle a sob, and sense Rann gone tense as a board, through that odd linkage they sometimes shared. Maybe—

He was jerked from reverie by footsteps approaching from the sunlit room beyond. Steps he recognized instantly, by the slow, deliberate tread.

Tyrill. Once Craft-Chief of Smith, now—though she was not the oldest mentally competent member of Clan Argen in Tir-Eron—Acting Clan-Chief as well. Her mouth twitched when she saw him, but Avall was unable to read the implications. Traditionally, she had little use for him, beyond a begrudged respect for his facility at metalwork. But *traditionally* she and Eellon had been bitter rivals, yet she barely left his side now—proof that the line between love and hate was thinner than supposed. Still, the uneasy truce that she and Avall had contrived in the days after his Acclamation as King was a fragile, desperate thing, and Avall always felt as though he were walking on quick-fire around her. King he might be, but he was also a man of her clan, if not her sept. Never mind that she'd taught him a good chunk of what he knew about smithing. It was hard to break that conditioning and be King, not the little boy Tyrill seemed always to expect.

"Avall," she murmured finally, with an absent nod of steel-gray hair, signifying by that a blood-bond of Chief to clansman, not the oath-bond of Chief to Sovereign.

"Tyrill," he gave back, motioning her to sit, which she did.

"There's only one question," Tyrill volunteered bluntly. "How long will he live? And the answer is barely more debatable. His healers say three days because they think that's what we want to hear. I say two—if that."

Avall exhaled a breath he didn't know he'd been holding. "So little? Still, it would be a blessing for all of us. Waiting isn't something I do well, and waiting for this. For the world to change . . ."

"It already has," Tyrill rasped. "The world just doesn't know it yet. And with that in mind, I've taken the liberty of summoning those chiefs not already in Tir-Eron—"

"*Are* there any?" Lykkon broke in, genuinely surprised. "I've been keeping a tally—"

Tyrill regarded him keenly, as though torn between praising his foresight and condemning the interruption. "The septchiefs from here, South, Half, and Mid Gorges are all present. The -el chief from North is ill and may predecease Eellon, from what I hear. The subchiefs from all those holds less than an eight-day's ride away are also either here or in transit. Not so much out of curiosity—we know who's older than who—but because powerful people are drawn to the smell of history in process. And there *is* the matter of mental competence. It's one thing to claim that, it's another to display it. Some days I'm not even sure I'm competent myself."

Avall could think of no reply. Tyrill seemed to need comfort, and he didn't know how to provide it. She'd never needed it before, and he'd never tried. Besides which, she'd always had her own favorite, Eddyn.

Eddyn syn Argen-yr, whose bronze likeness, newly cast by Tyrill herself, now stood in Argen-yr's water court. Eddyn, Tyrill's favorite two-son and protégé, one of the three best smiths of his generation—and a rapist, a murderer, an exile, a hero, and—some said—a self-deluded fool.

Yet Tyrill had lived for him, then through him, and Avall suddenly wondered how much longer she would last, once a successor for Eellon was named.

But he wouldn't think about that now. *Couldn't* think about it. It had been a mistake to come here.

"Do what you think best," he heard himself telling Tyrill as he started for the door. "When it finally happens and we sit in conclave, you know I'll do everything in my power to be present."

"But who will you support?" Tyrill shot back, with what almost seemed like glee. "The two eldest claimants are exactly of an age, and one is from -yr, and one from -a. Will you do the right thing, or will politics once more prevail?"

"I will do what seems right to me," Avall assured her from the door. "As, I'm certain, will you."

CHAPTER II:

DIGGINGS

(NORTHWESTERN ERON: GEM-HOLD-WINTER— HIGH SUMMER: DAY XL—MIDDAY)

~~~~~~~

Crim san Myrk, Hold-Warden of Gem-Hold-Winter, patted the topmost volume of the imposing pile on the podium before her and aimed a meaningful stare at the other six people facing her in this, her most private council chamber. The stack would've been knee high had it rested on the floor, and that array of tired old oak-and-leather bindings probably weighed half as much as she did, never mind what it contained, which was priceless.

But Crim, at that moment, would cheerfully have consigned them all to the flames in the forges fifteen levels lower. She could do it, too; she had that much authority—besides which, it wasn't as if other copies didn't exist—in the Lore hall at Gem-Hold-Main, for instance—or Lore-Hold-Main, though *that* copy could only be accessed by Gemcraft's Chief herself, or the Chief of Clan Myrk, that ruled it.

An eyebrow lifted on the lined old face of he who sat nearest: Ayll, Myrk's local Sub-Clan-Chief—which meant he was the oldest member of that clan on the premises. Beside him, Mystel, the Sub-Craft-Chief, dared a confused frown; then again, for all her crafting skill (which was what justified her title), she wasn't the smartest person Crim knew, and certainly not the quickest. The other four, however—Savayn, the deputy Hold-Warden; Ekaylin, the Mine-Master; and Nyvven and Tynn, the local chiefs of Myrk's two septs, -or or -izz, respectively—leaned forward with anxious, if honest, interest.

"I've read every word in these," Crim informed them, tapping the books again—which raised a cloud of dust made more visible by the window-wall behind her. "Every word in four hundred years' worth of Hold-Wardens' journals and most of the Mine-Masters' tallies as well—which I intend to complete this summer. And I'm here to tell you that if any reference to gems such as Avall found exists, I didn't find it."

"And if you didn't find it," Mystel noted primly, "it's unlikely to be found."

Crim nodded, a grim smile creasing her smooth, no-nonsense features. "I'm going to continue searching, however, and I'm going to set someone to copying these records—in case that turns up something I missed. But I can now say with reasonable certainty that gems such as Avall found in Argen's vein are something new in the world."

Nyvven, the younger sept-chief, puffed hollow cheeks, one of which was scarred from a pick handle gone awry in his youth. "There was the stone that Healer woman found—"

"The attraction stone? Actually, we've found a few more of those over the years. They're interesting, but mostly a novelty."

"Refresh my memory," Tynn mumbled in turn. "I've forgotten so much . . ."

Crim had to work to suppress her impatience. Tynn was twice her age and more, and close enough to senile that he often forgot to bathe, with distressing consequences. Still, it was important to provide everyone with equal information, and if that was painstakingly slow—well, so was cutting diamonds. "Briefly," she began, "they're red, like Avall's gems, but they don't have lights inside them like Avall's evidently do. Their main property of note is that if you break one—which is easy to do, across the long axis—each part points toward the other like a lodestone, except that these don't seem limited by distance."

"There's also the stone in the Sword of Air," Nyvven noted.

Again Crim nodded. "And I wish we had it here to study, or that I could see it there—assuming Avall would let me. Unfortunately, that stone was found so long ago no one from here knows *what* it is, and since it's part of royal regalia, we've no way to find out unless someone from Gem becomes Sovereign."

"Maybe we should move in that direction," Ayll mused, a bit too loudly.

Crim silenced him with a glare, though the notion had its merits. "What we need to know, first and foremost," she continued, "is whether more gems like Avall's remain to be found. As best we can determine, he discovered his in Argen's vein—and then Strynn found one, though she, by rights, shouldn't have *been* in Argen's vein, given that she's Ferr. And then Rann—who isn't Argen, either—somehow got hold of five more."

"All of which you only know by report," Savayn, her sharp-eyed deputy—and niece—observed.

Ekaylin cleared his throat and folded muscular arms across his brawny chest. "Maybe so, but I will swear any oath you like that Rann syn Eemon was never in Argen's vein. Once Avall and Eddyn disappeared, that vein was always watched, and every entrance and exit recorded—your orders, Lady Warden. As to any being found elsewhere, there's no way to know for certain without subjecting everyone who's ever been here to interrogation under imphor wood, which is impossible. Not that we can afford to offend every chief in Eron, anyway," he added.

"We're actually in a fairly precarious position," Crim agreed. "We control the source of what may be the most powerful substance in Eron, yet cannot—ourselves—our clan—lay claim to any of it without risking civil war." She tapped the books again. "Much as I hate to say it, it seems very possible that whatever

Avall found is peculiar to Argen's vein and legally beyond our control."

"So are you saying we should ally ourselves with Argen, just in case?" Tynn inquired archly.

A shrug. "I'm saying we should ally ourselves with the King, who happens to *be* Argen. Besides which—"

"Besides which," Savayn broke in, "we're effectively allied to him anyway, given that his mother was Clay, which was one of our septs until they split off; and that his bond-brother is Stone, which would still rule us if we hadn't asserted ourselves after we took control of this place."

"Which still doesn't tell us what these gems are," Nyvven huffed. "Nor whether they're unique to Argen's vein, nor whether someone else has also found some and is simply not telling anyone, nor what their nature is."

"Nor how they relate to the Wells," Ekaylin interjected. "We do know that vein is somewhat damper than most, and we know that the gems seem to confer abilities similar to those conferred by the Wells—"

"Which, beyond the common element of water, is stretching a point, I think," Crim replied. "Never mind that to pursue that line would require the cooperation of Priest-Clan, and I don't trust the Priests in this hold as far as I can throw them. Certainly not Nyss, who I *know* is carrying around enough secrets to strangle a geen."

"*How* do you know?" Mystel wondered.

"Because she disappears too easily," Savayn supplied, drumming her nails impatiently.

Crim suppressed a knowing smirk. "I've noticed that, too. She enters her suite, but then she's not seen for days. She summons no food to her room, yet has no way to cook there—but makes no claim to be fasting. The conclusion is that she's eating somewhere else that's accessible only from her suite. And given what an unmapped warren this place is . . ." She paused for a reply that didn't come. "Unfortunately, I dare not confront her. That could alienate Priest, and we're worse off alienating them than our other potential enemies."

Mystel looked puzzled. "How so?"

Crim spared her a tolerant scowl. "Because, Mystel, they control the weather-witch, and we are, let me remind you, a winter hold. We can do without witchings in the summer. Winter is another matter. We need the warnings the witches provide. And before you reply that anything that hurts us, hurts them, remember what I just said: that they've clearly got a mechanism in place to look after their own. I don't know how much you've heard about those people who attacked Avall, but they were almost certainly allied with Priest, if not actually part of it, and the only way they could've learned about that gem of his is if they had agents here, which, along with her disappearances, implicates Nyss."

"You could request a replacement," Savayn suggested.

"But I'd need better reasons than I could officially give. The real reason and the overt reason would be two separate things, and that's always dangerous."

"But . . ."

Crim slapped the books with an open palm, and rose. "Enough! It's clear that I know nothing about what I should know a great deal about, and that you know even less. It's equally clear that this situation has to change. I want each of you to take one of these books away with you and read it—and note anything that smacks of aberrant finds in the mines. I also want you to look for anything we don't already know that might cast doubt on Argen's claim to that particular vein, in case . . . Well, just in case."

And with that, she turned and swept from the room.

She did *not*, however, return to her quarters, as she usually did this time of day, to review the assignment lists and supply reports. Rather, she bent her steps by the straightest route to one of the eight principal stairways that spiraled directly down to the mines. What she hoped to find, she had no more notion than she'd had the last dozen times she'd been there. Still, it was always good to observe firsthand that over which her role as Hold-Warden gave her sovereignty.

Levels twisted past as she continued down, their walls changing mode of decoration as she descended—now fresco, now mosaic, now tapestry, now bas-relief—yet nowhere was the transition jarring. One day, she reckoned, she might even take time to stop and look at them.

But not today, not even when her legs began to protest. Which she chose to consider less a sign of age than of inaction born of responsibilities that kept her ever more confined to her suite or the adjoining office. Restocking the hold with sufficient provisions to see a thousand-odd inhabitants through the Dark Season was daunting at best. Never mind the recent war, which had played havoc with supply and production alike.

Down and down and down.

She'd chosen a route that terminated in the mines' "official" entrance, though there were other stairs that ended in the vaulted corridor that encircled it, and a few that gave onto the offices, storerooms, and vesting rooms beyond. The chamber itself was octagonal and roughly ten spans across, rising to a dome easily that high. Archways opened off it at regular intervals, most leading to the surrounding corridor, while eight major piers of stone ran up the walls to the center of the dome, all carved from the living rock of the mountain. It was through these piers the principal staircases ran, issuing from archways in their bases. The local stone being somewhat dark, all surfaces between the piers were whitewashed and void of ornament. Color came from the floor, where, beneath a slab of glass two fingers thick, a map of Eron and environs had been worked in gems and rare metals, the entirety framed by roundels bearing the sigils of all twenty-four clans and crafts. It was one of the wonders of craftsmanship in that part of the world, for each gem was faceted, so that even the smallest stream glittered with emerald fire.

Crim strode straight across it—as many people, she'd discovered, were loath to do—and entered the corridor beyond, which opened, in turn, on a much smaller, though still impressive chamber, the far door of which was bracketed by the assay desks of the Mine-Master and his deputies. Iron gates were set in slots above all major entrances here and elsewhere, including the room she'd just vacated, but beyond their yearly inspection and cleaning, they hadn't been lowered since the Hold's foundation.

Crim heard the mines before she saw them, and at that, the musty odor of raw earth and broken stone reached her before the noise. Still, the sounds waxed steadily as she approached: a grinding, most notably, but also a dull pounding, and the raspy jingle of the gears in the *trods,* as the vast, pedal-powered drilling machines were called. Before she knew it, she was passing the first of them, drawing curious glances from the sweaty, half-clad men and women pedaling beside the screw-shafts. An unlikely occupation for Eron's artist-elite, she acknowledged. On the other hand, it kept them fit and trim, and was a great equalizer besides, since most of this batch were, indeed, High Clan scions. Young, too: recently Raised adults in the first cycle of the Fateing, discovering that physical labor was a necessary adjunct to the crafting to which most of them aspired.

She paused for a moment, wondering whether—since the King was from Smith, which ruled machines—now might not be a good time to approach him about either replacing the oldest trod or adding a new one. Perhaps this coming autumn, when she made her first trek to Tir-Eron in five years. . . .

Assuming she didn't go mad before then. Dismissing such speculation with a snort loud enough to make the nearest treader fix her with a dubious stare—even if her Warden's cloak and hood did not—she continued onward, steering her way toward the private veins. They revealed themselves slowly, tunnels opening off other tunnels, that in turn opened off larger chambers hollowed in the rock of Tar-Megon itself. Argen's vein was to the right, the guard niches beside the entrance occupied by two weary-looking women in Gem-Hold livery. They straightened when they saw her, and nodded smartly, trying to look alert, and failing. Crim didn't blame them. This was dull work, most of the time. But now, regrettably, necessary.

"Any visitors?"

"Argen's Sub-Craft-Chief, about a hand ago," the right-hand guard replied

Crim grunted an acknowledgment and continued on.

The vein itself was fronted by a circular chamber three spans across, its walls covered with gold leaf and its marble floor marked by Smithcraft's sigil wrought of rustless steel. The same emblem was cut into the stone above the archway that gave onto the vein itself.

But where was the guard? Besides the two she'd posted in the corridor beyond, Argen had started posting one of its own here. Yet the niche by the door was empty. Still, *her* guards had said nothing about anyone leaving. Therefore . . .

It was with considerable determination that she strode through the archway and into the vein itself. One span beyond the entrance, the floor became dirt and began to slope upward. Soon enough she had to stoop to continue, which was when she began to see the irregular openings of the side veins, most of them entering the main one at roughly waist level—dark, uninviting holes so small a person must crawl to work them, which had led to their being called crawls.

Propriety got the best of her beside the first one. This was her hold, aye, and the hold of her clan. But it was Argen's territory on which she actually stood, as much theirs as Argen-Hall in Tir-Eron. She had no right here save by courtesy and with permission she'd neither sought nor expected to have granted.

Still, Tir-Eron—and Argen-Hall—were a thousand shots to the southwest, and while their local representatives were among the more forceful representatives of that clan, she had a fair bit of experience with force herself, much of it recent, when bullying had become a fact of life. Unfortunately, Brayl and Pannin, the old Argen chiefs she'd known for so long, were gone, having left the previous spring in ignorance of the war they'd found mustering upon reaching Tir-Eron. Their replacements had been two women who'd fallen from favor with old Eellon and been dispatched here. A new Sub-Craft-Chief had come with them.

Both Clan-Chiefs kept to their quarters, but Liallyn, Smith's much younger Sub-Craft-Chief, could often be found here, and was in fact in the vein even now. Which was just as well; Crim needed to talk to her. Indeed, she almost abandoned decorum in truth, and was actually removing her cloak with the notion of entering the nearest crawl in her shift, when she heard the sound of someone backing out of it. By the feet, which appeared first, it was male. The missing guard, in fact, looking embarrassed at being caught off his post and in such disarray. He wore no sword, but did sport a dagger. And given the closeness between Argen and Ferr, he probably knew how to use it better than most. Indeed his hands reached to it by reflex, before he realized whom he was confronting. A shadow of confusion crossed his face. This was his clan's vein, but Crim was the Hold-Warden . . .

He had already opened his mouth, when a second set of scrabblings issued from the crawl. He sighed relief and looked away—which implied that whoever he awaited ranked him, which meant he could abdicate responsibility.

More feet appeared, these clad in dirty boots and small enough to belong to a woman. Legs followed, cased in the leather breeches worn by both sexes when working the narrower crawls. Someone fairly young and supple, to judge by the way those hips were twisting.

Liallyn herself, as it turned out. The woman—she was roughly Crim's age, and they shared some history, years ago—brushed dirt off her tunic and was already inhaling the shaft's relatively fresher air, when the combined noise of the guardsman clearing his throat and Crim's pointed sigh made her start and spin around—but not before Crim noted that she held two small leather bags of the sort used to store mined gems. Both were bulging.

Liallyn followed Crim's stare. "Dirt," she said flatly. "Not that you have any right to know, here in Argen's sovereignty."

"Dirt," Crim echoed neutrally. "How interesting."

"I can show you, if you like," Liallyn replied, thrusting one of the bags at the startled guard, while reaching for the ties on the other.

Crim shook her head. "No need, though I suppose dirt is technically part of Stone—or Clay."

"Both of which are Smith's allies," Liallyn replied. "Still, honesty being better than subterfuge, I'll go ahead and tell you that we're curious as to whether there's anything special about the matrix in that vein. There's no reason to hide that fact from you, given that it's ours, anyway."

"Actually," Crim shot back, "I'm looking into that."

Liallyn's brows lifted in annoyed surprise before she could hide it. The guard's eyes darted back and forth between them as his hand found the hilt of his dagger.

To Crim's chagrin, Liallyn took the initiative. "That old business about the original vein grants? Let me remind you that it was a Smith who first found this place and dug the initial tunnel."

"Looking for ores, not gems," Crim countered, though she shouldn't have. It was an old, old argument, but one that wouldn't die. Priest and Lore had been assigned to work out a settlement two centuries back and still hadn't. In essence, the argument went, Smith had made the excavation—with Stone's help—and established a small hold here. But when nothing useful to Smith had been forthcoming, they'd ceded the hold to Stone, of which Gem had then been a sept. Gemstones had promptly been discovered, which had given their miners sufficient clout to form a clan and craft of their own, but only with Smith's support, which they'd granted on the condition they be ceded a vein of their own to mine in perpetuity. Gem had reluctantly agreed, but the ensuing furor had resulted in all the other clans likewise demanding private veins in exchange for supposedly equal considerations. The clincher had come when someone pointed out that, beautiful as they were, gems were essentially a luxury, the withholding of which troubled no one but their own.

All of which took Crim half a breath to recall. Which was still long enough for Liallyn to ready another volly. "You can bring it up at Sundeath," she said. "For now, this is Smith territory. There's one of me, and I'm probably your equal in a fight. I have a guard. You can leave, or he can escort you. I'm sorry to be rude, but present right and ancient precedent both support me. You can challenge, but until then, I still have to report whatever I find and tithe the same—to your Mine-Master. If you want to confront someone, let it be him, who let first Avall, then Strynn slip at least two of these gems you're so obsessed with past his nose."

"Rann also found some," Crim snapped. "And he could only have come down here with Smith's grace."

"He didn't," Liallyn replied coldly. "If you want to pursue that, I suggest you address your complaint to Lord Eemon. For myself, I need to clean up, then take this sample to our suite—where I doubt it will tell me any more than it would have told you."

And with that, she snatched the remaining bag from the guard and pushed past him, to stride back down the shaft, leaving Crim gaping in her wake.

"Lady—" the guard ventured, when they had returned to the entrance chamber. "Hold-Warden. I have to remind you that, as my Chief says, you are on Argen's earth. It would indeed be wise if you . . . departed."

And somehow, without her being aware of it, he had set himself between her and the entrance to the vein, with his dagger now fisted ominously. Crim glared at him, but managed a marginally courteous nod as she started for the exit. The boy was only doing his duty. As was his Chief. As was she. But Eight, why did doing one's duty have to be so troublesome?

She had a headache, she realized, as she reached the cooler air in the larger shaft beyond. Maybe from anger, perhaps from fatigue, possibly from the closeness of the mines or the pounding of the trods she had to pass again to make her exit. Whatever the cause, tending to it was suddenly uppermost in her mind.

When had she become so impatient? she wondered, as she strode past the assay station, passing an alarmed subchief in the process. And how would she deal with it?

Well, with wine, to start with, to calm her nerves a little. And a hot bath, and then . . . What? Music?

Kylin was back, she recalled, as she neared her apartments. Kylin, who was the best harper she'd ever heard. Kylin, who was also allied, very firmly, with that preposterous young power structure in Tir-Eron, by virtue, some said, of his being the Consort's lover. He'd arrived three days ago, with an escort of Royal Guard, ostensibly to retrieve his chief-harp. He'd also be leaving "soon"—but that was all he would say. But until "soon" arrived, Kylin was hers again. Her harper, as he had been before . . .

Before what?

Before last autumn's trek had brought Avall, Strynn, and Eddyn, and with them that which had changed the world.

But for a while, she could forget all that and listen to Kylin playing.

CHAPTER III:

COURTING DISASTER

(ERON: TIR-ERON—HIGH SUMMER: DAY XLI—JUST BEFORE NOON)

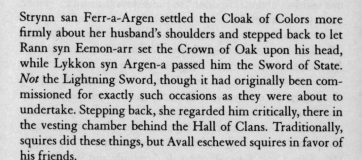

Strynn san Ferr-a-Argen settled the Cloak of Colors more firmly about her husband's shoulders and stepped back to let Rann syn Eemon-arr set the Crown of Oak upon his head, while Lykkon syn Argen-a passed him the Sword of State. *Not* the Lightning Sword, though it had originally been commissioned for exactly such occasions as they were about to undertake. Stepping back, she regarded him critically, there in the vesting chamber behind the Hall of Clans. Traditionally, squires did these things, but Avall eschewed squires in favor of his friends.

A glance around the room showed Strynn few enough of those, most in Warcraft crimson beneath the Argen maroon-with-crown of the Royal Guard: young Myx, with his bond-brother, Riff; Lady Veen; and Strynn's senior brother, Vorinn, newly returned from Brewing up past North Gorge, where he'd sat out the war nursing—and cursing—two broken arms. Only one of his younger allies was missing: Merryn, Avall's twin sister and Strynn's bond-mate. But Merryn was exactly where she wanted to be: guarding the Door of Chiefs. A position that actually required she do more than stand around looking ritually pretty.

Strynn dusted imaginary lint from Avall's arm and grinned at him. "Well," she announced, "you look magnificent."

Avall grinned back, part excited boy, part bemused adult being forced to play a game that was still unreal to him, part frightened youth caught somewhere between. "There's still time to join me," he murmured.

Strynn shook her head. "If you change your mind in the autumn—if you allow yourself to be confirmed as King at Sundeath, *then* I might consent to be Consort-in-fact. For now, I want this to be your decision alone. I don't want to get a taste for power and find myself urging you toward something for which you have no heart. And you've already said you've no desire to be *my* Consort, should they offer the Throne to me— nor will I sit it alone. Besides," she added with a smirk, "it'll be more fun to watch."

Avall tried to shrug, but the cloak was too heavy for that. Which might be an omen, Strynn decided. No one would argue that Kingship did not weigh heavily on her husband.

A rap sounded on the door behind them, and Riff, who'd recognized the distinctive cadence, opened it with a mixture of apprehension and relief, standing back to admit eight Priests in various robes and masks, who entered in solemn file to claim places on the inlaid sigils of the principal avatars of The Eight: Man, Fate, Craft, Law, World, Life, Strength, and Weather.

"The sun rises," the senior Priest, Grivvon of Law, intoned. And moved toward the door to the Council chamber.

It wouldn't open for Avall, Strynn knew. Only for the Priest of Law. She wondered how Law felt returning to this role after Eellon had taken him and his clan-kin captive. Certainly there was no love lost between Crown and Clan now. But that didn't negate the force of tradition.

Law inclined his head toward her, extending the gesture to include Rann and Lykkon. "Lady, if you are not to accompany His Majesty, Law says you must retire to the Consort's chair in the hall. If you hurry, you can still get there before court commences."

She almost protested; almost joined her husband anyway. Sense got the better of her in the end. Besides, as she'd already said, it was more fun to watch.

Sparing Avall a final kiss and a whispered "luck," Strynn whisked through another door, which in turn led her, via the corridor that encircled the hall, to the entry vestibule. As a member of the Council in her own right, she paused long enough to raise her ceremonial hood of Ferr crimson and to announce herself to the door warden. She needn't have bothered. It was Merryn, looking smug and happy in full armor, but with an Argen-a clan robe, hood, and tabard stored nearby, should she deign to avail herself of her option to sit with her kin. Merryn was taking to the power game a little too well, Strynn suspected.

Still, they exchanged knowing grins, and then Strynn composed herself and walked unaccompanied into the tall, if ill-proportioned, splendor of the Hall of Clans. She did not seek the wedge assigned to her husband's sept, however, or the Consort's chair, for that matter. Rather, she turned left and followed the spoke that ran beside her own clan and craft. Argen she might be, by marriage; and Consort-apparent by Luck; but she was Ferr by birth and blood, and that took precedence here. That she was probably the youngest woman in the room and was claiming a place with her kinsmen without leave didn't concern her. It was more than time that some of Eron's ironclad rules were tested.

Silently, she joined her father and her other brother, who themselves sat beside Craft-Chief Tryffon, called Kingmaker, and Preedor, the Clan-Chief himself, who was here in spite of his vow never to share the floor with Tyrill unless the King command it—which Avall had. Tryffon nodded acknowledgment; her father winked; Preedor scowled.

Others were scowling as well—but not at her. Rather, their brows were lowering at the sight of the new Ixtian Ambassador,

Tozri min Aroni mar Sheer, occupying a seat in the observers' gallery. In Healing's section, in fact, in token of the fact that his Eronese mother had been from that much-ravaged clan. Which might be wise or might not, depending on how fractious a mood the Council was in today.

And then the light of the rising sun struck the octagon of windows below the dome at a carefully contrived angle, and the Hall of Clans filled with the first strong rays of midsummer's light.

At that precise moment, a gong sounded, the Priest's Door opened behind the dais, and Grivvon of Law strode in. Seven more Priests followed, then Avall himself, then eight members of the Royal Guard—including, by courtesy, Myx, Riff, Lykkon, Rann, and Vorinn. Murmurs promptly filled the hall, for the King usually presided unguarded, though Avall had very publicly stressed to the Priests that he was honoring these people, nothing more. Did he feel threatened by Priest-Clan? Of course not! Did not they both serve The Eight?

Perhaps, Strynn concluded wryly, the same way one cup could serve either fine wine or scorpion poison.

Per ancient precedent, Avall paused briefly before the Stone, which was set in the center of the dais, then settled his cloak about him, laid the Sword of State across his knees, and sat motionless while his guard arranged themselves behind.

Law promptly stepped forward to roll the ritual die that would determine which Priest would officiate. It came up Craft, and that young woman took Law's place in presiding at High King Avall syn Argen-a's first Midsummer court.

Craft's mask was the most complex of all the Priests of The Eight, constructed, as it was, from a vast array of materials, notably inlaid wood and mother-of-pearl. But Avall, behind and to her left, could see little more than the fringe of feathers that surrounded it. What he saw clearly was the long, pure sweep of her robe, cloak, and hood, which put his own Cloak of Colors to shame, with their intricate embroidery, complex weaving, and the jeweled ornaments carefully placed to accent every fold, shape, and design. It was controlled chaos. It was also the perfect embodiment of the twenty-four crafts that, with the chiefs who ruled those crafts' ruling clans, constituted the elite of scholar-artisans that ruled Eron.

Avall listened attentively through Craft's formal opening speech, noting that her voice was softer than expected, and that it wavered more than it ought. Then again, Craft was young—as was he. But she was also Priest-Clan, and they were never to be underestimated.

With that in mind, Avall tried to appear suitably regal, in spite of being the youngest Sovereign in ten generations. While he had the support of all but one of the most powerful clans, he had few illusions of how tenuous that support might be, resting as it did mostly on marriage alliances and the goodwill of a few old men and women, any of whom could follow Eellon down the road to illness and death before the year was out.

Craft was finishing now, and he steeled himself for what was to come.

". . . Know, then," Craft intoned, "that by ancient right and privilege, the first order of business before the High Sovereign of Eron in this, the first court of Midsummer, is the petitioning of His Majesty by anyone of Common Clan who would claim hearing."

Avall barely heard the rest. He was more than a little trepidatious, and justifiably so. Common Clan were the great unpredictable factor of Eronese politics. Comprised mostly of lesser artisans, merchants, and landowners, they also comprised over half of Eron's population. Any Sovereign who wanted to keep his crown was therefore wise to keep them happy. Most had. It wasn't as though one were doomed to remain in that clan, anyway. Anyone with scholarly or artistic inclination could petition the relevant Craft-Chief for a hearing, and if accepted, join the ranks of those High Clan youths studying at the various holds. Conferral of a mastership upon adulthood also conferred legal High Clan status, assuming an appropriate sponsor could be found; and any children born or sired thereafter were deemed High Clan by birth. This had the double effect of placating Common Clan and assuring a steady infusion of new blood into the High Clans, thereby diminishing the dangers of inbreeding.

Still, not all Common Clan were driven or accomplished. Most were merely content—or not. Many were ignorant as well, in spite of easily available education. And the ignorant often took solace in overreaction.

An example of which he'd witnessed yesterday. And which he feared he would face in truth as soon as the Common Door was opened.

". . . by His Majesty's command," he heard Craft announce—and started, jogged from his reverie just in time to see her turn toward him expectantly.

He cleared his throat and spoke, though it almost seemed that another mouth and lips shaped the ritual words. "Let Common Clan come forward, in what guise, number, and order they would, so long as they not equal the number already present in this chamber."

A door opened at the end of the centermost of the radiating aisles that met around the dais. A man entered, then a woman, then two more men, at which time Avall stopped counting, as they advanced with stiff dignity toward him. All wore hooded tabards of Common Clan beige, signifying, as such things did, that they acted in official capacity. Beyond that, there was little to unite them. Unlike High Clan, the bulk of whom tended to look much alike, those Commoners already ranged before him included everything from women considerably taller than Avall, to men over a head shorter, showing hair of every shade and hue, and a variety of builds, save the very stout. Their leader was a blunt-faced, middle-aged man with a shock of hair almost the same brown as his eyes. The edging on his tunic indicated that his clan came from near South Gorge and that he was a merchant by trade, with a connection to Weaver-Hold. He looked confident but tense; concerned— almost angry—but polite. Clearly he was used to a leadership position, though probably not to appearing in such before the Council of Chiefs.

In any case, the man had an impressive entourage, and as they gathered around, Avall noticed that most wore pendants bearing the eight-sided die that signified particular devotion to The Eight. He also had a good idea what subject was about to be addressed.

Tradition said the man would not speak until the Sovereign told him to, and Avall was confident the man had been reminded of this at least thrice before being allowed to enter. He did not kneel, however; abasement was only required of unclanned or clanless, besides which, Avall's position on the dais required the man look up to meet his gaze.

"State your name, man of Common Clan," Avall intoned formally. "Then state what it is that brings you before me."

"Haggyn syn Masall," the man replied. "And with me the chiefs of Common Clan from a dozen towns between here and South Gorge, and the Common-Chief of Eron Gorge itself." He nodded toward a thin old woman who'd come up beside him. Avall recognized her as Kayvvin. She'd have had a seat on the Council in any case, and would have joined this group from among the ranks of those already seated.

"And your business?"

A deep breath. "We have come here in protest, Majesty."

"And what is it you would protest?" Avall inquired. "I have done nothing by conscious will to in anywise harm your clan, nor will I, for Eron's strength is in its people."

His sudden eloquence surprised him. Then again, Law had passed him a drink from Law's Well before he entered. Perhaps it was The Eight who spoke through him.

Haggyn frowned ever so slightly. "Eron's strength may well

be its people," he acknowledged. "But Eron Enthroned would do well to recall that the strength of the people comes from observing the will of The Eight."

"Which we of High Clan likewise strive to do," Avall observed.

Haggyn looked uneasy, but did not shift his gaze from his King. "As you say, Majesty. Yet we have heard it rumored even in South Gorge, and heard it rumored more often, with more conviction, and in greater detail the closer to Tir-Eron we came, and rumored most strongly in Tir-Eron itself, that there are those of High Clan—and higher—who have long striven to erect barriers between the common folk of Eron and The Eight, when such barriers need not exist."

Avall studied him in the ensuing pause. Haggyn was good at this—and probably a decent man in any account. He would volunteer no more than asked, but deny no information should it be demanded. But Haggyn was also playing by High Clan's rules in High Clan's Council. And doing it well, even if this verbal dance clearly irked him.

"Of which barriers do you speak?" Avall asked. "And in what way have we maintained them?"

"We do not know *how* you have maintained them," Haggyn retorted. "As to the barriers—let me speak plainly, Majesty. We have all been taught since birth that The Eight watch over all and direct our lives by Their plan. But we have also been taught that They speak only through Priest-Clan, and the King Himself at Sunbirth and Sundeath. We have been taught that man's soul is bound to his body until death dissolves that bond. We have been taught that beasts have no true thoughts as we know them; therefore, they have no souls. Yet now we hear that this may not be true: that some beasts—geens are what we have heard named, Majesty—have minds, and therefore souls, and must therefore be allowed the same rights as any man. We have heard—"

Avall cut him off with a wave of his hand. "I acknowledge that you have the right to speak until you are finished," he said.

"Yet what you have conveyed already could occupy this Council for a day, and that if everyone present had only minimal say. Let me therefore tell you in reply that nothing you have related is new to me. I have heard the rumblings of protest that we—myself, my clan, my advisers, and this Council—and Priest-Clan, of course, who are part of this Council—have conspired to withhold access to The Eight from the people—not only Common Clan, but High Clan, clanless, and unclanned as well. And I say to you this is not so—so far as I am aware. Certainly I have not ordered this thing done. Nor my advisers, nor this Council."

Avall paused, expecting the murmurings that did indeed fill the Hall, the bulk from Priest-Clan's wedge. At least three of the officiating Priests shot him sharp glances. None voiced protests, however, as they were still smarting from their incarceration during the war, when their talk of the very things these Commoners were addressing had got them accused of treason in the face of impending attack.

Avall knew he walked a fine line. The people needed their religion and they were used to getting it from Priest-Clan, and Priest-Clan was used to giving it to them. That a means *did* exist that *might* allow direct access to The Eight was also a fact—perhaps. But it was also a new discovery, tied up with the larger problem of the gems. And no one knew how large the fire beneath that glimmer of information was. Priest-Clan probably knew more than it was telling. Certainly at least one faction among them did. But even if the gems *did* allow direct access to The Eight—to Their realm, more properly—there was no way that access could be provided to the people, even with Royal and Priestly consent. There simply were not enough gems for everyone in Eron who would want to petition The Eight to do so directly. Never mind that he was King, and had not himself petitioned Them that way. So far as *he* knew, The Eight still made Their will known in Their own time and season, and answered no more to mortal demands than heretofore.

Still, these were matters that must be addressed, and it wasn't as though he hadn't anticipated this very confrontation. So it was that he set his sword aside, rose, and folded his arms across his chest, trying to look stern and thoughtful, and not twenty years old and scared.

"Haggyn," he said quietly. "I know of these concerns, and whether you believe it or not, I share them. They are also concerns far too large for a morning's work before the Council. Therefore, I have determined that a council to address these particular questions must and will be assembled. But since the traditional business of Midsummer court is itself bound by ritual, into which frame an issue as large as this cannot be effectively fitted, I have set the time for this council as an eighth from now: halfway between Midsummer and Sundeath. This will allow us all more time to prepare. And if, in the interim, The Eight make Their will known in this matter, you may rest assured that I will make Their pronouncements known in a timely manner."

Haggyn started to reply, then looked around him. A few muttered words were exchanged, whereupon he set his mouth and spoke again.

"This is not what we desired when we came before this Council, Majesty, but it is what we expected. If nothing else, we have named what has not been named and thereby made it real. And real things cannot easily be dispersed. We will abide by your word—for now. But we will be watching and listening—carefully. And, Sire, Common Clan do not like liars."

"I am no liar," Avall replied calmly. "Nor ever have been. Now, if you have no more business, I would ask that you withdraw so that other business might be heard."

Haggyn sketched a bow—all that Law required—turned, and pushed his way through his comrades, who then followed him from the Hall. One remained behind: Kayvvin—Chief of Common Clan.

The old woman looked very serious indeed—and deeply troubled. "Kayvvin?" Avall prompted.

"Majesty," she began, with quiet dignity, "you have heard one concern of Common Clan already—the one that is uppermost among all our minds. But we have another almost as serious, and perhaps doubly serious, now that you have told us of this council you have proposed." She paused, straightened her shoulders, then went on. "Perhaps this council of yours will succeed, perhaps it will not. In any case, whatever decisions are reached—if any there be, which I doubt, given that these matters have occupied our thoughts since we came here to Eron"—she cleared her throat—"whatever decisions are reached will depend for their implementation on who sits the Stone when those decisions are reached. Therefore, I ask you clearly either to dispel or confirm the rumors we have heard: that you plan to abdicate at Sundeath—and, if the latter, to name who your successor might be."

Avall had not sat down since his interchange with Haggyn, nor did he do so now, but he relaxed ever so slightly, if for no other reason than because Kayvvin had finally voiced what *had* been uppermost in his thoughts—and countless private discussions with his friends—since the throne had been thrust upon him two eighths back. Nor had he any illusions that his obvious reluctance had not been discussed—probably by everyone on the Council, if not in all of Eron.

Yet it was Tryffon syn Ferr who spoke, preempting Avall's right to first reply. Which was typical of Tryffon: bluff and protective as he was, by turns. "Of course he will retain the throne," the Chief of Warcraft cried. "We all saw him at the Battle of Storms. The Eight favored him that day, as They have never favored another King of Eron. They favored him in his craft—for the helm, sword, and shield were either of his making or his augmenting. Nay, They favored him before that, by allowing him to find the gems that ensured our victory. He—"

"Anyone could have found those gems," someone from Beast shouted. "If any clan has a right to them, it is Gem, not Smith."

"Smith did not seek them, however," came a woman's voice from closer in. "They were found in Smith's vein at Gem-Hold, and—so far as we know—in no other."

Avall gasped. *Strynn* had said that, which he hadn't expected—though why not, he had no idea. In any case, she was continuing. "So far as we know," she repeated. "If one wants to open up the entire affair and engage in valid, if incendiary speculation, one might well ask if *other* clans might not have found something similar in their veins and withheld that knowledge entirely. Certainly Gem-Hold should know to a mote of dust what the earth beneath it contains, in kind if not in number. And as has been noted, these gems such as Avall and his counselors have found, should not, in theory, be uniquely the province of that one vein." She did not continue, but fixed Priest-Clan with a pointed stare.

"Which has nothing to do with Avall's abdication," Kayvvin replied, "save, perhaps as he has knowledge of these gems. But even so, such knowledge would be the province of Gem or Lore, not of the Sovereignty. And the gems are themselves the property of the Crown not only by virtue of being incorporated into masterworks, which all who have seen them freely admit; but also by being part of the royal regalia, which likewise belongs to the Crown. Which *could,* in theory, be placed on the head of someone of Common Clan."

A general uproar ensued.

Avall started to reply, to cut through that hubbub by symbolically raising the sword. But just as he shifted his grip upon it, a tap on his shoulder from Lykkon drew his attention to the back of the hall. Merryn had entered, in full Royal Guardsman kit. But she was not alone. Someone stood beside her, clad in Argen's colors beneath the tabard of a Royal Herald. Avall didn't have to look twice to know that it was Lykkon's younger brother, Bingg. Nor would Bingg have entered had the news he conveyed been less than dire. And there was very little that was important enough to interrupt the first royal court of Midsummer.

Only one thing, in fact. "Hold!" Avall cried, thereby silencing the debate. Then, ignoring a veritable choir of protests: "Herald, come forward."

To his credit, Bingg didn't flinch as he strode down the aisle, for all he was only thirteen and legally too young for such a role. Still, his eyes had begun to tear by the time he reached the dais, and Avall knew then, with absolute conviction, the news his young cousin carried.

Somehow, he maintained a semblance of decorum as he spoke the ritual words. "Herald, have you news for this Council, or for the King's ears alone?"

Bingg's handsome young face was as grim as someone thrice his age as he replied. "What I would say will be common knowledge in Tir-Eron in half a hand anyway, and affects all on this Council in some way, but I would still say it first to you alone, if I may approach to whisper it."

Avall nodded and gestured his cousin forward. It was all he could do not to reach out to embrace his kinsman, yet the King kept the youth at arm's length as he heard the words pronounced.

"Majesty—and Avall syn Argen-a—it is with sadness beyond knowing that I tell you both alike that, at a finger past sunrise, Eellon syn Argen-a, Chief of all three septs of Clan Argen, took one long breath which was not followed by another. They . . . they thought he would last out the day," he blurted abruptly, all pretense of decorum fled. "Avall, I'm sorry. I know you wanted to be there, but the healers misjudged."

Avall didn't hear the rest, if there was any, for here, before all the assembled Chiefs of Eron, the High King of them all was crying.

"There will be time for debate, later," he heard himself say to the silent Council. "Argument can bear fruit anytime; mourning has a shorter season."

CHAPTER IV:

OUT OF THE WOODS, INTO THE DARK

(NORTHWESTERN ERON: GEM-HOLD-WINTER— HIGH SUMMER: DAY XLI—SHORTLY AFTER NOON)

~~~~~~

Kylin syn Omyrr, comfortably ensconced on a padded stool in the cedar-paneled splendor of his clan's best common hall, had been playing the ancient harp tune called "Winterqueen's Lament" for what seemed to be a very appreciative audience of one. It was one of the Hold-Warden's favorites, he knew, as it was likewise one of Strynn's. Two very different women, but linked by the bond of music. Then again, music *was* a bond: a force for unity and harmony—which could well be why he loved it. Of course, he was also objective enough to realize that he might love it simply because it was one of the few crafts at which he could actually excel. He *was* blind, after all—since he was three. But he'd also been born into the clan that controlled music, which he liked to think implied at least marginal involvement by Fate.

As for music's power to soothe—was that something he desired intrinsically, or merely another function of his blindness? A reaction to the fact that in chaotic times it was people like him who suffered most? Not that he didn't have effective patrons: Crim here, and the King and his comrades back in Tir-Eron. But he was already wondering whether it had been a mistake to return here, even to retrieve his chief-harp. Div had tried to argue him out of it when he'd first broached the notion of a journey west, and Strynn had added her own protests. Avall had remained silent, which might mean something and might not, given that the High King knew that he and Strynn were, in all but the physical act, lovers.

In any case, he was here, and Div, who had no use for the place, had abandoned him for the time being in favor of her own hold in the Wild, several days away. In fact, this was his second time playing for Crim. The first had gone well, though she'd had a headache then. This time she seemed . . . edgy.

He concluded the song with a plaintive "ping, ping . . . ping," and let his hands fall to his thighs, where he wiped his fingers on scarlet sylk house-hose and the hem of a purple velvet short-tunic, their textured fabrics chosen to please one sense in the absence of another. Across from him, Crim sighed happily, then took a sip from a goblet of wine she'd lately filled from the frosted carafe beside her. A *metal* goblet, he knew, because of the way it had sounded being filled. A sip, because he heard the sound her lips made on the rim and the soft gulp of the ensuing swallow.

"Do you have anything new?" Crim asked a little too casually, though Kylin caught the subtlety of the inflection. "That's my favorite tune—as you very well knew, wicked boy—but surely you picked up something new in Tir-Eron. Some ballad about Avall, perhaps? And that magic sword of his?"

Kylin felt a shiver of alarm. This was exactly what he'd feared. He was the person in the entire hold closest to the happenings last spring, and to those who had effected them—and Crim would want to know those things, since they affected her as well. Which knowing was her responsibility as Hold-Warden, if not her right as, so he'd supposed, his friend.

"They're mostly whistle tunes, Lady, or tunes for the lute," he replied offhand. "I haven't taken time to transpose them for the harp."

"You could, though," Crim replied with more of that studied

nonchalance that put Kylin so on guard. "It would be as easy for you as breathing."

"The tunes aren't that interesting, challenging, or original." He tried to sound as indifferent as she, absently removing his black-sylk blindfold and retying it around his long black hair.

"I'm not interested in the tunes. In cases like that, it's the words that matter."

"I didn't know you were interested in ballads at all—and that's what one mostly hears, never mind that one only hears the newest in the South Bank taverns, and I haven't *been* to South Bank."

Another sip. Carefully, as though she were watching him intently. "Avall won't let you go?"

He shook his head. "Avall denies me nothing—but South Bank is no place for a blind man."

"You can't mean that!"—her surprise sounded sincere— "No one would dare harm you. For what you are to the King, never mind that you're High Clan."

"That last isn't the shield you might suppose," Kylin retorted, trying to shift the conversation in a less controversial direction while still appearing naively informative. And hoping along the way to learn how Crim felt about certain notions.

"It isn't?"

"I assumed you knew. I wasn't the first to come here since the war."

A deep breath. "You've always been honest with me, Kylin. I'd appreciate you telling me what you can—what you feel, or suspect, more importantly. I won't ask you to violate any vows or confidences."

Because it would cost your position, he thought grimly. "I understand," he continued aloud. "The problem is simply that some of Common Clan—and clanless, more to the point— have found themselves at odds with the Crown and the King." He shifted listlessly. "Maybe not so much at odds," he corrected. "Conflicted. The King saved the country, but the King has also roused the ire of Priest-Clan, and the people don't want to have to choose between them."

"Will they *have* to?"

"Not if Avall can help it."

"Avall," Crim murmured after another sip. "It all comes back to him, doesn't it? I wish I'd had a chance to get to know him better when he was here."

Kyril relaxed a little. "He's not a bad man, Lady, nor a happy one."

"You wrote a song about him, didn't you?"

Kylin's heart skipped a beat, even as confusion invaded him. "I . . . Lady, I did not!"

"For his wife, then. 'The Dreaming Jewel'?"

Anger replaced confusion. Kylin's pulse started to race, even as a rush of heat roared up his cheeks. "You had no right!"

"It was in your quarters," Crim retorted stiffly. "You abandoned them without warning, permission, or explanation. It was my responsibility to investigate. I didn't know what I was reading until I'd read it. I didn't know what it meant until I heard about the gem."

Kylin stood abruptly. "I'd appreciate it if you'd—"

He broke off, cocking his head. Listening.

"What?" Then a confused, "I don't hear anything. If this is some excuse—"

"Hush!" Kylin hissed. "Someone's approaching at a run and asking for you. Surely you can hear—"

Crim rose in a swish of garments. Kylin followed her footsteps toward the threshold. She paused there, holding her breath, then slowly eased the door open. The sounds came louder—loud enough for anyone to hear, even one with sight: the hard, brisk tramp of heavy outdoor boots. And words that chilled Kylin to the bone. "Lady," a young male voice announced breathlessly, "there seems to be a . . . disturbance."

• • •

"What *kind* of disturbance?" Crim demanded as she let the door slip closed behind her and confronted the panting young man in Warcraft livery who'd just tracked mud onto Clan Omyrr's expensive carpet. He'd been outside, she knew already, by the flush on his cheeks as much as the layered clothing—this far north, the days were chill, even in High Summer. Too, he was Warcraft, in official livery, and the only function such folks served here was to keep watch and guard.

"Armed men in the woods," the youth gasped. "Moving toward the hold. We've seen the flash of their weapons."

"Show me," Crim demanded, already pushing past the breathless messenger in the direction his footprints indicated. He followed at a trot, as her own steps became a run. Fortunately, it wasn't far from Omyrr's suite to the high-arched east–west corridor that was the hold's main thoroughfare. And not far from there to a door that let, via the requisite weather-gate, onto one of the massive stone arcades that wrapped Gem-Hold-Winter on three sides this low down, and four higher up.

By the time she rushed out to join what she saw with dismay was a concerned mob in the arcade, she'd learned that there were "a lot" of these men, that they wore white cloaks above dark blue tunics, that they also wore helms and carried shields but sported no insignia. And that over half of them were mounted on very good horses indeed. *Eronese* horses and weapons. Which negated her notion that this might be a band of renegade Ixtians bent on vengeance.

Her forces were moving, too—such as they were—men and women alike, all clad in summer cloaks of Warcraft crimson, pouring out of archways at the arcade's either end. And if that was happening here, it was probably happening in the other arcades as well. But what could be going on? "Find Akalian," she told the guard, meaning Warcraft's local chief.

"He should *be* here," the guard panted, still winded. "We sent for him when we sent for you."

"*Find* him."

"I was told to guard you."

Crim started to reply, then thought better of it, though already she was wishing she'd snared at least a paring knife from Omyrr's suite. Instead, she seized the arm of the competent-looking woman next to her, not waiting for the woman to recognize her before she barked an order—"Go find Akalian of War!"—and was pleased to see the woman scurry off.

For all its enormous size, the arcade was rapidly filling up as rumor spread. If Crim wasn't careful, she'd have panic on her hands, for this was certainly an uneasy mob. Some were fresh from Tir-Eron, she reckoned, or from Half Gorge and South Gorge, which had born the brunt of Ixti's recent incursion. They'd be scared, nervous, and quick to act, when in fact, she had no idea what these supposed warriors' business should be—if any. Worse, if Akalian didn't appear soon, she'd have to act unilaterally, which, where martial matters were concerned, could be a mistake.

She'd reached the stone balustrade by then. Taking a deep breath, she climbed atop it—it was half a span wide but she had a good head for heights, and the important thing was to let herself be seen. Ignoring the murmurs behind her, she scanned the surrounding terrain, searching the fringe of pine woods atop the ridge that ringed what part of the hold wasn't carved into the mountain. There *was* movement there, she acknowledged with a sinking heart; and she could indeed see horses and the white-cloaked figures who rode them, coupled with the flash of metal that could be weapons as easily as armor. Even as she watched, a long line of those half-seen shapes stepped, as by some unheard command, from beneath the shadow of the trees to form a near-unbroken line from left to right—north to south—along the crest of the slope. And—a chill ran up her spine at this—three of every four were mounted. And everything she'd ever read about warfare agreed that infantry generally surpassed cavalry by a ratio of four to one.

So where were the missing men?

She had a terrible feeling she knew. "Back, inside!" she snapped at those who stood nearest. "Arm yourselves and search for anyone who acts suspicious or looks like they don't belong here. We've almost certainly been invaded."

As if her word were some sign, the encircling force moved closer. Eight! How many were there, anyway? A hundred? Five hundred? A *thousand*? It had only taken a thousand Ixtians to overwhelm War-Hold, and it had been well fortified. Her hold was mostly warded against the winter, and far too many doors gave access to the ground, all of which had weather-gates that could be sealed at need but probably weren't this time of year.

In any case, these horsemen weren't there to get in; they were there to assure that no one escaped. They would intimidate and distract, while the infantry picked off stragglers.

And then she heard what she'd both dreaded and expected: shouts, cries, and screams, and louder than them all, the heart-stopping clang of metal on metal. From behind her.

Those around her were yelling, too, but an encouraging number were turning to fight the white-cloaked men now issuing from every door in sight. As best she could tell, the invaders were fighting their way upward, securing sections as they reached them, which did not bode well, given that this arcade was two-thirds of the way up the hold's face.

Without thinking about it—or waiting for Akalian, who she doubted would do much good anyway, assuming he still lived—she leapt down from her perch, which put her in a circle of milling kinsmen, and started toward the juncture of two massive stone buttresses where the arcade kinked outward to the left.

She had no doubt what had happened. Some force—probably those mysterious folk who had attacked Avall—were now attacking Gem-Hold. They'd most likely entered by stealth at night—maybe several nights. Not all of the entrances were guarded, after all, and she was certain there were some of which even she was unaware, notably the rumored "Gods' Door" Priest-Clan referenced now and then. Which fit with her suspicions about internal collusion perfectly.

But why? she wondered, as she thrust aside a panicked

woman, then neatly sidestepped a teenage boy trying to comfort a hysterical sister. Yet logic had already provided an answer. Gem-Hold controlled the source of the magic gems, and those gems were the most precious—and powerful—things in Eron. Whoever controlled them controlled the kingdom. And those who stood to gain most by maintaining the established order—which likely meant deposing the present King—were easy enough to name.

Priest-Clan.

Still, Crim knew her responsibility to a fine degree, and it was to her country, her King, her clan, and her hold in that order—and that left no choice as to her next action.

She'd reached the buttresses now: massive piers of stone two spans to a side, rising to the distant ceiling and merging into the wall below. A band of low-relief interlace encircled it at waist level, and her hand quickly found a niche within it that exactly fitted her Warden's ring. This was supposed to be a secret, she reckoned, but this was no time for subtlety, and so she pressed her signet into its place and gave her wrist a quarter turn. Stone grated and grit drifted down on her head, as an opening gaped, revealing a narrow spiral staircase that extended both up and down. She slipped inside at once, though guilt at abandoning her people when they needed her almost made her pause. No, it was too late for them, she concluded. If the invaders had let themselves be seen, the hold was already infested with them, and she knew what she'd do in their boots: take everyone of importance hostage and disarm the rest. And the armory was on the ground level, because no one had ever thought the hold would actually be assailed, the weapons there most often being used for hunting.

"Lady," came a voice behind her, and she realized she wasn't alone. It was the guard who'd first alerted her.

"What are you doing here?" she rasped, as a stone panel slid home behind her, leaving them both in darkness.

"Guarding you."

"Stupidly, but I've no time to argue. Do you have a name?"

"Bayne."

"Let's hope that's not a name of omen. Now go or stay, but don't even think to hinder me. I've got to go down—and down and down." Not waiting for reply, she found the wall by feel and the steps on whose landing she stood by memory as much as anything, and started downward at absolutely the fastest pace her long Warden's robe allowed. Fortunately, the first full turn revealed one of a series of tiny glow-globes set in hand-sized niches every dozen steps. To his credit, Bayne didn't protest, but followed doggedly as they began their descent.

"Priest-Clan," she told him, because he surely wanted to know. "After the mines."

"You have proof?"

"I have sense; that'll have to suffice for now."

"But why . . . ?"

"Power. Pure and simple."

"But—"

She didn't reply, for they'd reached a landing and her fingers were once again seeking a certain niche in a certain design. Gem and Stone had once been one, and Stone had here wrought well for Gem. She heard the click at the same time she smelled the forges.

And would've rushed out into battle had Bayne not restrained her. "Lady, you've no weapon—"

"I have now," she replied brusquely, snatching the sword from his hand before he could stop her. "You've armor; I've none, but I can't delay. There should be something you can use out there. Now come on!"

With that, she strode out into what was normally a vast, whitewashed room, against the walls of which easily two dozen forges were arrayed, most usually occupied by someone from Smithcraft. Avall had shaped the helm's panels here, as had Eddyn portions of the shield, and Strynn most of that wondrous sword. Now, however, it was Crim's own folk being tempered—and losing—mostly over to the left, by the door, where two dozen bare-torsoed and sweaty kinsmen battled a tide of silent invaders in white cloaks, far too many of which bore telltale splatters of red. It took Crim but a breath to dismiss theirs as a lost cause. "Back," she told Bayne, shoving him toward the door from which he'd just emerged. He barely had time to snatch a sword blank from a nearby rack before complying. "Lady—"

"We can do no good here," she snapped, as she followed him in. "We *might* in the mines. They may not have reached there yet."

"The mines—"

"There are ways to seal them," she said shortly. "I'm going to do that. It gives me a bargaining position, where otherwise I have none. It's a risk, but it's all I have."

And with that she set her signet to the wall behind, letting the darkness that followed her down the stairs ensure that it had closed. Maybe she'd been seen, maybe not. It didn't matter. What mattered lay many levels lower.

She was sweating now, and her lungs felt like bellows from the forges she'd just left, pushed too hard and too long to fan too hot a fire. Her heart thumped like the hammers there, or like those on the trods, that loosened the stone for the drills to pierce more easily. Yet ever down she went, feet slapping the treads like the beat of an unheard song. Which reminded her of Kylin, whom she'd abandoned to his fate. Not that she'd known what awaited her. It was amazing, she reckoned, how fast reality could change. Not even a finger had elapsed since Kylin had heard those steps.

Down and down and down, with Bayne still behind her, loyal as a dog, which might not be a virtue if it got him killed. He wasn't War-Hold born, she reckoned, else he'd have been more assertive yet more subtle. Someone had told him his duty, which had absolved him from thinking, and he was doing it. He'd have a clear conscience when this was over. If he survived.

Down and down and down.

She could feel the mines as she approached, for the stair was hewn from the rock of Tar-Megon itself, and the grinding and pounding in the veins rode through that stone to speak of endless efforts to acquire what was beautiful but ultimately useless, save as objects over which to argue—or make war.

Down and down and down—and then there.

Bayne stumbled into her back before he realized she'd halted, but she ignored the minor discomfort of armor striking her shoulders while she fumbled, yet again, with a hidden catch.

This time she emerged into something no more remarkable than a blind niche in the Mine-Master's common room, the true nature of which had hopefully eluded him. Not that it mattered, for a cautious check showed the room unoccupied, with no sign yet that battle raged beyond it.

Setting her shoulders, she opened the door opposite the arch, which put her in the Master's duty chamber—empty as well. In any case her business was farther on: at the entrance to the mines themselves, one more door, an archway, and a very large room from where she stood. There were still no sounds of battle. Or maybe she simply couldn't hear them.

With Bayne in tow, she stepped out into the corridor that surrounded the octagonal entrance chamber—exactly as footsteps echoed on the lone "formal" stair to the right. Someone was evidently in as big a hurry as she was, with more steps following, these heavily booted.

Through the facing archway, then, and onto the inlaid map in the main chamber, aiming for the entrance to the mines themselves . . .

A figure appeared on the stairs a quarter way around to the right, and proceeded to dash down them two at a time—a woman in Smithcraft livery, pursued by men in white cloaks.

"Fool," she growled, as she recognized Liallyn. "That damned fool's led them here."

Of course they'd have found their way here anyway— eventually. Still, whoever the invaders were, they'd been unable to penetrate this far before their attack. At least that much of her security force was working.

Liallyn had reached the bottom now, and looked more angry than relieved to see Crim moving to intercept her. Crim wondered vaguely whether those working the present shift in the mines even knew what was happening—until the sounds of more feet approaching from that direction, coupled with cries of "attack" and "invaders" gave answer. Word had spread like fire through the hold, but this place was farthest in, and thereby last to know.

They all met in the stone octagon: Crim and Bayne entering from the east; Liallyn, still ahead of the invaders, from the north; a force of grim-faced miners issuing from the arch that marked the actual entrance to the mines in the west.

But what was Liallyn doing? Paying no mind to Crim, she was running toward the entrance as fast as her heavy robe allowed—which made no sense.

Unless, Crim realized with a gasp, her agenda was neither Crim's nor her own, but her clan's. Smiths were famous for their loyalty and pride. And if *she* were from Smith . . .

Crim's heart sank. And sank farther when she realized what Liallyn carried. A leather bag marked with a certain warning sign she could make out even here.

Quick-fire.

"Nooooo!" Crim shrieked, even as the Smith reached the wall nearest the mines and snatched the glow-globe there, only to smash it ruthlessly to the floor, freeing a flood of heat imprisoned by the glass. Light slammed around the room, so that Crim could barely see the woman empty the bag atop the burning fluid.

Then light and heat in truth, as the chamber exploded.

"That fool!" Crim had time to scream, before Bayne snared her from behind and yanked her back into the surrounding corridor. His gesture saved her, but Crim scarcely cared. She heard, rather than saw, the mines' entrance collapsing in a heap of fallen stone, and barely reached the Master's suite intact before the whole ceiling came down atop the inlaid gemstone floor, burying the entire entrance chamber and most of the surrounding corridor beneath a mountain's weight of rubble. Burying Liallyn of Smith, too, and hopefully a good many invaders.

But also trapping who-knew-how-many folk in the mines.

"I assume there's another entrance," Bayne managed, wide-eyed and gasping as he wiped dust and sweat from his face with a corner of his tabard.

Crim shook her head. "No, and damn Liallyn, Smith, and Argen for it, too."

"You mean—?" Bayne dared breathlessly.

She nodded grimly. "Anyone still in the mines is as good as dead."

"But that woman . . ."

"From Smith. She was looking out for their interests, but what she got . . ."

Bayne nodded sadly, as they squeezed past masses of rubble on their way to what was left of the main stairs. "What she got was one more stick on the fire of civil war."

Crim didn't even protest when five white-cloaked figures emerged from the third landing up, disarmed her and Bayne, chained their wrists together, and escorted them away.

It wasn't her responsibility any longer. She'd done everything possible, and it hadn't been enough, but those who would judge her were very far away, and to stand before any judgment they might give, she had to survive. She dreaded sleep, however, for already she could hear—in spite of all rationality—the panicked screams of those now trapped below.

A very short time earlier, Kylin had heard screaming, too, but it was screaming born not of fear, but of anger. Crouched as he was where curiosity had placed him after Crim's departure—beneath a wall-table in the corridor outside his quarters—he only hoped the thick folds of black velvet with which the table was draped rendered him invisible to what had proven to be an invading army. Composed of his own countrymen, he assumed from their accents; and definitely soldiers, by the sound of their boots.

These soldiers were evidently looking for the Hold-Warden,

too—and not finding her, to judge by the altercation he'd just overheard between an officer and one of his subordinates, which had resulted in someone being slapped and an angry protest from the recipient. He'd been keeping a close eye out, the soldier said, but the Warden had disappeared from the arcade, so he'd thought she might return here—which explanation was interrupted by the arrival of someone else, who by the sound of her soft indoor shoes and lighter tread must be a woman. Lady Nyss, the local Priest-Clan-Chief, as it turned out. Kylin knew her voice all too well—and also Crim's suspicions regarding the woman's clandestine activities, courtesy of a conversation between Crim and Mystel he'd "accidentally" overheard.

And now Nyss and the invader were engaged in as vehement a contest of authority as Kylin had ever witnessed.

"You were to make sure the Warden was in her quarters," the invader snapped. "Half this hold sees her daily or waits upon her. You were to have made sure the door was locked when I told you. This one," he added, evidently referring to the man he'd slapped, "was supposed to have done it."

"She wasn't supposed to go visiting or have warning," Nyss retorted. "One of your men must have moved too soon or too carelessly. He was seen."

"Aye," came the accused's cautious reply. "I was on my way here when I saw someone from War also approaching. I knew at once what he was about, and I . . . I suppose I should've challenged him, since I'd lost the initiative of surprise. But that would've made noise, which would've alerted the Warden in any case, and increased the odds of her success."

"And your death," Nyss inserted sourly. "But go on."

"I thought I might find another chance," the man panted. "So I followed them. I was moving toward her on the porch with my dagger drawn, hoping to kill her in the confusion, since capture no longer seemed viable. But then she reached one of the buttresses that support the arcades, and before I knew it, an opening had appeared there, and she—and that soldier from War—had ducked inside, and she was gone."

"Eight!" Nyss spat, even as the invader uttered a coarser word.

"I would've followed!" the man protested.

"Silence!" from both others at once. Then, from Nyss: "We both know how riddled with secret corridors and stairs this place is, else you wouldn't be here. But that one—I did not know of it. Still, if it was in a buttress, it can only go up or down, and down would make more sense, since that way lies escape, if that was her goal, or the—"

"The mines," the invader replied heavily.

But he said no more, for at that moment, the entire hold was shaken by what had to be an explosion in its depths. Even where Kylin crouched, many levels above the ground, he felt the floor jump beneath him. Worse, the table threatened to topple, and would have, had he not braced it. The air filled with the dreadful grating of tortured rock, mingled with distant shouts and much closer curses, and finally by the shriek of splitting stone. A loud rumble followed, and more shouts— one from Nyss, yelling for her companions to get in the doorway, and then, with a deafening roar, a section of ceiling came down. Something struck the tabletop, and Kylin heard wood splinter. He wondered, briefly, what had become of his chiefharp, but that concern lasted only long enough for him to realize that the harp, without him alive to play it, was not a thing that mattered.

More rubble fell as the building settled, but Kylin didn't want to ponder what that signified, save that something or someone had surely wreaked havoc deep in the bowels of the hold.

A final shake-and-shift, and the stone wall split right beside him. He flinched away in horror, expecting some terrible fate, but what he found was merely a rush of cool air. Which meant that however much destruction reigned beyond his hiding place, he probably wouldn't suffocate.

But he didn't want to be taken prisoner, either. Fortunately, the tabletop above him listed to his left, and the force of falling stone had dragged part of the cover down with it and pinned it to the floor, effectively prisoning him in a fabric cage. Which was just as well, since the last thing he wanted was to be detected. The wall to his right, however . . . He probed it with his fingers, seeking the source of that fresh air. Nor was he long in finding it. A split ran as far as he could reach up and down, neatly bisecting one of the intricate metal ventilation grills that brought outside air into the hold's inner regions. It had loosened the grill, too, and it was a simple matter to remove it.

Freedom was suddenly the most important thing to him: freedom and survival. With the hold apparently under siege, any free man was valuable. There might still be allies somewhere in this pile, after all; and in any case, Div was due back soon and would surely sense the situation. Hopefully, he could somehow connect with her. In the meantime, he would learn what he could about these invaders. He'd try not to be seen, but if he *was* seen, anyone who didn't know him would only see a harmless blind man. Which meant he had to avoid being seen by anyone who knew him, which was best effected if he availed himself of this gift from The Eight he'd found right here. The vent ducts led everywhere, and they had many openings. Some even opened onto shafts that terminated close to ground level. If he could reach one of *those*—Well, he'd worry about that if he survived to confront it.

At least the building seemed to have settled, though he could smell smoke now, which was a good reason *not* to try the vent ducts yet. The hold was largely impervious to flame, but that didn't mean parts of it couldn't burn. As soon as the air cleared, he'd make good his escape—from this level, at any rate. Just twist his way into the duct beyond the grill and pull it to behind him. And hope there were no more explosions and that the domain behind the walls was not more dangerous than the one beyond them.

CHAPTER V:

DECISIONS

~~~~~~

Perhaps, Avall reflected, as he strode away from Eellon's death chamber, there *were* advantages to being King. If nothing else, the title gave him an excuse to absent himself from that cold, dry thing that had once been his two-father, mentor, adviser, goad, and friend. As, he reflected, Eellon had also been to Eron—and three generations of Kings, not the least of them the one whom Avall had succeeded.

But he wanted to think about Gynn even less than about Eellon. At least Eellon was dead; therefore, he was at peace. Any decisions concerning him would be determined by rite, tradition, and the Death Priests. Gynn, however, still lived—if sitting wide-awake with half his brain gone constituted life. Avall didn't think so. Better a clean death for his predecessor— a sword through the heart in the heat of battle, or a clean slice across the throat—than a chunk of stone shrapnel flung high by an explosion that, upon falling, crushed the back of the High King's helm and the head beneath it. A finger's difference in distance that fateful moment, and Avall would still be back in Eellon's chamber, free to mourn.

He froze in place, then spun around to face the Guardsmen

following discreetly three paces behind. Strynn was there, too, with Rann and Lykkon. Most of his inner circle, in fact, save Merryn, whom he'd left as his surrogate to guard the corpse until the Death Priests came. Scowling, he motioned them farther back; then, having no other choice, turned again and strode numbly on, his vision increasingly veiled with ill-fought tears, until he came to what had been his own suite before he'd assumed the throne. Abandoning his companions to the sitting room, he slipped into the bedroom, locked the door, and for the next hand lay staring at the ceiling, knowing there was one less good thing in the world, and one less resource on which Fate would let him rely.

By rights he should cut his hair and change into mourning black. But that would acknowledge the reality of what had happened, and he wasn't ready for that. Instead, he flung himself off the bed, unlocked the door, and rejoined his friends. But not to mourn.

Their ranks had swelled, he noted. To Rann, Lykkon, and Strynn had been added his mother, Evvion; Veen; and a redeyed Merryn—now off duty—along with Vorinn and Tryffon of War. Preedor was standing honor watch over his old friend, Merryn murmured through a hug. Avall wondered what those two old men had been like as boys. They'd been bond-mates, he knew, until something had torn a rift between them. It was long since healed, but they'd never renewed that vow. And now they never would. Maybe someday Preedor would tell him the entire tale. In the meantime, there were more pressing things to ponder.

The company had claimed seats around the room, some even on the floor, for all he was about to turn this into a royal council. Bingg appeared a moment later with food and drink, causing Avall to wonder yet again whether the boy and Lykkon might not share some mental bond that was more than ordinary, if not as strong as that wrought by the gems.

In any case, they got themselves settled, with Avall in his favorite chair beside the fireplace. "I need to be distracted," he informed them frankly. "Probably we all do. But I *don't* need frivolity. Therefore, as much as I hate to discuss politics, this might be the time for it. Most of you saw what transpired at court today. You must also know that I had no more notion of convening that council I promised than I had of holding court while painted blue. Which is not to say that I don't think such a council is needed, nor that, now I've committed to it, one won't be forthcoming. Still, I preempted myself to buy time in an awkward situation, and now I have to throw myself on your mercy"—he grinned at that—"and ask your advice after the fact. Specifically . . . what *are* we going to do about Priest-Clan?"

"Assuming we do anything," Strynn added. "If we play things carefully, we can let them destroy themselves. They have as much to answer for as we do, if we can only get Common Clan to see it. Whatever we've been hiding from them—which, as far as I'm concerned is nothing—Priest-Clan has been hiding far longer."

Avall chewed his lip. "So you're saying that we should try to redirect whatever questions are put to us to Priest-Clan instead? Let them bear the brunt of whatever . . . rebellion, to name the direst option, Common Clan contrives?"

"The problem is," Lykkon observed, "there isn't one single, united Priest-Clan, and I'm not sure there ever was. There are the folks that tried to kill you and Rann, for instance. We've no idea if they're officially sanctioned, or if the bulk of Priest is no more aware of their existence than we were. From what little Eddyn told us between his return and death, I'm inclined toward the former."

Tryffon scratched his short gray beard. "And I wish we'd thought to query him more thoroughly, since he was our main source of information about them. As it is, we know very little. Mostly that they're very canny, very competent, and have at least one citadel between here and Gem-Hold-Winter."

"But if they're that canny," Merryn retorted, "they're likely to have *more* than one. Fallback positions are a necessity for extralegal groups like that. It would be nice," she added with a sour grimace, "if we at least had something to call them."

"Eddyn called them ghost priests," Avall supplied. "Because of those white cloaks they wore. That'll do until we learn otherwise."

Lykkon cleared his throat. "Actually . . . a means *does* exist to learn otherwise—maybe."

Avall looked puzzled, then glared at him, as realization dawned. "You mean Rrath?"

Rann and Lykkon nodded as one. "He's still alive," Rann continued. "Whatever happened to him doesn't seem to have involved brain damage—not like what's afflicted Gynn. His healers say his coma is more like a retreat from the world. The gems in the regalia kept him alive after what should've been a fatal fall. There's no reason they shouldn't also have saved his mind, given that they seem to protect whoever wields them."

"Which raises the question of whether the gems are active or passive parties in all this," Merryn noted.

"Which is damned far from the question of Priest-Clan," Avall growled, "and more properly subject for open debate before this new council I now have to organize. In the meantime, I think Lyk's right. There *is* no single Priest-Clan now, and maybe never was. Eight, I can think of three factions without even trying.

"The first," he went on quickly, counting on his fingers, "are those who want to preserve things as they are, but for positive reasons. They're the arm that honestly wants to serve the people—*all* the people, but especially Common Clan, and clanless. They care less about dogma or power than about expressing the will of The Eight in ways that can actually help people. If some heavy theological debate a quarter from now suddenly has us acknowledging that geens have souls, the cosmic implications of that decision will matter less to them than the practical matter of how it would affect the supply of surplus meat, since geens would then have to be kept from starvation, just like people. If there's a rebellion—which I pray won't happen, but which we must admit might occur—we can probably count on that faction to go their own way calmly, and play as much as they can for both sides. They won't fight against us, but I doubt they'll fight for us, either. And they'll minister spiritually to anyone who requests it."

"Good thinking so far," Tryffon conceded. "Optimistic—but that's your age talking. Still, it's in line with what I've seen and heard."

"Second faction," Merryn prompted. "Let's define the structures, *then* fill in the details."

"Second faction is the opposite of the first," Avall went on. "I'm talking about the ghost priests, of course. We know they're the radical political arm of the clan. We know they're powerful and have resources at their disposal that we can't begin to suspect. Beyond that, we know nothing."

"I do," Vorinn volunteered, speaking up for the first time. "I've been talking to some of the Ixtian defectors, and one of them says that some people he assumes were representatives of these very ghost priests came to Barrax's camp one night with some kind of bargain to offer. From the very little he overheard or pieced together later, it appears that this faction told Barrax that they—and, by extension, Priest-Clan—wouldn't oppose him during his invasion, in exchange for assuring their own position."

Avall felt heat rise in his face. "Now you tell me!"

Vorinn regarded him calmly, his smooth features carefully controlled—yet vaguely at odds with the rest of his body, which evinced a kind of restless power, even in repose. "I only just learned myself. And let me stress that a lot of it is guesswork."

"Makes sense, though," Tryffon rumbled. "Those to whom power is important will work to secure that power any way they can. If it involves throwing in with the enemy—well, they might just as well regard us as enemies, and with better reason, if implicit threat is what defines an enemy to start with."

"The third faction—" Lykkon reminded them, looking up from his ever-present journal, "I assume it's the middle ground?"

Avall shook his head. "I don't think there *is* a middle ground. The primary variable really seems to be how much a given faction values power in the abstract over their clan's stated goal. One faction evidently doesn't—much. The second values it above all—I suspect for its own sake. The third is the 'no-change' sept—except that what they're hoping to maintain happens to be very powerful anyway, simply because their clan 'controls' religion. And since religion equals both hope and comfort for a large part of our population, that isn't to be underestimated."

Strynn steepled her fingers before her. "Which means that in case of rebellion they'd advance their own causes before they'd advance ours."

Merryn nodded gravely. "Given that we're probably the ones they'd be rebelling against to start with, I think that's a fair assessment."

"*Rebellion,*" Lykkon echoed harshly. "We keep throwing that word around like it was something very abstract, much like we did 'war' two seasons back. But I wonder how abstract it really is. I assume that this rebellion, if it comes, will be Common Clan against High Clan, with Priest sitting by to pick up the pieces?"

Tryffon leaned back and folded his arms. "Not necessarily. Common is no more united than anyone else—less so, if anything, simply because it's so diverse. They've got people poor as mud who'll side with anyone who'll give them a meal, preferably for free. And, on the other extreme, there are those who are so precisely similar to us in every way but lineage that we marry them and think nothing of it."

"But we're not united, either," Rann retorted. "Even before the war we were factionalized. There's the ancient Smith-War-Lore triumvirate, to start with—with Stone almost included as well, since we've married into the others so often;

and Gem as a somewhat shaky adjunct: not strong enough to go against the powerful three-and-a-half, nor yet wanting to be overrun by them—and important because they're rich."

"In other words, they'd like to be courted," Avall summarized. "I wonder if anyone actually has. Remind me to set someone watching their hall and hold, to see who enters."

"I'll tend to it," Merryn volunteered before Veen could preempt her.

The discussion continued in ever-more labyrinthine detail as the day waned. Eventually, it progressed to every single clan and craft being named and its strengths, weaknesses, alliances, loyalties, and countless other traits assessed. It was tiring work, and represented only one set of admittedly biased opinions, but it proved to be a useful and much-needed distraction from confronting Eellon's passing. That was properly a clan matter, anyway, to which Avall would merely give royal assent. He could sit in on the deliberations, but only as a clansman, not as King.

Finally, Avall took a deep breath. "Well, that's about as much as we can accomplish today—mostly to put us all on equal footing in terms of information. I'm sure Tyrill will be needing several of us soon, which means we won't get anything useful accomplished until after Eellon's funeral. I'll have to participate, of course—in a double role. But the actual logistics are for Priest and the Argen chiefs to work out. In the meantime, I have a bit of personal business I need to conduct." He rose at that, which everyone but Rann, Strynn, Merryn, Lykkon, and Vorinn took as a request to leave. Those five lingered. He eyed them wearily, loath to abandon their company, which was comfort in itself. "Merry and Lyk," he sighed at last. "Stay here and be my spies in Argen—and my mouth, should that be needed. I trust you both to know my will if a ruling is needed. Strynn, I'm about to do something you may not like, but I don't want to leave you out of any more than I have to, so you can accompany me or not, as you choose. Same for you, Rann. I know you're preoccupied. Vorinn—"

"I have my own plans," Vorinn replied cryptically.

"And this errand is . . . ?" Strynn inquired with a troubled scowl.

Avall shook his head. "I don't feel like defending my actions just now."

Rann shot him a conspiratory grin. "Count me in," he murmured. "I have to go to the Citadel anyway."

"That was odd," Vorinn announced a moment later, into the sudden silence of what was now an empty room, save for his sister. He stretched his long legs languidly and helped himself to a handful of nuts from a silver dish beside his goblet. His eyes never left Strynn, who'd wandered over to stare out the window.

She felt that gaze, too, yet started when he spoke. "What was?"

Vorinn inclined his head toward the door through which his brother-in-law had just departed. "Avall. Is he always that—"

Strynn turned full around to face him, caught, as she often was these days, between agreeing and disagreeing with the same issue. "Dismissive? No. But there are things that are his, and things that are mine, and we tend to keep them separate."

A brow lifted. "*And,* so it seems, things that are the King's that are separate from your husband's."

Strynn's reply was to claim a seat beside her brother on the low couch he occupied. He was seven years older than she: enough that he'd never been part of her primary reality, a situation compounded by the fact that she'd been little more than a child when he'd first entered the Fateing, at twenty. He was midway through his fourth cycle now, which had seen him posted in a variety of distant holds and halls—for the last three years, as Sub-Craft-Chief of War in North Gorge and environs. Not that it wouldn't have been convenient to have had him around after Eddyn had raped her. The Eight knew he'd have saved Smith a world of diplomacy by the simple expedient of killing Eddyn while Eddyn was still open to challenge by her next of kin. Of course he'd have had to fight Merryn for that privilege, but even Merryn would've deferred to Vorinn's cool, considered wrath. As it was, he'd arrived just too late—as he'd arrived too late for her wedding, but not for her Raising to adulthood—or another Fateing, which had posted him to Brewing, up past North Gorge, where he'd promptly fallen from a horse, broken both arms, then taken a winter's worth of chill. This was, she realized, the first time they'd been alone together since he'd come striding into Avall's coronation in full armor, regalia, and road sweat; beside himself that he'd missed the war—then promptly disappeared again, to assess the damage at War-Hold.

"You've missed a lot," she acknowledged. "I can hardly believe it myself: the things that have changed in the last year."

"Less than that," he corrected, with a dry chuckle. "Last time I saw you, you were getting on the barge to head downstream to meet the trek that took you to Gem-Hold."

She chuckled back, but her laughter held an edge of regret. "Where the world changed. It must be worse for you: to leave here with the kingdom running as it always has, then return to find that a war has come and gone in your absence; that magic—or something—is suddenly a reality, and has turned interclan politics topsy-turvy; and that someone you remember as a serious, dreamy boy is now your King."

Vorinn eyed her soberly. "It still doesn't seem real, any more than it seems real that he's your husband."

"He needs people like you, though," Strynn murmured. "People who are loyal and reliable, but don't want anything out of him."

Vorinn scowled. "How do you know I'm either of those things? I am—as it happens—but it's also an absolute fact that I'm more qualified to be King than Avall is."

"Perhaps," Strynn agreed, helping herself to some of the

nuts. "But when you're this close to the duty that goes with the title, you soon see that it's nothing for anyone to desire. You're a subchief, Vor; you know what that entails, and that's with you working with people who are either conditioned by birth to work with you, or who are so hungry to learn what you have to impart they'd give up their birth-clans to acquire that knowledge. Avall has very few truly stable pillars on which to lean. So much rests on tradition and conditioning, yet he—we, I should say—must challenge that foundation every day."

"He could abdicate."

"He might."

"And you? I still don't like the way he dismissed you. The sister I remember wouldn't have allowed that."

Strynn regarded him levelly. "I didn't allow it. I have my own agenda, Vor, and it's very complicated. There was no reason for me to go with him just now, except to *be* with him. I don't really like working with magic, and that's what Avall's about. Rann's much better equipped to protect him in that context than I am, because Rann's had more experience with such things."

"You always were trusting—too much so."

Strynn's gaze never wavered. "Maybe. But I trust Rann because he loves Avall more than anything in the world, and he knows that by protecting Avall, he's protecting me, which in turn protects Avall. It's hard to understand unless you live it."

"But still—"

Strynn silenced him with a hand on his wrist. "Don't assume anything, brother, except one thing: I'm free to do anything I want right now. If I don't do something, it's because I choose not to do it."

Vorinn patted the hand in turn, then grasped it fiercely. "If you say so, sister. And because you've said it, I'll be Avall's man absolutely—but only because he's your man."

"You don't like him?"

"I don't know him. I intend to get to know him. I'd like to

respect him, but he hasn't earned that yet—him, not his title. For now, I'll play Tryffon's game: watch, wait, and be a power behind the throne without the headaches that throne entails."

She smiled a challenge. "For now?"

"Things change," Vorinn replied. "But remember one thing, too: I will never, ever hurt you."

Strynn started to reply, but a knock sounded on the door: Riff's cadence. "Yes?" she called.

The stocky blond Guardsman stuck his head inside. "Lady," he began formally, "the Ixtian Ambassador requests an audience."

"Admit him," Strynn called back, shooting her brother a regretful look. "One day we'll get to catch up," she assured him sadly.

He started to rise. "Should I go?"

"Not unless you want to. If Tozri's here, it's in search of Avall, not me, and probably for a nondiplomatic reason."

By which time the door had opened, to admit Tozri min Aroni, Ambassador from Ixti.

Like Eron, Ixti had suddenly found itself ruled by a sovereign who was young for the position and had not sought the title—though Kraxxi *had* been groomed for a throne since birth. And like Avall, Kraxxi had surrounded himself with retainers roughly his own age—one of whom had just entered.

Originally one of Kraxxi's personal guard, along with being his closest friend, Tozri—with his sisters-of-one-birth, Elvix and Olrix—had come north with Kraxxi when he'd gone into exile. Already half-Eronese and loyal to Kraxxi as only childhood friends could be, they'd had a colorful, if stressful tenure in Eron—first as prisoners in War-Hold, where Tozri and Kraxxi had shared the room next to Merryn's; then as fugitives, which adventure had ended when they'd chanced upon Eddyn during his own winter exile; next, as prisoners of their former king; and finally as fugitives again, this time seeking to free Kraxxi from his father's plots. They'd defected to Eron during the Battle of Storms, but only because Eron's side seemed more likely to aid their lifelong friend. Olrix had been killed in that battle, which was still a point of tension between certain parties, even if logic forced forgiveness. Which was why Tozri's coambassador was plying the road between Eron and Ixti, rather than standing here in Avall's room. Some injuries took a while to scab over, never mind flake away.

In any case, Tozri was here now, in the formal black-and-gold ambassadorial robe that so nicely complemented his dusky skin, brown eyes, and short-cropped black hair.

"Lady," he began solemnly, with a slight bow. "Is His Majesty—?"

"You just missed him," Strynn replied curtly, hoping to salvage the conversation she'd been having with her brother.

"As I did at the Citadel."

"Is it important?"

"Only if condolences are important," Tozri answered. "I heard of Eellon's death when everyone else heard, but thought it inappropriate to intrude too precipitously on family sorrow. I also thought it inappropriate to neglect paying my respects too long."

"Politics is balance," Vorinn inserted, rising to join Strynn.

"As is everything, I'm beginning to think," Tozri conceded. "I don't believe I've had the honor."

Strynn cleared her throat. "Since you're here in official regalia, I suppose I'll have to introduce you first, Tozri. Tozri min Aroni mar Sheer, Ambassador from Ixti, allow me to present my elder brother, Vorinn syn Ferr-een."

Tozri grinned, as he took Vorinn's hand. "Ah, yes, the man who would've turned the tide at South Gorge, if he'd only *been* at South Gorge."

Vorinn's face clouded.

"Not an insult," Strynn assured him quickly. "Tozri was seeking sanctuary in Eron at the time. Remember?"

"I was prisoner of my own king at the time," Tozri corrected. He looked around casually. "But now that my errand is dispatched, I find myself with time on my hands and good folk with whom to spend it." He studied Vorinn speculatively. "I've heard you're quite the strategist. I'd be interested in hearing what you'd have done differently had you commanded either side at South Gorge."

Vorinn smiled wickedly. "Is that something I should be discussing with the Ixtian Ambassador?"

Tozri blushed in spite of his dark skin. "I concede the error of my query. Very well, then; what do you say to a game of *toriss?* That way we can include your sister, and I can still see if the rumors about you are true."

"I'll get the board," Strynn volunteered, rising.

Vorinn laughed aloud. "I can see you haven't been around my sister nearly long enough."

"Why?"

"Because, if you're talking *toriss,* the one you need to fear is her, not me."

And, until Bingg reminded them it was time to prepare for the mourning dinner, they forgot about politics of any kind entirely.

Until he'd become Sovereign, Avall would never in his wildest dreams have guessed how many secret passages, chambers— even levels, in some sections—honeycombed the Citadel. Even now, after consulting the plans in the archives and setting the ever-alert Lykkon to studying them as well, he wasn't convinced he'd located all of them. In any case, having them about was nothing if not helpful—and might be more so, if, for instance, the oft-discussed rebellion actually occurred.

At the moment, he'd found one particularly useful for keeping certain things hidden far from the public eye. Especially when that particular arm of the public was very powerful—and sneaky—indeed.

Priest-Clan had—reasonably enough—demanded Rrath's return after the Battle of Storms. But fortunately for Avall and his partisans, Priest's most powerful advocates had been incarcerated in the Hall of Clans at the time, so that, though the battle had raged at the very door of Priest-Clan's summer hold, there'd been no one about with sufficient authority to claim what all but a very few assumed was a lifeless corpse. And while nearly every bone in Rrath's body had indeed been broken by his fall from the heights, and his chest laid open to the ribs by a geen claw, he had nevertheless survived. And since Avall knew more than most how much the priest had suffered and to what end, he'd felt honor-bound to see that Rrath got the finest care available. And if he also nursed some guilt about that occasion last autumn when he'd failed to protect Rrath from a potential birkit attack, that was more cause to see to Rrath's good, not less.

And, of course, there was what Rrath knew.

Avall halted halfway down a dead-end corridor not far from his own suite, and pressed three blocks in the wall before him in a certain order while standing on a fourth. A grinding sound to his right marked a bas-relief panel sliding back in such a way that the resulting opening was obscured by a pilaster from the rest of the hall unless one stood very nearby indeed. "Hmm," Rann murmured, not having been there before, though he knew Rrath was secreted somewhere in the Citadel.

"I know about it," Avall confided. "Strynn knows; Veen, two other Guards, and three healers know, one of whom is Gynn's daughter." He motioned Rann through before him, then followed, pausing to close the portal behind.

"One wonders what else you're not telling me," Rann grumbled good-naturedly. "Remind me to do more prowling next time you and I share minds."

"I offered to show you when we brought him here," Avall shot back. "You were busy with Div. Oh, and someone else knows he's here, as of yesterday."

"Anyone I know?"

"His bond-brother. A lad named Esshill. He first thought Rrath was dead, then wasn't sure what happened to him. He got no satisfaction from Priest, and finally petitioned me—in private. I had to tell him, Rann. I know what it would be like if it was you and me."

"It *was* you and me," Rann replied soberly. "Remember? Four eights ago I thought you were dead. The only thing I could do was try to preserve your work and your memory."

"Except that Esshill didn't *know* about Rrath's real work. In any case, I granted him sanctuary on the condition that he wouldn't return to Priest-Hold, and would agree to remain locked in the suite next to Rrath's when he wasn't visiting him."

"The one where the healer from War-Hold used to stay?"

"Still stays," Avall corrected. "I'm not so stupid as to leave him unguarded."

"But—"

"Later," Avall broke in. "We're there."

Two keys inserted in three locks in a certain order opened a plain oak door, which revealed a bright, sunlit chamber that looked out on the wall of the gorge fifty spans away. They were fairly high up, as testified to by their sore legs and Rann's panting, but that, again, was a security measure. They were also about as far as one could get from the secret armory. Just in case.

A woman rose as they entered: slim and dark-haired, dressed in healer white and looking far younger than Avall knew her to be, given that she'd attended his arrival in the world. Beejinn was her name, and her movement merely made room for him beside the bed on which Rrath lay, beyond which a large window stood open to admit the fresh summer air.

Rrath was exactly as Avall had last seen him: flat on his back, shrouded to mid-chest with white sheets, beneath which his body was no longer bound in casts, wrapped in bandages, or discolored by extravagant bruises. His eyes were closed, his hair neatly combed, his face shaved, and his body waxed. But the cheeks that Avall remembered as smooth were sunken, and his eyes had fallen back in his head.

All at once it reminded him far too much of Eellon—so

much so that he had to look away—even as he wondered what secrets the old Clan-Chief had taken with him to the Overworld.

"Any change?" Avall asked without looking up.

Beejinn eyed him frankly. "Not really. He eats, he breathes. He functions as he ought, but doesn't awaken: doesn't groan, doesn't respond—you know how he is. We've asked him over and over to give some sign that he could hear us: move a finger once for 'yes' and twice for 'no'—that sort of thing. Nothing. Something's driven him so far into himself he won't return. And he's now been there so long he might not be able to, even if he wanted."

Avall nodded grimly. "If you'll give us a moment alone with him, we'll call when we're finished. No harm will come to him," he added, unnecessarily.

"No, it won't," she assured him. And eased through the nearer of two adjoining doors, which she shut behind her. No lock clicked in her wake.

Avall claimed Beejinn's chair beside Rrath's head. He reached over and touched the Priest's brow gently. "What's in here? I wonder," he whispered.

"The secrets of the ghost priests, for one thing," Rann muttered, as he folded himself down on the floor at Avall's feet. "I assume that's why you came."

Avall nodded, already fishing in his tunic for his gem. Not the master gem—the death gem, as he sometimes called it— but the other, lesser one that Rann had found and given him. "I've tried this once before, when you weren't around to stop me—and accomplished nothing. I don't know if this time will be any better, but I have more reason to pierce the shell of his coma than I had before, and I know desire affects how these things work."

He'd secured his gem by then. It gleamed in his palm like frozen fire. "I also—" he began, then broke off, scowling, before soldiering on again. "I also thought it might help if we both tried to get through to him. You and I would be stronger together, plus you might also be able to go somewhere I can't."

Rann shrugged amiably. "I'm game."

"Fine." Avall glanced at the door. "We'll need to hurry. I don't want to have to explain this to Beejinn."

Rann had anticipated him. His own gem already glittered in his hand. He'd also snared a paring knife from a bowl of apples on the small bedside table. Mashed apples were one of the few things Beejinn had been able to get Rrath to eat, but she preferred to do her own preparation in his rooms. Avall saw no reason to argue.

"Will we need to cut him?" Rann wondered, surveying Rrath's limp form. "Or—"

Avall traced the angle of Rrath's jaw and shook his head. "Someone nicked him when they shaved him and there's still a scab." He picked at it with a nail, and was rewarded with a thin line of brighter red. An exchange of nods, and Rann made a small incision in the palm of his left hand. Avall wouldn't have needed to follow suit, had it merely been he and Rann who were bonding, but including Rrath required more direct contact among all three bloodstreams. Fortunately, he still had small scabs in his palm from when he'd tested the ingots, which should prove sufficient. A deep breath, and he and Rann clasped hands, with Rann's gem between.

And with that touch, Avall felt power flow out of himself, yet without feeling in anywise diminished. Along with that flow, he felt the barriers that walled away his self dissolve, as Rann's consciousness surged into him. He resisted the urge to merge with Rann, for this was about power, not emotion, and Rann would need to work *through* him if they hoped to accomplish anything.

It was difficult not to bond with him, however, for that closeness was a wonderful thing, and something they'd allowed themselves far too rarely of late, lest it become—as they both feared—addictive or prosaic.

Fortunately, Rrath chose that moment to groan softly, which was enough to stir Avall from reverie. Another breath, and Avall curved his other hand along the smooth line of

Rrath's jaw, with his personal gem touching both the Priest's blood and his own.

Closing his eyes, he steered his awareness toward Rrath, then into him—and met resistance that was more than physical. Rann, who rode with him, thrust his strength against that barrier as well, and together they explored what language would've described as a wall around Rrath's mind. Had the Priest been conscious, or even asleep and dreaming, there would've been a twitch of recognition, followed by a bonding—if they were friends—or rejection—if they were not. Here, there was nothing.

Avall pushed harder, seeking to insinuate his consciousness into Rrath's. And succeeded—but only to the degree that his awareness reached a place where Rrath's awareness had *been*. It was like walking through an empty house: One could tell that those rooms had once held things—memories, feelings, emotions—yet he had no idea what those items might have been.

In a way, too, it was like using the master gem, in that he sensed the presence of some other self waiting deep within. But where using the master gem was like falling, this was like roaming an endless maze. And though he knew life awaited at the end, he also knew it would take more time than he had—and maybe more time than he could ever spare—to reach whatever essence of Rrath remained. Even with Rann to aid him, it would take a very long time indeed to search each wall-less room of vanished memory for the touchstone that might reawaken Rrath, who was the only one who could refill them.

Hopeless—for now, came Rann's silent whisper.

For now, Avall agreed. *But that doesn't mean I won't try again—eventually.*

Eventually, Rann echoed, and withdrew. Avall went with him. As one they opened their eyes; as one they unclasped hands. Avall left his other one on Rrath's jaw a moment longer before returning his gem to its mount.

Wordlessly they rose. Rann continued gazing down at Rrath

while Avall stepped to the door through which Beejinn had passed. "We're finished," he called softly. "We neither helped nor hurt him. Beyond that . . . just keep him clean-shaven. It might help more than you think."

She stared at him quizzically—almost angrily, but nodded.

"You're doing a fine job," Avall informed her from the door. "Thank you. Oh, and tell Esshill we were here. He might appreciate it."

And then Avall followed Rann into a chamber that was far more physical but no less empty than those he'd found in Rann's mind. And shivered. Rann was shivering too, and for a long time they simply stood there, embracing, still lightly bonded. And passionately glad to be alive.

CHAPTER VI:

IN THE WILD

Div gave the lock one final tug and turned away—from door, wall, and hold, all three.

And from her past. The lock would hold—or not. It was largely symbolic, anyway: a means of informing whoever happened by that what had once been a summer hunting hold belonging to her late husband's clan was not, however it might appear, abandoned, but under active claim, which ought to be respected. Of course if someone really needed it for shelter overnight, it would be simple enough to enter the place. The shutters were rotting, after all, and there was always that hole in the west wing where a pine tree had smashed through the roof.

In any case, she had what she'd come for: a good supply of furs she'd been forced to abandon last winter when what had begun as a simple hunting expedition had changed her life forever. She'd met Rann and Avall then, and through them a whole host of interesting and—she had to admit—powerful folk, and had found herself subsumed, without conscious volition, into the ranks of the mighty.

It was because she was smart, strong, and reliable, they said.

Which one had to be in order to survive here in the Wild, as she'd done for half a dozen winters. It was also because Rann loved her—or said he did—and Rann was bond-brother with the new High King, whose body she had likewise known.

And how many other Common Clan women could say they'd lain with a King? Still, she sometimes felt she was allowed among them on sufferance—not that either of her closest female friends, Merryn and Strynn, ever put on airs. High Clan women were not so spoiled as that, since every one of them did a share of menial labor in the halls and holds. Not for High Clan Eronese was privilege without responsibility or effort.

But she wondered if her clan, as a whole, knew that. She'd seen many things firsthand that few, if any, Commoners had witnessed. Far too many of them, she reckoned, remembered mostly that it was their ranks that had swelled the army and taken the brunt of a series of bloody defeats before that final victory. Worse, it was those same ranks that were most threatened by Priest-Clan's rumored interdict, which would, in effect, deny them access to The Eight unless the King made concessions she knew he'd never make.

But that was in the future, and whatever decisions Avall made, she'd sworn to follow him, and had a Royal Guardsman's tabard to prove it. That the future also meant returning to Rann was no bad thing, either; but she was no closer now than when she set out to achieving another goal, which was to determine, once and for all, how she truly felt about her relationship with Rann syn Eemon-arr.

She loved him. That was a fact.

Her womb was damaged, so she could never give him the children Law required he sire. That was also true.

She would therefore need to share him with at least one other woman.

And she already had to share him with Avall.

Would enough remain to keep her satisfied?

She didn't know.

For now, however . . .

Now she had to cross the worn wood of her porch and take a dozen strides across the forecourt to where White Star, the fine new stallion the King had given her, waited, along with a pack animal he'd likewise provided. She could've had an escort as well—Avall had advised one, given that the woods thereabouts were not as safe as had long been assumed. But she'd pointed out that she knew them as well as anyone, and one person and two horses were less likely to be noted than the same plus a dozen Royal Guards.

Whom she'd summarily dismissed to escort Kylin to Gem-Hold.

Kylin . . .

She wondered again about the wisdom of his returning to a place where he had so many conflicting memories. A friendship with Rann, for instance, that had led to a stronger one with Strynn, which had led, in turn, to her gifting him, however fleetingly, with the power of sight through the newfound gem. Trouble was, word of *that* had leaked out, and Eddyn had tried to force information about the gem from him, which had prompted Kylin to move in with Strynn, who was by then the only person in the hold he trusted, save perhaps Hold-Warden Crim. But Crim, whom Div had met exactly once, treated Kylin more like a pet than a human being. So he said.

He might be right, too. Kylin was blind, granted, but that didn't mean he was stupid, though the ignorant often assumed as much. In any case, there were things he needed to retrieve from the hold, and High Summer was far and away the best time to attend such things.

Besides, it gave her a reason to visit Gem-Hold. It was, after all, accounted one of the most beautiful outside, and *the* most splendid within. It was also two days' steady ride from her hold, and she'd be returning to Tir-Eron by a different route, which was another reason she'd locked the door. She would not, she suspected, be coming back.

Sighing, she paused one last time, sweeping her gaze around

the tiny clearing that she had, for so long, called home. And then she looked northwest, toward Angen's Spine, where lay her destination.

It was a fair long way to those mountains, yet the air was clear today, where yesterday had been rainy. Even so, she wasn't certain, but it *seemed* that a line of smoke rose up from among those ragged peaks. And for smoke to be visible at such a distance, it must mark a very great burning indeed.

Still, she'd gain no answers here, and she had to meet Kylin regardless. But it was with more concern than heretofore that she set her heels to White Star's sides and pointed his nose toward that tiny, thin line of troublesome darkness.

CHAPTER VII:

MEMORIALS

~~~~~~~~

Avall stared at the whipping flame of the torch before him, grasped so firmly in his right hand he feared the brass band that bound the pitch-soaked reeds might buckle beneath his fingers.

Yet he had no choice but to hold it that tight, lest his occasional tremors become too obvious. Beyond the flame, wavy in the haze of heat, he could see the packed seats that framed the enormous, stone-paved lozenge that comprised the Court of Rites, which filled the space between the River Walk and the Citadel proper. The sky glowered, dark clouds matching the black cloaks and tabards that every single person present wore, by Law.

He could force himself to look at those folks—barely. More often he looked left or right, where Rann and Strynn flanked him, black-clad like everyone else, and with their hoods drawn far forward above their faces. He alone went bareheaded, the better to display the crown that was mark of Sovereignty, for it was in that role he now officiated at the funeral of Eellon syn Argen-a.

Eellon's bier stood six strides before him, raised on a

portable marble dais that lifted the old man's body just far enough above the level of Avall's head that he could not see the corpse's face above the fabulously embroidered corpse-cloth of Argen maroon and Smithcraft gold. The wind twitched what little of Eellon's white hair still showed beneath the hood of his Clan-Chief's tabard and the circlet that marked him as High Clan. If there was rain, four young kinsmen stood ready to raise a canvas awning above him—until the fire ignited. And once the flame caught hold, there were substances within the bier to assure continued burning even in a downpour.

Avall had endured the formal eulogizing in the Hall of Clans, which had occupied most of the morning. Indeed, he'd managed to sit stone-faced while chief after chief of clan after clan spoke of the man who lay dead before them. Nor did anyone speak ill, which didn't surprise him, given that Eellon, though he could be as hard, petty, and manipulative as any other person gifted with his talents, charisma, and power, was much loved by High Clan and low clan alike. Even Tyrill, speaking on behalf of Clan Argen, which had not yet chosen a successor, had waxed eloquent on how love and hate were such close kin one could not always distinguish them, but how she was a better woman and a better craftsman for having had Eellon to set a standard for her to emulate.

Avall had suffered her comments stoically, for all he'd heard them voiced before, in private. But what had brought tears to his eyes that he hadn't bothered to hide before all those assembled chiefs was Preedor syn Ferr's eulogy. He'd spoken of Eellon as a boy, and of their childhood together, and how Eellon had once thought of challenging for a seat in War instead of Smith, when Tyrill had bested him in a competition. Tyrill had started at that, and Avall had guessed she'd never heard the tale. And then Preedor spoke of their bonding and the dispute over the woman who'd become Eellon's wife that had sundered that bond, and that woman's death from plague that had reunited them.

And through it all, Avall had sat the Stone unmoving,

resplendent in the Cloak of Colors, over which he wore a mourner's tabard, hood, and—briefly—mask. And when the eulogies were done, it was time for Priest-Clan to take over, each Priest in turn addressing his or her aspect of The Eight, and espousing Eellon's virtues in terms of it.

And still Avall had said nothing. But when he'd marched out to the Court of Rites at the head of the mourning file, he'd carried the new helm with him, as Merryn had carried the shield and Lykkon the Lightning Sword. And when the time had come for him to speak as King—which was his prerogative, though he had none within his clan—they'd simply raised those three wondrous things on high and he'd shouted for all to hear, "Without him who lies there, none of these would exist, and most of you who sit witness to this rite would be dead."

They'd then relinquished those items to trusted kinsmen, and he'd taken the torch the Death Priest offered. He'd considered using the Lightning Sword, but that would both irritate Priest-Clan and remind Common Clan—and others—of issues still far from resolution.

Besides which, Eellon despised such display, and were it not for massive arguments to the contrary from everyone Avall respected, he'd have followed custom and made this a private affair in Argen-Hall's own small court of rites, with only the clan and a few close friends to witness.

Yet somehow Eellon had become a national hero. And in that, the clans and the common folk alike must be mollified.

So it was, that with a strange separation from himself that was almost like being drunk or high on imphor wood, Avall slowly stepped forward, gaze focused intently on the torch in lieu of the bier that rose ever higher before him. And then someone—it truly did not feel like him—was lowering that torch to the basin of volatile oil at the bier's base, which would feed the flame where needed to ensure rapid and complete combustion.

The world went yellow-red, then white. Thunder boomed that was not of Avall's summoning. Heat washed his face, and he felt the skin stretch taut across his cheekbones as necessity forced him back. Yet even then, he could only stare fixedly as the Death Priest pried the torch from his still-locked fingers, while Rann and Merryn gently led him back to where Strynn and Lykkon—and others of his clan he'd asked to join the royal party—waited, and there watched with tear-stained faces as the most powerful man in Eron not to wear a crown surrendered his mortal shape to ashes.

Only when the smoke of that burning was a thin spiral damascening the heavens did Avall finally turn away. And only then came the rain, dripping from his crown to wash his tears away.

It was still raining when Avall found Tyrill. The old Craft-Chief was sitting, as she often did these days, in the water court behind Smith-Hold-Main. A high-arched dome stood there, sheltering a life-size bronze statue of Eddyn that stared down at a slab of rustless metal that had been mingled, when molten, with a portion of his ashes, which was all he would ever have for a tomb. Even so, she'd had to fight most of the clan to have that edifice erected. Oddly enough, however, she hadn't had to fight Avall. "He was flawed, but still a hero," Avall had told her. "Without him, Ixti would have had the victory."

Avall came upon her quietly, where she sat unmoving, a cup of brandied cider cooling between hands still gloved in the thin black sylk of mourning. Save a sash of Argen maroon twined with Smithcraft gold, she wore only black these days—for Eddyn had been of her immediate line, and it was for him, as much as Eellon, that she mourned.

Why Avall sought her out, he had no idea. Perhaps it was simply that she was one of the few ties remaining to the life that had vanished like the smoke of Eellon's burning all in a season. A time when the old Chiefs' rivalry—and the surrogate continuation they propagated among their two-sons—was one of the fixed points in the universe, along with winter snow.

Silently, he mounted the marble steps that put him beneath the dome. A stroke of his hand wiped water from his face and swept his hood back with it, as he took a seat close enough beside Tyrill to be heard without raising his voice. She acknowledged him with a murmured "Avall" and filled a cup for him without asking. It was High Summer, but the rain had brought a chill that reminded him far too much of the colder seasons to come.

"You've lost a lot," Avall whispered finally, wincing at the inanity of the words, though he knew there *were* no words that could comfort Tyrill now.

"I've lost nothing," the old woman retorted without rancor. "Everything has lost me. It's all gone—*all* of it. My husband, my children, my one-children, and most of my two-. My friends, my lovers, my foes, and my rivals. People tell you they want to live to old age. Some are even so stupid as to crave immortality, but I tell you, it's not worth it. I've watched the world grow and seen civilization advance. I've seen the plague come and go and take half the people I cared about with it. And then I watched people grow to adulthood to whom the plague is only words in books, images in paintings, and lines in plays. You're seeing that now, but you don't know it. History starts out as a thing remote from you, and then, all at once, it surrounds you. You're the center of the world—for a while. Take that book Lykkon's writing—the chronicle of the war and the documentation of the power of the gems. Have you ever stopped to think what that book will represent a thousand years from now? It'll be like Allegri's *Treatise on Falconry* or Calayn's book on honing edges. It'll be something that's as much a part of those future lives as breathing. Yet it will have no connection with us at all. We'll be names, but not flesh, blood, and bone, love, hate, and jealousy. We'll—"

Avall silenced her by edging closer and easing his arm around her. "Eddyn's the past, and Eellon's the past, and—"

"I'm soon to be the past," she broke in. "I don't know when, but soon. But the funny thing is that history will mention you and me on the same page, if it mentions us at all. I'll get a line, and you'll get a paragraph, but no one will get *any* sense of how we're from different generations. I was born when adherence to rite was uncontested. Then came the plague, and necessity forced flexibility, and with that came questioning and dissent. You're from a more liberal age, though it doesn't seem that way to you—it never does. But those who read about us a thousand years from now won't know the gulf between us, or the bond. They won't be aware of the distance between our ages, because history books don't emphasize such things. I'll simply be your mentor's rival; you'll be the man who wielded the sword that won the war with Ixti. And *maybe* they'll mention Eddyn and Strynn, and how you were all barely more than children, and you were the youngest King Raised in tenscore years. If you learn nothing from this, Avall, learn that nobody is ever apart from history, but always a part of it."

Avall could think of no good reply, and so kept his peace, as did Tyrill, for a long yet comfortable time. "History," he murmured eventually. "It all spins on such small things: a discussion I had with Lykkon that made me angry, that made me place-jump to Eddyn's cell, where he got the gem and jumped away himself, into—eventually—a worse kind of captivity. But if Lyk hadn't asked that one question—"

"Eddyn would've finished the shield sooner and saved some lives. Or he might've refused to work and cost us everything."

"Which do you think?"

A shrug. "I don't want to think, because I'll have to recall a bad thing about someone I loved. But I do know that if he hadn't had that final forging in the south—if he hadn't fallen in love, then been captured, tortured, and raped—he'd never have valued what he saved enough to make the sacrifice he did."

Avall shrugged in turn, patted her hand, then drained his cider. "Well," he said "this has done me some good, whether you know it or not. But now I have to return to being King."

"And I," Tyrill echoed, likewise rising, "have to return to something as well."

"Being chief?" Avall inquired.

"No," she sighed. "Being old."

Merryn wasn't surprised by the summons that Bingg delivered to her suite in the Citadel, only that it hadn't arrived sooner. Bingg's footsteps were still echoing down the corridor, and she caught the flash of the Royal Herald's tabard he wore so proudly just before he disappeared around the corner to the right.

It was an official summons: That much was clear from the paper, the seal, and the fact that Bingg had delivered it. She also knew what it contained before she tore it open. It showed only a place and time—Avall's suite in the Citadel for dinner, at sunset. Its existence implied the rest. Her brother had finally been pushed to the limit on one of the crises that had been simmering all summer. This scrap of paper meant that he'd decided to act, but needed—or thought he did—the input of his counselors. So, she supposed—as a glance out the window showed soggy workmen already removing the soot-stained marble dais that had held Eellon's bier—she had best be there.

Avall surveyed the faces of those arrayed around the table at which they'd just dined on the most sumptuous repast he'd yet had set before them. They'd needed it, too, to put paid to the stresses of the day, but also in payment for what he was about to inflict on them. Problems were presenting themselves faster than he could resolve them, and he had to get some of them off his plate. Not the most important or most troublesome, perhaps, but removing any of them was progress.

Still black-clad from the morning's rite, they were gazing at him expectantly, across that expanse of damascened velvet, expensive gold dinnerware, and the remnants of roast venison, fresh lobster, fried shrimp, wild mushrooms, tame rice, and fruit grown under open sky. Wines had been consumed and cordials sipped and savored. But that was the salve; now came the punishment.

One last time he surveyed them, from left to right around the table: Rann, Merryn, Tryffon, Vorinn, Veen, Lykkon—and Strynn, at his right hand. Those he trusted most, with five of them born outside his clan, and thus, in theory, more objective. Bingg was there as well, but only to make notes. His two favorite guards, Myx and Riff, stood outside. Avall would've liked to have Kylin and Div on hand as well, but that was impossible. He missed both of them most keenly.

A deep breath, a sip of walnut liquor, another breath, and he spoke. "If you were me," he began, "ruler of a kingdom—any kingdom—and you had in your control weapons so deadly they assured your victory in any battle, but also assured your defeat if they fell into other hands, what would you do with them?"

Merryn gnawed her lip for a moment: she who, as Avall's twin sister, had known him longest and knew him best. "For the sake of clarity, I suppose you should specify *exactly* what you're talking about, brother."

"The new regalia," he retorted through a weary glare. "The sword Strynn made, Eddyn's shield, and my helm."

"Only one of which is actually a weapon," Lykkon noted. "For accuracy's sake, I mean."

"And none of which is dangerous without the gems," Strynn added quickly. "I'm not even sure you should consider them as one thing—the regalia—or as two—the regalia and the gems."

Avall exhaled heavily. "I'd like to think they were separate, but the more I use them—and let me stress that I *have* used them more than anyone else, and am the only person alive *and conscious* to have used the whole ensemble—the more I think you can't have one without the other."

"Meaning what?" Veen inquired.

"Meaning that, to state what we're already dancing around, the gems and their receptacles really are, in essence, one thing."

Veen shook her head, and Avall wondered about the wisdom of including her. Still, she'd been involved in this affair virtually from the beginning and was older than all but Tryffon by a half score years. She was also from Ferr, which was loyal anyway, but was one of those rare people who split generations, being old enough to value tradition and young enough to acknowledge its abuse. Vorinn—who was holding his peace for the nonce—was another.

Tryffon, however, was scowling mightily. "That might make sense if you were a Smith," he rumbled. "Or if you made these things or saw them made. I didn't. Veen and Vorinn didn't. Lykkon and Rann saw only a little, and Merryn was prisoner most of the time. Only you and Strynn actually worked on the things—of those to hand, I mean."

Avall steepled his fingers before him, mirroring Merryn's favorite council pose. "That's true," he acknowledged. "All of you know—or should—that the gems have many powers, among which is the ability to modify the perception of time so that one can do better work than is possible otherwise. I'm the only person here who's actually applied that skewed perception to crafting, but trust me, it's a fact. In any case, you also know that the gems, in a sense, bond with their owners and protect them. They like some people and dislike others—apparently based almost entirely on how those people relate to me, I assume because I found the original gem."

Everyone was nodding now, which Avall hoped meant they understood what he'd said so far. "So," he continued, "I have some reason to assume that these gems are themselves sentient beings, working for their own good by ensuring mine. And since my good was—and still is for a while, I'm afraid—bound up with the good of Eron, they seem also to have influenced events in that direction."

Veen frowned above folded arms. "I'm not following you."

Avall managed a wry grin. "And I can't really explain, since much of this involves concepts for which we have no words—especially as Gynn implanted a fair bit of it in my mind without speaking at all. But what I'm trying to say is that all the regalia—the helm especially, and the sword—was created under the influence of the gems—"

Merryn shook her head vehemently. "Not the shield. Eddyn had completed most of it before he ever heard of the gems, and Tyrill rebuilt the frame from scratch."

"But I showed Eddyn how to make the connections between the gems and the shield," Avall shot back. "And that information came, in part, *from* the gems."

"Which isn't getting us anywhere," Lykkon muttered.

"Briefly, then," Avall retorted, "the regalia is what it is because of the gems. Assuming we could remove them easily—which I doubt, though they were easy enough to install—and tried to set them in another sword, helm, or shield, I don't think they'd work as well. It would be like wearing clothes made for someone else. Parts might fit, but the whole would bind in odd places and be loose in others."

"The point of which is?" Rann grumbled through a grimace.

"What you've all been thinking. If the things are so dangerous—and they are, both at a real and symbolic level—why keep them here? Or why not simply disable them and no one the wiser? Remove the gems; substitute others, lock up the components in remote locations and be done."

"All of which assumes they're the threat you think they are." From Merryn.

"But they *are* a threat, sister," Avall shot back. "You should know that better than anyone. It was you that leveled half a cloister when the sword got the better of you—and you're as strong-willed as anyone I know."

"But I wasn't wearing the whole ensemble," Merryn countered.

"No, but we can't guarantee anyone else who got hold of them would, either. In any case, while they're here they're a terrible temptation to anyone who wants power—unclanned

thieves and paroled Priests alike. I'm a fool to keep them anywhere around, and at that I've got them multiply guarded. But
if you think there aren't a hundred plots already afoot to steal
them, to whatever end, you're fooling yourself. Everyone from
North Gorge to Ixtianos knows that the givens of power have
changed, and that a boy has changed them and now controls
them."

Strynn reached over to take his hand. "Obviously you're
voicing things you've pondered long and hard. And I suspect
you've already reached a conclusion you're afraid to reveal. I
think you want us to reach the same conclusion, then suggest
it. But you—"

"You have to trust us enough to tell us what's on your
mind," Rann finished for her. "We care about you because
we're your closest friends, and we care about the Kingdom because of how we were raised. Do I have to say any more?"

Avall buried a grin in another sip of liquor. "Very well," he
said. "What I've been thinking is this. On the positive side, the
regalia gave us victory over Ixti. Part of that was due to Rrath,
granted. But it *was* a victory, and, whether I like it or not, it
gave me my throne."

"Which you didn't want," Lykkon grinned in turn.

"Which I didn't want, but nevertheless have. But to return
to where I was. The negatives are in one sense more nebulous,
but in another sense more real. The gems have cost us. They
cost us Eddyn absolutely; they cost us Rrath, maybe; and they
quite possibly cost Eellon his life. They've made Priest-Clan
jealous, made Common Clan distrust us, and done who knows
what to those between."

"All of which we knew," Merryn sighed. "Get to the point."

"The point is, those who *don't* control them would, for any
number of reasons, like to. And we, who *do* control them, fear
them on the one hand—and rightly—and on the other cherish
them as what might be construed as security, but which I consider to be temptation."

"In other words," Rann summarized, "if the people riot, you're afraid you'll resort to the regalia instead of more traditional channels."

Avall nodded. "Eron has never been ruled by fear, and I won't let it start with me. In a very real sense, we've moved too far too fast, and we have to retrench a little."

"Which means?" Vorinn inquired, speaking for the first time.

"Which means, much as I hate to say it, that we—I—have to remove this massive source of temptation from any possible abuse—or use, either."

Lykkon's eyes were huge. "You don't mean . . ."

Another nod. "I do. Part of the regalia's value is symbolic, but that function can as easily be filled by something that *looks* like the regalia as by the regalia itself."

Lykkon's eyes went even wider. "Which is why you've been making molds of it. You said it was for 'archival purposes'—"

"It was, and is. But it also allows easy duplication by anyone skilled in casting and gold leaf—at which, let me remind you, half the people in this room excel."

"And the real regalia?"

A final deep breath, and he said what could not be recalled. "We hide it. I can't trust myself with it, and I won't live in fear for the rest of my life."

"And *where* will you hide it?" Tryffon snapped gruffly.

Avall didn't bother suppressing a smirk, though he sensed that if anyone defied him now it would be Warcraft's Chief. "If I knew that, it wouldn't be hidden." Then, before anyone else could interrupt: "I'll give it to you, Merry. You take it, and you spirit it away in the night. Put it somewhere none of us knows nor could reach easily. But do it as soon as possible. The important thing is that only one person alive know where it is."

Silence filled the room. Stunned silence. Then, softly, from Lykkon: "What about your personal gems? They're as much a threat."

Avall glared at his young kinsman. "That's another debate

for another time," he said eventually, aware even as he said it that it was something he should have considered himself—and a problem that would not be dismissed easily. "For now . . . I wanted you to know my thinking on this thing, and I wanted to know yours. We can talk as long as you like, but the decision rests with two people: Me—as King, not as your friend, Avall—and Merryn, who has been asked to undertake a preposterous royal commission, but is still free to refuse that request."

More silence, from everyone, caught, as they were, between their roles as friends of a man and subjects of a King. It was Merryn that finally spoke. "Give me the keys to their keeping place," she said. "If I return them tomorrow, you'll know how I decided."

Avall smiled wanly. "Which is all I could ask."

Merryn looked very, very troubled. "Unfortunately," she replied heavily, "it's not all *I* can ask." She gazed up at him, a grim sadness in her eyes that had not been there a breath before. "If I'm going to do this thing, I want it done once and for all. For that reason, I want to save us all a lot of trouble I can already see starting to fester." Her gaze slipped sideways to Lykkon. "I want you all to relinquish your personal gems to me as well. Now. Before I leave this table. This means you, Avall, and you, Strynn and Rann."

A murmur of amazement rumbled around the room. Avall opened his mouth to reply, but Merryn silenced him with a raised palm. "No, hear me out," she demanded, in a voice like steel in ice. "I have two reasons for asking this, and let me assure you, neither has anything to do with any personal power plays. The first is simply another aspect of temptation. If you're going to remove such dangerous things from reach, you have to do it absolutely. It does no good if, an eighth or a year from now, you decide you want another, more powerful sword or shield, and simply stick your personal gems in new mountings. Additionally, it does no good for me to hide the regalia if you can contact me through the gems. Hidden is as hidden does."

Avall scowled at her, rubbing his chin. Strynn looked troubled; Rann looked dazed. Even Lykkon looked mildly stunned.

"It makes sense," Strynn conceded slowly. "My gem certainly helps in some cases. But in the balance . . ."

"It's hard to fault your logic," Rann agreed, already fishing inside his tunic.

"Avall?" Merryn prompted, none too gently.

"You can have it," he rasped at last. "I may regret it, but I'm sick of worrying about the things—and the fact that Lyk's already brought it up means we'll be thrashing it until the Last Winter if we don't address it now. But," he added, "you can only have my second gem. The master gem stays with me. That's not subject to debate."

Merryn raised a brow, her face gone tense with anger. "You're undermining your position."

Avall stared back at her, suddenly incredibly weary. "Perhaps, but I'm fairly certain I'm the only person who can control it, and, I fear, the only person who can cure it."

"And if you do? Cure it, I mean?" Vorinn challenged.

"Then Merry gets a second royal quest."

Merryn rolled her eyes, but nodded and extended her hand palm up. *"Now,"* she snapped. "If I have to ask again, you'll have to find someone else to make your journey. I may refuse anyway. You may have your gems back tomorrow."

Avall shook his head, but reached into his tunic anyway. Rann's gem already gleamed in his hand. Strynn was fumbling with the clasp on hers. Avall looked at his briefly, then laid it in Merryn's palm. No words passed between them, but tension was palpable in the room. "You're now the most powerful person in the world," he told his sister softly.

"I know," she whispered back. "You won't regret it."

Avall broke eye contact first, and let his gaze drift slowly around the chamber. "And now," he murmured, "I think we've all had a very trying day, so I would wish you all . . . good evening."

Only Tryffon lingered at the door, face clouded, brow

furrowed with concern. "I knew it would do no good to tell you this," he told Avall finally. "I know a man with a certain mind when I see him. But, forgive me when I say this, lad— but I think you're a fool."

"I may be," Avall acknowledged, with a sad smile. "But at least I know what I want to worry about." And closed the door behind him.

CHAPTER VIII:

WALLS WITH EARS

It had taken Kylin far longer than expected to reach what had been his nominal goal ever since sufficient smoke had cleared from the ventilation ducts for him to dare moving at all. Indeed, he'd had *no* goal at first, save to get as far away as possible from the place where he'd entered that maze of narrow shafts and cramped passageways, driven by what he now acknowledged was a largely irrational fear of being caught.

That assumed anyone was looking for him, for one thing, which was far from given. Granted, he'd arrived with a royal escort, but that had been late at night, so the event had gone largely unmarked, except by Crim. And since then, he'd kept to himself, but for a pair of audiences with that formidable lady. As for the few friends he'd managed to make within his own clan, most of the ones he'd once claimed had left with the last trek.

And afterward—well, everyone knew the ducts existed, but few actually thought about them, and there was so much noise after the initial invasion and follow-up explosion that any odd sounds were ascribed to clumsy invaders or the hold's settling.

Which had freed him to make his way downward. But that had presented another set of problems, for the ducts, like the rest of the hold, had suffered major damage, with some passages being blocked by rubble and others sporting gaping holes in the floor that forced him to back up. Fortunately, he had a near-perfect memory, and had possessed sense enough when he began his exploration to count paces—if crawling on hands and knees constituted paces—and turns left and right. In spite of that, he was no longer certain his retreats had returned him to points he'd visited before or merely similar ones.

It was therefore no surprise that it had taken most of the first day to find somewhere he could move downward instead of horizontally. Not that he'd known, at first, for a rough-cast metal grille had blocked access to what sound and scent merely suggested was a tight spiral stairway. Many of the vertical shafts *did* in fact contain stairs, both for stability and to better regulate the flow of heat up and fresh air down. Most were simply sealed off and thus not very well finished. That this one even had a grille closing it off from the ductwork had been something of a surprise, though perhaps it had something to do with controlling rats, of which he'd heard several but met none. And glad he was about that, too.

The *immediate* problem had been that he hadn't known if that particular stair was in use. Finally, he'd decided to wait four hands, as best he could tell, and if no one passed his hiding place, to venture out.

Unfortunately, sleep had ambushed him where he lay, and he had no idea how much time had elapsed while he sprawled there in a stupor. He'd thus waited a while longer, hearing nothing but the rush of air through the stairwell and noting no change in light (for he could discern major differences in illumination). Eventually impatience had got the better of him, and he'd pried the grille free with an abandoned mason's chisel he'd found some way back, and wriggled out.

To find himself where he was now: in what he assumed was the hollow core of one of the massive piers that flanked the central court. Happily, going down was relatively easy—until his careful progress ended when a shuffling foot tapped out into nothing. He sat down at that, breathing hard, and harder yet when a probe with an outstretched hand showed at least three steps fallen through to the turn below. And since there was no way to tell what waited down there, he didn't dare proceed, much less jump. Which meant a retreat into the horizontal system, from which he hoped to find his way to another, similar stair, since all the piers in the Grand Court were reported to contain them.

And so he crawled onward, increasingly aware of a gnawing in his stomach, which reminded him, now he'd slept, that he'd not only lost track of what time it was but of how long it had been since he'd eaten.

On and on, and he began to wish he was wearing more substantial clothing, because the thin sylk of his house-hose was already wearing through at the knees, and his slippers weren't prospering either. In any case, he forgot about both as a turn brought him the distant scent of hot meat and warm bread. Suddenly ravenous, he let the shaft lead him that way, following a series of bends toward those heavenly odors. Voices reached him, too, waxing as he approached, and louder again as he softened the sounds of his own movements. If he was lucky, the diners would eventually depart, leaving something he could snare for himself. Or they'd go to sleep. Or—he didn't know. All he knew was that hunger was uppermost in his mind. And so he crept onward, stretching his body long against the stone, for there was no way to tell whether this duct met the adjoining chamber high or low.

So it was that, long before his fingers finally found the grating, his well-tuned senses informed him that he'd not only happened upon diners, but—more importantly in the long run—some conclave of the invaders. Their voices came from above and were muffled, from which he guessed that the grille was set near the floor behind a piece of furniture. By the sounds of cutlery against crockery and the click and slosh of pouring, he assumed that a meal was in progress. Not breakfast, by the smell of the food, but that was all he could tell. Scarcely daring to breathe, he listened.

At first, the conversation was about the quality of the meal, the difficulties in assuring the cooperation of those set to prepare it, questions regarding how the rest of the hold's inhabitants were to be fed, and whether they should be allowed to continue their established routines or some new system be set in place now that the mines had been sealed. Before long, Kylin managed to attach names to two of the speakers: a young-sounding man named Ahfinn, who was evidently some sort of secretary or scribe, to judge by the lists and records from which he frequently quoted or was asked to quote. The one who addressed him most often was a man with a voice full of authority, rather like Lord Eellon sounded when he chose. That man's name was Zeff, and Kylin suspected he was the commander of this expedition, if not of the Ninth Face itself. Another chance remark made him think that this room was somewhere in Priest-Clan's quarters, maybe even Nyss's suite.

In any case, he heard a good many things and filed them away for when he might possibly encounter someone who could put them to use. But not until at least two people had left, and he was beginning to fear he might have to depart as well, lest a growling stomach betray him, did he hear something that truly set his heart thumping.

"Have you made those revisions I requested?" Zeff inquired, over the sound of more goblets filling.

"I have, Lord Chief. They await your approval and we will send them."

A pause, then: "Let me hear them one last time, since that's likely the way they'll be presented—if not by our agents, then by Avall himself, when he receives them."

Kylin heard a sigh, followed by the sound of parchment rattling, then someone swallowing and clearing his throat, then more rattling.

" *To his Incipient Sovereign Majesty, Avall syn Argen-a, High*

*King of all Eron, greetings unto you from those who would not be
your foes unless you make them so. Know you that on the forty-first
day of High Summer, forces loyal to The Most High God, of whom
Eight Faces have been shown to man, and acting in the name of
that God's minions in this land, have taken guardianship of Gem-
Hold-Winter with minimal insult to man, beast, or building, and
now claim it as their own protectorate, with full and total sway
over its folk and fold alike, even unto the dispensing of life and
death in the name of The Most High God, after proper trial, should
occasion arise.*

*" 'Know you that our intentions in so doing are our own, but
should be obvious to a Sovereign so quick to act and so well
equipped and advised as yourself. Yet know you, as well, that our
acts were perpetrated solely to protect the land and people of Eron
from any danger within and without. But know also that we have
been made aware that a threat indeed exists to the land and people
of Eron, and to the sovereignty of The Most High God and those
who serve Him in all His aspects. And know that said threat is now
confined to the hands of the High Sovereign of All Eron, and that
said threat consists of a helm, a sword, and a shield of fine and noble
design and craftsmanship, wrought by Avall syn Argen-a himself;
his bond-wife, Strynn san Ferr-a-Argen; and Eddyn syn Argen-yr,
each item set with a particular distinctive red gem, for which cause
exists that they might be deemed the Lawful property of Gem-
Hold-Winter.*

*" 'Be it therefore resolved that said items, hereinafter referenced
as "the regalia," have been deemed by those possessed of sufficient
wisdom to make such judgments, to be too dangerous to be entrusted solely to any one man, office, rank, or title so subject to dispute and change. And be it therefore stated as a function of this
resolve, that Avall syn Argen-a, acting in his state and function as
High King of All Eron, will, as soon as may be accomplished, deliver and surrender the above-mentioned regalia to Priest-Clan, as
represented by those now in possession of Gem-Hold-Winter. And
should His Majesty fail in this request, be it known that Gem-
Hold-Winter and all those who inhabited it at the time the agents*

of The Most High God gained sovereignty over it, will be razed to the foundations, and no one left alive, regardless of clan or conscience. Be it so stated, signed, and ordained, this forty-second day of High Summer, in the first half year of the reign of Avall I (Incipient).'"

A pause, then: "It waits only your sign and seal to make it so."

Another pause, a deep breath, and, "Give me a pen."

The rattle of parchment followed, then a scratching, then the slosh of more drinks being poured and what sounded like a toast.

"Whatever happens, they'll blame it on Avall, you know," Ahfinn observed.

A mirthless laugh gave answer. "That's precisely what we intend. Though what Avall *doesn't* know is that we may well level the place anyway."

Kylin's blood ran cold at that. Logic demanded that he hasten away as soon as possible and make every effort to relay what he'd just learned to his Sovereign and friend, though it cost him his life. Yet still he lay there, unmoving, scarcely breathing, as fascinated as a wild beast caught in a lantern's glare.

"Shall we send it now?" Ahfinn inquired.

Silence followed, broken by the sounds of drink being slowly sipped, as if Zeff were considering his reply. Then: "It *should* leave tonight. But first—"

A knock sounded on the chamber door: a distinctive cadence that likely identified whoever sought entrance. "Enter," Zeff called irritably.

A door opened and someone strode into the room. Someone smaller than Zeff to judge by the weight of the tread. "Nyss," Zeff acknowledged, in greeting. Something in his tone told Kylin that their relationship was no longer entirely cordial.

"Chief," Nyss replied formally. "You summoned me here at this time," she continued. "I await your pleasure."

"The extent of which," Zeff replied, "has yet to be determined."

"I am *not* some neophyte," Nyss huffed, all pretense of

formality fading. Steps followed, then ceased. A cushion sighed as someone sat down. "My time is of value, if not to me, to our cause. I—"

"Your presence here is by my leave," Zeff snapped back. "I heard good report of you and I listened. Perhaps I shouldn't have."

"We are all equal before the Ninth Face," Nyss replied, in the cadence of someone quoting.

"Ah, but The Ninth has given me this place, and it is now my task to determine how I might best secure it."

"And so you hesitate."

"And so I hesitate."

"Because once you've sent forth that parchment there, the course is set. And you fear you haven't explored your choices as thoroughly as you might." An edge had entered Nyss's voice, Kylin noted: hostility and perhaps contempt, if not true challenge. It was good that he'd remained there, he reckoned. And if he lingered longer, perhaps he could learn more. It would be a balance, however; too long and anything he discovered might reach Avall too late. And that assumed he was able to reach his Sovereign at all, which was a *very* large assumption indeed.

But pondering that was for later. For now . . .

Bodies shifted. Yet more drinks were poured and one, by the sound of it, offered. "I don't like contention," Zeff sighed, somewhat more amiably. "For all Contention has a Well, it's my least favorite aspect of my least favorite Face."

"You do have an option," Nyss observed carefully.

"And what might that be?"

"If you had gems of your own, you could argue from a position of strength."

Zeff's breath hissed. He set his goblet down hard. "What do you think was my intent in coming here myself? I hadn't reckoned on what happened. Everything I knew of Crim suggested she was wise and very, very circumspect. I thought perhaps she was someone with whom we could do business."

"And she isn't?"

"She's not proving so," Zeff grumbled. "I keep hoping."

"And time flies on hope's back," Nyss retorted with a grim chuckle.

"I know. And yet I fear. If I send that message, Avall will almost certainly attack this hold, and he'd be a fool not to bring the Lightning Sword. If he wins, that's the end of us. But an attack on us, if it is perceived as an attack on *Priest-Clan,* could well bring civil war, and Avall has sense enough to know that. He may choose to cut his losses."

"Which leaves us if not stronger, then no weaker."

"Stronger, I hope. We'll still command the source of the most powerful objects in Eron."

"If there *are* more, of which we have no proof." Nyss filled her goblet and drank again. The atmosphere was becoming less charged by the moment; indeed, was assuming that of two old friends working for a common cause.

"Which doesn't matter anyway," Zeff acknowledged, "if we can't access the mines."

"Is the damage that severe?"

"Worse even than I feared. That's also why I'm waiting." A pause, another sigh. "When I came here, I assumed Crim knew about the gems. I assumed she either had some of her own or could find them. I assumed that if I sent challenge to Avall, I would be in a position to meet that challenge. I still know, in the way I know the sun will rise tomorrow, that more gems exist here. But I can't get to them—yet. Suppose Avall risks war and comes to face us? Will I be able to face him in turn?"

"It won't be you alone that faces him," Nyss replied dryly.

"Which is why I want to try one last time to force Crim to reveal everything she knows about the gems, and, more to the point, about ways to access them."

"It will have to be tonight, then," Nyss retorted. "If I wait longer, I may have to answer to someone higher in the clan than you. There are limits to what I will risk."

Zeff stood abruptly. "Well, then, if all this hinges on one point, I suggest that point be assessed."

"A wise choice."

"My only choice, given the time frame in which I'm forced to function. Ahfinn," Zeff called, more loudly, "fetch the prisoner."

"You'd bring her here?"

"It's her hold, under Law," Zeff shot back. "And she is High Clan, and a lady. Besides, comfort often makes one lower one's guard."

Kylin released a breath he didn't know he'd been holding and closed his eyes in a vain effort to banish the image that had entered his head. He'd heard nothing of Crim since he'd begun hiding out. She was probably the closest friend he had in the hold, he reckoned; and the fact that she still lived was encouraging. But she was also a prisoner, and from what he'd heard of these men's methods . . .

There was no way on Angen he'd leave now. And if he could find out where she was kept and there was access to the ductwork there, why, maybe, just possibly, he could free her. In any case, the best thing he could do for his cause, clan, and Kingdom was to continue listening.

But Zeff and Nyss seemed to have found some point of equilibrium and lapsed into a discussion of the relative merits of last year's vintages over those of the year before, which Kylin found both boring and nerve-wracking, for all he fancied himself a connoisseur.

Indeed, so long was Ahfinn in returning that Kylin dozed, only to awaken to the sound of voices and a door opening. It closed again, and Kylin heard the lock click. As best he could tell, Zeff and Nyss had indeed been joined by two others in house-slippers, one of whom was certainly Ahfinn, and the other, by her lighter tread, Crim. She sounded tired, but that was to be expected.

Unfortunately, two more men accompanied them, and these wore sturdy boots that branded them as soldiers on duty. One seemed to station himself by the door, the other not far from where Kylin hid behind his grille. They were armed and armored, too; Kylin could hear the rustle of their mail and the rasp of gauntlets against sword hilts.

Crim was clearly confined, for every time she moved, he caught the muffled clink of metal, which meant they'd shackled her wrists—probably with soft-chains.

"Lady Crim," Zeff intoned formally, "please sit down and be as comfortable as you can, considering the situation in which you have found yourself."

"Into which *you* have put me," Crim shot back with a vehemence that surprised Kylin. "You could end this instantly, which I know perfectly well."

"I also know that you, being a much-esteemed Hold-Warden, are aware that one sometimes finds oneself entrusted with certain duties."

"Duties in defiance of clan and King are no duties."

"How do you know I defy them?"

"How could you not? You've claimed their property; that alone puts you in rebellion."

"Have you considered that my clan might sanction this?"

"They'd be fools."

"The line between genius and idiocy can sometimes be razor thin."

"I doubt you had me brought here to match tongues or wits," Crim snapped. "State your purpose and be done."

"Very well," Zeff replied amiably. "I want power. I betray nothing by telling you that. The fact that I already command you implies it."

"I can't be bought," Crim retorted with absolute conviction, as though she hadn't heard. "There's nothing you could give me that I desire."

"But there might be things I could take from you."

Silence, for a moment. Then, from Crim: "You still risk more than I. Everything I've done since you came here, I've done for my honor and the honor of my clan and King. Nor have I taken any risks that my clan and King do not sanction, and which have not the backing of Law."

"The Law of man, or the Law of The Eight?"

"They're the same."

"They are not!" Zeff countered. "That assumes that The Eight have but eight Faces, and that is not a given."

"To think otherwise is heresy and puts you at odds with your clan."

"A mask conceals a face," Zeff replied, "and a face conceals a skull. And sometimes one cannot tell mask from face. Perhaps something lies behind the faces you know, which my clan has chosen not to reveal."

"They've revealed it now!" Crim snorted recklessly. "Whatever mask you've worn—by your clan's leave or in defiance of it—has now been torn asunder! Whatever happens, there'll be no going back."

"Not to the world that was, perhaps. But why go back at all? Why not move ahead to a world that might be? One in which—"

"You control the strings?" Crim finished for him.

"Enough!" Zeff snapped. "You asked what I want, and I'll tell you. I want to know where you've hidden the other gems."

"What other gems?"

"The gems you surely have found over the years and kept secret from us all—until that fool of a boy brought them to light."

"You invent what isn't true," Crim replied, utterly dumbfounded. "Do you think I would support him if he'd acted in defiance of the good of my clan—which betraying our secrets would certainly be?"

"It doesn't really matter, does it?" Zeff chuckled. "Because what I want more than any gems you have is their source."

"The mines, of course."

"Which are blocked," Ahffin growled.

"Nothing is forever," Zeff went on smoothly. "Besides which, there must be as many ways into the mines as there were into this hold."

"So you say."

"So you *will* say."

"You've wasted enough time," Nyss broke in roughly.

"There's only one way to get truth from this woman. Words have failed, for words are born of thought. The body speaks more eloquently and more loudly, as do the emotions."

Zeff paused thoughtfully. "That's true," he conceded. "And we, who practice no formal crafting sometimes forget . . . certain things."

Kylin could almost hear Nyss's lips curl in a fiendish smile. "This woman values her honor," she purred. "But I've no doubt she values her pride more. For one such as she, pride is linked with skill in making. And if she could make no longer . . ."

"Crush her fingers," Zeff commanded. "A joint at a time, starting with her left hand."

Kylin heard Crim gasp, which he imagined she regretted. The woman he knew would not display even that small weakness before anyone by choice.

"It's actually very humane," Zeff continued. "We'll damage nothing she needs to live, only what she needs to be happy."

"In other words," Nyss laughed, "we'll destroy her access to her craft."

Heavy boots sounded, as Crim was hauled, none too gently, to her feet.

"Use that table," Zeff ordered.

It wasn't until he heard boots approaching that Kylin realized that they meant the table behind which his grille was hidden. He had no choice but to back away. And was just as glad that choice had been made for him, because it meant he was two turns away before he heard the screaming.

He moved in truth then. Heedless of the noise he made, he backed down to where the duct in which he crouched met the larger one he'd planned to follow. If his intentions had been unclear initially, they were that way no longer. He had to get out, and quickly, and he had to get word to Avall.

As to how that might be accomplished, beyond some notion of trying to connect with Div—well, he supposed, that was for Fate to determine.

CHAPTER IX:

PARTING IN THE NIGHT

(ERON: TIR-ERON: ARGEN-HALL-MAIN— HIGH SUMMER: DAY XLIII—EVENING)

Strynn found Merryn in Argen-Hall's war court, clad in full armor and wearing the colors Law required of her: the maroon of Argen, which was her birth-clan, quartered with the crimson of Warcraft, which was her skill of choice; beneath, over all, the embroidered crown that marked her part of the Royal Guard even when off duty. There was another tabard specifically for that more formal role, but Merryn never wore it.

Black-cloaked and stealth-shrouded, Strynn watched her patiently from the darkest corner of the arcade that squared the court. Beams from three moons cast strange shadows upon the pavement there, while providing light enough to see without a lantern, though torches flared anyway, at the center of each wall.

That brighter light flashed off steel, brass, and gilded bronze. Most particularly, it flashed off the long, keen edge of a sword. Strynn recognized the set of moves Merryn was rehearsing. "Dancing with dust motes," it was called, from the intricacy of the pattern. And indeed it was a dance, for every part of Merryn's body moved in a complex weave of dodge, twist, and parry.

It was what her bond-sister did to relax, Strynn knew, as she also knew why relaxation was necessary.

She dared not interrupt now. The dance was not yet over, and Merryn would never forgive her if she destroyed her momentum. Not that Strynn wanted to, for she'd never seen that suite of moves executed with such violently elegant precision. She tried to fix the image in her memory and lock it there: silver-blue walls embracing jet-black archways; a sky of royal blue dappled with stars; and Merryn in the middle, a symphony of muted red and flashing silver, bound by shadows that rippled like black moonlight on water.

And then it was over, and Merryn was walking straight toward her, the sword a bar of light before her, still unsheathed. "I knew you were here," she panted, when she reached the requisite span that polite speech required.

Strynn grinned back. "I'd be disappointed if you didn't. It's part of your Night Guard training, isn't it? To see everything, even while your attention is focused on one thing alone."

"You have beer, I assume?" Merryn replied pointedly, neatly sidestepping the query.

The grin widened, but Strynn shook her head. "I have walnut liquor."

Merryn sheathed the sword. "Even better." And with that she sank down where she was, shoulders against one of the arcade's pillars. Strong, deft fingers skinned off mail gauntlets, then fumbled with the fastening of the helm.

Strynn squatted in turn, reached over to undo the buckle for her, then flopped back against the other pillar while Merryn removed the helm and arming cap beneath, revealing black hair so soaked with sweat it looked like enameled metal.

Neither spoke. Though this was in part a spontaneous moment, there was still ritual to be placated. Reaching to her hip, Strynn unhooked a padded leather pouch from which she removed a hand-sized, blown-glass bottle, protected by a cage of bronze filigree. Matching cups went with it. Merryn would recognize them, too: the first things she had made for Strynn, back when they'd sworn sisterhood. A pause, while she undid the hasp that held the cork closed, and the strong smell of walnut filled the air.

And still no one spoke until Strynn had filled both cups and both had been drained once.

"I knew you'd be here," Strynn smirked when the ritual was complete and the cups had been refilled for sipping. "I also know you're planning to leave tonight, because you haven't seen anyone today, and I know you hate good-byes."

Merryn frowned at her. "Then why are you making me say one?"

"At least I'm sparing you the one you dread most!"

A brow quirked up. "You know me that well, do you?"

Strynn regarded her levelly. "Look at me straight and say it's not your brother. Whatever we two feel, it's him you don't want to leave, because—"

"This time it may be forever?" Merryn drained her cup with a flourish. "There: I've said it. What you don't want to hear."

"I'd rather know than wonder."

"So would Avall."

"Which is why I'm here: so I can tell him. When it's the proper time to tell him."

"When I can't be recalled?"

"That's right."

"I didn't think it would be like this, sister," Merryn sighed, folding her arms across her breast. "I don't know what I thought our last meeting would be like, but this isn't it. Still, things never work as you expect them. Life isn't a painting or a play you can revise over and over."

A deep breath, and Strynn said what she'd long been thinking but nevertheless feared to say. "This *isn't* our last meeting, is it?"

A shrug, which was just like Merryn: reducing strong emotions to subtle gestures. "It might be. Once I leave the Gorge, I only know that I'll know where I'm going when I arrive. And no, I'm not fool enough to think you don't have some idea where I might begin. You know I've always wanted to go west. But 'west' is a big place, and most roads from here lead west, one way or another. But I may not be taking the roads."

"But you will come back?"

"I *want* to come back," Merryn conceded. "But I probably won't *be* back until I've settled my mind about some things."

"Kraxxi?"

A tiny pause, but one Strynn noticed. "That's one of them."

"*Krynneth?* You know he'll think you're running away from him."

"Haven't you heard?" Merryn snorted, shifting her back restlessly. "He's run away from me! He's been gone a whole eight now. Headed south with a trek of masons bound for War-Hold, and that's all I know, except that I think Elvix was with them. In any case, I've never *had* him—in any way you want to construe that. I liked him a lot, and during the war we often kept company because we'd both been at War-Hold when it fell. And then afterward, I guess we were each other's anchors. We shared the bond of being outsiders in War-Hold but pledged to that clan. And we—"

She broke off. To Strynn's surprise, she was crying. "I'll say it for you, sister. You shared what you thought was betrayal. You both thought you could've stopped what happened."

Merryn's eyes were bright when she looked up again. "Truth."

A deep breath, from Strynn. "So that's another thing this is, then: another reason you may not come back. You want to assuage your guilt for the destruction of War-Hold, and to do that, you have to do something bigger than that, but it has to be a *good* thing. You're out to make yourself such a hero that no one will remember what happened down south."

Merryn managed a wicked smile. "Ah, but you're forgetting something, sister."

"What's that?"

"That this is a *secret* mission. When I ride out—in two

hands, if things go right—I won't be riding out on a royal errand. I'll be going as a Common Clan woman—which is more than I should tell you right there. Not that it matters, since I've plans to change disguises like you change clothes."

"But you expect to return a hero," Strynn retorted. "And the only way you can do that is if you discover something important."

Merryn grinned again. "I *could* return as queen of Ixti."

Strynn nodded, only then noticing the ring Merryn wore on her right hand. A red stone: one of three. Avall had one just like it: a gift from the man they were even now discussing. "But you've told Kraxxi otherwise. Have you changed your mind?"

Merryn shook her head. "No. But that doesn't mean I *won't* change it. A year ago, I couldn't have imagined that my brother would be King. Nor that we'd have proof positive of magic—or something. Nor that we'd be on the brink of civil war."

"You think it'll come to that?"

"Not before I return, I hope."

"And if you don't return?"

"Well, obviously if my brother goes to war without me, I won't be happy."

Strynn chuckled grimly. "So if we want you back, we have to start a war?"

Another shrug, while Merryn studied her empty cup. "I just want to do this right, sister. If I do as my King bids me, I'm doing what's right, by Law. If I remove the regalia from reach, I'm doing everything I can to make things like they were, which will be good for the Kingdom. Avall wants his legacy as King to be that of the man who fixed things when they'd been broken. I don't entirely agree, but I understand."

Strynn drained her own cup. "So do I." She rose abruptly, giving her bond-mate a hand up. "What, I wonder, did my husband do to deserve two such wonderful women?"

"What did *I* do," Merryn countered, as she clasped Strynn

in a rough hug they both knew was all they dared, "to deserve so wonderful a sister?"

And then, harsh as a sword cut, she broke the embrace, turned, snatched up her helm and sword from where she'd left them, and strode off down the arcade, leaving Strynn alone in the moonlight with a new ache in her heart to join those already lodged there.

CHAPTER X:

WALLS AND WATER

~~~~~~

The timeless period after he'd overheard the invaders' plans and the torture session that concluded it was the worst of Kylin's life. Thwarted in his efforts at finding a way closer to ground level than he'd already ventured, and frightened beyond reason of being discovered—which could only result in him being interrogated and possibly tortured himself—he was reduced to a furtive existence a rat would not have envied. At least a rat would've risked showing itself for food. Kylin couldn't. Many times, as he made his way through the duct-work maze that had become his world, he caught the sounds of voices he could not approach and the scent of food he could not access. Fortunately, he did manage to find a rift in the wall of one of Woodcraft's private pantries, where he'd snared enough dry bread and cheese to sustain him, along with a skin of good ale. He made a special point of remembering where that place was, too, in case he needed to return—which he did, twice. Unfortunately, the suite beyond was occupied by the invaders, which ruled out assistance from that quarter. He was trying harder than ever to be systematic now, to explore every twist and turn and remember it. But his greatest frustration was that he'd found no more stair-shafts.

All of which was of minimal import when reality was rapidly collapsing beneath a weight of urgency he could not assuage—because he could not escape. So on he went, exploring this way, probing that. Sometimes he crawled over mounds of fallen stonework or squeezed around them. Twice he found standing water, and three times came upon places where the sewage drains had ruptured, with attendant awful odor. Once, too, he smelled what could only be rotting human flesh, from which he divined that the damage, while not truly extensive, was far from minimal in some quarters.

And, always, he listened: straining his hearing for voices he could trust, but finding none. From the rest, the invaders, he determined how the explosion had occurred, and that efforts were being made to reach those trapped in the mines, but that Liallyn, who'd *caused* the cave-in, had been far more thorough than even she had anticipated. It would take eights to reach the mines, not days.

And, of course, he slept. But he came to dread those lapses into timelessness as he once had welcomed them, for he always awoke wearier and hungrier than when he'd begun, and more disoriented. He had a constant headache, too, and his body was a mass of scrapes and abrasions.

Even so, he wasn't prepared when he awoke from a particularly dull and heavy slumber to find something nibbling his fingers. He flinched reflexively, only to be rewarded with a sharper pain as his knuckles scraped rough-dressed stone. Forgetting where he was, he screamed. His voice echoed in the closed space, but of more concern was the soft scrabbling of whatever he'd hit, which indicated it hadn't gone away. It had been warm and furry—or at least not cold and sticky—which was some relief. But the only warm, furry things that ought to be sharing his space were rats, and hold rats could reach more than a quarter span in length.

He flinched again—and his foot impacted something soft. The recoil brought him in contact with another, and the recoil from *that* struck something hard enough to evoke a squeak before teeth bit down on his leg just above the big tendon at his heel. Something squeaked back, close to his head, and that was more than he could endure.

He had no idea how many rats were attempting to share the crawl space with him, but one was one too many. Still half-asleep and closer than he dared think to being terrified, he thrust himself forward. The duct was low here, and he had to worm his way along with his forearms—which, he suspected, meant that this was one of the older parts of the hold and probably a good way from the bulk of the edifice. The air was warmer, too, for no reason that made sense, but it smelled musty where it didn't smell of rats.

The bad thing was that he couldn't turn around. Worse, this was new territory, so he had no comfort from anticipation as he continued onward.

Nor were the rats ignoring him. More than once he felt one nip at his toes or heels, and one even dared run up his leg to stand atop his shoulders. Fortunately, the duct was high enough there that he could arch upward to scrape it off against the ceiling.

Unfortunately, when he flopped back down, it was atop another that had tried to crawl beneath him.

He screamed again, and then once more when it bit him savagely on the chest. Blood washed warm down his belly, even as he reached beneath him and, in an effort worthy of an epic poem, snared the wretched beast and threw it with what little strength remained back down the duct behind.

The result was not what he expected. Rather than being cowed, the rats gave chase. And though his bulk blocked most of the passage, that didn't prevent them taking increasingly frequent and stronger nips from his legs and buttocks. Before he knew it, he was crawling as fast as he had since coming there, with no concern for logic, no attempt at counting paces.

All that mattered was escaping the wretched rodents.

He was still bleeding, too, and that seemed to have triggered some reflex in what passed in the beasts for brains, so that they became more venturesome yet. And then one sank its teeth into his left calf and absolutely would not let go. Not only that, it was gnawing; more blood trickled past those sharp little incisors.

"Go away! Go away! Go away!" he shouted recklessly— even if the invaders found him, they'd be unlikely to eat him alive. And while his rational aspect reminded him that they'd also try to torture him into betraying his friend and King, he could not make that matter.

Another bite, as a second rat joined the fray, then another, and he could feel his strength start to fail. He was twisting every way he could think of, trying to crush them against the walls or scrape them off, but it seemed to be doing little good.

Abruptly, the air changed, and he felt the duct expand around him. Not that it was much wider, but he sensed more space above his back and head, which let him move faster. And then more again, and he could stand. Suddenly, he was running. The rats followed, but the constant jarring proved too much, even for those that held on most tenaciously. As soon as he dared, he slowed enough to reach down and slap away the few that remained. His legs were slick with blood, and he couldn't count the points of pain from his hips down, yet still he staggered onward, utterly lost, utterly tired and hungry. Utterly aimless.

And so was paying no attention when a mislaid step unbalanced him. His palms brushed rubble as he pinwheeled briefly on the brink of what sound and more subtle senses told him was a vast gulf. Something snared his tunic and steadied him for a moment before the fabric ripped free. And then he was falling, in truth.

The fall seemed to last forever, but in fact took less time than it took to draw one breath, ending when his hips slammed into what proved to be a steep slope that changed pitch again soon after, sending him sliding down some kind of chute.

And he knew what *these* chutes were, for Strynn had considered using them when they'd planned their escape back in the winter. These were the master shafts that brought air from close to the ground outside and ducted it to the hold's interior. And if he remembered right, they ended in grilles recessed into the hold's outer walls at twice a man's height above the ground.

As if to confirm that supposition, the air turned warmer yet. Fresher, too, with the spice of conifers overriding the stench of burning. And then, in final confirmation, he found himself brought up short when his feet slammed into something with sufficient force that shock and pain became all of reality. Abruptly stationary, his body folded down around itself, so that he found himself wedged, half-sitting, half-lying, half-standing, atop something very solid indeed. Probing fingers found a pierced stone grille set at an angle in the wall. But even his most energetic efforts loosened it not a whit—while serving to tire him further.

At least he'd evaded the rats—for a while. He wondered, grimly, if he'd remain there, unable to crawl upward, until he died and began to stink. Or maybe they wouldn't find him until he rotted enough for his small bones to fall through to the ground.

One thing was certain: He wasn't going up—at least not very far. And he didn't think he'd be going down, either—alive. Worse, there were even odds whether he'd wound up on the east side of the hold, which meant he was two spans away from freedom, assuming he could reach the ground, or on the side that faced the mountain, where a number of tiny enclosed gardens occupied the hollow between the hold and the mountain proper. He suspected the latter, if only because he didn't think he'd slid long enough to have traversed the six or so levels between where he'd begun and the grilles in the eastern wall. Which meant he was farther down than when he'd started, but farther than ever from freedom.

He awoke to the sound of running water. It was raining; he could tell by the way the air felt, and the patter of heavy drops against the bare earth below the grille. But water was running elsewhere, too, and not, though he feared it, down the shaft in which he'd become lodged. No, this was somewhat muffled, yet at the same time it echoed, as though it flowed through channels. He could even feel it, as a vibration in the surrounding stone. The hold had drains, he knew, that fed into cisterns throughout the edifice. It also had drains that flushed out the garderobes. In either case, water close enough to hear was water close enough to investigate.

Drawing himself up to his full height, he stretched along the shaft down which he'd fallen, gratified to hear the sound intensify as he rose. He closed his eyes, too, for entering that deeper dark helped focus concentration. Slowly, methodically, he slid his hand along the walls of his stony prison in the direction in which the water lay. Right! Then farther to the right. The slope was steep, but not so much that he couldn't force himself up it, progress aided by a thin growth of lichen that had rooted there. The water sounded louder now, and definitely to the right. He stretched his hands that way, seeking some opening—some crack in the wall—anything that would provide one more choice than he'd had heretofore.

Twice he slipped and slid back down, but the third time he gathered what strength remained and hurled himself as far up the shaft as he could reach, flailing right as he did. And this time his fingers found something useful.

A ledge, as it turned out, and one that was dry enough and big enough that he could ease his other hand there. The water sounded louder, too, and he guessed the hold was being visited by one of those torrential storms that characterized summer in the mountains. Pushing with his feet, he forced his way higher, twisting his torso so as to give his fingers better purchase on what he hoped was the lower edge of an opening onto that invisible watercourse. It was artificial masonry, not hewn native stone—or maybe not, for it began to narrow as he slid his arms through into a nothingness that was nevertheless cooler and wetter than any he'd encountered before.

In any case, it was worth the chance; besides which, he'd managed to work his feet to the other side of the shaft, so that he could brace against it and push.

A particularly strong thrust, coupled with a strained twist, put his upper half into the opening, and from there, it wasn't hard, all things considered, to wriggle the rest of the way in.

Water roared in his ears, but with it came the thunder that marked a truly magnificent storm outside, coupled with occasional gusts of chill wind that found him even there.

But the place he'd lodged was cramped—not that he was certain he could continue anyway. Besides which, he couldn't really swim, though he'd managed enough training at War-Hold to be able to float with reasonable confidence. *If* he set his mind to it. If panic didn't overrule rationality.

Well, he concluded, he could either lie there worrying and dreading, or he could take action. And he *was* privy to information Avall desperately needed. Information that had cost Crim her craft.

That decided it. Fumbling forward, his fingers found the opposite end of whatever this opening was that linked the air shaft and the drain. One minute his hand lay on solid rock, the next it flopped in air. Running water brushed his fingertips when he strained an arm downward, and a similar check above showed at least as much space overhead. Good: There might be enough air in the space beyond to allow him to breathe. Also, whatever he'd found was close to the hold's outer walls, which was where the main cisterns lay. More importantly, there was a series of overflow gates near the hold's south end, which diverted any surplus into the Ri-Megon, which ran *under* the hold for most of the hold's length before exiting past the south court and the water garden.

Which would probably not be watched now.

But which were also at least three levels lower.

Still, he had to die eventually, and drowning was better than starvation.

Without further contemplation, he took a deep breath, pushed himself forward—and fell into water half a span below. The cold shocked him, making him belch out half his cache of air, but by then a current had him. He started to fight his way to where he imagined the surface to be, then realized that was stupid and relaxed as much as his hovering panic allowed, letting his body rise of its own accord. Fortunately, the runoff drained through man-made channels; thus, there were no rapids such as made rivers perilous, so that an instant later, he felt cold air across his back and realized he'd bobbed to the surface. In his efforts to flip over, his feet touched something, and he discovered that the bottom wasn't very far down at all, so that he could actually walk, though with his head less than a hand's width from the ceiling. With no energy left to choose another option, he let the current thrust him where it would, which he fervently prayed was out.

It seemed to take forever, but actually required no more than a quarter hand, for the hold, though enormous, was still no more than a shot long, measured at its major axis.

Besides which, he could hear a change in the outflow's pitch, which told him water was pouring through some opening into a larger space ahead.

And then he stepped on something slick, and fell—and was still trying to find either the bottom or the surface when he began to fall in earnest, surrounded by water that was also falling.

He *did* panic then, and was starting to breathe more water than air when something solid made him see colors he hadn't seen since going blind, and then he simply gave himself up for lost and let ultimate darkness claim him.

• • •

Kylin's breath was coming harsh and ragged, and his pulse seemed none too steady, but at least he had them. As he also had more scrapes and abrasions than Div had ever seen on a live man, even during the war. And she'd seen most of Kylin's, too, because his clothes—nice indoor velvets, she noted absently—were torn to ribbons, and he was missing his shoes entirely.

Setting her mouth, she scooted to a more viable position on the steep rock shelf atop which she'd just hauled the harper's body and slid her elbows beneath his armpits. It wasn't so much that he was heavy as simply deadweight, which, with the slope, made standing with him both unlikely and dangerous. She was therefore reduced to edging backward up the stone, while Kylin gasped, wheezed, and finally began choking and—to her relief—trying to knock her hands away.

She let him go and scrambled farther upslope to wipe rain-soaked hair from her eyes and cast a wary glance through the slanting sheets at the portion of hold visible beyond the intervening screen of laurel—which was as close as she dared approach, lest someone note her spying. It was exactly as it had been a finger ago—which was to say that it was overtly the same as it ought to be, down to the Gemcraft standard flopping soddenly above—save that no one walked its many arcades but men in white cloaks she knew far too well. As well as anyone, in fact, since men in that same livery had tried to kill her and left a scar on her hip to prove it.

And, of course, there was that substantial crack running from the hold's foundations halfway up its eastern wall, on which smoke stains had still been visible when she arrived. And a good thing they had been, for that had been the final proof she needed that things *weren't* as they ought to be when she'd come riding up shortly after noon intending to retrieve Kylin and head back to Tir-Eron.

She *had* retrieved him, too, but not in the way expected.

He was moving more vigorously now, and trying to cough, while his fingers scrabbled at the rock. She eased down to help him—an action rendered awkward by the rainwater that slid unabated over the outcrop, courtesy of a storm grown fiercer yet.

"Kylin," she called, having remembered that he was blind and therefore unable to recognize friend from foe save by voice. "It's me, Div."

"Div . . . ?" he managed through a mouthful of water. "Where . . . ?"

"On a rock, south of the hold. I have to get you to higher ground."

He sat up at that—and promptly slid half a span back down the shelf. She grabbed him frantically, heard fabric rip in what was left of his tunic. "Steep slope, Kylin, below woods. You'd best back up crabwise, but there's no good way for me to help without falling. Just take it slow. It's maybe three spans."

To his credit, Kylin didn't protest. Obedient as a child, he leaned back and did as instructed, scooting ever upward, with Div positioned above to assist how and when she could. Only when they'd reached the shelter of a copse of laurel strung between a span of oaks did he find his feet again, and that only long enough to collapse against her in a soggy, bony bundle. At least he was clean, if massively abraded. "Div," he gasped, "I— we have to get away from here. We have to tell Avall. We— Where are we, anyway?"

"About a shot south of the hold, where the river makes a turn and there're sandbars—which you didn't have the grace to wash up on."

Kylin released his grip abruptly and slumped back against a tree. "Is it . . . ?"

"I've got a camp two shots south of here. A cold camp, I'm afraid. I didn't dare build a fire for fear of being seen. We can talk there."

"But . . ."

"We can talk *there*," Div repeated, hauling Kylin to his feet.

"You're alone?" he ventured, as he found reasonable footing and she got her arm around him, the better to lead him along.

"Not anymore," she grunted. "But if you're asking whether I have a dozen armed knights with me, the answer's no. I have myself, my horse, and a packhorse for the furs I was going to trade away at the hold."

"Maybe that's just as well," Kylin sighed as he trudged along. "That way we can make better time to Tir-Eron."

And then the rain came harder and conversation turned to the more basic demands of overland travel through storm-wracked woods.

Kylin shrugged the blanket loosely around his shoulders and reached down to unknot the drawstring that snugged his drawers, letting them fall in a heap at his feet before stepping clumsily out of them. At that, he lost his balance and flailed out—until he felt Div's strong grip behind him, steadying him. "Thanks," he murmured as he regained his balance, then hugged the blanket more closely around him. At least it was dry. So was the ground underfoot—a blessing, that, after what seemed like an eternity of slippery leaves, dripping branches, and the rain itself that still came down in torrents beyond the edge of the rocky overhang beneath which they sheltered. It was too shallow to be called a cave, Div said, merely a shaded indentation in the ledge above the river they'd followed to get there. They were south of the hold, which made sense, for not only did *her* hold lie in that direction, but the land was wilder there. The South Road followed the opposite bank of the river above which they were sheltering, while fishing was usually confined to the cleaner water north of the hold, since, in spite of all efforts to the contrary, a thousand people housed in one building produced a lot of wastewater that had to go somewhere.

"You're welcome," Div replied offhand, as Kylin folded himself down in place and waited. "If you don't mind, I'll get dry; then we'll talk."

Kylin nodded mutely, accustomed to waiting, though he didn't like it. To his right he heard the sounds of Div stripping, and decided that from her point of view there were advantages to sheltering with a blind man. Not that she was very modest anyway. More sounds ensued, likely her laying out clothing on rocks. He wished the rain would abate. The steady rush of the drops themselves, coupled with the roar of the wind through heavy summer foliage, made it hard to catch the more localized nuances of sound that helped define his environment. He compensated with his other senses, though touch was mostly confined to the roughness of the blanket against bare skin and the occasional trickle of water from his hair down his back. Drying his hands as best he could, he patted the ground round about, finding it an even mix of naked rock, sand, and small stones. Probably material that had washed in during the spring floods, which explained why birkits hadn't denned there— though it might also be too exposed.

His sinuses were still too clogged with river water for smell to be very reliable, but he did catch the scent of horse from the blanket and what might be sharp cheese and some kind of liquor.

Div had evidently finished changing now, and eased close enough for conversation. He could feel the warmth of her body near his and was insanely grateful for it. A final bit of fumbling on her part, involving leather, glass, and metal, followed by wood being filled with liquid, and she eased a cup into his hand. "It'll warm you inside, if not out," she informed him tersely.

Kylin drank, recognizing the fumes of one of Brewing's more potent products—a thrice-distilled whisky, if he wasn't mistaken, mixed with honey and some kind of herb that could be either mint or tarragon. It numbed his tongue, soothed his throat, and flashed through his nose like cold fire, even into his eyes. He blinked away tears, but found his head far more comfortable.

For the rest, he was bruised and beaten, but alive.

Div was slicing bread, so he thought. An assumption that was confirmed when she passed him a slab, augmented with some of the cheese he'd smelled earlier. "Your tale first, or mine?" he asked, after a pair of very welcomed bites.

"Mine's simple enough," Div replied with her mouth full. "I was coming to the hold to retrieve you, pick up our escort, and head back to Tir-Eron, just as we'd planned. I'd already seen smoke where there shouldn't be that much smoke and become wary. I'd also seen horsemen riding toward the hold, all in white cloaks I recognized as belonging to those who attacked Avall, Rann, and me last winter. Unfortunately, they were too far ahead of me to catch, and in any case, the smoke was all the proof I needed that they'd already taken the hold, or at least attacked it, and that these were simply reinforcements. I assume they wanted to control the source of the gems," she added, "if not the gems themselves."

"You're correct there," Kylin agreed, through another mouthful. "Go on."

"At that point, my intentions became twofold. I wanted to find out as much as I could without betraying myself, so I picketed the horses in the safest place I could find and put the place under surveillance." A pause for another drink, then: "I also knew you were in there, and I doubted things would go well for you if anyone found out that you were one of Avall's intimates, so I decided to try to find out what had happened to you, and free you if necessary. If I'd known about the water gate, I might've tried earlier, but the fact is, I wanted to take it slow. I was trying to get a sense of when sections are guarded, when they're not, and when the guard changes—and that takes time. I'm sorry if you suffered while I scouted."

"You couldn't have found me," Kylin assured her, rubbing

absently at a particularly vicious scrape on his wrist and wondering if it looked as bad as it felt. "I was holed up inside the walls. Speaking of which, how *did* you find me?"

"Luck, if you want to call it that—or Fate. I'd been favoring this direction because this is where my camp is, and where the best shelter is that's still reasonably close to the hold. I'd just gone out to see if the rain changed anything about the patrol habits and saw something floating down the river. Turned out to be a certain harper."

"Without the harp he came for, I'm afraid," Kylin sighed.

"No time soon," Div agreed wearily. "But I'm thinking I won't be going back with the things I came for, either."

"Not after you've heard what I found out."

"You've been spying, too?"

Kylin grinned in spite of himself. "Let's say I've been in a position that *allowed* spying. But maybe I should tell you from the beginning . . ."

Div listened without comment to the tale he relayed, speaking only to clarify a few points, most having to do with how he'd found his way around the hold. "I was trying to determine what quarters the invaders were using," she admitted finally. "If we're going back in there, that'll have to be our goal."

"Going back!" Kylin all but shrieked. "I can't! Not that I'm afraid, but you have to know how urgent this is. We have to tell Avall the real story: that there's a good chance they'll destroy the hold anyway, so he'll be blamed for it."

"Now repeat what was said again," Div urged.

Kylin did, word for word, for the art of complete and accurate recall was one of the skills a musician mastered early on, though it was properly the province of Stagecraft.

"We'll have to hurry if we're going to be of any aid," Div conceded finally. "And the only way we'll be of much aid is if we get to Avall before these folks deliver their ultimatum. After that, it'll be a hard call. Avall may take the battle to them; he may not. He may try to call their bluff; he may not."

"But he's got the Lightning Sword," Kylin protested. "They'd be mad to stand against that."

"They might not have to, or they might have weapons just as deadly by then. We're in a double race, Kylin. We have to reach Tir-Eron before the ultimatum, and Avall has to deliver a quick and decisive reply before the invaders can find gems of their own. That's his key advantage right now. They want him to think they have gems and are willing to use them. We know that, as of a day ago, they don't. We also know that they'll do anything to access the mines. It'll take at least three eights to get word to Tir-Eron and bring an army back here. They can do a lot of digging in three eights."

"You're forgetting that Avall can space-jump. He could be here two breaths after he gets word."

"He can jump with the master gem," Div corrected. "But he can't *use* the master gem—or won't. The others—I understand he's tried but failed. They're not all alike, but we don't— yet—know how they differ."

"But Merryn . . ."

"Merryn, very recklessly, used Strynn's gem and the Lightning Sword *once* under extreme duress and jumped, *with Strynn,* to where Eddyn was—and half destroyed one of Barrax's camps in the process. It scared her to death and almost drove her mad—madder than she's ever told her brother. So no, I don't think she'd act unilaterally, even assuming she could get hold of the Sword, which she can't. In any case," she finished, rising, "those are decisions for Avall's council to make, not us. And if we're going to have any input on that council, we need to ride."

"I hope you've got sturdier clothes than I've been wearing," Kylin muttered wearily.

"You're close to my size," Div gave back, "and I wear men's garb when I can. I've probably got something that'll fit you."

"Right now," Kylin replied through a nervous chuckle, "I'd wear a dress all the way if it was dry."

"I've got one on my horse," Div retorted, matter-of-factly. "You can decide when you get there."

A quarter hand later, and once more clad in rain-soaked clothes, they were walking again. Three hands after that, marginally dryer and better fed, they were galloping for all they were worth toward Tir-Eron.

CHAPTER XI:

STRANGE DIPLOMACY

(NORTHWESTERN ERON–HIGH SUMMER: DAY XLVIII–LATE AFTERNOON)

Kylin sniffed miserably and shifted in his saddle, trying to free enough cloak from the wad behind him to pull his hood farther forward. He succeeded too well, for the wet fabric could not support itself and flopped down in his face, which would've blinded him had he not been blind already. As it was, it was merely another minor discomfort in a file of days that had been full of them. Not once since they'd left Gem-Hold-Winter had they been completely dry. Indeed, it was as though the storm was following them from the mountains toward the coast, though logic told Kylin that most summer weather came out of the mountains anyway, just as winter weather came off the sea.

"It's times like this I believe in The Eight," he grumbled through another sniff.

"The Eight are supposed to be on the side of the King, which is the same side you're on," Div chided. "Anything They do to inconvenience you is incidental to some larger purpose."

"So Priest-Clan would say."

"Not everything they say is wrong, Kylin. I—Look out!" she warned abruptly. "Branch, to the right."

Kylin leaned left reflexively, but even so caught the impact of twigs and needles as the branch Div had thoughtlessly pushed aside threatened to unseat him—and did unseat his hood, which he had to adjust again. Still, it was the only way to travel: her in the lead on White Star, with him behind on Etti, a pack animal that was proving to be a doughty companion indeed. As for the route—he had to trust her. There were ways through the Wild that had nothing to do with established roads. Whether Priest-Clan's minions also knew those ways, he had no idea. Still, they were four days out now, and had found no sign of either scouts or the messengers that should long since be en route to Tir-Eron. By the road, not this—presumably—faster way.

He hoped their haste was worth it, because it had been among the most miserable four days of Kylin's life—so much so that at times only the knowledge that comfort waited at the end made it tolerable. Even their last trek from Gem-Hold to Tir-Eron had been more pleasant, fading winter though it had been; for at least then there'd been less sense of urgency.

And less pain. Though he was already scraped and abraded, this ride was adding new calluses to his sensitive harper fingers, never mind the raw patches inside his thighs where ill-fitting breeches against a make-do saddle waged a war of attrition against hair and skin alike. Nor that his handicap had always exempted him from the hardest labor (though he'd taken a tour on the trods in the mines like everyone else), which meant that his suddenly overstressed muscles were at least as sore as his much-abused skin. And that wasn't even counting the bruises he'd suffered in his fall and subsequent tumble in the river. More than once he'd wished Avall were here, or at least Avall's master gem, with its healing powers. Strynn's could heal, too, of course—enough to quell the sickness and pain of pregnancy, at any rate—but wishing Strynn there was not wise, for any number of reasons. As for the other gems—he wasn't certain, though the ones in the regalia Rrath had stolen had definitely saved that troublesome Priest from literal death, if only to precipitate a figurative one.

"A weather-witch would be good to have right now," Kylin opined finally, to distract himself from pondering his aches and pains—and maybe, possibly, make this miserable journey seem to pass faster.

"They could only tell us how long we'd have to endure," Div retorted. "Not turn the weather itself."

"Some of them *can* change the weather," Kylin shot back. "Strynn said that Merryn said that Avall said that Eddyn said that Rrath said—"

"A string of 'saids' long enough to hang a man," Div snorted, slapping White Star on the neck—which sound carried clearly, even above the patter of rain. "What I'm worried about isn't *our* comfort so much as the horses'. We've been pushing them extremely hard with no letup save when *we* rest or walk them. They can't continue like that indefinitely."

"Your point being?"

"That I know a place nearby where we could shelter for the night, but it wouldn't be a good place for our mounts."

"Why not?"

An exasperated sigh. "Because it's a birkit den, Kylin. And we both know what birkits like to eat better than anything."

"Horse," Kylin sighed back. "I suppose this is the same den where you, Avall, and Rann sheltered last winter? I could understand you being hesitant. I know I . . . am."

Div nodded so vigorously Kylin could hear her hood move. "And that's allowing for the fact that I know the birkits there—if one can say one 'knows' what I'm still half-convinced are wild animals."

"But they saved you, and they mind-spoke to you, Rann, and Avall, and they showed Rann how to get to Gem-Hold, and one came around your hold—so you said."

"Sometimes I talk too much. In any case, that was while the gem-glamour was still upon us. They swore not to hunt us, but I'm not sure who that included or how widely it was to be applied. We can't just march into a birkit cave and claim kinright, much less expect that right to include our mounts. We were on skis last time, remember? This time—we'd be expecting a lot of self-control. I don't have that much faith."

Kylin frowned. "They only exempt us because we're hunters, correct?"

"Something like that. It's more complicated, but you have to have linked with one to understand that, and I never did—not really. That is, they tried, and I kind of wanted to, but it scared me, so I never did it fully. I've never even mind-talked to them, really. And for us to den with them, I'd need to negotiate some kind of pact, and I might not be able to."

"Still," Kylin persisted, "you wouldn't risk much by trying—"

"—only my life—"

"—and I sure would like to have a real fire tonight, and a hot bath—you did say there was a hot spring in that cave?"

"You're asking more than you know," Div growled. "And that's assuming we even find any of the wretched beasts. The Eight know we didn't see any last spring!"

"Raising their cubs, you said. Occupied with their own affairs."

"Never where you need them," Div grumbled. "Not when I hunted them, and not now."

"Uh, I don't think *that's* going to be a problem," Kylin muttered, as a shift of wind flung rain in his face. "Something's following us. I just heard footfalls behind and to the left. Soft, but something big."

"Watch your reins," Div hissed back, suddenly all business. "I'm going to slow but not stop. It's getting dark, and there's no way we can outrun birkits in this terrain, besides which—oh, Eight, there's one in front of us!"

"Well," Kylin replied calmly, though chills trembled up his spine, "let's hope their memories are better than the memories of our kind."

"That's like expecting a child to speak fluent Ixtian," Div grumbled. Then: "Whoa!" to White Star.

Etti stopped, too, of her own will, leaving Kylin no choice but to stay where he was and wait. Div however—he'd just heard the liquid rasp of her boots slipping out of the stirrups and her voice, very tentatively, calling out, "Hail to you, oh Hunter."

It was her own voice, yet Div scarcely recognized it, the words sounded so strange—stiff and stilted, as though this were no real situation but a part in some play she was enacting. Nor did she know where the beasts had come from; they had simply . . . appeared.

Not that the image before her seemed real in any case: darkening woods, with trees looming heavy to either side, many draped with long tendrils of summer moss, with the rain still coming down, but lessening even as she spoke, and backlit by an actual, visible sun that turned the drops to lines of silver.

While straight ahead, a steel-gray shape as big as she and Kylin together sat catlike on haunches that would've done most bears proud, gazing at her with calm green eyes, while a tongue that could rasp flesh from bone licked a pointy muzzle, revealing fangs whose effectiveness it was not wise to contemplate. A birkit. Somewhere between a cat and a bear, but more deadly than either. And now, she knew, at least somewhat intelligent. If she could but contact that intelligence.

Something buzzed in her brain, a sensation like the clogging and popping of ears when one reached a certain altitude, or having one's sinuses plugged by a cold. Except that *this* clogged her thoughts, as though other thoughts sought to insinuate their way among them—and failed, save that it made her feel drunk and muddled.

"Hail, Hunter," she repeated from reflex, trying to think what to say next, while praying this creature could read her thoughts, for all she could not read . . . *his*—for by its size, the beast before her was definitely male.

"Div . . ." Kylin gritted behind her, sounding nervous. "Div, what's . . . ?"

"A birkit," she whispered back. "It's sitting in the trail directly in front of us, blocking the way, but not threatening. I don't think it'll attack, but I don't know what it does want, except that it's prowling around in my head or something, so it might figure out my intentions from that."

"Which are good, are they not? A desire to seek shelter for the night? Safety for our mounts?" He sounded alarmed, but in control. So far.

"That's what I hope I've been thinking. What I hope they *haven't* found is my distrust of them—for all they've been good to me—as company, if nothing else. There was one that came to my hold every day for eights last winter. But then one day it left. *Damn,* but I wish we'd met some on our last trek. If we'd only known—"

"But there has to be some way. Maybe I—" He broke off, cocking his head. "There're more, Div. One behind me, stalking. One to our right, two to the left."

"Their den is to the right," Div muttered through her teeth, wondering why she bothered, if the beasts could read her mind.

"Maybe they're—"

"Cutting off our escape to the left? That's what I was thinking."

"And there's *no* way you can talk to them? No way to establish communication?"

"Maybe—if I had one of the gems."

"But the gem residue might still be in your blood."

"We don't even know there *is* residue."

"But if there is . . ."

"What're you getting at, Kylin?" she snapped, awash with sudden anger. "We're in a dangerous situation, in case you haven't noticed. I don't think the big lad ahead of us is going to let us pass, and the others seem to have agendas of their own as well. I'm helpless to do anything about it." A pause. "Unless you—"

"I'm not a hunter. But I'm thinking about what Lykkon read me from that book of his—the one where he's put down everything anyone's said, thought, or speculated about the gems—and the only thing that makes sense to me is that they must leave some kind of residue in a person."

"And if they do?"

"Didn't you say that Avall first managed to mind-speak with one when one came into contact with his blood?"

"Yes, but—" She broke off, feeling a terrible clutching in her stomach. She knew what was coming next, yet it still chilled her when he said it.

"Blood," he repeated. "You need to let them sample your blood. Maybe that way whatever's in you that lets them mind-speak with you will become stronger."

Her only reply was to continue looking at the beast before her. Indeed, her gaze had never left it, though she'd avoided making direct eye contact for fear that would be construed as a challenge. Yet as she stared, the clogging in her head changed character in a way that suggested—though it was only the vaguest of suspicions—a kind of approval.

Even so, the notion frightened her—more than it should, she admitted. She'd be risking pain, though far less than she'd risk if the beasts attacked. But to draw blood, she'd have to expose a knife—and that might also be construed as a threat. "I don't like this," she muttered again. "If we die here, we'll not only have failed ourselves, we'll have failed the Kingdom."

"From what you said," Kylin shot back, "the only alternative is to provoke confrontation. Besides which, in case you haven't noticed, the horses are getting *very* nervous. I think mine's ready to bolt."

"And if they do, we'll be delayed even longer."

"True."

"I'll do it," Div announced abruptly. "And The Eight have mercy on my soul."

With that—without thinking, because thinking lead to fear and fear to irrationality—she gave White Star an encouraging pat and, very slowly, slid out of the saddle, keeping one hand on the reins. To his credit, the horse stomped and fidgeted but held his place. She wondered if the birkits had some kind of hold on them. Probably not, else they'd be able to trap prey that way. Which meant the horses' calm was due to training, and these *were* well trained, there was no mistaking that. Royal steeds were the best that could be found.

In any case, she was on her feet now, and dropped the reins. To her dismay, White Star *did* bolt then: jolting away to the left, crashing through the laurel there, and continuing on. She waited for the birkits to give chase but none did. She only hoped she could retrieve the horse eventually. In the meantime, Etti was getting even more fractious. "Kylin! Get off now!" she rasped. And heard him obey.

Heard, because she was still trying, very hard, not to take her eyes off the beast she was about to approach. Slowly, oh so slowly, she squatted, which put their heads nearly on a level, and with clumsy caution, began to ease forward on all fours. The birkit had been roughly two spans away when she'd begun. She covered one of those and stopped, then rocked back on her haunches and extended a hand, palm upward, wondering even as she did whether there wasn't some better way to access her blood.

None came to mind, so she tried, very hard, to think the word and image "knife," while at the same time keeping her brain empty of any desire for violence.

And as she did, she reached for the blade at her belt—a gift from Merryn and Strynn upon her departure. If she was lucky, it would accomplish the task assigned. If not, it would be an interesting curio for someone to find. Eventually. Or not, for this way was rarely traveled.

Her hand had just brushed the hilt when the birkit moved. A breath, and it was before her; another, and those claws had raked her outstretched hand so quickly she barely felt the pain.

And so carefully there was no damage *but* the pain—and enough blood to serve their purpose.

She flinched back from reflex, and by then the beast was atop her, and Kylin, who must have heard the scuffle, was crying out and fumbling forward. "No!" she yelled—to him, the birkit, and the situation in general. Instinct made her bat at the huge head above her, while she felt her lower body pinned by massive legs. And it was opening its mouth, and all she could see was fangs sparkling in the sunset light, and a cavernous maw like the night to come.

"No," she repeated, barely more than a whisper. And with that, the clogging in her brain intensified to the level of a headache, and the birkit's tongue lolled out and casually wrapped itself around the bleeding hand she discovered she'd extended toward its muzzle in a vain effort to fend off those fangs. It licked her flesh and with it her blood, and then, with a spring that took the wind from her, it leapt away.

For a moment nothing happened, and then, like a landscape slowly revealing itself through melting ice on a windowpane, came words.

You are We. You are the We who leaves and returns and has silences in Your head where We used to be, where We still are, and yet You are not. This confuses.

It is something My kind of We cannot help, Div gave back. *We speak loud when We speak this way: when the blood is fresh. But when the blood grows old, We speak softly, and then We do not speak at all.*

This confuses.

So does it confuse My kind of We. We are still learning to speak this way. We ask patience.

You remember We?

I think I do. I remember a We much like the one I see before me. I remember a den in the land near here.

That is Our den. That is the den where You and He-Who-Speaks-Loud and He-Who-Was-Weak denned with Us last Cold Time.

I—

This One with You . . . We do not know Him, but He is broken. Should He therefore live?

Only His eyes are broken. I would have no harm come to Him.

If You say so. We would put Him from His misery.

It is His choice. For now . . . We would crave shelter for the night. And We would crave the right to build a fire.

The one is Your right. The other We will endure.

And Our mounts—

Big Tasty Ones. Have You brought them—?

We cannot give them to You, for We must have their aid. We regret this. We ask that no harm come to them.

You ask much. They would feed the cubs for—

There was no word for the image that ensued, but Div got a sense that it meant something like "as long as it lasts."

We would ask You not to. We are . . . hunting to aid He-Who-Speaks-Loud. We must hurry, or He will no longer be able to speak loud at all, and the friendship He has wrought between Our two kinds may end, for Those Who Would Harm Him would rule Our Tribe, and they would not be friendly to Your kind.

Silence followed—or the absence of the heaviness in her head, which was much the same. Div was startled to note that real sounds still existed in the world: water dripping from leaves, the harsh breathing of the birkits—three more of which had made their presence known and were even now crowding closer—and the sharper breaths Kylin was taking. She imagined he was scared to death.

"I've established communication," she told him. "I think they'll give us shelter, and not hinder us. But the horses are a problem."

Kylin didn't reply at first. Then: "How far is it to Grinding Hold?"

"Around three days this time of year, but it's out of our way."

"Could one horse carry us that far?"

"If it was rested. But I don't like killing horses."

"But you're under royal warrant, you could requisition more. Think of the men—and horses—who'll die if you don't."

"So you're saying—"

"That you should offer them one of the horses when we leave. And—Wait, I'd forgotten that there's a ghost-priest messenger in transit somewhere out here. You should alert them that there's someone afoot who might do harm to us *and* them. We don't know when or if he'll be near here, nor what route he's taking, but if we could arrange for them to attack him . . ."

"You expect a lot from luck, but I'll tell them—later. For now—"

"Offer them the horse," Kylin repeated stiffly. "I think it's the only choice."

We accept Your offer, the birkit agreed unexpectedly. And that was that.

The other horse—

We will find it for You. We will fear it back this way. It will be there for You when You leave.

That must be soon.

It will be when it will be. For now, be warm. Sleep well. Den with Us and be happy.

"Kylin," Div sighed aloud, "prepare for what may be the strangest night of your life."

(NORTHWESTERN ERON—HIGH SUMMER: DAY XLVIII—NEAR MIDNIGHT)

Bekkin could wait no longer. He'd hoped he was over the sickness—the gripping in his gut and fluidity in his bowels that had come upon him and his Fellows-of-the-Face three days into this journey, and which had cost them two days already. Most things one could endure on horseback—flux, one could not. So it was that they'd spent as much time out of their saddles as in them, and the only thing that made it tolerable was that Nyss was as badly afflicted as her squires. It was balance, Bekkin sup-posed: The Ninth Face had attacked Gem-Hold unawares, and sickness had caught its emissaries unawares in turn.

Still, there was nothing to do but accept it. If nothing else, the ailment seemed to be shifting focus from his bowels to his stomach—which was suddenly threatening to rebel. He could feel the sweat starting now, the tightening in his throat, as pos-sible approached inevitable—

Setting his jaw against the sour taste already flooding across his tongue, Bekkin scrambled out of his bedroll, sparing but the briefest attention to his three companions, who bracketed the other sides of the fading fire like logs. Birch logs, he sup-posed, what with the white cloaks they'd rolled around them-selves.

Not that it mattered—as he clamped a hand across his mouth and staggered toward the deeper woods that surrounded the camp. A laurel hell walled it on three sides; he thrust through the fourth, angling toward the road, a shot away from which they'd camped—

He managed a dozen paces before his body overruled his mind and set him vomiting: long, aching spasms that brought up nothing but thin yellow bile that tasted like bitterness dis-tilled. On and on and on—endlessly. Eventually, he finished—but had barely taken two steps toward camp before nausea ambushed him again. He slumped against a tree, seeking strength that had all but left him.

And in the ensuing pause, he became aware that new sounds now stalked the night. Troubling sounds, though no more, at first, than the patter of raindrops shaken from leaves that still held water from the earlier storm. But then came a pad of heavy feet, a snort from the horses; then a mad, loud scramble of leaves and twigs, followed by three thumps that merged at once with growls and tearing sounds, and one choked word that might've been "birkits."

Then—worse—a set of screams from the horses, and—worst of all—a pad, pad, pad coming toward him. Quickly.

Blind with fear, he fled, hearing the deaths of horses, followed by a wild thrashing, predator yowls, and a louder crashing.

On he ran, blindly in the woods; forgetting his sickness, his fear—everything but the fact that he had to survive, because he was the only one who *had* survived, and Zeff's ultimatum had to reach Tir-Eron no matter what.

Twigs tore at him, laying his cheek open. Breath hissed harsh and loud in his ears, but atop it came the woody thunder of something smashing through the undergrowth behind. Something too big to be a birkit.

Horse, instinct told him. He turned to confirm, not believing his luck. And doubted it again when the darkness spat out his very own steed: faithful Wyle. He whistled Wyle's special note—and saw her slow but not stop. Even so, she swerved close enough, for long enough, at a sufficiently viable pace for him to grab her mane as she passed and hurl himself atop her.

Already fearing attack from above, she bucked. Bekkin hung on grimly—and then there was nothing to do but let Wyle run herself out.

At least they were alive—for now.

Even so, he didn't return to camp until a hand past sunrise, and only then armed with a spear he'd made from a sapling. Wyle hadn't wanted to approach closer than a quarter shot, but he forced her, unwilling to go afoot longer than necessary. He found what he expected, too: his companions dead, with their throats torn out by carefully calculated bites from massive jaws. Even Nyss was dead—which would not please Zeff. The horses were dead as well—and *they,* Bekkin noted, were missing flesh.

Which was still strange, he reckoned. Birkits killed no more than they needed. Usually they killed men solely to get at horses, and then only one horse at a time. In any case, what mattered was completing the assignment. Steeling himself, and grateful that his stomach no longer rebelled, he searched the bodies, finding the document where he'd last seen it, in Nyss's saddlebags. He also found other things that he might need to survive, and—efficient lad that he was—was on his way again a hand later, with three dead companions and three dead horses lying unburied behind him. He was hungry, he realized, and thirsty. But this time food and drink stayed with him, as he turned Wyle's nose toward Tir-Eron.

(NORTHWESTERN ERON—HIGH SUMMER: DAY XLIX—MORNING)

The sun was shining in his face when Kylin awoke, warm, well fed, and dry, with stone invisible above him, beneath him, and curving up to either side, save that which faced the light. Div was there as well; he could hear her breathing and stirring a pot of what smelled like stew. There was a scrambling at the cave's mouth, too, followed by a series of padded footsteps, that had to be a birkit returning from some all-night endeavor.

"What have *you* been doing, beast?" Div murmured amiably. Then, with alarm: "How'd you get all that blood on your fur. Are you hurt, or—?"

Perhaps it was the fact that Kylin was still half-asleep, and thus receptive; or perhaps it was simply the intensity of the birkit's reply, but he "heard" the reply even as Div did. *Three dead,* alien thought whispered through his mind. *One survived.*

Then gone. From him—but not, apparently, from Div.

"Something seems to have delayed the messengers," she informed him a moment later. "If we hurry, we *may* still reach Tir-Eron in time. The birkits say they—some of them—will follow us all the way to the Gorge."

Two hands later, they were traveling.

CHAPTER XII:

SMOOTH THINGS, AND ROUGH

(ERON: TIR-ERON: ARGEN-HALL—HIGH SUMMER: DAY LIV—EVENING)

"It's the smoothest thing in the world," Avall murmured, letting his fingertip glide along the soft curve of Averryn's chubby cheek, where he lay, velvet swaddled, in Argen-a's family creche. The surrounding room was soft, too: soft with shadows wrought by a tiny glow-globe's dim but steady light.

Strynn, beside him, was a face melting into the warmer shadows of her maroon robe, shadows that merged with the dark folds of his own house-robe. She gazed a moment longer at the child—her child, by Eddyn's rape—then shifted her gaze back to him, a sly smile on her face. Lifting a slender hand that could nevertheless forge blades, she traced the line of his jaw. "Not much rougher here—for an old man, but a very young king."

Avall blushed in spite of himself. For all the intimacy they'd shared, of body—and mind, through the aegis of the gems—Strynn could still make him feel like the beardless boy who had been so enraptured with her when he was fourteen. And, in spite of three seasons of marriage, he was not yet reconciled to the fact that she *was* his, to touch when he would, where he would, and that she had the same—and oft-claimed—right to

him. At times like this he could almost forget that he was a reluctant King, a political father, and a smith denied his craft. He
could almost forget he had a bond-brother he loved as much as
anyone alive, and live only to be with Strynn. He wondered if
all married men felt the same. Bond-mates were usually taken
young, the bond born of adolescent pain, insecurity, and passion. Marriage was an adjunct of adulthood, and—typically—
the result of much more careful consideration, for marriage
forged links between clans as well as people. Who would
Strynn have wed, he wondered, if left to her own volition?

"What are you thinking, Vall?" she murmured, taking his
hand. With the query came a nuzzling around his mind—
which didn't surprise him. She would never invade his thoughts
without permission, but the mind sometimes did its own wanting, and one had now and then to rein it in, lest curiosity satisfy
itself unasked.

"I'm just tangled in the complexity of it all," he replied, not
moving. "Love, sex, and friendship, and how they can all
merge and mingle; and how trying to set priorities among
them is much more involved than trying to run a kingdom—
and just as scary."

"Dangerous, too."

Avall nodded vigorously, then took a deep breath, not looking at her. "Which brings up a dangerous question. One I keep
finding myself having to ask again and again, though I don't
know why, but . . . are you ever jealous of Rann?"

Her grip tightened ever so slightly. "Are *you* ever jealous of
Merryn?"

"Merry's my sister!"

"And my bond-mate. Which means that we're allowed to
be closer than you and she could be."

Avall shook his head. "But you and I have been as close as
Rann and I have been . . ."

She regarded him frankly. "But you two have been that
close longer. I knew your bond existed when I agreed to marry
you. I knew you . . . liked me and I knew you'd wanted me at

one time, and I knew you'd try as hard as any man alive to love me, and I knew you were a man I could love. But I wasn't sure you were the *only* one I could love, because that choice was stolen from me."

"It's so easy to forget that."

Strynn gnawed her lip. "I forget it myself, sometimes. I no longer feel his touch, when I'm with you. I no longer look at Averryn and think at once that he's Eddyn's child."

"Nor do I," Avall admitted. "It's not hard for me to think he's mine—for now. But I . . . I guess I'm afraid that, though I love him now, I . . . might not as he grows older. He *is* made from Eddyn's seed, and that seed will manifest one day. Maybe he'll be taller, or more reckless, or more vain, or—"

"More talented than you?" Her voice had gone sharp and cold. "You're afraid of that, aren't you? That he'll surpass you the way you surpassed Eellon."

A snort. "I didn't surpass Eellon."

"Yes, you did. And Tyrill. There's no point in denying it. *I'm* accounted Tyrill's equal, and I wasn't even born a smith."

"But if two mastersmiths have a child, that child is bound to surpass either of its parents . . ."

Strynn's harshness succumbed to a wicked grin. "And if another smith, better than the first, should sire a child on that same mother . . . ?"

"It would be the best smith ever."

Strynn chuckled. "Would you risk it, Avall? Would you dare sire the child of legends?"

His smile gleamed even in the half-light. "You're saying we're legends?"

A shrug. "We don't seem to have much choice."

"And now might be a good time to try?"

"I'm saying that, King or no, you're required to give Eron three children, and that I would be honored to bear them."

Avall felt a stirring in his loins which he didn't try to suppress. Yet something still gnawed at him. Maybe it was the environment: the softness of the shadows shaping a kind of dreamlike otherworld in which it was safe to say what could not be said under harder light. And so he asked that which could shatter it all.

"What about Kylin?"

She didn't falter, though something like pain flickered in her eyes. "He . . . loves me, I think. And I'd be lying if I said I didn't . . . care for him. But, believe me when I say that I would never, ever put him above you."

"But do you *love* him?"

A long pause, then: "I love different things about him. And—" She paused again. "And you and he love different things about me, I think."

Avall cocked his head, genuinely curious. "How so?"

"You love the hard things in me: my strength, my skill . . . my honor. Kylin—loves the soft things. But you know what's really funny?—which I only just realized. I love you two the other way around. I love the soft things in you—the part you let me see that you reveal to no one else except Merry and Rann—the boy that's still in you, I guess. But Kylin—I love that solid core in him he doesn't know he has: the fact that he just goes on. He's blind, and people want to feel sorry for him and make allowances for him, but he doesn't let them. He's iron sheathed in sylk, I guess. You're sylk sheathed in iron."

Avall exhaled a breath he didn't know he'd been holding. "That's as much as I dared hope," he conceded. "Though I'm just as glad he's far away tonight."

"So am I," Strynn smirked, "because I've got some *very* interesting ideas about how we should spend the rest of the evening, and I want *no* interruptions."

Avall grinned back. "I think we can manage that. It's one of the advantages of being King."

"Maybe I was wrong about Averryn," Avall murmured into the nape of Strynn's neck, an indeterminate but very pleasant while later. He was curled around her on a fur rug they'd dragged onto the north balcony of their suite. She lay before him, naked, as was he, and utterly exposed to the cool night breeze that made her skin shiver and her nipples tense even when he didn't touch them. It was other skin he touched now, palms cupping the fullness of her breasts when fingers didn't venture lower.

She stopped one such foray with a hand, yet not so much as to forestall caresses. "What do you mean?"

"That parts of you are at least as smooth as parts of him."

Her hand found his upper thigh—all she could easily reach, the way they lay—and stroked it in turn, first sensually, then critically. "You're in need of waxing."

"I haven't had time since the war," he whispered into her hair, as he freed his fingers again.

"You haven't *made* time. You and Rann should do each other. I'll watch. That way we could all learn something."

"So now I have to worry about him as well as Kylin?"

"You have to worry about no one, love," Strynn gave back seriously. "But he does have to sire his three sometime, and Div can't give them to him."

"Do you have any suggestions?"

Her hand guided his a certain way.

"Not *that* kind of suggestion—though that one's interesting, too!"

"Foolish boy! You're as full of questions as—"

"As you were full of me a while ago? We didn't talk then."

"We'd no need to. Even without the gems there's that incredible closeness they give us unaware. I am so sorry, Avall, for all those other lovers who can't know that. It—Oh! Do that again!"

He did, and for a fair long while they spoke with their bodies alone. Eventually, however, they fell apart, sweaty and sated.

"Mates for Rann," Strynn recalled abruptly. "I'd give him a child if you consented—once I've provided your three."

Avall leaned up on his elbow. "And maybe one for Kylin? You're expecting a lot of your fertility."

"My fertility owes me after what it got me into with Eddyn."

He laughed in spite of the reference.

"As best I can figure," she continued loftily, "there're at least two others, whom I suspect Div would also approve."

"And who might they be?"

She rolled onto her side to face him. "Don't tell me you can't guess."

"Humor me."

"Someone you're very close to."

He tried to shrug. "But I'm not close to any women except you, Div, and . . . oh, Eight, Strynn, you don't mean Merry?"

"They could both do worse, given that she's unlikely to wed. And it shouldn't bother him overmuch, seeing how she looks so much like you."

Avall blinked back surprise. "Well, maybe . . . And the other?"

"Elvix, for variety."

"I thought she and Krynneth—"

"For variety."

"Speaking of which, what about Myx and Riff?"

"They're the closest set of bond-brothers I've ever seen, except for you and Rann. They're also both betrothed, though I've never met either of the very lucky ladies in question—thanks, in large part, to the Fateing, which seems determined to keep them apart. They—" She broke off, cocking her head. "Avall, I thought you gave orders."

"What?"

"Someone's at the door."

He sat up quickly, the wind cool against his bare skin. At first he heard nothing, but then he caught it: two doors away, faint but clear, and in the cadence that signaled emergency. "Eight!" he spat, and rose, snatching up a maroon wrap-robe as he strode through the adjoining bedchamber. By the time he'd reached the common hall, the cadence was sounding again, this time accompanied by a voice.

Myx, by the sound of it, and very, very agitated.

"Majesty!" Loudest yet, and barely muffled by oak. He'd

have to have a word with the man about discretion. Scowling, Avall wrenched the door open.

It was indeed Myx. But Riff was with him, and between them was a boy Avall had never seen. Clanless, to look at him, fourteen at most, and frightened out of his mind.

"They told me they'd kill me if I didn't . . ." the boy wailed. "They told me—"

"Who told you *what*?" Avall demanded furiously.

Whereupon the boy flung himself flat on the floor, sobbing wretchedly.

Taking a deep breath, Avall sank down beside the boy and laid his hand gently on his back, to comfort, not condemn. And though he'd never bonded with the lad before, some of the boy's emotions found their way through that link. Fear. *Raw* fear. Fear of what was and what had been and what would become, all three.

Riff joined Avall at the boy's other side. "Veen said he approached her at the main gate, scared out of his mind, but that he had something with him that alarmed her more than the boy's fear did. She didn't dare leave her post, so she sent for me."

"And what was this thing?"

"I don't know," Riff retorted anxiously. "He wouldn't tell me, nor would Veen, beyond the fact that it was important. She simply told me to see that he reached you at once."

"There's something in his hand," Myx noted.

"Lad," Avall prompted softly, "you've done your duty now. Whoever gave you something to give me—I'm here to receive it."

"It's two things, Majesty," the boy sobbed, slowly sitting up.

"Two things?"

"I only showed the lady guard what they told me to show her so they'd let me in to see you."

"Who is 'they'?"

"The men who said they'd kill me *and* my family if I didn't do what they said."

Avall took the boy by both shoulders, trying to resist the temptation to give him a good shake. "What did they look like? Did they have on any livery?"

A helpless shrug. "Men. It was dark."

Avall bit back a sharp reply. No point terrifying the boy more than he already was. "Let's see what you showed Veen. I'm interested to see what could make her countermand a royal order."

The boy wouldn't look at him, but he finally opened his hand far enough to reveal something that gleamed gold in his grimy palm.

A ring.

A Hold-Warden's ring, by the configuration. But whose? Avall plucked it gingerly from the grimy palm and held it into better light.

"Gem-Hold-Winter," he said dully. Strynn was at the door, he noted, wondering when she'd joined them. He passed the ring up to her. "I don't want to know what this means."

"I have a message that tells," the boy replied, patting the front of his filthy tunic.

"I'll take it, then," Avall told him softly. "With thanks."

The boy promptly fished a sealed copper message cylinder from within his ragged clothing. "They said they'd watch until I went in the Citadel," he volunteered. "So I had to, Majesty. I *had* to."

"No one here will harm you," Avall assured him, rising. "But I may have to do some harming sooner than I thought." He eyed his companions speculatively. "Riff, go find Rann and Lyk, then take this lad to Bingg and tell him to get him fed and pampered, but not to let him go until I say so. Myx, get Veen and send her here at once, while you relieve her. She ranks you, I'm afraid, and I need her level head just now. Have her pick up Vorinn, if she can find him. I'll tell you everything when I can, I promise."

"As you will, Majesty."

Riff was hesitating. "Anyone else, Majesty?"

Avall rounded on him. "Whom would you suggest?"

"Given that's the Warden's Ring of Gem-Hold-Winter," Riff replied bravely, "I'd say the Chiefs of Myrk and Gem."

"Tomorrow," Avall grunted. "Someone needs to get some sleep tonight. Now, if you don't mind, I've got a message to read."

And with that he and Strynn returned to their suite and locked the door. Only then did he realize that he'd left no one on watch outside.

But he forgot about that entirely when he read the message the boy had brought. And he almost forgot the message as well when he found what was inside a smaller cylinder within the roll of parchment, attached to it by a ribbon as though it were a pendant seal.

A finger: tan, slim, and of indeterminate age—but female, by the carefully shaped nail, and with a pale band around it that exactly matched the ring.

"Crim," Strynn breathed. "Oh, Eight."

"At least we have a name for them now," Avall growled. "Look here." He pointed to the bottom of the document. It was signed "Zeff, in the name of the Ninth Face."

"Ninth Face of what?" Strynn wondered.

"The Ninth Face," Avall replied grimly, "of The Eightfold God. Or so I would assume."

"Priest-Clan!" Strynn hissed.

A shrug. "Maybe. *Probably*. But somehow I don't think they know—not all of them."

She yawned heavily. "And you really have to address this tonight?"

He regarded her wearily, through an untidy forelock. "I won't sleep regardless, and neither will you. Our guardsmen deserve answers, and I've already sent for half the council. I promise not to act until I've sounded everyone out. But I *have* to have ideas. This is—"

"Someone's coming," Strynn broke in.

An instant later the door sounded with Rann's familiar cadence. Avall hauled the portal open, blinking in confusion when he realized that Rann was not alone. Two other figures stood with him, robed and hooded to disguise forms and faces, yet even at a span's distance he caught the stench of sweat, dirt, horse, and unwashed bodies. "These folks reached the main gate just before your summons reached me," Rann explained, hair still wild from sleep, though he'd taken time to don a formal clan robe. He sounded unaccountably excited, and his eyes were alive with secrets. "Veen took one look at them and sent them straight to you. We met on the way. It's—"

"Div," Avall finished for him. "And . . . Kylin?"

"Majesty," Kylin managed through a sketchy bow, sounding as tired as a man could sound and live.

"Come in," Avall cried, delighted, dismayed, and confused all at once. "All of you. And tell me what—"

"I *know* what," Strynn announced behind him. "I'll bet anything I own they've just come from Gem-Hold-Winter."

"With all their fingers?" Avall muttered absently.

"What's that supposed to mean?" Rann snapped. "She—"

"With a message that can't wait," Div dared, loud enough to override him. "I'm sorry." She took Rann's hand, perhaps in compensation.

Avall could only shake his head and usher them all inside. By the time he'd found them seats and stuffed their hands full of food and drink, Lykkon and Veen had also arrived, with Vorinn on their heels. Div looked more than a little startled at that, but it was Kylin who spoke first. "We appear to have arrived in the midst of crisis," he ventured at last, sounding far too apologetic for someone as tired as he obviously was.

"And we bring word of another," Div continued, trying to keep her hands steady as she sipped her drink.

Avall shook his head, then slumped down in a chair opposite them. "If it's what I think it is, it's another side of the one we were already addressing." And with that, he spread Zeff's ultimatum upon the refreshment table, atop which he added, with deliberate conviction, Crim san Myrk's ring finger.

PART II

CHAPTER XIII:

DECISIONS BEFORE DAWN

A proper council chamber adjoined the common hall of Avall's suite, and it was there that his council reconvened shortly past midnight, with half of them in night robes and most of the rest looking sleepy. By the time everyone had assembled, sense—and Div and Kylin's arrival—had overruled Avall's initial desire to keep the matter confined until morning, for which reason he'd dispatched heralds to summon Tyrill, along with Nyll of Gem, Eekkar of Myrk, and Preedor and Tryffon of War. Bingg was there as well, sleepy-eyed, but not complaining as he assumed the role of squire. The boy-messenger was sleeping off his fear in Bingg's quarters, full of calming posset. And under lock and key, pending further interrogation.

Avall waited until everyone had food and drink—spiced cauf, for most of them—before he cleared his throat for silence. "Some of you know what's happened, some don't," he began, "but we'll all be equals, as far as that goes, as soon as I read this message I received a short while back." He went on to detail the circumstances of its delivery, then cleared his throat again and read the entirety of the Ninth Face's ultimatum.

By the time he'd finished, Tryffon was having trouble

restraining himself, and since he was the senior person present—saving Tyrill, Eekkar, and Preedor, who would all, as always, watch and wait—it was to him Avall appealed first.

"I don't want another war," Avall said flatly. "But do you see any other choice?"

"There's always diplomacy," Nyll offered. Which was reasonable, given that his craft had the most to risk.

"Which always goes better with an army at your back," Tryffon retorted.

"That does seem to be the case," Vorinn agreed.

"And Zeff's played this very well," Tryffon went on, sparing his protégé a tolerant stare. "He's left us just enough time to get an army there and back before the cold season, thereby saving face for us, and making him look good in the bargain. Assuming we do what he asks."

"But why should he save face for us?" Riff inquired, forgetting himself.

"Because it's the character of aggressors to try to look like the offended party—the other side of which charade is that they need to appear magnanimous," Vorinn answered a little too quickly. "He's put us in a pretty trap, too: If we stay here, we're branded cowards, or else we're branded insensitive to the needs of our captive people, who are certainly suffering already, and who may die—"

"Though, to be blunt," Preedor put in unexpectedly, "if he destroyed the hold now, we'd probably lose fewer folk than the army would lose from a siege."

"But soldiers take those risks by choice," Strynn shot back. "Prisoners don't."

"And if he destroyed the hold—by which I assume he means that he'd blow it up—that would certainly paint Priest-Clan's face very black indeed," Vorinn concluded.

"And mine," Avall added. "I'd look callous at worse and weak at best."

"It sounds like you've already decided to go," Veen ventured.

Avall leaned back in his chair and stared at the edge of the table. "Maybe I have, though the point about diplomacy is well taken. There's always a chance, after all, that we could come to an understanding. We give them what they want—with the whole army of Eron at our back—and they go their way."

"Thereby restoring to Priest-Clan power they've lost—or think they have—and more on top of it," Tryffon rumbled.

"In any case," Avall sighed, "I think a quick resolution is best. Either we stay here, which effectively gives them total control over what happens, or we go there and try to force the issue."

"My, my," Tyrill drawled. "It's quite the little soldier you've become."

Avall glared at her. "I've become a pragmatist, Tyrill. Greatest good for the greatest number. Don't forget that if things go entirely in our favor—which, of course, they won't— we could utterly discredit Priest-Clan. If nothing else, we could certainly break the power of this secret arm."

"Besides which," Bingg broke in eagerly, "since we don't have the regalia anyway, we can give them the fakes and they won't know the difference."

Avall rounded on him. "How do *you* know about the fakes?"

"I saw them being made," Bingg replied innocently. "And I . . . it wasn't hard to figure out the rest. I saw Merryn leaving with something that looked like them, and—"

"They'll demand proof," Tryffon thundered. "You can offer them the fakes if you want, but they'll want proof they're the real thing."

"And I'll give it to them—on their rooftops," Avall snarled, thrusting himself forward again, and slapping his hands on the table hard enough to rattle cutlery. "Let's see how they like having lightning called down on them. All I have to do is recall Merry."

"You could," Tryffon chided, through a grin that suggested he'd enjoy exactly that. "Unfortunately, if they're threatening to blow up the hold, they'll certainly have explosives in place, which lightning—or whatever that is the sword calls—would ignite."

"And then it'd be my fault the place is destroyed—and I have revolt on my hands." Avall flopped back in his chair again, glowering at the room in general.

"Not that it matters," Tyrill put in. "You don't know where Merryn is."

"Then I'll—*someone*—will have to find her!"

"I'll go," Div volunteered at once. "You've done more for me than you'll ever know, simply by accepting me. This is my chance to return that grace."

"Div!" Rann protested desperately. "You just got back!"

"And I'll leave again as soon as I can. There's no way I'll be able to rest with this hanging over us, and if I'm looking for Merryn—"

"You don't know her habits! You have no idea where to start."

"I've tracked birkits," Div retorted. "Besides, which—"

"I've got a finding stone," Strynn put in. "Kraxxi gave me his because he said it reminded him too much of Merryn. And Merry's got Tozri's old one, if she didn't give it back before she left, which would be simple enough to discover."

Vorinn raised a dubious brow. "So we *could* find her?"

A nod.

"But she's had a considerable start." From Riff.

Another nod, this time from Avall. "Right. But I'm afraid it's something we're going to have to do." He paused, shook his head. "I don't believe I said that," he added quickly. "It's like I've completely ignored the human cost of such a venture. To Div, to Rann—"

"You're becoming a King," Tryffon told him calmly. "That's all. And I, for one, am glad to see it."

"And if *I* were to go," Strynn broke in, "we'd be even more likely to find her. I know her habits. And if there's any need to persuade her—"

"There won't be," Rann and Lykkon chorused as one.

"I don't think so either," Tryffon agreed.

"So that much is *settled*?" Strynn breathed, blinking in surprise. "I don't believe it."

"That much is *tabled*," Avall corrected through his teeth, not looking at her. "We've still much to discuss. Like why, for instance, Div and Kylin are here—not that I'm not glad to see them. I think we've made them wait long enough."

Div glanced at Kylin, who'd remained silent since the actual council had begun. To Avall's surprise, it was the harper who spoke. "We're here to tell you what you already know," he began. "But with one modification. That letter is just a sham: They don't intend to make a bargain at all; they almost certainly *do* plan to destroy the hold regardless, so that you'll get the blame whatever happens."

"They'd just prefer to have the regalia in hand when they do it," Div added, through a scowl.

"They do, and they've lost Gemcraft forever," Nyll exploded. "I've tried to keep out of all this," he continued, glaring at Eekkar. "But this! All I can say, Avall, is that if you *don't* go, I still will. I'll summon every gemsmith in Eron, and call in every favor, I'll—"

"You'll do nothing," Eekkar broke in mildly. "*We,* however, will do all those things—if it please the King that we do them. Don't seek contention when you already have potential allies— *probably* have them," he amended. "That's exactly what Priest-Clan wants. And if it costs us favors, we're also owed favors." With that the old Chief fell silent, though his gaze was fixed firmly on Avall.

"I assume," Tyrill put in acidly, "that they won't destroy anything until they've evacuated their own. They don't need to be there for that."

"Eight damn it!" Tryffon all but shouted. "They've got us both ways, then. If we stay here, they'll destroy the hold, and we get blamed for inaction; and if we go there, they'll still destroy it, and we'll get blamed for pressing the issue."

"Which means that we have to recapture the hold without it being destroyed," Vorinn observed pragmatically.

"Any idea how?" Riff wondered, looking at Avall.

"No," Avall sighed, "but I'm sure we can think of some once we're under way. No one here is stupid, and we know things the Ninth Face doesn't—and vice versa."

Rann shot him an appraising stare. "So you're saying we should muster out—"

"As soon as possible," Avall finished. "Decisive action would be to our advantage right now."

"And don't forget you're popular, Avall." From Veen.

A shrug. "I'm not so sure, after a few days ago."

"They'll follow the King," Veen assured him. "And if not him, they'll follow the Lightning Sword."

Avall looked her straight in the eye. "Even if it's *not* the Lightning Sword?"

"By then there's a good chance we'll have the real thing," Strynn countered. "And all that goes with it."

"Speaking of which," Lykkon broke in. "I hate to mention this, Avall, but there might be a way to expedite this situation."

Avall raised a brow in his direction. "And what might that be?"

"You could try to contact Merryn with your gem. Barring that, you could even space-jump into Gem-Hold and put an end to things that way."

Avall's face went white. "You don't know what you're asking."

"And why not?" From Tyrill.

"First of all," Avall explained, "for the benefit of those who didn't already know, we no longer have the other gems. Merryn took *all* of them—except the master gem, which I've retained, only because it's effectively insane, and therefore too dangerous to entrust to anyone right now."

"So, use that one," Tyrill snapped.

"You don't know what *you're* asking, either."

"I know what you're risking if you don't!"

"She's got a point, Vall," Rann agreed. "You've said yourself that it's slowly getting better. And we already know that it's need that drives it to extraordinary efforts. Space-jumping itself doesn't matter so much—you can attempt that anytime, even on the road. But if you had the sword, and could jump into the hold with *it*—"

"They'll have thought of that," Tryffon rumbled.

Avall studied him keenly. "Maybe not. We've been very circumspect about who knows about *that* little bit of witchery."

"—Except most of the Ixtian army," Tryffon snorted.

"But it was mostly the rank and file who saw Merryn's attack," Strynn shot back. "They won't know how she got there, and—"

"They had contact with the Ninth Face," Rann reminded her. "The Face was already selling us out before any of their present move began."

"What do they want, anyway?" Bingg yawned.

"Power!" From several mouths at once.

"They've *got* power," Riff retorted.

"We're letting ourselves be distracted," Lykkon inserted pragmatically. "If Avall *can* contact Merryn, now would be a good time, before she gets even farther away. If she can't meet us here with the regalia, she could still meet us in transit."

"A hand from now we could know," Veen agreed.

Avall felt a fist of fear clamp around his heart. This wasn't real, simply wasn't happening. These were his *friends,* yet they were trying to force him to do something he feared beyond all reasonable fear. He was King, too, and they his council. If he said no, his word had the force of Law.

And if there was civil war in Eron, it would be his fault.

There was not, he realized dully, any option that didn't result in pain. One way or another, he was doomed. It only remained to work out what form that doom would take. Trouble was, he wanted to *be* a good King, to be *remembered* as such, and wanted his friends and counselors to be recalled that way as well.

Still, as someone pointed out, a hand from now they'd know.

He recalled how, the last time he'd worked with the master gem, it had sucked him in, though not quite as badly as the previous occasion. And he also remembered what a short while that link had lasted. And one could endure anything if one knew how long it must be endured.

"I'll do it," he announced. "But I'm not responsible for the consequences."

"Consequences?"—from Tyrill.

Avall regarded her levelly. "This could kill me or drive me mad," he informed her flatly. "I'd suggest you start considering my successor—if you aren't already."

Strynn rose abruptly. "Avall, are you sure about this? We can wait until you're more relaxed. Rann and Lyk and I can link with you, maybe, and—"

"Me too," Kylin volunteered.

"No," he told them softly. "Now that I've decided to do this, I just want to get it done. But I will say one thing. Once I make the effort, that's the last thing to be said about it unless *I* bring it up. And it's the last thing any of us does tonight. We have to get some rest, people. Tomorrow will be a difficult day, and we need to be alert. Anyone who wants to stay in the Citadel tonight is free to do so; The Eight know we've got more than sufficient quarters. But by noon tomorrow—if I'm still King—I want a muster list drawn up, starting with what forces I have on hand now. There should still be some about who missed the *last* war. Vorinn, would you mind handling that? And I want everyone to know exactly what's happened and who's behind it."

"Everything?" Riff inquired.

"Not the plan to level the hold regardless. We need to be seen to act, not only by the folks here, but by the Ninth Face. They don't need to know that we know about their deception, and if they see an army approaching, which is what they expect to see, they're less likely to suspect."

"And if you're *not* still King?" Rann teased with forced good cheer.

"Be kind to my successor."

Silence, then, as no one found anything to say that wouldn't shift conversation into new, but equally troublesome, directions.

"Well," Avall inquired eventually, "who has the sharpest knife?"

More silence. Then, from Kylin: "I didn't think you needed to do that anymore."

"I may not—but I think in this case, since I've got an actual goal in mind, I ought to. Don't forget, too, that mind-speaking eats up massive amounts of energy unless the target is immediately to hand."

"Sorry," Kylin yawned, "I did forget."

"You're tired," Div told him sweetly.

Avall studied the square of faces dubiously. "Most of you have seen this done," he began. "If you haven't, I need to warn you about a few things. What I'm about to do will take more energy than I have by myself, and that's at the best of times. It will therefore draw on your strength—probably most strongly from those who are physically strongest and from those to whom I'm most closely bound emotionally. The other thing, is that there may be some spillover. I've bonded with several of you enough times that I may pull you into the link even without the other gems. Everyone here will probably feel something, and it's unlikely to be pleasant. And——"

"You're stalling," Rann said. "Let's get to it."

Avall didn't reply. Rather, he lowered his eyes until all he could see was the bit of table before him, on which a golden dish gleamed, empty of all but crumbs. With one hand he fished into his tunic for the master gem, but it was Rann to whom he passed the chain and globe once he'd found it. "You seem to have an affinity for this. You open it."

"I would be honored if you would use my knife," Preedor murmured, from the other end of the table. "Strynn made it for me, and it seems right that you use it now. That way I can say Warcraft and Ferr were in this from the start."

"It will be my honor to accept it," Avall replied formally. Preedor rose at that, moving briskly to where Avall sat. By which time Rann had freed the gem, handling it carefully with a double-folded napkin. "I had gloves," Avall chided him, under his breath.

Rann simply blinked at him and tried to smile.

"Very well," Avall breathed, and accepted Preedor's knife. Another breath, and he closed his eyes and drew the blade across his palm. The edge was so keen, he didn't feel the pain at first, and by then he was acting—quickly, so as not to lose his nerve. It was easy enough, really. He simply extended his bleeding hand to where the gem lay in the napkin, snared the ruddy stone, then folded his other hand across it and set both hands before him on the table. And by then, the gem had hold of him.

If it had been greedy before, it was twice as greedy now. Already death was gibbering at the gates of his mind. But where before he'd simply tried to link with it, this time he had a specific goal, so perhaps the gibbering could be overruled. Trying his best to ignore the nothingness that gaped just beyond his self, he sought to fix his desire firmly on that other goal—to ignore the warnings and the madness as one ignored jeers on an orney field.

Instead, he tried to picture Merryn's face as he'd last seen it. And with that, he tried to call to her: to fix her name above all other names in his head, her face above all other faces, his desire to contact her above all other desires—and all other fears.

He had it—maybe. Certainly he felt that strange wrench of consciousness leaving the bonds of body. But as he reached eagerly for what he'd not expected, something else found him instead. It was like reaching for a friend's hand across a yawning chasm, only to have that chasm yawn wider as he started to leap—so that he fell.

The madness surrounded him: the worst part of his own fears and Barrax's fears and pain commingled, so that the former enemy king was suddenly the only thing in the world, roaring around him like a whirlwind of furious thought. It wanted him to share its own death. It wanted—

Pain—light—and a floating that was like the fall turned inside out, and he was *nowhere* for a moment, then saw light again, and felt hands upon him, even as he felt such cold as he hadn't felt since that timeless time in the Ri-Eron. And then more hands touched him, and someone was dragging his eyelids open, forcing him to see—to receive stimuli, at any rate—and someone else was pouring wine down his throat. The fumes exploded through his head like the lightning called down by the sword. And then he heard voices, and had sense enough to realize that he was back in his own world, and that Rann had one hand and Lykkon the other, and they were dragging them apart, even as the gem rattled and rolled on the plate before him, demanding that he take it up again, and rejoin that trip to death.

"Get that thing away from me," he choked. "I don't want to see it until tomorrow. And no, I didn't contact Merry. Now go! All of you! I've done what you asked, and it's cost me dear, and for now—I don't care—just go!"

For once, no one argued.

Two hands later, with dawn fast approaching, Avall was still awake and pacing around his common hall. He couldn't believe how much reality had changed since—since sunset, he supposed. Why, as recently as supper he'd had no firmer plans than trying to fix a date for his planned conclave regarding the succession and related problems. Oh, he'd been worried about Merryn a bit, but who wouldn't be? And he'd leavened even that concern with the knowledge that she was probably as happy now as she'd ever been, being completely on her own for the first time in her life.

And now another war loomed—or something like a war, something that would require him to function as the commander of an army, in any case. Only it wouldn't be foreigners he'd be fighting, it would be his own folk. Granted, it was a new thing in the world, and he still had time to think of creative solutions, and people at his call who could surely provide them. But he'd still have to make the decisions and give the orders, when the only decisions he wanted to make concerned which gauges of metal to use in smithing projects. It seemed unreal, too, coming as it did in the middle of the night, with such an unlikely mix of people—Nyll and Eekkar, to name two, but also Div and Kylin. And what would they do with Kylin, anyway? Take him with the army, he supposed, since he was certainly the best source they had to hand of the particulars of the invasion and the state of the actual hold itself. Assuming, of course, that Kylin would be willing to return to the site of so much pain.

In any case, he'd have to work on it in earnest—tomorrow, for he didn't dare let much time elapse before making his intentions known. Every day he delayed put Merryn farther away, and that was something he didn't want to face, for all that every King before him had faced battle with no more resources than Avall already had to hand, and less reputation.

He paused in mid-stride, considering. If he were ruthless—or brave—or stupid—or all three—he might indeed call the Ninth Face's bluff. Sanctioned or not, they were part of Priest-Clan, and Priest-Clan was based in a dead-end canyon off the main gorge, not far away. He could always lay siege to *them,* if the Ninth Face didn't release Gem-Hold.

But that would be a public move against one of the people's primary sources of comfort—and that, he feared, they would not tolerate.

So what *should* he do?

It was in the hands of The Eight, he supposed.

But he *was* King. And, outside the ranks of Priest-Clan, only the King had the right to drink of the Wells of The Eight, and only then on specific occasions as part of a formal rite. But typically one also drank of them before battle, if one was brave enough to face what they might show. Gynn was reported to have done that, though he'd never learned what the King had foreseen.

In any case, Avall had little to lose by trying. If nothing else, it would be one more piece of advice he could choose to heed or not.

And tomorrow was fast approaching. He had to act now or wait another night, and who knew what another day might bring?

It took but a moment to find outdoor boots and a light hooded cloak that didn't proclaim his status. Yet even as he paused at the door, he heard someone stir in the shadows of the guard niche beside it.

"Majesty?" a sleepy voice inquired.

"Bingg?"

"Where you goin'?"

"Out."

"Alone?"

"I have to."

"You shouldn't."

Avall didn't know he'd decided until he said it. "You can come, too, but only so you can report in case something happens. No questions, understand. And no conversation. Not because I don't like you or appreciate your company, but because I don't need any distractions."

Bingg's only reply was to draw himself up and say, very softly, "I am Argen-a. Argen-a supports the King; therefore, I support you."

Four main corridors, three side staircases, and five levels later, they stepped out a postern gate into the River Walk.

It was the soft time between midnight and dawn, but three moons were shining so that Avall needed no torch to light his way, though torches flared at intervals, here by the Citadel's wall, and there by the wall that divided the pavement from the river. Always steamy from the hot springs within it, the Ri-Eron was veiled in frothy white, though real fog from the cooler land by the Gorge walls vied with it here and there.

Beside him, he heard Bingg's breath hiss in what might be a nervous shiver. But he was King, and had nothing to fear—not here.

Still, he had to hurry. Setting his shoulders, he strode off at an angle to the left, following the wall for most of a shot south, to where it was pierced by the only bridge on North Bank that led to the Isle of The Eight, which lay within the Ri-Eron. A Priest stood guard at the inner end—which Avall had expected. The man stepped out smartly as Avall and Bingg approached. By his mask, he was a priest of Law, and a fairly high-ranking one, but everyone in that clan stood guard eventually, regardless of age or rank. Avall flipped his hood back when he came within the span dictated by courtesy for acknowledgment. The man started when he realized who faced him, then tensed. Avall thought he might challenge his right to approach the Isle so unconventionally, but he did not, though his folded arms and stiff posture spoke clearly of disapproval.

"I have an appointment with Fate," Avall murmured as he passed. "This is my herald, should Fate likewise have an appointment with me."

"May Fate show you what you seek," came the reply.

Avall left the man behind.

The Isle itself was so cleverly laid out that, though it contained the fanes of all eight Faces, and fairly close together, none was visible from the others. Fortunately, Fate's fane was nearest. A copse of hollies surrounded it, their trunks so closely planted that the temple at its center was visible from beyond them only in sporadic glimpses of rough-piled stone. The path wove among the trees, its frequent branchings symbolizing the turns Fate made in men's lives.

And since it was bad luck to stray from those paths, Avall stayed on one until, later than he liked, he came at last to the stone-paved plaza before the fane itself.

But that was not his destination. His interest was in the Well that rose waist high in the center of the pavement. He started toward it eagerly, then remembered himself. He had a choice now. He could approach as King, in the prescribed regalia, and Fate would presumably recognize him as King and provide a response appropriate to that role.

But he could also approach the Well naked, so that Fate recognized him only as a man. So did he come here now simply as Avall syn Argen-a, or as the High King of all Eron?

It was his choice, and he feared to make it.

But Fate itself had several aspects, he recalled, Choice and Chance among them. Perhaps Fate had its own idea about how he should proceed. Squatting where he stood, he reached into his pouch and withdrew a coin—one of the new ones, with his face on one side and Strynn's on the other. It was a good likeness, but it made him feel strange. In any case, the male side was traditionally Chance's face, because men took chances. The other side was for Choice, because women made more considered decisions. Chance would represent Avall the man; Choice would represent the Sovereignty of the Kingdom.

With no other thought than that, he flipped the coin into the air. Torchlight caught it and made it gleam, and then it was falling again—to land, half on the pavement, half on the soft moss on which he stood.

Which might itself be an omen.

The face he saw was his own.

That was all he needed. With a soft "wait here," he divested himself of his clothes, handing them to Bingg to fold away. If anyone else was about at this time of night, it would be a Priest, and most of the Priests had seen him naked when he'd stripped for final proving of his physical perfection before they'd made him King.

A final pause for breath, and he stepped out into the plaza, feeling the stones pleasantly cool against his bare feet, as the wind was cool against his body.

Too soon he reached the Well and gazed down into it. He'd tasted of the Wells before, of course—at his coronation—but they'd told him little. Sometimes they didn't. Hadn't The Eight made their will known clearly enough by giving Eron victory in the war, and making Avall, untried as he was, King?

Well, that King needed guidance now! No, he countered, *Avall* needed guidance. He could abdicate tomorrow if he chose. But he knew already that he would not.

His face looked up at him when he peered into the darkness. The moon was behind him, which made him seem crowned with golden light. Perhaps the Well was telling him that regardless of his coin toss, it was his Sovereign aspect it was addressing. Or maybe it was saying that it would address the man, but that the Sovereignty would be an underlying factor.

He wouldn't know which without trying. Steeling himself, he slid both hands into the cold, clear water, cupped them beneath the surface, and drew up enough to drink. It tasted sweet, with maybe a hint of moss, stone, and earth.

But it tasted of something else as well. It tasted of moonlight on stones, the way an imphor high could rearrange one's senses, so one could taste colors, feel tastes, and smell textures.

"I am here, oh Fate," he whispered, his voice loud as thunder in the silence, though he knew that only he heard it, so softly did he whisper.

Nothing replied, though he could feel the wind caressing each hair upon his body, like the mist creeping up the gorge. For a moment he *was* the gorge, and then he was all Eron, and then he was himself again, and the Well had shown him nothing.

Disgusted, he started to turn away, then realized he hadn't begged The Eight's pardon for the intrusion. Scowling, he stared once more into the depths.

And saw that water stretch, flow, and expand, until he gazed upon a lake of clear blue water, and inside that lake, an island. And upon that island, people.

And then the image shattered, as something cold lanced into his shoulder like a dart of direst pain.

It took a moment to realize that, though it had already been foggy when he'd set out, it was actually raining now—scattered drops, true, but big ones.

Bingg was asleep when he returned to where he'd left the lad, and only when he checked the glimmer of the one moon that still struggled with the massing clouds, did he realize that a full hand had passed while he stared into the Well, though it had seemed to him that his vision had lasted barely a breath.

"Did you learn anything?" Bingg dared, as Avall dressed.

"I don't know," Avall replied sadly. "I got an answer, but it wasn't to any question I thought to ask."

Sometimes, Avall discovered two fingers later, as he trudged up the stairs to his suite, one didn't truly consider something until long after one had first thought it. So it was now. Back at the council, the notion had crossed his mind that they *could* lay siege to Priest-Clan, or at least confront its chiefs directly. And while that was far too risky, he nevertheless had a member of that clan to hand right here in the Citadel, if only he'd cooperate. In any case, it would take half a hand to find out—that and turning right at the top of the stairs instead of left.

He opened Rrath's door carefully—but not carefully enough, it appeared. Someone rose from the floor almost at Avall's feet, all in a scramble of blankets, night robe, and startled countenance beneath tangled hair. Hands fumbled for a paring knife, even as Avall reached for his own sturdier blade.

"Don't—" Esshill began. Then paused, blinking, as he realized who he faced. But he remained where he was, blocking access to Rrath, who seemed not to have moved since the last time Avall had seen him.

"You always sleep on the floor?" Avall asked casually, though his hand never left his knife hilt. "Devotion's a fine thing, but—"

"Don't hurt him," Esshill hissed, still blinking, and shaking his head uncertainly.

"What?" came another voice from Avall's left. The door there had opened as well. Beejinn stood there, a dagger sparkling in her hand. Avall weighed the odds and didn't like them. There was caution, and there was threat, and Esshill, at least, had little cause to love him.

"It's me, Beejinn," Avall said carefully, trying to keep an eye on Rrath's official nurse and his unofficial one at once, and finding it impossible. "I need to talk to Esshill, so I'd appreciate it if you'd leave us alone a few moments. You can sit in the hall, if you don't trust me."

The knife wavered, then lowered. Beejinn managed a wary— and weary—smile, then padded toward the door through which Avall had just arrived. "I didn't tell him he could stay there," she murmured. "But I didn't think it would hurt. As for Rrath . . . no change."

Avall nodded absently. "Nor did I expect any."

Not bothering to observe her exit, Avall reached out and steered Rrath's bond-brother toward the door to the right, which opened on his quarters. It was no more than a cell, really, but Esshill was still a novice in Priest-Clan and therefore used to austerity.

Closing the door behind him by feel, Avall motioned Esshill to sit on the bed, while he claimed the single chair. Light from the torches on the battlements trickling through a window to the right was the only illumination, yet it glanced off Avall's blade like sunfire. Esshill dropped the paring knife on the rug, and folded his hands before him, head bowed.

Avall started to ask him to raise his head, to stare him straight in the eye, then reconsidered. "The Ninth Face," he said instead, keeping the inflection neutral.

Esshill did look up then, but his face showed nothing but confusion.

"What? Majesty, I'm sorry, but I don't understand. What—?"

"Rrath never told you?"

"What?"

A pause, as Avall wondered how much he should reveal. "Who his allies are," he dared at last. "Those who got him into this."

Esshill's face went hard with conviction. Anger and indignation pulsed off him so strongly Avall could feel them as a thrust against his consciousness. More of the gems' doing, he supposed. Even apart from him they were still of him, never mind the master gem. "If I knew who they were," Esshill said clearly, "I would kill every one of them I could."

"Though it cost you your own life?"

Esshill nodded toward the door to the room where Rrath lay. "The best part of me is dead already."

Avall started to tell him he was a fool to invest his feelings in one as flawed as Rrath. But then he remembered that he'd liked Rrath as well, and had himself been hurt when Rrath had transferred his friendship to Eddyn. More to the point, he remembered how he felt when anything threatened his bond with Rann.

Abruptly he stood, wondering why he'd bothered coming here at all. Wondering, more to the point, if he should trust his intuition and believe Esshill's vow of ignorance. Well, it wasn't as if Esshill was going anywhere. "If you think of anything," Avall said, from the door, "anything at all—or anyone who might know more—let me know at once."

He was already a stride into Rrath's room when he heard footsteps behind him. "Nyllol," he heard Esshill whisper into the gloom. "Not a fact, but a guess. That's all I can offer."

"It won't hurt," Avall sighed, and left Rrath's chamber. Beejinn was sitting on the floor blocking the door as he entered the corridor between it and the world outside. She rose fluidly, but in her own good time.

"No one was hurt," Avall muttered as he passed her. "No one here will be, if I can help it."

The lock snapped shut behind him. It was less than a hand until dawn.

• • •

The note on Avall's pillow didn't surprise him, only that it had appeared so soon. He snatched it up and read it one-handed as he fumbled with his dagger belt with the other. No surprise in it, either; the silence had already told him what it said, though not the physical silence of his and Strynn's suite, but the more subtle silence inside his head that told him without thinking that she was nowhere nearby.

The note had to have been written hastily, yet the script showed no sign of that. Rather, Strynn's script was as neat and measured as ever.

My dear Avall,

Perhaps I should address this to Your Most Sovereign Majesty, for it is in service to that title that I write this, not my dear and treasured husband. In whatever case, I have decided to save us both the anguish of another parting as well as the anguish of endless arguments that lead to that same parting, when we both know the conclusion is inevitable, and in fact one to which you have, in principle, agreed already. In short, I have determined to act now, while I am still flush with the fire of determination, and you are likewise aflame with indignation, for if daylight shows you to me again, I may fail in my conviction, and I dare not. In short, I have gone—already, this night—to seek Merryn. Div and I will travel together, leaving you, Rann, and Kylin to console each other, as I have no doubt nor dread you will do. Perhaps I am acting precipitously, but—again—what other choice do we have? You must lead the country and probably the army. I have nothing to add to that; therefore, I do that for which I am best suited in order to serve our common good. And I find that I am rambling already, stating things poorly that should be expressed with eloquence, and for every word I put down I reject hundreds, even as more arguments crowd upon me to make their precepts known. But I will silence them all now. I am gone. The discussion, if discussion there must be, will come after, when you and I and Merry and Div and Rann are all reunited in an Eron I pray will be free from strife—to prevent which I bid you yet another farewell . . . my love.

Strynn

The note still in his hand, Avall fell, fully clothed, onto the bed and remained there, oblivious, until two hands after sunrise, when Vorinn arrived with the first of the muster roles.

CHAPTER XIV:

ORDERS, WELLS, AND ORDERS

Zeff flung down the pickax he'd been wielding, with a dozen others of the Brotherhood, and wiped his hands on his robe with more than a little irritation. It wasn't the labor that irked him, however—labor was good for a man of any station—it was the futility. They'd been digging for days now, but every stairway down to the mines ended the same: in seemingly endless mounds of rubble. Well, except one, which ended in water, courtesy of a cistern the explosion had breached. That might be their best choice, too—if they could ever figure out how to drain the wretched thing.

He wondered why he bothered. Everything he'd learned—which wasn't much—suggested that the gems were not common, that Avall and his cadre had found the only ones to be found, and that Clan Argen's vein was the only one that held them. Even worse, Argen's vein was, inconveniently, farthest from the entrance, so that even if they won through to the actual mines, there was no guarantee they'd reach the presumed source of the gems anytime soon.

Of course Avall didn't know that, as he didn't know many things. But this difficulty, while not unexpected, was proving far more troublesome than anyone had predicted. Worse, the Face's ancient legacy of egalitarianism demanded that Zeff toil with the rest of his brothers and sisters toward that common goal.

At times like this, he wished their charter allowed slave labor. Murder was fine, if effected to the Face's greater good. But murder merely put the victim back in the Cycle, to be reborn better than before, as recompense for having his choices removed. So said the charter. So, also, said both The Eight and The Nine.

Zeff wondered if Lord Death would be amenable to a wrestling match right now, the better to renegotiate the terms of their devotion. But Death was not the Face they worshiped, any more than Life was. Their god—their Face—was that most shadowy one that transcended—yet united—all the others. *Time.* Of which everything else, both tangible and ephemeral, was a part. Including patience, which aspect Zeff sometimes had trouble accommodating.

In any case, there was nothing more to be gained here now. Not for Zeff, First Subchief of the Ninth Face.

Yet still he lingered, as though patience alone would prompt some breakthrough. But what he saw was the same: a dozen of his knights stripped to their breeches, with their hair bound back, and their shoulders showing scars where clan tattoos had been effaced when they'd sworn higher allegiance; a dozen of his knights crowded halfway down one of the wider stairs, working steadily at a wall of rubble with pickaxes, while others carried away their leavings. Stone mostly, but three times, so he'd heard, the shattered remains of bodies. He'd given those to their clansmen, with all the solemnity he could muster. And sent their finders back to digging.

"Eesh," he called, snapping his fingers toward the youngest among them: a skinny, clanless lad they'd rescued from a foolish hunting party, and who was now this stairwell's water-bearer.

Eesh approached silently, eyes downcast, as he presented

the dark-glazed jug. Moisture dewed it, which was good, for the shafts were proving hotter than expected. Zeff refused the proffered cup, however, and drank straight from the jug as a sign he did not set himself above those he commanded.

Water gushed out faster than expected and drenched his face. Impulsively, he splashed his chest, then each hand in turn, thereby depleting the jug. "Sorry," he told Eesh. "You'll have to get more."

"It's the dust," Eesh replied solemnly. "It gets in everything."

"Wash yourself," Zeff told him. "When you finish. I only regret the explosion blocked access to the main baths. They're supposed to be magnificent."

"What I have suffices," Eesh murmured. "—Lord," he finished with a bow, and pounded up the stairs in search of the nearest cistern.

Zeff followed him more slowly, though still at a vigorous pace. He'd stayed too long, he feared, hoping to have some real answer to relay to those who waited to hear. Hoping the orders he was soon to give would not be given too precipitously.

Being a commander was more trouble than anyone suspected. But sometimes one had to endure trouble in exchange for power.

Up and up and up.

He found the level that the Ninth Face had appropriated, and was pleased to see it thoroughly and competently guarded by grim-eyed men and women in long, blue, hooded surcoats, worn above the best mail anyone outside Smithcraft could fashion. Their mouth-masks were raised, too, obscuring their identity—not so much from their fellows, as from any kinsmen, renounced though they might be, that they might chance upon in the hold.

A moment later, he was striding into his quarters. Ahfinn rose when he entered the common hall, blinking as though his eyes were tired. He also looked irritable, which was not to be encouraged, and certainly not in an underling, however accomplished at organization, record-keeping, and the drafting of ultimatums he might be. Ahfinn's gaze swept toward the time candle in the corner, then back again, before he looked down. Zeff caught the gesture anyway.

"I know I'm late," Zeff snapped. "I'll tend to my business before I bathe rather than after. What I need from you is to know whether you've found anything."

Ahfinn exhaled anxiously and shook his head, indicating the open volume on the desk behind which he stood. "This looks promising, but it's a duplicate—a rough draft, actually, and mostly scrawled. What we really need are the Mine-Master's records, and they're—"

"I know. Sealed somewhere beneath us."

Ahfinn nodded sagely. "And I think it's safe to say that when he says he knows nothing he hasn't told us already, he's not lying."

"The imphor worked, then?" Zeff inquired, offhand.

"So it seems, but you know how long it takes to break someone when they've been conditioned."

Zeff spun around in place. "Conditioned? He was *conditioned*?"

Ahfinn regarded him steadily. "He started out at War-Hold, then came here with his wife, liked what he saw, discovered he had a knack for it, and told Preedor—who was some kind of subchief then—that if they wanted him back, they could come here and dig him out. That was around the time of the plague, and Preedor had other things to do—like policing the cities—and the Master managed to get himself forgotten."

"Very interesting," Zeff mused, helping himself to a goblet of wine. "But not really useful." He started for the door of his private chamber. "I am not to be disturbed for the next hand, is that clear?"

Ahfinn nodded and started to sit back down, then seemed to think better of it and remained where he was until Zeff departed.

Zeff noted his relieved expression in a well-placed mirror. And shrugged. No matter—not now. Not when he had things to do and was late beginning them.

With that in mind, he wasted no time stripping off his filthy robe and the hose, shirt, and boots beneath it; then, as an after-thought, let his drawers follow. Naked, he snared a towel, wet it at a bowl of water, and managed to clean his hands and scour the worst of the sweat off his body before knotting the towel around his waist and sinking down in his Chieftain's Chair.

A pause to compose himself, and he reached to the panel between his ankles and pressed a hidden stud. A tray slid noiselessly forward, bearing a number of small phials, bowls, and jars. He selected one, peered at it intently, squinting a little to make sure it did indeed bear the sigil of Weather. That confirmed, he set it aside while he located the other two he needed, which bore the sign for Man and Time. These, too, he set aside in order to withdraw the smallest of the bowls. It was a tiny, delicate thing, yet potentially very powerful—and very dangerous. What he was about to assay was not to be ventured lightly, and he was already uneasy about his lack of preparation. Well, the Ninth would either forgive him or not, and if he did nothing, that would require even more forgiveness.

Another deep breath, a brief invocation to Lord Time, and he unstoppered the phials. A dozen drops from each went into the bowl and mixed and mingled there. Maybe the air in the room stirred. Maybe he was sweating more. It didn't matter. What mattered was completing the rite correctly.

He wondered what Avall would think if he saw Zeff now. Avall was newly come to Kingship, and thereby required by rite to drink of the Wells at certain times and seasons. He would know how that felt.

But no one save the Ninth Face itself, and then only its chiefs and wardens, knew what happened when one mixed water from the Wells of The Eight with that from the Well of the Ninth. One of the phials Zeff had just opened contained water from Weather's Well, one from Man's, one from Time's. Even now they were mingling, and with it, mingling their powers.

He let the bowl sit for a moment, observing the way the waters merged with each other, delicate arabesques of texture forming ever more complex designs atop the surface, as only he and two others had training enough to see.

It was time.

Closing his eyes, he sank back in his chair, then found the bowl by touch alone and raised it to his lips and drank.

It had almost no taste, and what it did have was rather sweet than bitter, but the fumes filled his brain like fire flung upon a sheet soaked in naphtha.

He saw light, then darkness, and then saw all of Eron as though from a very great height. He was, he knew, on the threshold of the realm of The so-called Eight, about to call upon the power of the Ninth.

To contact another nine.

The conjuring of their faces in his mind's eye was simple enough, but only because he'd done it many times. The difficulty lay in maintaining contact with all of them while still treating each one separately. It was like thinking nine things at once. Difficult, but not impossible.

He had their faces etched in his mind now: nine men and women of Eron, some of whom would've been easily recognized, some of whom were obscure. Not one was High Clan, however, and only two were Common.

He knew them all, but he called their names anyway, and one by one they looked up from where they were dispersed across the Kingdom and stared into space, no matter what they were about—though they were supposed to be alone this time of day, primed for exactly this kind of contact.

Blessedly all of them answered. Zeff waited a moment to confirm the surety of those nine bonds, then passed on the message he'd hinted for days might be delivered that very night, for which purpose these people had been set in place for three seasons—ever since Gynn had uttered the prophecy predicting a winter—and summer—of blood.

"We will do it," he told those people, letting the wind carry his voice to all those other minds. "We will do it when and how we planned. I hope your blades are sharp, your arrows keen, your hands strong, and your poisons virulent. If you fail me, you fail the Ninth Face, and if you fail the Ninth Face, you have failed the God who unites your Gods."

"Aye," came that silent unison. "That which you have commanded will be done."

CHAPTER XV:

PLOTS AND PLANS

(ERON: TIR-ERON: NEAR PRIEST-CLAN-MAIN– HIGH SUMMER: DAY LVIII–MORNING)

~~~~~~~~

"I still say Avall won't like this," Veen muttered, as she followed Vorinn toward the rough stone trilithon that comprised the gate to Priest-Clan's compound. It was broad daylight, if early. Reason enough to support the fiction that they acted officially, though they didn't.

In the afterglow of his frustration at finding Strynn gone, Avall had told Vorinn what Esshill had told him——in part to explain where he'd been at so odd a time, and why. Vorinn had nodded sagely, and, when opportunity presented itself, passed that information on to Veen, with whom he'd concocted the plan they were presently enacting. They were functioning as private citizens, however——if citizens who also happened to be the brother's-son of Warcraft's Chief on the one hand, and Chief of the Royal Guard on the other could be said to have private lives.

In any case, procuring useful information was preferable to endless rounds of meetings back at the Citadel, in preparation for the army's imminent departure. From that point of view, this little foray was a lark, and indeed Vorinn and Veen were like two children, for all they were twenty-seven and thirty-five, respectively.

"Vorinn?"

"Avall doesn't like dithering over situations that have only one resolution, either," Vorinn retorted finally, almost as an afterthought. Even without royal livery he moved like a soldier, Veen thought. Far more than she did; then again, he'd been born to it. "If we can get him one jot closer to finding the Ninth Face's power base in Tir-Eron, we could forestall civil war. If nothing else, we gain a bargaining tool we don't have at present."

Veen shrugged, and by then it was too late for further discussion, because they'd reached the gate proper. "Vorinn syn Ferr-een to see Nyllol," Vorinn informed the gate-warden promptly, not naming Veen, which not so much excluded her as shifted responsibility for the visit full upon his shoulders. Nor was there any reason to refuse Vorinn entry unless Nyllol was ill—which, as of the previous evening's report, he wasn't.

The warden consulted a duty tally, then nodded. "He is teaching at this time, but he should be finished soon. If you would like to wait, I would suggest the forecourt of the Lore hall." She pointed to his left, along a line of what looked like raw cliffs but weren't—once one got inside them. A series of piled stone walls fronted them, dividing the space at their base into a series of courtyards, interspersed with masses of shrubbery.

"Thank you," Vorinn acknowledged, and moved on as directed for maybe half a shot before claiming a seat built into the wall that faced the slab of ruddy sandstone masking Priest-Clan's Lore hall.

They waited patiently, speaking little, but observing everything. "Do you suppose this . . . calm is real?" Veen murmured. "I keep looking for conspiracy and not finding it. It seems to be a hold doing exactly what it's supposed to be doing."

"Which reinforces what we suspect: that the Ninth Face doesn't have official sanction. I think it mostly uses Priest-Clan as a source of recruits. Think about it, Veen: Few people are *born* to Priest-Clan, so there are few deep clan loyalties to contend with, never mind that anyone who's left his birth-clan to join Priest is likely to have weak roots in that clan anyway. And if one is going to exist outside authority, one doesn't *need* things like clan loyalties to complicate affairs. But since Priest also has strict entrance requirements, what we've basically got is a clan made up of misfits—and I don't have to tell you that people like that can be dangerous."

"And Nyllol?"

"He and Rrath were spending a lot of time together before Rrath entered his first Fateing. He was from Beast, but left as a child—rumor has it because he thought no one there was smarter than him. He's got a reputation as a fine scholar and teacher of the ethics of animal husbandry—I sat in on a few of his lectures on that when I rotated through here. And he knows a lot about geens—maybe more than anyone alive, now that Rrath's effectively dead."

Veen nodded, then started as a bald, brittle-looking man matching Vorinn's description of Nyllol strolled out of what looked like the entrance to a cliffside cave but wasn't. Vorinn rose as she did, trusting her that much. "I see," he muttered under his breath.

By which time Nyllol had also seen—and apparently identified—Vorinn, and was striding toward him, an easy grin on his face. A grin that faded as he noticed Veen. She could almost hear him working out the connections between former student and present Guard.

Yet the facade never crumbled. "Vorinn!" Nyllol cried at the requisite distance, extending his hand as he cut that span in half.

"Priest," Vorinn replied formally, dipping his head. He stepped aside, as though to introduce Veen, but the movement let him slip beside the Priest in such a way that he could seize Nyllol's arm in a grip that was at once excruciating and unobtrusive. "This way, Nyllol, and apologies in advance for any pain we must inflict, for it is not pain we seek, but information."

Fortunately, Vorinn had chosen their location carefully, so it wasn't difficult to steer Nyllol through a hedge-framed archway to the right, and into a small meditation garden. Veen closed the gate one-handed, indicating that the garden was in use.

"Veen," Vorinn prompted. Whereupon Veen withdrew a length of dark, fibrous wood from her pouch, broke it in half, and thrust the broken ends beneath Nyllol's nostrils. His reaction alone would tell them something. He *should* possess no more than minimal immunity to what was both a euphoric and an anesthetic. The presence of any sort of conditioning would be hard to hide.

Not surprisingly, he flinched away, but Vorinn shifted his grip, while Veen found the pressure points behind his jaw that made his mouth pop open. She thrust one broken end inside and squeezed so that the juices would run out and thus have maximum effect.

"The Ninth Face," Vorinn whispered. "If that term means anything to you, you would be wise to tell us now. And if it doesn't, we'll know soon enough, and tender our apologies with appropriate compensation. But we don't think it will come to that, because we think you *do* know."

Maybe the fumes had had time to produce the desired effect; maybe they had not. Veen and Vorinn would never know. Because even as they stood there, on the threshold of discovering the truth, Nyllol managed to free one hand long enough to seize the stump of wood from Veen's fingers, ram it into his throat, and swallow. Death came quickly, though whether Nyllol drowned in his own blood from savaged vessels in his throat or suffocated from a plugged windpipe they could not unclog, neither of them ever knew.

They left him where he was, though Veen protested. In any case, while Nyllol himself had told them nothing, his death had told them quite a lot indeed.

"They swear he did it with his own hands," Avall told Grivvon of Law, two hands later, in Avall's private audience chamber. More properly, he told the Chief of Priest-Clan, who happened to *be* Grivvon, for Priest-Clan's Chieftainship rotated through the eight chief Priests with the seasons. At least Grivvon was more reasonable than some, for all he'd come storming into the Citadel like a hurricane. They were alone, save for a vigilant Riff.

"Can you prove it?" Grivvon huffed. "Avall, I don't have to tell you that they're a breath away from being charged with murder."

"They say they'll testify under imphor if I ask them to," Avall shot back. "And given that they're Warcraft conditioned, you know how much risk *that* entails. For that matter, I'll testify that I didn't send them, as long as I've got three other Chiefs here to witness that you take no advantage of me. Don't even *think* I'm happy about this," he added through his teeth. "Now," he continued more calmly, "since you're here, I might as well save us all a lot of trouble and ask *you*: Does the phrase 'the Ninth Face' mean anything to you?"

Grivvon didn't reply at once, but Avall didn't particularly want him to. He was watching for more subtle signs: a tensing here, a hesitation there, a tic or twitch somewhere else, or some change in his breathing. He was also alert to any unexpected sensations in his mind that might be the result of strong emotions expressed spontaneously.

"It does not," Grivvon replied stiffly. A little *too* stiffly, Avall thought.

Avall studied him keenly. "Let me rephrase that. Have you heard anyone in your clan utter the phrase 'the Ninth Face' before today?"

Grivvon smirked mirthlessly. "You're getting good, boy."

"I'm also good enough to notice a clumsy evasion," Avall snapped. Then: "Grivvon, I'd like to trust you, but I can't—not yet. I could subject you to imphor, but that would require force, and we already know what happens when that's misapplied. But I have a simpler, though no less binding, solution."

Grivvon's brows shot up; he regarded Avall suspiciously. "And what might that be?"

In reply, Avall reached behind his throne where he'd casually concealed a certain object and brought it forth: the Sword of Air, used to compel Sovereign Oath. It had been used more recently by poor High King Gynn in his last battle when the sword that had been made for that battle had gone missing. Avall hoped it was none the worse for that. He also hoped Grivvon didn't know how it had been used. It was effectively a sacred object, after all—with all that implied about casual usage. Never mind that it had neither been tempered for use as an actual weapon, nor meant to be used that way. Indeed, it's purpose was solely to affirm the truth of, and then bind vows, through some unknown force not unlike the power of the gems.

"I will have your oath of you," Avall said simply, tilting the sword so that its light flashed down the hall. "I would prefer to have it privately, but I can produce witnesses besides Riff if you like. I would also prefer to be able to trust you, but that, again, is up to you. You must be aware by now that I am mustering a force to take to Gem-Hold-Winter, which is now in the hands of members of your clan. I find it unlikely that you do not know of such a thing, but I also find it unlikely that you would betray your country in such a way, whatever you may think of my recent discoveries. Therefore, I ask you simply to place your hand on the point of this sword and swear to me that you are not complicit in this thing. Such things are perfectly possible, and I will try very hard to believe you when I hear you say it. I will also expect you to ferret out this cancer that has infected your clan as soon as possible, for it can do none of you any good. Now swear! Place your hand on the sword's naked tip and swear. Choose your words; the sword will know."

Grivvon swallowed hard, even as anger drew shadows

across his face like an approaching summer storm. He glared at Avall, and Avall feared he was about to turn and stalk out of the room—or strike him. Instead, he knelt, as was appropriate, but his eyes never left Avall's as he stretched forth his hand and rested it on the blade.

"I, Grivvon, Priest for this time of the Face of The Eightfold God that rules both the Laws of The Eight, and the Laws of man, do hereby make oath before Avall syn Argen-a, for this time High King by proclamation of all Eron, that I have no knowledge—neither overt, secret, nor clandestine—of any group operating within the confines of my clan under the name of the Ninth Face, or any similar name. Nor do I—"

He didn't finish, for the sword had moved of its own volition, or so it seemed to Avall. But where before, when Avall had sworn the sole Sovereign Oath that Gynn had forced upon him, he'd felt the sword twitch and found his hands bloodied; this time the sword had made a stab at Grivvon's wrists, as though it intended to slash them.

Or as though Grivvon so intended. Which could mean any number of things, not the least of them being that Gynn's unorthodox use of the weapon during the war had somehow sullied it past redemption. Or perhaps Grivvon himself had used it to attempt suicide in such a way that Avall would be blamed.

But that didn't explain Grivvon's startled expression as he flung himself away from the sword while blood splattered in an arc across the floor.

Avall dropped the sword as though it had burned him. "I don't know," he said flatly, rising. "It didn't like what you said, but you act like a man surprised when a pet turns on him. If you would have me believe your innocence, find it and bring it to me. In the meantime, if you won't help me, don't hinder me, but beware your own clan, Grivvon. There's a cancer at work in this land, but cancer can sometimes be cured by amputation. See that you are part of the body if that happens, not part of the infected limb."

"Majesty," Grivvon murmured stiffly, which, though technically a reply, said nothing. And then, with one hand still clamped around the more freely bleeding wrist, he rose, bowed slightly, and started for the door.

"My chirurgeons will attend you," Avall called.

"I have my own," Grivvon spat. "I can travel two shots without aid."

And with that he was gone, leaving a trail of glistening red in his wake. And leaving Avall with a slightly clearer conscience—but no answers.

(THE CITADEL—MIDAFTERNOON)

"Avall?"

Avall looked up from where he was rather listlessly packing a selection of half-finished smithing projects from the shelves of his private workroom—which were practically the only things they'd let him pack for himself.

Rann was peering through the doorway, looking harried, with what passed on him for a forelock falling winsomely toward one eye. "You look busy," Rann teased, easing the rest of the way in. He was in Eemon livery, Avall noted, undifferenced by the crown of royal service—which meant he was here as himself, which was a relief.

Avall chuckled wryly, even as his ears caught the sounds of chaos from the room beyond. Packing, it seemed, was always noisy. "Actually, I'm as busy as anyone will let me be," he sighed, following Rann to the room's lone sofa. Both Lykkon and Bingg were absent, so Avall snared a jug of ale himself, passing it to Rann as he joined him.

"It's a funny thing about being King," Avall mused. "Once something like this is set in motion, it more or less takes care of itself. I don't have to decide anything, really, except what I'll take to distract myself—excluding you, of course."

"Of course."

"The rest—well, it's not like War didn't have plenty of practice back in the spring. They've got 'moving the King around' down to a fine art by now. Lykkon's taking notes like crazy. Says he's going to compile it into a concise form in case some other King ever has to do it again."

"That's our Lykkon."

"Always where you need him—unlike some."

"That's an odd remark."

"I'm an odd King—as we both know all too well. But I really do feel kind of useless right now, Rann. My job, ultimately, is to provide a figurehead and a scapegoat as necessary, and to make decisions when decisions of a certain sort are required. Right now, the only decision anyone needs from me is how many changes of clothes to take, about which I could care less."

Rann grinned. "Given that you're a middle-sized man from a populous clan, that's unlikely to be a problem. If you run out, you can always borrow. Maroon is maroon, after all."

"There're things like crowns, though. I keep finding new ones for particular purposes, but there doesn't seem to be one for civil war."

Rann's face darkened. "Are you going to take the Sword of Air?"

"In case I have to command another Sovereign Oath? I don't know. Do you think one would hold if someone swore on The Eight but believed in The Nine?"

"The Nine might have something to say about that."

"Bullshit," Avall snorted, allowing himself the rare luxury of profanity.

Rann shifted beside him, reaching over to fling an arm across his shoulder as he relaxed against him. Which, given the order of the day, was probably not purely for comfort.

"Something bothering you?" Avall murmured.

"Just wondering if Strynn got away all right."

A shrug, as Avall felt a jolt of anger. "You *know* she left without telling me good-bye."

"I know she's had to tell you that a lot of late. Maybe she's tired of it."

"Maybe."

"You should be used to it. That's how it is with Merryn. And they *are* bond-sisters."

"They are."

"Faster gone, faster returned."

"So I've heard."

Rann eased away and took a long draught from the jug. Avall regarded him dubiously. "That's your 'I've got something controversial to say, and I need to find strength in alcohol' style of drinking."

Rann lowered the jug and wiped his mouth. "I have a controversial proposition."

"I'm a controversial King—as well as an odd one," Avall retorted. "Perhaps I'll hear it."

"I can't say you won't like it, but it'll be trouble to execute. But you said yourself you really have nothing to do."

Avall shifted so as to look at him more directly. "I'm listening."

Rann took a deep breath. "Two things, Vall. One is simply that if we *can* identify our enemy's stronghold, we can take the battle to them where they don't expect it. At best, it could break their back without requiring us to go all the way to Gem. At worst, we'd know more than we do, and in the middle we could find ourselves with another bargaining tool, or at least a useful distraction. Ultimately, there's no way they can put as many forces on the field as you can."

"It is fervently to be hoped."

"But all this depends on finding their citadel, and we don't know where it is. Not without subjecting everyone in Priest-Clan to interrogation under imphor, and anyone who's affiliated with the Face would probably go mad before he'd volunteer anything."

"Or kill himself—as we've already seen."

"Or be killed."

"Your point being?"

Rann cleared his throat. "There *is* someone else who may know where their citadel is, and who has no cause to love Priest-Clan—or the Face—at all. Someone they, in effect, abandoned."

Avall knew whom Rann meant even as they both said it. "Rrath."

Rann nodded. "From what Eddyn said before he died, they've both been inside one of the Ninth Face strongholds—probably the main one, since Eddyn met one of their chiefs there. Unfortunately, we were all preoccupied when Eddyn returned, so no one ever bothered to find out particulars of place from him until it was too late. The Eight know we've both worn out the maps of the area between here and Gem-Hold in hopes of identifying anything that might serve the Ninth Face as a hold—any place where a large number of people could hole up in secret. And all we've come up with is that there are a *lot* of rock formations in that area, many of them riddled with caves, and we've no time to check them all on the way."

"What're you getting at?"

Another breath. "What I'm proposing is that we take Rrath with us to Gem-Hold just in case. It's possible that simply being in the proximity of a place linked with that group might jog him from his coma."

"It's also possible he might serve as bait," Avall replied slyly, wondering even as he spoke why he found that idea so appealing.

Rann grinned fiendishly. "I hadn't thought of that, but you're right. The Face doesn't know what's happened to him unless they've got spies closer to you than either of us would like to think. Therefore, they don't know if he's alive or dead, conscious or unconscious. Therefore, they don't know what he'll have told us."

"Nothing," Avall growled. "But they won't know that."

Rann grinned again. "The question then becomes how do we actually effect his . . . removal, and how widely do we let his presence with the expedition be known?"

Avall eyed him wryly. "You probably have an answer to that, too."

A vigorous nod. "Lykkon and I do. But it was Bingg's idea. It's simple, actually."

"I'm listening."

Rann paused for another swig of ale. "You already know that the plan is for one of the wagons in your train to be the designated treasure wagon—the one containing the presumed regalia. It'll be housed in your own compound—probably in an adjunct to your own tent, so it'll be under heavy guard at all times, one of which guard will always be someone you know personally, and one of them always Night Guard. As for the regalia itself, we've already had a safe made for it, which no one can carry off, and it's quite . . . large."

"Large enough to contain a person?"

Rann nodded eagerly. "A small one, like Rrath. Long enough to get him into the treasure wagon, at any rate."

Avall gnawed his lip. "It's risky."

Rann snorted. "To whom? You're the King, Avall. All we have to do is keep Priest-Clan at bay when we load the regalia."

"And his healers? He's a sick man, Rann."

"Beejinn's probably too set in her ways to risk such a journey, though she'd go if we asked, but Gynn's daughter used to be Royal Healer and has a bone to pick with those who helped work her father's doom. I don't have to tell you that she's loyal as they come."

Avall shook his head. "No. But what about Esshill?"

Rann gnawed his lip. "That's a hard call, but I think we'd be mad to try to separate them. He'd probably be content to hide in the wagon with Rrath. If not, we could always keep him sedated."

Avall raised a brow, then shook his head. "I see you've thought of everything."

"You approve, then?"

"I don't disapprove, and it increases our choices. When do you propose to do this?"

"Tonight, optimally. With the help of the Guard, we can seal off corridors and stairs at need. And since no one knows where the regalia is housed anyway, or even if it's all in one place, that alone will be an enormous assist right there."

"Won't Rrath smother in the safe?"

"Maybe. But it's not like the thing's airtight, plus he's barely breathing anyway. And let's not forget that it's residue from the gems that's keeping him alive to start with."

"So he'd be at risk—"

"Maybe half a hand. Once he's in the wagon with a healer, we can let him out."

Avall exhaled deeply and rose. "I'm not sure we can actually gain anything from this, but I don't see that we've got much to lose, either. And Fate seems to smile on us most brightly when we take foolish risks."

Rann rose as well. He favored Avall with a hearty hug, followed by one of his rare kisses, and sauntered out the door, jug still in hand. "To Luck," he called cheerily.

"Luck," Avall called back. But before he could return to his packing, Tryffon had claimed an impromptu audience to discuss final plans for their departure. It would be tomorrow—at dawn, because that was an auspicious time. There would be a preposterous amount of panoply, but that was necessary; the people needed to see their King, and the King, frankly, needed to see his people. He would also have to wear the regalia, because they expected to see it—which might actually facilitate their ruse. Avall only prayed they wouldn't want him to call the lightning.

CHAPTER XVI:

TREKS AND TOMBS

(SOUTHERN ERON–HIGH SUMMER: DAY LVIII–LATE AFTERNOON)

Merryn reined her horse to a halt half a shot short of the gap. Mountains rose around her, a jumbled, broken pile of them soaring up on the right to form the massive range called Angen's Spine, which paralleled Eron's coast at varying distances until it disappeared beneath the ice cap far to the north. That ice formed Eron's northern border, the Oval Sea its eastern one. The Spine itself defined the west—for now.

For now.

She paused in the saddle, steeling herself for what lay ahead. For the last three hands she'd been riding the crest of a ridge, heading steadily south, with the Spine to her right and a less threatening assortment of peaks tumbling down to the left to join the narrow strip of lowland that divided the Spine from the sea. The water was blue, as was the sky, for the day was clear and as hot as it ever got in Eron. She wore no cloak and went clad as a Common Clan woman—overtly, though mail she could not bring herself to forsake lay snug about her thighs and torso beneath a plain beige gown. Her hair was unbound, too: more freedom there. As for the regalia, which rode on the packhorse behind her: The helm was tucked inside a large cookpot; the sword nestled among a brace of tentpoles. The shield was too large to hide, but she'd masked that intricacy of metalwork within a plain leather case—masked it so well, she suspected, that unless someone actually hefted it, there was no way to tell it wasn't ordinary.

Besides which, it was the safest of the three pieces of regalia, and the only one she'd dare to wield herself.

She hoped she wouldn't have to.

As for the personal gems—Avall's, Rann's, and Strynn's—those she'd sewn into a false lining in the leather pouch she wore chained at her hip.

The air stirred her hair as she sat there looking. Her mount—a new mare named Hammer, overtly for her steady gait, but more likely for her hard-headedness—had taken her hesitation as permission to wander, and was happily investigating the short grass that grew beside the road. The Eight knew *nothing* grew in the road itself—not with the steady traffic going south to the site of the great rebuilding. So much traffic, in fact, that she'd had to spend most of the last two days traveling by night, in the woods.

She probably shouldn't have come here, anyway; it wasn't really advancing her mission, though she had no firm timetable.

More to the point, it was a risk.

Still, she had to know, and this was a good time for knowing. After this—after tonight—she would disappear, in truth.

And so she picked up the reins again, set heels to her horse's flanks, and urged him toward the gap.

The ruins of a gatehouse rose to either side, but they were ancient and covered with Ixtian graffiti. Mostly, now, they served to frame this approach to what lay beyond.

Had lain beyond, rather.

War-Hold-Winter.

Eron's southernmost bastion against its neighbor, Ixti, which lay even farther south, beyond the empty desert called the Flat.

War-Hold-Winter.

Now in ruins.

Because of her.

She paused between the weathered stones, looking out, for War-Hold stood—*had* stood—on the next peak down, a good four shots away. Yet even at that distance, Merryn could make out the changes the recent war had wrought.

Attacking in the night from within, Barrax's army had intended to keep the hold as intact as possible, merely killing its defenders or taking them prisoner. But some fool lower in the chain of command had ordered the machines that controlled the heat plant slighted. And since the heat plant ran off steam from a fire mountain nearby, the hold had effectively exploded. The central keep had come down, and with it both adjoining sections of curtain wall, so that its eastern flank now stood exposed and bare. Fire had rampaged through some of the rest, but much of it was stone, and fire spread slowly, so the bulk of the hold had been spared.

Ixti was rebuilding it. Ixti's gold, resources, and food, rather. Merryn's brother was not fool enough to trust even the most obtuse Ixtian laborer anywhere near such an important fortification. For though the Spine extended a fair way farther south, in humps and ripples, Eron effectively ended at War-Hold.

Then again, many things ended at War-Hold, not least among them Merryn's honor.

In spite of herself—in spite of the firm admonitions she'd given herself that she'd made peace with what she'd done and was now strong enough to confront the results of her actions—tears burned in her eyes. Maybe it was the wind—stronger on this side. Or smoke from the cookfires of those workmen camped outside the walls because there was no more space for them within. Why, it was a veritable carnival out there, with tents a shot beyond the walls in three directions, all catering to the needs of the workmen.

And it was all her fault.

For it was she who'd been shown the secret way out one

night half a year ago, and that itself in a clandestine effort to repair another stupid thing she'd done. Not that she'd known Kraxxi was crown prince of Ixti in exile then. Still, she should have suspected. And not that she hadn't tried to set things right once she'd let him escape. But she'd played everything about that wrong. She should've simply gone to Hold-Warden Lorvinn, told her everything, and let Lorvinn handle it.

Then again, Lorvinn had found out anyway, and almost as quickly as if Merryn had approached her first, so maybe that much wouldn't have changed.

Maybe Lorvinn, acting, in all honesty, to repair an indiscretion of her own, wouldn't have asked her along on that fateful final mission in search of Kraxxi, so she wouldn't have known the secret exit. And if she hadn't known it, she couldn't have revealed it to Barrax's spymaster. Granted, they'd broken her with imphor, but she should've been able to endure that. If she'd stayed in the hold, she'd have built up a stronger resistance by now. If she'd stayed in the hold—well, the attack would probably still have come, but it would've been much more direct. She could've fought an enemy she could see, and maybe she'd have died, but she'd still have had her honor.

She'd been forgiven, of course—by everyone from Preedor and Tryffon on down. Avall had forgiven her, as had Strynn and Vorinn. But she still hadn't forgiven herself. Maybe she never would.

In any case, she'd seen enough for now—more than enough to drive the dagger of guilt satisfactorily deep into her heart and let it twist and turn there. She was ready to move on, to begin her quest in earnest.

West, into these mountains—and beyond—just as Avall and Strynn had predicted, the only uncertainty being where she would begin that turning.

After that, who knew? The only direction she'd ruled out was farther south. This was close enough to Ixti, thank you very much. And not only from the real, if unlikely, fear that the regalia might somehow fall into Ixti's hands, which could be very bad indeed, but also because that way lay Kraxxi, and he was another source of guilt in her life.

After all, had one conversation gone differently, she could now be Ixti's Queen. Kraxxi would love her like a man possessed, and give her everything she could reasonably desire.

And guilt would gnaw her heart raw.

No, this was the right thing, she had no doubt of that.

And when morning came, she would, indeed, turn west.

She found the cairn by accident.

Unable to sleep so close to the source of so much distilled pain, she'd crawled out of her tent at midnight, intending simply to stare up at the sky, which always seemed to calm her. It was a cloudless night, if somewhat humid. Mist hid the land around War-Hold, though the hold itself reared above it: stark, angular black above the glowing white. Her campsite was clear, as well. For while the idea of companionship after eight days on the road appealed to her, the need for solitude was stronger. She'd therefore camped in the lee of an outthrust scrap of mountain two shots from the hold.

And for the last half hand, had been walking.

She hadn't really been thinking about it, had simply been striding along the ridgetop, letting her feet take her where they would, which was mostly east and south, for the brighter sky there beckoned.

Still, she carried a sword, though not *that* sword, and followed the ridgeline but a little below, so as to paint no silhouette upon the sky. The ground was rocky underfoot, more stone than grass, but that was typical of the area. Now and then, however, she caught a glimmer of rusting steel or had to sidestep a helm or—once—a sprawl of bones, all of which served to remind her that not all deaths at War-Hold had occurred indoors.

And then she made her way around one of the random

rocks that thrust up here and there, and saw, not five spans ahead, at the crest of a low hill, a carefully laid pile of stones. A stick had been set at one end, and upon that stick sat a helm; while below it a swath of fabric flapped in a rising wind: a tabard of Warcraft crimson, differenced with two arrows *in saltire*.

Which could only belong to one person.

She looked on the grave of the former Hold-Warden. Lorvinn, who was Strynn's aunt and almost Merryn's friend. A woman in the prime of her life who'd trusted her enough to entrust her with the secrets of her hold—to her doom.

For Merryn had built this cairn as surely as if she'd set each stone with her own hands. Another heart-wound stabbed with guilt's dagger.

For a long time she sat there, silent at first, but eventually she began to talk, in a low voice that yet was not a whisper. She didn't apologize—it was too late for that—nor did she make excuses. Rather she spoke of what Lorvinn had meant to her, and what she'd learned under her tutelage, and how being asked to join the Night Guard had been the biggest thrill and greatest honor of her life, and how much she regretted the fact that Lorvinn would never be able to see the new Eron that her brother, in spite of himself, was building. She spoke, too, of her friend Krynneth, and how he'd ridden north like a madman to discharge his last promise to Lorvinn, and how he'd served so well in the war, for all he'd gone strange afterward. And finally she spoke of how the greatest regret in her life was that any children she might bear would not get to meet War-Hold's greatest Warden and how—for one could speak frankly to the dead without risking offense—they would only know Lorvinn as the person who'd cost War-Hold its one defeat, and never grasp the complexity of the woman.

"I'm going on a quest now," she concluded, rising to her feet and feeling automatically for the hilt of her sword. "I've decided to head west—but I might change my mind in the morning. You've met Kraxxi; you know how charming he can be. And maybe the light of day will make me remember that charm, and I'll go south just to see him one more time, in spite of the risks that entails. I need you to send me a sign, if you can, while I'm close enough to be tempted. I need you to use whatever influence you have with the dead and The Eight and any other powers to which you have access, to keep me from going south. This is my chance to redeem myself, and already I find myself tempted, and I can't let that happen. I have to do right for Eron."

A pause, then, as she found herself walking away. "They haven't found you yet, have they? They've been too busy looking to the future to seek the past, and I guess that's good. I think you'd like this place, too—for your cairn. But you deserve better than a pile of rocks, for all they probably consigned your body to ashes. So this will be my last gift to you. Tomorrow when those folk arise, one of them will find a message in a stranger's hand directing them to this place. It's as much as I can risk for now. I'm sure you understand. But risk is what makes life worth living—and I'm sure you understand that, too."

And with that, Merryn marched into the night.

The next morning a young man from Wood named Baylyn syn Mozz found a sealed scroll addressed to the acting Hold-Warden outside his tent door. Footprints were found where expected. But she who had left them was gone.

CHAPTER XVII:

CAUGHT IN THE ACT

(NORTHWESTERN ERON: MOSS ROCK STATION—
HIGH SUMMER: DAY LIX—AFTER SUNSET)

~~~~~~~

"What're you *doing*?"

Rann's voice made Avall start violently, coming as it did without warning from the silent shadows of the darkened room. He twisted around where he sat cross-legged on the floor with a chest full of secrets open before him. For a moment he debated closing it, but he'd already been found out, and if Rann knew this much, he wouldn't stop until he knew everything. There'd be a row, he supposed, but then there'd be peace between them. In any case, it was too late to worry about that now, for Rann was already standing in the only exit, with a lantern in one hand and a gaping darkness behind.

"How'd you find me?" Avall growled.

Rann swept his free hand around to indicate the room. "This is the only real privacy for shots; it wasn't hard to figure out."

Avall quirked a brow upward. "You saw me leave?"

Rann took a step into the room, then paused and relaxed against the rough log wall beside the door. The lantern made his features look pale, but did nothing to disguise the irritation that rode on them. He started to speak, but a noise sounded from the darkness beyond the door. He scowled in that direction, as did Avall.

"Tell Lyk to come in, too," Avall grumbled, rising only far enough to claim a seat on what remained of a desktop in this, the warden's quarters of an abandoned way station he'd found half a shot from the nice, clean new one around which the army was bivouacked.

Rann chuckled wryly, then stepped to the door and called out, "Lyk, it's okay, we've been found out."

Avall chuckled in turn—in spite of himself. He'd come here for secrecy, but part of him acknowledged that he did not want to face what he was about to undertake alone.

Rann rounded on him, a little angrily. "What's funny?"

"That a moment ago you were claiming you caught me, and now I've caught you instead."

At which point Lykkon appeared in the corridor beyond the door. "Close that," Avall told them. "Extinguish that thing, and sit down."

They did as commanded, blowing out the lantern before setting it by the door. They didn't need it anyway; the moons were all but full and shed a fair bit of light through a considerable rent in the roof of the room's southern corner. The shutters were sound, however, which was what really concerned Avall.

Rann exhaled explosively. "You can't hide from me, Vall. After all that linking we've done—all that prowling about in your brain one time and another—if I don't actually sense where you've gone, it's easy enough to second-guess you."

"Then you don't have to ask what I'm doing."

"I'm not *that* good," Rann shot back. "But logic says the only reasons for you to sneak off would be to commune with Rrath, work with the gem, or both. And since Rrath's nowhere near here . . ."

"Veen's on guard," Lykkon supplied, before Avall could ask.

"Which brings us back to the original question: What are you doing here?"

Avall shook his head. "I suppose you'd consider it an evasion if I said I was trying to ensure my survival?"

"I'd ask for specifics," Rann retorted through a yawn. "I'm tired, Vall. Whatever you were doing, do it and let's all go to bed for the night. I'd still like a hot bath, if that can be arranged."

"I'm not stopping you."

"No, but if whatever you're up to got you killed, I'd lose many a night's sleep. It's worth the trade."

Avall rolled his eyes. "All right, then, I'll come clean. You were right, dammit—I've come here to work with the gem."

"That's still a rather large topic," Lykkon muttered.

Avall glared at him. "I had a reason for wanting to work alone, beyond not having to explain everything to you two."

"We're listening."

Avall squatted before the small wooden chest he'd brought with him and withdrew a ceramic jar no larger than his hand. "You won't have seen this before."

Rann shook his head, as did Lykkon.

Avall passed it to Rann, who accepted it with the care with which it had been bestowed. "Open it and sniff."

Rann did, grimacing when he caught the odor issuing from inside. Avall caught it, too, or maybe his memory did. "Blood," Rann spat, passing the jar to Lykkon.

"*My* blood," Avall corrected. "A few drops a day since we set out, diluted with water."

Lykkon stared at him. "For what possible purpose?"

Avall retrieved the jar but didn't reseal it. "Because I had an idea I wanted to try, and since it involved no threat to me, there was no reason to tell you until I had results."

"Which you were hoping to have tonight?" From Rann.

"Maybe. I intended to add another dose of blood, then decide."

"Decide what?"

"I bet I know!" Lykkon broke in excitedly. "You've been feeding the gem blood."

"Smart lad," Avall acknowledged sourly. "The presence of blood clearly has some effect on the way the gems work. Something from the user's bloodstream activates something in them, and they, in turn, activate something in the user, generally to his or her benefit—which is also, I might add, generally to the benefit of the gem."

Lykkon puffed his cheeks. "You mean like we protect food animals?"

"More like animals we use for wool and other renewable resources. It's to our advantage to keep our sheep well and happy—and to their advantage, if they only knew it, to keep *us* happy, since we're the ones who stave off predators and so on."

Rann shook his head, scowling. "So you think the gems are . . . animals?"

A shrug. "I think they display properties that are consistent with that idea. In any case, I knew that when I've fed that one blood, it's always been blood that was in direct contact with my bloodstream. Trouble was, anytime I did that, I was subject to those horrible memories of Barrax's death. I thought if I fed it blood that wasn't in contact with my *self*, it might . . . heal itself."

"And has it?" Rann inquired archly.

Another shrug. "I don't know. All I know is that when I touch it with my bare skin—being careful that I don't allow it access to my blood—it seems to feel . . . better."

"And tonight?"

"If it still felt better tonight, I was going to try bonding with it again. If I could cure it—if I could use it like I once did—it would solve a number of problems, not the least being allowing me to contact Merry, optimally to bring her here, along with the regalia."

"A reasonable thing to want," Rann agreed. "But why here?

Why not do what you've done before? Let us watch and observe."

"Yes," Lykkon broke in, as angry as Avall had ever seen him. "I'm supposed to be compiling a precise record of how the gems work. I can't do that if you withhold information."

"But having you here means I might not be able to do what I was going to do."

"Which is?"

"Fine," Avall sighed. "To tell it from the beginning, it's this way. We all three know that the thing works, in part, on strong emotions—strong desires, one might say—and the strongest of those we can imagine is self-preservation. When it jumped me out of the Ri-Eron into Eron Tower, it probably knew it couldn't sustain my body in the cold much longer, that letting me die there would be bad for the gem as well, and that the only way to prevent that was to send me where I could get help. But it needed *me* for that: *my* desire, down there in the bottom of my brain, to survive, and my knowledge of where help could be located."

"You think it knew all that?"

"I'm not sure. We know so little about jumping. We can't even make it happen when we want it to, most of the time. But I know that the desire has to be really strong. Too, I *think* one has to have been at the place to which one jumps. As far as I know, no one has ever jumped anywhere he hasn't been before, though we *have* had some luck jumping to a person *at* a place we've been."

Rann shook his head. "But if you're hoping to contact Merry, and you don't know where she is . . ."

"I'm hoping to find her mind with mine," Avall replied. "Then get her to tell me where she is, or establish a meeting place where I've been."

"But again," Rann persisted, "why here?"

"Because it scares me to death to work with the thing!" Avall flared, rising and starting to pace. "But every time I *have* worked with it, I've had the security of you or Lyk or Merry or Strynn nearby to save me if things got out of hand. I was thinking that the fact that help was close by might be preventing me from doing more with it. In other words, that if I bonded with it alone, and it dragged and dragged at me, and I got really scared—I might get scared enough to jump somewhere else, with or without it."

"How do you figure that?"

"It would be in the best interest of the gem to have me sane."

"And you're also thinking this might help cure the stone?"

"I don't think it would hurt it. In any case, my assumption was that it would read my desire for escape and jump me to where you two were."

Rann folded his arms across his chest. "So why not tell us?"

Avall spun around to face him. "Because I was afraid that the fact that I *know* I can get help might keep me from wanting help as badly as I'd need to in order to produce the effect I want."

"So you came here—"

"—Hoping that, about now, if things had gone as they should, I'd be appearing wherever you lads were, optimally, in my quarters."

Rann scowled darkly. "I don't like it, Vall, yet it makes a perverse kind of sense."

"Good, because I'm not going to let you stop me."

"How can we help?" From Lykkon.

"By leaving."

"That's not an option."

Avall gnawed his lip. Time was wasting; that was a fact. And he had no energy for this. Rann and Lykkon had no idea how much discipline it took to make himself do even as much as he did. Bleeding oneself *hurt,* dammit—which people tended to forget. And every time he tried to bond with the gem—well, that was absolutely the most frightening thing in the world. Didn't they realize that? Maybe he should yield to Rann's suggestion and let *him* bond with it. Maybe the shock would do the gem good—as Rann had more than once proposed. Or maybe it would do Rann good—by making him see, once and for all, why Avall felt as he did.

Or maybe Rann *did* know. Their emotions tended to slop over on each other these days, especially when they were in close quarters.

In any case, it didn't matter. And since it was taking all the discipline Avall possessed not to bolt, he had none left for arguing. Besides, a solution had just occurred to him.

"I have to do this my way," he said. "It won't work if I know you can step in and save me if things get bad. And a lot of what I plan is contingent upon me having an all-encompassing desire either to get away from the gem or to reach someone who will help me. So what I want you two to do is to sit in the common hall of this place. *And wait*. If I don't appear there within a hand, come get me."

"That long?" Rann cried incredulously. "It's never taken that long before."

"We've never let it," Lykkon retorted. "We've always interceded."

"I've noticed," Avall drawled.

Rann and Lykkon exchanged glances. "I presume it'll draw on us," Lykkon mused. "I guess we'll feel the chill if it works. That'll be some kind of sign."

Avall nodded. "But remember that time runs strangely when I'm bonded with the gem. That's why I said you should wait a hand."

"You could die!"

"I don't think the gem will let me," Avall countered. "Frankly, I don't really think it'll let me go mad—in spite of how it acts—but I'm not eager to test that theory."

Rann snorted but stood away from his place by the door. "You owe us after this."

"Yes," Lykkon agreed, with atypical candor, "you do."

"The best wine you have on this trek."

"Chilled, and drunk in the hottest bath we can find."

Rann chuckled grimly. "Something tells me we'll need it, too."

"None of which you'll get if you don't leave," Avall told them, shooing them out.

Abruptly, he was alone with his fears.

A deep breath and he returned to where he'd been sitting, pausing to loosen his belt, lest even that constriction provide an unneeded distraction. That accomplished, he set the jar of blood on the floor between his knees and reached for the chest, from which he produced the sharp paring knife that he and Strynn typically used when working with their gems. Only one more thing was required.

He tried not to think about the actuality of what he was about to attempt as he fished the gem from within his tunic and freed the stone onto his unscarred right hand, where he pondered it briefly before setting it on the scrap of figured velvet atop which the jar already sat.

Setting his jaw in anticipation of pain that was familiar, but no more pleasant for all that, he drew the knife along his other palm, opening the scar that was always healing there courtesy of this very rite. Another pause, a prayer to The Eight, and he grasped the gem in his right hand and clasped both gem and hand atop his left.

It seized him like a thwarted lover intent on rape or revenge in lieu of pleasure or satisfaction. It was like a pack of ravening birkits invading his body, and he could feel every dire thought they possessed as they roared into him in their millions. And every one savaged some part of him, tearing it free from his *self* and dragging it back to the gem so the greater madness there could dine.

Then came the warning, where before the warning had come first. He ignored it, as he'd always done. The falling followed. And fall he did, into the expected madness, the expected pain, and—worst of all—the expected fear. But this time the warning went with him; this time he was not completely alone as he fell. Rather, there were presences with him that shielded him from the worst of the fear, the worst of the darkness. Better yet, for the first time he could tell what were Barrax's fears and what were his, where before they'd seemed to mingle. Or perhaps to resonate: Barrax's anguish rousing an equivalent, if hidden, anguish of his own.

In spite of that, it was terrible beyond description.

And, as always, he found himself beginning to dissolve: parts of himself slowly winking out as memories dispersed. But this time he tried to watch those memories, and he realized it was not Strynn's face that was fading into oblivion, but the face of some unknown, dark-skinned woman who could only be Barrax's wife.

Or perhaps his concubine, something supplied.

And then a name: *Etall*.

And then other names flashed across his thought before they winked out like sparks from a winter fire.

Yet with every winking, Avall felt a twist in his heart—of regret, of longing, of things he could no longer want or think or say.

Yet all the while, he continued falling. And while that was the most dreadful sensation he could imagine, there was no way he could stop watching Barrax's life flash before him as, over and over, he began to die.

And then there were no more memories. Only fear. Only a sensation of being unable to breathe; of being trapped in sand, earth, and water all at once; with his senses being pressed upon, then clogged, then compressed into an ever-smaller space, where they had to compete with everything else he was.

Nothingness loomed: a thing with no color, no sound, no size or volume. Small as dust and huge as the universe.

It sucked at him with far more force than simple falling had done.

And it scared him—both of him—beyond reason.

If it touched him, he *would* die; that was an absolute. Barrax would die again and again, but this time Avall would die with him. The gem would contain two deaths, and one was one too many.

He had to escape, *had* to. There was nothing in the world he wanted more than to be out of there. Away from there. Done.

Was the nothingness drawing away?

He couldn't tell, but relief that it might be fueled his desire to escape it forever. And so he wished, not with his intellect, or his learning, or even his emotions. He wished in that most primal part of himself, deeper, even, than his soul.

And he fled.

Take me! something that might've been a splinter of Barrax cried.

Without pondering how that was to be accomplished, Avall did. But death was a terrible weight for fear to carry, and he could not sustain the effort.

Something ripped—or perhaps he let go.

Something—someone—*many* someones—screamed.

And then he was retreating. Out. Away. Gone.

Gone where?

Out. Away. Gone.

Where?

To the only source of aid and comfort close at hand.

Reality split, exploded, and recombined. Every tiny part of his body burst into invisible flame and was extinguished. Breath fought at his mouth and nose. Something ordered his heart once more to beat.

A final explosion of something that transcended pain as the sun transcends the light of a match . . .

Then his ears rang with noise, in truth.

Something hard came up and slapped him on the back, even as cold gripped him.

"Avall!" A voice like thunder.

"Vall!" Another, barely softer.

"I did it!" His own voice, then. It felt like rocks tumbling down a mountainside, as chaotic thoughts gathered noise and twisted them, by raw force, into sense.

"You did it!" Rann agreed, but then his eyes grew huge. He swatted at Avall's fist.

Already half-numb from cold, the gesture shocked Avall, so that he opened his hands.

They were empty.

"I'll go look," Lykkon managed, shivering as he rose and staggered toward the other room.

"Something's changed," Avall choked into Rann's shoulder as the two embraced—from relief, for comfort, and not the least for warmth. "But I have no idea what." They spoke no more until Lykkon returned, with the gem carefully recased in its crystal prison.

"You owe us a drink," Lykkon smirked, "and a bath."

"I won't argue," Avall conceded weakly. "I feel like I've been cold forever."

"Merryn?" Rann dared.

Avall shook his head. "I can't. I dare not. I don't think I could survive that again until I've had a chance to rebuild for a while."

"But you *will* try again?" Rann retorted. It was impossible to tell whether that was a request or a warning.

"I will," Avall agreed sadly. "I don't have any choice."

CHAPTER XVIII:

A MEETING BY A RIVER

(SOUTHERN ERON—HIGH SUMMER: DAY LX—LATE AFTERNOON)

Merryn stopped one last time to look back at War-Hold—
from the west this time. She'd spent most of the last two days
skirting around it, taking her time, and trying very hard not
to be seen, never mind recognized. She was in no particular
hurry, anyway—which was good, because the rough terrain
discouraged all but the most careful navigation, especially with
the horses. Alone, on foot, she might actually have been able to
maintain a better pace, for she could've gone over obstacles
she'd been forced to detour around.

Still, the view was worth it. Not only did the western angle
show the hold's least damaged side, it also allowed the rare
pleasure of looking down upon it, which gave her a chance to
appreciate the lavish use of movable gold-foil panels on what
roofs were still intact—foil placed there not to evoke opulence,
but for the more practical purpose of absorbing and reflecting
sunlight when snow threatened to cover the skylights that lit
the indoor sparring courts in winter.

Winter . . .

The thought of it chilled her even in High Summer. Nor
was cold an idle threat. She was fully into the Spine now, and

everywhere she looked, she saw snow. Not nearby, granted, but the entire west was mountainous, and all those peaks were crowned with the frigid stuff. Even the fire mountains that were so common thereabouts that she could see the smokes of six from where she stood—one very close indeed, for War-Hold was built on its very knees—sported caps of white. She had no idea how far west they persisted. Report said it took two eights to cross the Spine, but that was farther north. Here—Well, she had maps, but they were old ones. Eronese curiosity stopped dead in its tracks when confronted with the west.

Idly, she reached up to scratch her head where she'd finally yielded to temptation the previous night and cut her hair short, the better to fit beneath a warrior's cap helm. She'd passed the bounds of civilization now, and was free to be herself—which meant serviceable fabrics, supple leathers, and, more to the point, no dresses. A final moment to take in the view and fix every detail in her memory so that she could tell Strynn and Avall about it, and she picked up the reins again, and gave Hammer the heel. The pack animal—Boot was his name—followed gamely as she started down the other side of what was more a high meadow than a pass. Blue sky rose above, and mountains likewise reared up in her wake as the slope increased. Ahead, shot on shot, as far as she could see, more mountains showed, with the one she'd just traversed among the smallest.

Still, big things were made of small things, she reckoned, and it was still a quarter before the snows. If she only made eight shots a day, that should see her past this barrier well before then—if she even had to pass it. After all, her errand was simply to hide the regalia in a place only she would know. There were hundreds of likely prospects just in the landscape visible from where she stood. Why, she could probably hide it tomorrow—tonight even. But even so, she would've only accomplished part of what she'd set out to achieve.

Besides which, the meadow seemed to extend quite a way,

sloping ever so slightly downward to a copse of evergreens, beneath the shade of which it might be wise to camp.

Two hands later, she was seeking a likely place among them—still in sight of the meadow, but not so close that a fire would be visible to any nighttime patrols from War-Hold that chanced to pass that way—not unreasonable, given that she was still only a day's hard ride from the hold. More troubling was the fact that she'd also seen hoof marks bearing the unmistakable central crossbar of Ixtian horseshoes.

That wasn't unreasonable, either. The largest army mustered in five hundred years had passed near there on its way north the previous winter, and the collapsed remnants of it were still making their way south.

But while she was as good at combat as anyone she knew, the idea of fighting for her life against even one irate Ixtian did not appeal to her. Circumspection was therefore in order, so she chose her campsite with care—shielded by a trio of boulders, one of which overhung just far enough to shelter the back of the tent, while the other two fanned out to either side like protective, if heavily lichened, arms. Laurel interspersed with pine trees framed the rocks, while the ground before them was thick with pine straw, so that she had little to remove to find a comfortable place on which to make her bed.

There was even water—a nice freshet a dozen spans away that disappeared downhill to terminate in what she suspected was a waterfall. Which would be a good place to bathe before dinner.

It was while investigating that very option that she saw the crazy man.

She'd found the waterfall, all right—a magnificent example at least twelve spans high, sliding down rocks into a pool three spans across. The land was wilder thereabouts, thick with laurel and pocked with stone outcrops. And sitting atop one, calmly watching her—from the other side of the cataract—was a man.

Eronese, by the look of him, and young—her age, more or

less. Beyond that, well, his clothing—which should've offered some cue to identification, since each clan had a distinctive color Law required they wear somewhere upon their bodies— certainly gave no clue to his identity whatsoever.

Everything *this* man wore seemed to be greasy gray and grimy tan. Which was no one's livery. He wore a cap, too: a tight-fitting item that hid his hair.

How did she know he was crazy? Because he was outdoors, fully clothed, and yet was barefoot, dirty, and sported a short, scruffy beard.

No Eronese man except Tryffon ever let his whiskers grow if he could help it, and certainly not long enough to obscure his cheeks and chin. And no one ever went barefoot outdoors, either, save when swimming; to do otherwise was considered rude, if not actually obscene. The dirt was the clincher. No sane Eronese with access to water—which this man plainly had—would ever let himself get so filthy.

Still, he was here, Eronese, and she was armed and he wasn't. That said, she was well advised to investigate any threat, real or imagined.

"Hail," she called formally, lest his situation have been born of circumstances she hadn't considered.

"Hail," he called back cheerfully. "Be careful, Lady, they'll get you."

A chill ran up her spine, not so much from the words themselves, but because the voice sounded familiar.

"Who are 'they'?" she called back, seeking more than one set of answers.

"The burners."

"The burners . . . You mean the Ixtians?"

"Aye. They burn things."

"They do, and I've lost many a loved one to them," Merryn shouted back, nodding vigorously while trying to resist the temptation to reach for her sword, since the man was still five spans away, with the head of a cataract between them. "Do you have a name?" she added, which was rude, but not so much as demanding that name directly. But then she recalled that she was in this man's territory, or so he would likely perceive it, and so she took a deep breath, and yelled, "I am Merryn san Argen-a, on an errand for His Majesty, the King of Eron, Avall syn Argen-a."

"Merryn," the wild man shouted back, standing now, and shading his eyes the better to look at her. "I once knew a woman named Merryn. She was—"

"Krynneth!" Merryn blurted, having to restrain herself from starting across the precipitous rock. "You're Krynneth syn Mozz-een. What are you doing here? Last time I heard you were—"

"Fine? I was. Long enough to bear word to the King that War-Hold had fallen. Long enough to carry every image from that last siege in my head every waking instant of every day, and live it again every time I slept."

"But you were there at the end. At the Battle of Storms. And after."

"And after," Krynneth echoed. "But so were the memories."

She started to reply, then changed her mind. "We could talk better if we didn't have to yell. This thing"—she indicated the waterfall—"makes a lot of noise."

"So do swords and shields," Krynneth replied amiably.

But he came. Wading through rushing water up to his knees, as though the fact that a misstep could precipitate him to injury or death was of no concern.

Maybe it wasn't. Merryn had met men like Krynneth before—a few. Men who managed incredible feats of endurance in order to execute a duty or fulfill an obligation, and who gave all sign of living normally, until, one day, something inside them broke.

Krynneth had been at the Battle of War-Hold. So had she. But she'd only watched, tied to a chair at Barrax's bidding, so that she had no other choice. Krynneth had been inside. That could do strange things to a man. She'd meant to talk to him about it, too, for she had her own demons from that time, and Krynneth had lived in the suite next door to hers, and had had the keeping of one of the Ixtian prisoners, the same as she. They had history, they did: ancient, if not so honorable, history.

And frankly, had Kraxxi not appeared, she might well have taken him for a lover. In any case, things had clearly not been as right as she supposed. Last she'd heard—and she regretted not trying to hear more—he'd been among a party going south to survey the damage to War-Hold. He'd evidently abandoned it at some point. Probably the report of that was buried among many of similar kind on Avall's desk.

He'd reached her side by then, and she was at a loss as to what to do. He made that decision for her—by collapsing against her, weeping.

"Krynneth," she managed, in some alarm. "What—?" Then, as the sobs grew stronger, "Are you all right?"

He didn't answer, just stood there with his face buried against her shoulder and his hand clutching her sides. She stroked his head clumsily, at a loss how to react to a grown man come apart so suddenly. He was still strong, she noted absently, but she could feel more bones than she should beneath his ragged tunic. He also stank, but after spending most of a quarter in one or the other of Barrax's dungeons, she was used to that. Maybe later, she could tend to that. For now . . .

That was a problem, actually. The man clearly needed help, but she was on a secret mission and couldn't turn aside from it to provide that assistance. The smart thing would be to take him back to War-Hold, but he had to know it was nearby; therefore, if he'd wanted to go there, he could have done so himself.

Still, she had her quest, and that could only be accomplished alone. Well, there was no hurry, regardless. It was getting late, she still needed a bath, and he was a friend in need. Besides, she needed to make a more complete assessment of his situation.

"When was the last time you had a good meal?" she whispered, trying, very gently, to ease him away. "You're thin."

"I'm sorry," Krynneth mumbled through his tears, rejecting her efforts to disentangle herself, and, indeed, holding her tighter. "I'm sorry, so sorry, so sorry."

"It's not your fault," she murmured numbly. "You did your duty. Lorvinn gave you an order, and you carried it out, and maybe saved many, many lives—maybe the whole kingdom, since we barely got the regalia finished in time as it was."

"I could've ridden faster," Krynneth sobbed wretchedly. "I could've waited to visit Lorvinn when the attack came. If I had been—"

"You can't play the 'if' game, Kryn," Merryn whispered, even as she knew her own thoughts and actions gave the lie to that. "It'll drive you—"

She broke off before she said the word she probably should *not* say under the circumstances. Not until she knew more.

"Mad?" Krynneth chuckled. "I may be mad, Merryn. But that's a relative thing, isn't it? Killing people is generally considered the work of a madman—unless you happen to be working on someone's orders."

Merryn shook her head. "It's only mad when you do it without remorse, and I can't imagine that you don't feel sorry for every single man you killed." She tried to ease him away again—and to draw him away from the waterfall as well, which was suddenly too close for comfort.

"Kryn? Do you have a place to stay? Surely you're not living in the Wild?"

He motioned to the surrounding woods—a general sweep of what was still a strong and graceful hand. "I have a different house every night. A different tree or rock or cave. That way they can't find me."

"Who can't?"

"The burners."

"Kryn, there are no burners anymore."

He cocked his head. "Part of me believes you. Part of me

isn't so sure," But he let her thrust him far enough away that she could hook an arm in his and slowly steer him toward her camp.

"We'll have dinner," she told him. "We'll talk. You'll tell me your adventures, and I'll—"

She broke off again. She couldn't reveal her errand, but she didn't know if she had the energy to lie, besides which, she'd never *been* a good liar, and Krynneth was one of her most trusted friends. Maybe she should simply tell him what she was up to and be done. Given that he seemed scared to death of War-Hold, it might be best for him to accompany her on her quest. She had no illusions about her own ability to heal a damaged mind, but she had no illusions about anyone else's abilities that way, either. It took time, love, and circumstance.

"Dinner?" Krynneth murmured, sounding like a little boy.

"I've some smoked venison I've been saving. We can have that, with some rice and herbs."

"Ale?"

She tensed, then relaxed again. "Aye—some. I'm not certain you should drink, though."

"Of course I should drink!" he shot back fiercely, all his former meekness vanished in a breath. "That's the only way I can forget. The only way I can sleep."

"When *did* you last sleep? Really sleep, I mean. Without fear or worry."

"Before the burners."

"How about since you came here?"

"Never for a whole night. I dare not." He yawned abruptly, as though talk had awakened the impulse.

She gnawed her lip. "Very well, then. It sounds like you need sleep more than anything. You sleep in my camp tonight, Kryn. I'll get you fed and warm, and you can sleep, and I'll watch over you and . . . and I'll let nothing happen to you, I promise. Not even in your dreams. I'll guard your dreams too, Kryn."

He gazed at her askance, adoring, yet distrusting. Like a

child or dog. How many Krynneths were there? she wondered. In the world at large and here with her? Was this one madder than she thought? Or did a Krynneth who was totally sane still survive somewhere beneath that greasy hair?

They were approaching camp by then, and the shadows were growing long. It would be dark soon, and she'd wanted to wait until then to build a fire, lest the smoke be seen from War-Hold or any random Ixtians who might happen by. She had to tend the horses, too: get them properly fed, rubbed down, and picketed for the night. Fortunately, she'd already pitched her tent, laid out her bedroll, and found stones for a fire ring.

Releasing Krynneth with some difficulty—he didn't seem to want to let go of her—she unfolded a second set of blankets and pointed to them. "Sit there, Kryn. Or sleep. You need it. I'll cook and look after you."

"Ale," he repeated petulantly, more like a child than ever.

She sighed, but searched for some. Maybe if he drank enough, it would knock him out—which would give her more time to decide what to do about him.

"I've got brandy," she announced a moment later. "That might be better for you, but go easy, it's strong."

He snatched the bottle, uncorked it, and took a hearty swig. He'd started to take another, but she grabbed it back. "Not yet! You'll get sick. You don't want to do that, and I don't want you to."

"Sick . . ."

"Get some sleep, Kryn. I'll cook."

"Sleep."

She pushed him down on the blankets, smoothed his hair out of his eyes, and gently patted his eyelids closed. As an afterthought, she kissed him on the forehead. Like a mother. Thank The Eight that Strynn couldn't see her now. She'd never hear the end of it.

To her amazement, Krynneth started snoring at once. She took that as a good sign—that he trusted her, if nothing else—

and bent herself to preparing the promised meal. He was still snoring when she finished, and she had trouble waking him. When he did, his eyes were clearer, but he was very subdued. He took the proffered food without protest, and ate with gusto and surprisingly good manners.

"What's happened in Tir-Eron since I left?" he asked eventually, sounding perfectly normal. And though Merryn wanted more than anything to learn as much about his situation as possible, she decided that for the moment she'd best let him lead the conversation. Which he did, sounding as sane as when she'd met him, even joking now and then.

It was full dark now, and Merryn was tired and sleepy. She hadn't had her bath, either, but that would have to wait until morning. If Krynneth was still improving then, she'd see if she could get him to take one, too. Or maybe they could—

No! She wouldn't let herself think about that. Her life was too complicated as it was, and Krynneth needed no more stress brought to bear on already fragile emotions. "I'm enjoying this," she told him finally. "But I've been traveling all day and I need to rest. You need it more, though, so you sleep, I'll keep watch. And don't worry, nothing's going to happen to you."

"Nothing?" he replied softly, sounding like the boy again.

"Nothing," she assured him.

He didn't reply, for he was asleep already.

Daylight woke Merryn. Or perhaps it was the anxious whickering of one of the horses, or the soughing of the wind through the pines as the morning breeze began to dispel the night. Possibly, too, it was Krynneth breathing beside her, the sounds soft, even, and unconcerned. She smiled at that. It had been a long time since she'd awakened beside any man but her brother or one of his comrades, and that in soldiers' quarters on a battlefield. Leaning up on her elbow, she studied Krynneth's face, noting lines of worry that shouldn't be there at his age. The beard would have to go if they were to continue together.

Which made her frown. She'd intended to reach a decision about that last night, but sleep had surprised her. In any case, he was sleeping soundly, and she still hadn't got that bath, and was in dire need of one. She thought of making a fire first, and putting water on to boil for cauf that she needed and Kryn would probably appreciate, then decided that the noise might rouse him, and she wasn't prepared to deal with him yet.

Having so decided, she slipped silently from her bedroll, found her spare clothes where she'd laid them out the previous night, and padded, barefoot (scandalous notion!) through the woods back to the pool at the base of the waterfall, where she wasted no time finding a rock shelf and stripping, wincing as she slid into what was amazingly cold water. Not that she couldn't endure it, hadn't expected as much, or was likely to get better for a very long time—unless she found a hot spring, or went to the trouble of boiling a great deal of water indeed.

She therefore made short work of it, paying particular attention to her hair. And was just giving her head a final toweling, enjoying the fact that the new short locks seemed already half-dry, when she caught a movement out of the corner of her eye. Sound went with it, and she was already scrambling to her feet when something hard hit the back of her head just behind the ear. Instinct identified that blow—location, implement, and angle—as one she'd learned as part of the Night Guard. It was supposed to do minimal harm, but ensure instant unconsciousness. In fact, the blow, as much as what she actually saw before darkness swam in her eyes, confirmed her attacker as her fellow Night Guardsman, Krynneth.

She tried to fight him off, but surprise had sufficiently dulled her reflexes that the first blow made another possible. This one connected more surely, and the last thing she remembered before darkness claimed her was that one should always turn one's back to a river if there was a waterfall nearby to dull one's hearing.

When she awoke again, it was to find herself back in camp,

clad only in her undertunic, with her hands tied securely before her and her ankles trussed up like a roasting pig.

Krynneth—fully dressed and sleepy-eyed, but intently focused for all that—was sitting across from her, calmly sorting through her gear one pack at a time.

Her heart sank. The shield was where she'd left it, hidden within its nondescript cover. The pouch with the gems was piled with the clothes she'd worn to the pool. But the sword and helm . . .

He found the former exactly as she thought it, and pulled it from the bundle of which it had been part, staring at it quizzically. "I know this sword," he gasped, fingers brushing the peace ties that also, fortunately, covered the gem's trigger. "It's the Fire Sword." He paused, cocked his head. "Fire Sword," he repeated. "Or Lightning Sword. Doesn't much matter, 'cause they both burn things—and I've had enough of burning."

"Put that away!" Merryn snapped. "It's more dangerous than you can imagine. It could kill you without you even knowing."

"Then it's safer if I keep it," Krynneth replied solemnly. "You think I don't know that it was you who caused the burning?"

"I never—!" Merryn began. But he was right. It *was* her fault, in a way. But he had the regalia now, and that was the imminent problem.

"You stole this, didn't you?" he accused. "It belonged to the King, and he'd never let anyone take it away. Not even you."

"I'm his sister."

"You're also the king of Ixti's lover. And you're going south in disguise. What would that make you think if you were me?"

Merryn blinked in blank amazement. What had gotten into Krynneth, to prompt such accusations? They might not have been so bad had he been angry. But to have him lay them out so calmly, as if they made perfect sense . . .

"I've never lied to you," she said slowly.

His eyes flashed fire. "Yes you have! You've tricked me, anyway—which is the same thing!"

"When?" she dared.

"When you and Lorvinn helped Kraxxi escape."

"We never—!"

"You did!"

Merryn started to reply, then thought better of it. The smart thing to do was watch and wait. Krynneth had already changed personalities several times since yesterday. It was more than possible he might change again. She hoped he did it soon. In any case, he was running on his own momentum now, and she knew better than to interrupt someone as angry as he obviously was.

"You think silence will save you?" he raged "It won't. You've got the Fire Sword, and there's only one reason you should have it, and that's to take it to Kraxxi, so he can make more fire."

"And what will you do with it?" she challenged.

"Cut out your tongue, if you say another word!" Krynneth shouted. Something about his tone made her believe him.

"I'm tired of this," he growled abruptly, whereupon he kicked her onto her side, then knocked her out again with the bone hilt of her cooking knife. When she regained consciousness, he'd struck the entire camp, and very neatly, too. But his eyes, when she saw them, were still mad.

"Krynneth—" she dared again.

"I'll cut your tongue out," he spat. "Be silent."

Merryn thought it best not to argue.

CHAPTER XIX:

HIDDEN AGENDAS

(ERON: TIR-ERON: ARGEN-HALL—MASK DAY—EARLY EVENING)

Tyrill hated Mask Day and always had. Even as a girl, she'd hated it. Possibly that was because she'd been obsessed with order even then, and Mask Day was the one day of the year when the ritual-loving, Law-respecting Eronese utterly abandoned any sense of propriety, expectation, or order. Or maybe it was simply the fact that when everyone wore masks—by Law; there was that much order in the celebration—she could no longer distinguish friend from foe, and thus didn't know how to act. As a gawky girl, that had been important.

Now, however, she simply hated it because it was one more thing to complicate a life that was complicated enough already. She watched the preparations from the windows of her suite— her old suite: the traditional Craft-Chief's suite in Argen-Hall. The revelry wouldn't start until a finger after sunset—which was an odd time, just as it was observed in the middle of an eight-day, without reference to cosmic proprieties such as equinoxes or solstices. In fact, the date itself was irregular, being chosen by random lot two years in advance, with allowances made to preclude two Mask Days falling close together.

She'd be glad when it was over. As it was, she'd spent most

of the last eight-day finishing things, not the least among them, business with Avall. She'd seen him ride out amid all that panoply. And she'd not even been able to argue with him when he'd told her that, in spite of his best intentions, he wouldn't be able to sit in the conclave that had—finally—Proven a new Clan-Chief. The Kingdom was more important, they both agreed. Lives were at stake, not mere power structures. And, by the way, did she mind sitting as Steward while he was gone?

She hadn't wanted to, but with Tryffon and Preedor both off with the army, she was the person he trusted most—more than the Chiefs of Stone and Lore, even, who were the other two likely candidates. She supposed that was a compliment, but she wondered, sometimes, if it weren't simply a way of riding her to an earlier grave than she'd have succumbed to otherwise.

But *that* would never have occurred to him, foolish, guileless half-boy that he was. Maybe he even considered it compensation for his absence at the conclave. But that was like spreading jelly on burned bread. In any case, she had no choice but to wear the Steward's circlet tonight, when she was required to put in an appearance at the Masker's Ball in the forecourt of the Citadel.

But that was still more than a hand away, and, to her surprise, she didn't seem to have any productive way of filling the intervening time. She tried pacing, reveling in the fact that the warmth of summer had made the pain in her joints subside. But pacing made her squires anxious, so she substituted walking the corridors of Argen-Hall.

That, in turn, brought her to the doors of the Clan-Chief's Audience Chamber. On impulse, she eased in there. The high-vaulted room was one of the most impressive in Argen-Hall, with every surface faced with some kind of cleverly worked metal; but she'd seen it so many times over the years that its splendor barely registered. The Chief's Chair stood on a low dais at the opposite end, and she found herself wandering toward it. When she'd been acting Chief, she'd presided from this chamber more than once, but she'd sat in her traditional Craft-Chief's chair, one step lower than the Clan-Chief's, since her role in the Chieftains Hall was born of courtesy, not right. The seats in *her* Hall were reversed.

Before she knew it, she'd reached the dais. She ran a hand along an arm of her chair, then along one of the Chieftain's. No one but a Clan-Chief could sit there, by ancient Law, but she'd *been* Clan-Chief in all but confirmation, at least briefly, and was close to ninety years old, and Death would likely visit her sooner than later—so, she considered, she had little to lose by yielding, just once, to caprice. Besides, wasn't this Mask Day, when rules were supposed to be flaunted?

A deep breath, a pause to listen, as though tradition like-wise held its breath in anticipation of her indiscretion, and then, in one quick burst of movement, she sat down in the Clan-Chief's Chair.

"Lady!" her squire—Lynee was her name, and she'd been born to Common Clan—gasped.

"Lady indeed!" someone echoed behind her. Tyrill started to rise, but the speaker was beside her by then, pushing her gently back into the seat. It took a moment to recognize her assailant, and when she did it was by sight, not voice. Mavayn. Lady Mavayn san Argen-el, to give her full name; now Chief-Elect of Clan Argen. Eellon's successor, confirmed the previous night after she'd finally, against numerous challenges, Proven herself more competent than Lord Trymm syn Argen-yr. They'd both been born the same day, and while Law would still have given precedence to the firstborn, they'd also been born precisely at sunset, so there was no way of telling who had preceded whom into the world. It had taken a match of wits to determine. Mavayn had won, after two hands of queries on every imagin-able topic.

"It's all right," Mavayn murmured with a wry smile. "In your place I'd be tempted, too—and what better day to yield to such temptations?"

"Chief, I apologize," Tyrill protested, trying again to rise.

"It was unseemly. I, of all people, should keep my pride in check."

"You have as much to be proud of as anyone in this kingdom," Mavayn shot back, though she withdrew her hand. "Perhaps if I sat here after you, we might be equally wicked." For all her age, she grinned at that, showing yellow teeth. What she proposed *was* wicked, too—and preposterous. There was no luck worse than to sit in the Chief's Chair before the appointed time of one's Raising to that title—which would not be until tomorrow's sunrise, after all masks were shed.

"So you're saying we would each owe the other a secret?" Tyrill dared. "I think not. What you do when I leave here is your business, of course. And it would be unseemly for me to try to stop you."

And somehow, in the midst of that rejoinder, which had commenced so casually, Tyrill's old iron-hard adherence to tradition had returned. She started back down the aisle toward the door, but paused halfway there and turned again. "I will expect a reprimand from you tomorrow," she said quietly, and departed.

Lynee was looking anxious when Tyrill finally reappeared in the corridor. "You must hurry, Chief," she said. "You've barely enough time to reach the Citadel before the ball begins."

"Ah," Tyrill chuckled grimly. "But wouldn't that be appropriate, too?"

Yet two fingers later, she and Lynee had climbed into the transport they had chosen for the evening: the poorest coach they could find in Argen's stables, pulled by the poorest horses. Indeed, had Tyrill not been so infirm, they properly should have walked, but she'd drawn the line at that. Still, they wore motley, as everyone was supposed to do, with no clan insignia anywhere about. And their masks were the standard issue everyone began the evening wearing across their eyes and noses, adding decorations as impulse directed, from piles of feathers, glass gems, furs, and other baubles set up at intervals around the city.

The sun had just vanished below the edge of the gorge, so it appeared, which was the signal for the bonfires to be lit—which they were, in front of every Hall and Hold from the Citadel all the way down to Farewell Island. In spite of herself, Tyrill felt a thrill as the nearest flame flared up, followed at once by the first of the revelers jumping through it, which was supposed to ensure luck.

The River Walk was already thick with people flooding out of the Halls and Holds, as well as from the bridges to South Bank, where most of the lower clans lived and had their businesses. Not that anyone could distinguish High from low now, save perhaps by height or build, since few High Clan men or women were notably thin, stout, tall, or short. True to form, many sported straw daggers and paper shields, and more than one mock combat was already taking place, to the enthusiastic cheers of those less inclined to play the fool.

Before Tyrill knew it, they'd reached the largest fire of all: the one that blazed before the open gates of the Court of Rites. She'd have to traverse the last part of the way on foot, however, so she ordered the coach to stop and let Lynee help her down. With that, she dismissed the coachman, who was clearly eager to begin his own revelry. Nor did it matter, really. The Eight knew there were quarters aplenty she could claim in the Citadel. Squaring her shoulders, but giving Lynee her arm, she made her way through the open gates of the most important public space in all Eron.

A makeshift parody of a palace had been erected there, three stories high, not including the towers, and wrought of every kind of discarded item one could imagine. Once the basic structure had been constructed by apprentices from Wood, anyone else in Eron had been allowed to contribute what he would to that most fanciful of buildings. True to form, however, the front was left open so that everyone could view the Chief of Masks, who even now held court from a hay bale throne.

A table stretched before him, covered with food donated by

anyone who wished, with ale from the royal stores by Avall's command. Many were drunk already, and so much noise roared within the place that Tyrill could barely hear. She was supposed to make her way to the Chief of Masks, present herself, remove her own mask, so that all could see that order was indeed being passed, then retreat into obscurity once more.

She was late, however, and knew it. Worse, everyone else seemed to know it, and the Chief of Masks, in particular, was clearly irked by her tardiness.

It would still take a while to make her way to the dais, too. But since chaos was supposed to rule tonight, perhaps it would be fitting to follow another plan.

"Chief!" she called from where she stood, rising on tiptoes, then pausing to seize a horn from a passing reveler. Scowling all the while, she set it to her lips and blew.

At first she was ignored, but Lynee had a particularly loud voice for a young lady, and soon made her shouts of "Heed! Heed!" heard above the din.

The Chief of Masks stood abruptly, looking her way, taking a moment to find them.

To Tyrill's chagrin, two young men promptly hoisted her up on their shoulders. Half-breathless, she nevertheless managed to rip off her mask, so that all could see that it was indeed she who addressed them. "The Steward has arrived!" she shouted through rising fury. "The Steward gives the court to the Chief of Masks. Let his reign begin!"

"Until sunrise," the Chief promptly shouted back. "Let the *revelry* begin!"

An explosion of shouts echoed around the court, punctuated by much banging of straw knives against paper shields, which produced a sort of raspy rattle.

More than one person stabbed his fellow, precipitating more mock battles, for such feigned combats were much the order of the day. Thus, Tyrill was not in the least alarmed when, just outside the gates, the young men set her down, laughed—and stabbed her.

Only when she felt cold steel slide along her side did she realize that one of the stray daggers had merely been a mask for a far more lethal one. Nor, as she sank to her knees, did she realize that all across the Court of Rites, High Clan men and women who had been carefully identified by certain people who made it their business to know such things, were likewise feasting on steel and death that night.

But she *was* aware, as the ground rose up to hit her, of Lynee flinging herself atop her, whispering, "Lie still, Lady, if you be not dead already. Safety lies in shadows"—followed by outraged wailing.

And Tyrill, once a careful assessment had determined that she'd only received a flesh wound, was willing to go along with that. After all, if she were lucky, no one would bother killing someone who was presumably dead already.

Meenon syn Nyvvon, Craft-Chief of Glass, poured himself a mug of dark wine and ambled toward the hot pool in Nyvvon-Hall's baths. He wore a loose robe of Nyvvon green that floated around legs still strong with youth—unlike that flapping against his Clan-Chief's spindly shanks before him. Their other two companions, Sallaro of Weaving and his Chief, Ganall syn Vrine, who was also bond-brother to Nyvvon's Chief, were waiting for them already, sitting naked in the pool while vapors rose up around them to soothe flesh grown stiff with age—though at that, the two elders looked little different than they had twenty years before. Meenon sighed as he approached. This was ritual on a day when rituals were supposed to be denied. Yet the four Chiefs had been meeting like this, once every eight-day, since the two Clan-Chiefs were boys. The only change was who bore the Craft-Chief's title—for either clan. And even that had not changed for the five seasons since Sallaro had succeeded Lady Orzheen.

He supposed he could endure. These sessions didn't actually take very long, if one controlled the conversation with care. And the ale, which Weaving provided, was always different, but always good.

So it was that Meenon's thoughts were on nothing in particular as he discarded his robe on the bench provided and eased his tired body into the steaming water. The others welcomed him with toasts. Small talk followed. Before long, Meenon was sufficiently relaxed that he'd lost any desire for haste. Oh, he'd have to make an appearance at the revels eventually, but that could wait. In the meantime—well, in the meantime more wine would be nice. And scented oil.

As if the lad had read his mind, a hall page appeared. He wore a half mask—obviously he was on his way to some revel and was sparing them one last consideration on a night when he owed them none. Meenon didn't recognize the face below the mask and motley, then again, there was no particular reason he should. The lad carried an ale pitcher; that was the important thing. And was grinning as he approached.

Meenon raised his cup to receive what the lad was about to offer, but to his surprise, the boy upended the jar atop him, then swirled it around, to splatter them all with what was certainly *not* ale.

"A poor joke that, lad," Sallaro protested. But by then Meenon had identified the scent of what covered his head and torso and lay as a skim across the water. Fire oil, so named because it was so easily ignited and so difficult to extinguish.

"What . . . ?" he shouted in alarm, trying to haul himself out, but finding the edge too slick to grasp. The page kicked him with a booted foot, revealing a sole studded with short spikes. And then ran, pausing only to toss the torch by the entrance into the bathing pool, and close the door.

Meenon didn't hear the bolt click home because his ears were burning.

"To your health!" cried Lady Vroo san Criff, Chief of the clan that ruled Clay. "Chaos may rule without, but indulge me in order a little longer." She paused with her mug still raised, surveying the other ten faces ranged around the table. They wore motley already, but their masks lay piled on a chest by the door. Both sexes were represented, and their ages ranged from twenty-three to eighty-seven. They were the subchiefs of her craft, with a few sub-subchiefs thrown in.

"How much longer?" someone called cheerfully.

"Long enough," Vroo called back. "Assain, how is it that you're always so eager to begin the breaking?" she continued, referring to the fact that, while on Mask Day her clan donated a year's worth of failed efforts at their craft to the Chief of Masks' banquet, they always kept a supply of imperfect crockery to break themselves.

"Because that's how she covers her mistakes," Kynall shot back, with a raucous laugh.

"More wine, I say," Intaro added, lifting a mug himself, then draining it, and flinging the empty vessel to the floor.

"And more cups!" someone appended, following his example. Whereupon chaos ensued in truth, with every drinking vessel in sight—including some that were properly too fine to suffer the fate that met them—summarily drained and broken.

"Wine!" Vroo called again, lifting her own fine vessel, then casting it to the floor. "Bring us the best, and then be about your play. We will drink one final toast, then see how the rest of the city fares."

The hall page did his best to obey the order, filling ten fresh cups in succession, while another page distributed them.

Clan Criff started to drink as one, but Vroo paused with the cup at her lips. "Perhaps it is best that the page propose this toast, since this is the day when all rules are inverted."

The page hesitated, clearly embarrassed, but another page entered just then, this one masked and obviously drunk already. Not that it mattered, as he gamely raised his cup on high. "Lady, I hope you enjoy that vintage, which was sent to you by my master, and now let us drink a toast!"

"A toast," they cried in unison.

"To life!" cried the visiting stranger.

"To life!" came the responding chorus.

And the drinking, all in one long draught.

"And to Death," the stranger added, and swept away.

"To Death," someone echoed, then broke off. Vroo started to reprimand her, then paused herself. Blackness swam before her eyes, and she had only time to gasp out one word before death seized her in truth. And that one word was *poison*.

The last thing she saw was the hall page's anguished face as he screamed, "Oh Eight, no!" then pounded in raw panic out the door.

The last things she heard were the sounds of her kinsmen, one by one, expiring.

"Lady, oh, Lady!" came Lynee's urgent whisper. "You have to stand up now, you *have* to! They've gone, but they may come back. We can't let them find you."

"Let *who* find me?" Tyrill huffed, as, with Lynee's help, she found her feet, though she didn't shy away from that helpful arm beneath her shoulder. She gasped when she came upright, as the wound in her side reminded her of why she was lying on the ground to start with.

"Them! I don't know who, Lady, but it's chaos out here. I . . . I don't think you were the only one, but they may come back. You have to be gone by then."

"Where?"

"I don't know, Lady, but . . . but this seems planned. It had to be."

Tyrill's heart double-beat, and not from fear for herself. "Eight, you may be right! What better time than when the King is away to stage a coup? But who, and how far—?"

"Priest-Clan, I would say," Lynee grunted, as she continued to haul Tyrill along—south, she noted absently. "Or that group within them that's seized Gem."

"It would make sense," Tyrill agreed. "But if I was a target, there have to have been others."

"You think?"

"It makes sense."

Tyrill stood as straight as her old bones and bad joints would allow. "I'm hurt; I won't lie about that, but I can manage. Right now, we have to learn two things: How far does this coup extend, and is there anyone around to stop it?"

"Lady . . ."

Lynee didn't get to finish, for the first question was already being answered. A reveler had rushed up to them, stone sober, but wild-eyed behind his mask. "Ladies, you should—it's terrible. You have to get away from here!"

"What?" Tyrill demanded.

"They've killed the Chiefs of Glass, Clay, and Weaving. And more, I fear. Forget masks, see to your skins!"

"Lady?" the squire asked again.

"He's right," Tyrill said firmly. "We have to get out of here. With all the confusion tonight, there's no telling who's alive or dead. But there's no way we can regain control of Tir-Eron quickly, and maybe no one to control it if we did. They won't listen to me without the Guard, and the Guard are all off with Avall, save my honor guard, to whom I foolishly gave the night off—and I'll bet they've all been assassinated. Anything I do, I'll have to do outside what's now passing for order. Priest-Clan have won—for now. Beyond that—we need to know how far this extends, and then we need to escape."

Learning the former was easy, Tyrill discovered, as Lynee steered her east toward Argen-Hall, but also south toward the river. Fires were everywhere, the bonfires having served as breeding grounds for far more dangerous offspring, as building after building was set alight. Rumors ran thick and fast as sparks: the King had done this; no, the King was returning at a gallop. It was Priest-Clan's fault; no, only *part* of Priest-Clan's fault. All eight Priests of The Eight were dead; no, they were holed up on their island or in their gorge. Every single Chief and subchief was dead. Ferr-Hall-Main was on fire (true); Lore-Hold-Main was on fire (false). Argen-Hall had been set ablaze but it had been extinguished. Yet still fires leapt and roared, and the people on the street suddenly wore masks of fear that rendered disguise redundant. The pavement was littered with paper faces and straw daggers—and some of the more dangerous kind. More than once Tyrill trod on someone dying.

"How can this have happened?" Lynee pleaded.

"By not watching where we should," Tyrill snapped. "By seeing what we expected instead of what was.

"It wouldn't take many to murder the Chiefs," she continued, "if their movements and habits were known. It wouldn't even require that every clan be infiltrated. When this is over, you can bet that scores of pages will be found trussed up in corners, alive if they're lucky, but just as likely to have their throats slit. I—Oh, Eight!"

She'd just caught a flash of white to the east, and heard a thunder of hooves on stone. Through billowing clouds of smoke, she could make out scores of mounted riders pounding across the next bridge down, obviously having come from South Bank. They rode in order, too, with swords flashing and white cloaks whipping above surcoats of midnight blue. All wore masks, but all those masks were blank. Their numbers seemed endless as they peeled off in groups of five, going east and west.

"The Ninth Face shows itself," Tyrill spat.

"Hurry, Lady. They're rounding up people. It's like they're looking for someone."

"Survivors, probably. High Clan survivors."

Somehow, in spite of the confusion, they'd reached the river wall. They paused there, panting. The night had gone utterly mad, had become a vision of red and black against which figures dashed and danced, laughed and screamed, all the while white-cloaked men forged order out of chaos.

"I will forge them back," Tyrill muttered to herself, though Lynee heard.

"Aye, Lady, but not tonight. To forge, one must live. There's a boat below, if you can reach it."

"My luck isn't that good," Tyrill sighed.

"It is tonight, but it won't be if you don't take it. Now go! Over the wall. I'll follow."

"I—"

"Die, High Clan scum!" Lynee roared in Tyrill's face, ramming her fist toward Tyrill's stomach as if to thrust in a nonexistent blade, then throwing her body atop her supposed victim so that they both pitched over the wall and into the river.

For an instant, Tyrill thought she'd been betrayed. But then water came up and hit her, and she was breathing waves, and a soaking-wet Lynee had seized her arm and was heaving her up into what seemed a small rowboat. "Play dead," the girl hissed. "If we're lucky, our enemies will see what *they* want to see— for a change."

"Yes," Tyrill coughed. And then, for a while, all she saw was night sky framed, quite beautifully, by the light of burning buildings.

CHAPTER XX:

WOMEN'S TALK

(SOUTHERN ERON: THREE OAKS STATION– HIGH SUMMER: DAY LXI–EVENING)

"There's something to be said for comfort," Strynn sighed, leaning back in one of several deeply upholstered chairs in the common hall at Three Oaks Station. She and Div had it to themselves, for which they were both grateful. Two nights under the stars were fine, but a nice soft bed was finer. Unfortunately, the last two stations they'd reached had been occupied, and while they themselves were traveling incognito, the colors splashed across the caravans outside had identified the occupants as having come from Warcraft, which meant Strynn was bound to encounter someone she knew, thereby raising questions she had no urge to answer.

"There is indeed," Div replied happily, rising from where she'd set cider to heat by the fire. Stew already boiled there; while yeastless way-bread baked in the adjoining oven. "Somehow I never thought traveling with the Consort of the King of Eron would be quite so much like—"

"Ordinary trekking?" Strynn finished for her, grinning. "Believe me, this is better. This way we can make our own decisions, never mind that we can make much better progress."

"Maybe," Div grumbled sourly. "It would be nice to know we're making *real* progress, though."

"At least we know what direction," Strynn murmured through a yawn. *Eight, but she was tired!* Why, she could probably doze off in a dozen breaths, given the opportunity. Her stomach was somewhat uneasy, too—and had been for the last two days, which she'd assumed was because the nights had been cooler than normal, and she was susceptible to that sort of change. Still, it was barely sunset—far too early for sleeping, especially with such good company.

Div raised a brow. "Shall we do it now or after we eat?"

Strynn suppressed another yawn. "Now, I think. I just want to eat, then go to bed."

"No bath? We may not get another hot one for a while."

"You have a point. Food, then bath, then bed."

Div patted her stomach meaningfully. "As hungry as I am, I'd be glad of any distraction from the waiting."

"Another point," Strynn agreed, fumbling at the ring on her right hand. It didn't come off as easily as heretofore, which troubled her a little. Maybe her fingers were swollen.

Div's eyes narrowed, but she said nothing, though she rose from her stirring to claim the chair opposite. Strynn had the ring off by then. It glittered in her palm. Once it had belonged to King Kraxxi of Ixti, which was an irony if there ever was one. Merryn had another—from Kraxxi's best friend, who'd once used it to follow Kraxxi as they were using it to locate Merryn. There were at least two more—somewhere.

"I only pray this thing knows which one it's supposed to be looking for," Div muttered, indicating the gold-set red stone. The arms of an Ixtian Landing House gleamed there, which were odd to see in an Eronese hand.

"It seems to," Strynn assured her. "Merryn said hers took her straight to Kraxxi, even though another one was closer by."

"It is to be hoped," Div sighed. "I'm not sure I like all this trafficking with magic."

"Me neither," Strynn agreed. "I get around it by not thinking of it as magic. It may not be. It could be some kind of undiscovered science, or an extension of the science we have. It could even be something that's somehow alive. That's what Avall thinks the gems are—sometimes."

"If we time this right," Div drawled, "we can finish just as the bread needs to come out."

Strynn nodded, taking the hint. From her pouch, she retrieved a length of red string which she knotted through the ring. If one ring were close to the other—or sensitive—one didn't need to use the string; the ring alone would tug one in the direction in which its specified fellow lay. But Merryn was still far away, so it appeared, and if the ring ever exerted any tug while on her hand, Strynn had never felt it.

Besides, she felt more comfortable this way.

Holding her breath, she extended the string over the flagstone floor, stilling the ring's gentle undulations with her other hand. Then, closing her eyes, she set it spinning in a circle, all the while trying to picture Merryn's face in her mind's eye. At first she sensed no change, but a quickening in Div's breathing told her that the ring was doing as expected. "Is it—?" she prompted, scarcely daring to breathe lest an idle breath upset the magic.

"I think so," Div muttered back. Then, "Yes."

By which time Strynn could likewise feel a difference. She opened her eyes, and saw, sure enough, that the initial circle was narrowing into an oval that was growing more attenuated by the moment, as it quickly decomposed into a curving line. Nor was that arc even; one end tended higher and tugged more strongly.

"Southwest," Div affirmed. "Just like before. At least Merryn's consistent."

"I'd be willing to bet she's decided to check by War-Hold," Strynn said, folding the string away. "It would be just like her."

"Returning to the scene of what she thinks is a crime?"

Strynn nodded. "That's just like her, too: to take guilt on herself she doesn't owe."

Div laughed grimly. "You're right there. What is it Rann

says about her? The three things she cares most about are honor, honor, and honor."

"She'd disagree with that," Strynn mused. "But only because Avall and I are somewhere up there as well. She's doing this at least as much for us as for the Kingdom."

"I wish," Div announced suddenly, "I had a brother."

Strynn cocked her head. "I'd have given you either of mine until about three years ago, when I finally decided they were human—or they decided I was."

Div regarded her keenly. "I'd settle for a bond-sister."

"You didn't have one?"

"I'm Common Clan, remember?"

"That doesn't change anything."

"It changes your parents' thinking about such things. Taking a bond-mate can be construed as putting on airs."

"Why? Common Clan has a seat in Council."

"But we're not High Clan. High Clan *dogs* have been known to come to Council."

Strynn was frowning. But not at Div's last comment. It wasn't as if they hadn't hashed out the differences between the clans more than once already. But perhaps the fact that Div was in love with a High Clan man made her particularly sensitive about it. It didn't matter to Rann, because he first of all loved Avall. But she couldn't convince Div of that.

But why wouldn't her ring go back on? Surely her fingers hadn't swollen that much. Maybe it was something to do with her cycle, which had always been erratic. In any event, she'd got it on now. And Div was easing a nice round of bread out of the oven. Strynn busied herself finding bowls from the station's stash and ladling stew into them. It smelled heavenly. Whatever else she was or wasn't, Div was a damned fine cook. Then again, she'd had years in the Wild to make her so. Strynn could cook, too, of course—everyone could—but the only thing for which she'd shown any real aptitude was sweets, and this wasn't the time for them. Maybe for breakfast, however . . . She'd see what was in the larder.

The bread was delicious, especially spread with butter from the station's horde, and the stew was wonderful as well. Div had seasoned it with something sharp and pungent that wafted up her nose to open her sinuses. There was also ale: local draft in lieu of the darker beverage Brewcraft issued to the stations as part of its tithe to the Kingdom.

She ate a second helping of the bread—but that was a mistake. This time the butter didn't taste right. Perhaps it was rancid. Had it been that way before? she wondered, setting half a wedge aside. Had the stew she'd eaten with it simply overridden the taste of rottenness?

Div scowled. "Something wrong?"

"Maybe the butter. I don't feel right, all of a sudden."

Div sniffed her own buttered slice, then the crock from which it had come. "Smells fine to me. Maybe—"

Strynn didn't hear the rest because a slight queasiness had suddenly become an all-too-familiar tightening in her throat. She was also sweating, and her face felt flushed. She knew what that meant.

"I'm going to—" she managed before she leapt to her feet and bolted for the garderobe. She made it in time, but only barely. When she rose from disposing of her meal, it was to find Div standing in the door, offering her a chilled mug of water.

Strynn took it hesitantly, wondering why Div was looking at her so strangely.

"I need that bath," Strynn announced, wiping her brow.

Div seemed to relax at that. "I'll scrub your back if you'll scrub mine."

"Done," Strynn agreed, already feeling much better. It really must have been the butter.

Unusual for an Eronese way station, the bathhouse was outside, attached to the main body of the station only by a covered walkway, walled with panels made of strips of interwoven wood. Div shot the bolt, then stood aside for Strynn to enter the chamber at the end. It was much as she'd expected: a weather gate to keep the worst of winter away, with a layer of straw matting over the cobbles, and more against the walls. A series of glass bricks near the ceiling provided minimal illumination, but they didn't linger there. The vesting room adjoined, and Strynn was glad to see that whoever had sheltered there before them had cleaned and folded the station's store of towels. Div snared one from the shelves by the door before moving right to undress. Strynn followed her example to the left. A moment later they were naked, and this time it was Div who preceded Strynn into the actual bathing room in order to light the candles, though there was also a skylight. Three Oaks was a small station, so cold and hot pools were set up in the same room, along with the shower. Strynn had always preferred the progression from room to room. In any case, what concerned her now was getting off her feet and giving her body a long, hot soak in the steaming pool in the center of the chamber. A moment later, she eased into the tiled pool, finding the soakers' bench by feel, as she watched Div jump bravely into the opposite end, where the water came up to her breasts. She swam there briefly, ducking her head to wet her hair before paddling over to sit beside Strynn. "Feeling better?" Div inquired a little too casually.

"Much."

"I have a theory about that."

Strynn grimaced sourly. "I'd prefer not to think what you're thinking."

Div grinned. "Easy enough to prove."

"Not if you're going to ask me about my bleeding. That's even more erratic than most High Clan Eronese women."

"As opposed to what? The women of Ixti? I hear they bleed twice an eighth."

"Which is why their men aren't as fertile as ours."

"That why Merryn felt safe to take one as a lover?"

"One of the reasons. But she really did love Kraxxi."

"And Avall?"

"What about him?"

"What kind of lover is he?"

Strynn blushed at first, then felt a flash of anger. "You should know that as well as I!"

Div shook her head. "We were linked by the gem at the time. Rann was there—he and I started it, actually, but Avall looked so sad we had to invite him to join us. That's when the gem really came into play, and we—the two men mostly, if you want the truth—bonded with the birkits as well. So yes, I've seen your husband naked and had him inside me, but I couldn't, at the time, have told you what was him and what was Rann."

"I've no anger at you for that. Under the circumstances."

"It had been a long time," Div confided wistfully. "And they were both so beautiful . . ."

"They were," Strynn agreed. "And still are."

"So why do you fear to name what you think?"

"That I might be pregnant? I'm not afraid."

"Yes you are!"

Strynn shook her head, but now that her demon had been named, she knew she'd told a lie. "Because if I am, I'm not merely carrying my child, I'm carrying Avall's child. More to the point, I'm carrying the High King's child."

"Does that matter? The succession doesn't work that way."

"But it could. He—or she—will be raised as a smith, first of all. But if Avall remains on the throne—which is *not* a given— then his children will grow up watching a Sovereign at close range. They'd therefore be more qualified than most, which would increase the odds of one of them being Sovereign in turn."

"You're forgetting something."

"What?"

"That you've already got a son who'll be in exactly the situation you describe. If he's allowed to be."

Strynn cocked her head. "That's true. But I don't think Avall will discriminate, at least not for a while."

"Not until Averryn starts to remind him of Eddyn?"

"We've had that exact conversation."

"Which is sidestepping the issue. Assuming you *are* pregnant, whatever else you're carrying, you're carrying the heir to two very talented people. That isn't a bloodline that should be risked lightly."

Strynn gnawed her lip. "If I'm pregnant—well, it's not from the last time we actually tried—it's too soon for that. It's from sometime further back. An eighth or more, at least."

Div merely looked at her.

Strynn frowned irritably. "If you're getting ready to ask about my breasts, I'll concede that they're a little tender when they really shouldn't be, but that outfit I've been wearing—"

"I think you are," Div said flatly. "Don't ask me how I know, but I've just got a feeling."

The frown deepened. "I hope you're wrong, then. Not about the fact of pregnancy in an abstract sense," she hastened to add, "about that being the case *now*. See, the problem is, if we abandon this journey and return, there may not be a throne for Avall to sit on, never mind the child."

Div, too, looked troubled. "And if Avall has no throne, that means things won't have gone well for Rann, either."

"No."

"No indeed."

"Well," said Strynn, decisively. "The child, at this point, is only a probability. Avall and Rann are facts. And while I'd as soon not bear this child in the Wild, it wouldn't be the first time—as you well know. In any case, it's likely we'll catch up with Merry way before it's a problem."

Div laughed, long and loud and unself-consciously.

"What's funny?"

"I cannot imagine Merryn delivering a baby, never mind having one."

"Actually," Strynn confided with a smirk, "neither can I."

"Feeling better, aren't you?"

"Yes," Strynn replied, surprised to discover it was true, "I am."

CHAPTER XXI:

INSIDE AND OUT

"That has to be it," Avall acknowledged, shading his face against the glare of the setting sun. The light made his eyes tear, so that he had to look away, which was more comforting, anyway. Better by far to survey the faces of friends, armored or not, and the comforting greenery of the pines that crowned the hilltop where they stood, than to gaze at what lay before them. Or maybe not, for the fading light gave everything a ruddy cast, as if land, trees, and men alike had all been dipped in blood.

Beside him, Rann likewise looked away, meeting his gaze with clear eyes and a troubled brow. "Are you certain it's that one?" he asked dubiously. "It's not like there aren't others."

"Yes, but this one fits what little description we got out of Eddyn better than any of those," Avall told him, absently scratching an itch where what he hoped were merely dead pine needles had found their way beneath surcoat, mail, and padded gambeson.

Lykkon rattled the map he'd just unfolded. "More to the point, it's *not* on here, which is even better evidence."

"I'd say so," Avall agreed. "It was Priest-Clan that first surveyed this area. All the maps we have originated with them."

"Besides which," Rann took up, "wherever their base is, it has to be between Gem-Hold and Woodstock for them to have attacked us like that last winter. With the weather like it was, there's no way that information about our movements could've reached them in time otherwise."

"Unless they had gems," Avall shot back grimly. "They don't act like people who have them, but there's always that possibility." He shaded his eyes again, and once again looked westward.

He could see more clearly now: what their outriders had been seeking since they'd passed the ruins of Woodstock Station and entered the area where these vast uprisings of rock occurred with regularity.

And what he saw was certainly an imposing sight.

If the landscape thereabouts were a moldering corpse, with the ripples of hills and valleys representing ropes of underlying muscles, and alternating stretches of meadows and forests standing in for remnants of skin and hair upon that body; well, there were bones as well. For here and there for the last two days' travel—and at least two more in every direction—massive escarpments of native basalt poked up from the earth like stubby broken ribs, some so low one could see over them, yet extending for shots in either direction; others rising as high as the walls of Eron Gorge, yet narrow enough for a man to span with his outstretched arms. Most were in between—a shot to half a shot wide and roughly the same high.

Easily big enough to house any number of people if they were hollowed out, which the Eronese certainly knew how to do. True, there were no obvious signs of modification—no glint of windows, no smoke venting from chimneys; and any overt entrances were masked by the luxuriant stand of ancient pines that clustered around the monolith's feet—yet Avall had a feeling about it. And in recent eights he'd learned to trust such feelings.

Besides, glass could be secreted behind shutters, and even in Tir-Eron, many buildings were hollowed in rock formations that, externally, preserved their natural shape, down to placing windows only in the deepest cracks and fissures. Nor did the absence of smoke mean anything, for most of Eron—and a good hunk of the area around this possible Ninth Face citadel—was riddled with geysers, hot springs, and fumeroles, which they'd long since learned to harvest for heat. From what Eddyn had reported about his brief incarceration, there were plenty of amenities—inside. The outside, therefore, didn't matter.

Granted, Eddyn had been drugged and blindhooded when they'd taken him indoors, and again when he departed. In spite of his statements to the contrary, he might also have been drugged while within; he'd *admitted* to being drugged when he'd met the local Ninth Face Chief and told him everything he knew about Avall's gem.

Not for the first time did Avall wish he'd interrogated his cousin about the whole episode, but it wasn't as if he hadn't been occupied otherwise—recrafting that cursed helm, for one thing. Eellon and Gynn *had* questioned him, he knew—but one of them was dead in fact, the other in effect. Too, both had been heavily preoccupied at the time, so that neither had caused any details they learned to be set down. What Avall knew came mostly from talking to Eddyn in the forges. And since neither of them were friends, in spite of the common bond they'd shared at the time, those conversations had been minimal.

"Can we take it?" Lykkon murmured eventually.

"We'll have to ask those whose business it is to know such things," Avall replied.

Rann gnawed his lips thoughtfully before he spoke. "More to the point, I wonder if we should."

"I don't think so," said Vorinn syn Ferr-een. His specialty was tactics, and while he had little actual experience, for all he was twenty-seven, he had as much theoretical knowledge of the subject as anyone in Eron. Not for the first time did Avall wish he'd been available during the war. Lately, he'd attached himself to Avall almost like a third squire—after Lykkon and Bingg—when he wasn't serving as Tryffon's principal aid. Avall didn't know him well enough to consider him a true friend—he'd been absent from Tir-Eron most of the time Avall was growing up— but he held him in higher regard daily. And since he was as fond of accepting responsibilities as Avall was of delegating them, it looked as though their acquaintance would be long and profitable. For now—Avall was content to listen while those more knowledgeable than he plotted strategy.

Tryffon prodded the map with a finger and regarded the others in the tent: Avall, Rann, Lykkon, Myx, Veen, Vorinn, Preedor, and three other subchiefs from War. "And why don't you think so?"

"For any number of reasons," Vorinn replied calmly. "First, if we simply lay siege, they're operating from a position of strength—that's obvious. They command the high ground, and that's always stronger, if for no other reason than because it's easier to throw things down than throw things up. Second, we have no idea how long this place has been here, but it's clearly well-enough staffed and provisioned to put forth a force capable of capturing and securing a major hold. We could wait them out, but we'd still have to deal with Gem-Hold, which would either mean splitting our force or staying here, where we'd risk getting caught between."

"That's reasonable," Tryffon acknowledged. "But more cautious than I'd have expected from you."

"I'm only trying to present all sides of the problem," Vorinn retorted. "In any case, those weren't the only reasons. We all know that a large part of winning battles is warfare of the mind—play on the foe's ignorance or fears. And we have a problem there. The foe knows a lot about us—they'd have to. We, on the other hand, know almost nothing about them. We have no idea what we might find inside that hold. We've some reason to suspect that the Ninth Face has access to gems at least as strong as Avall's if not stronger. If they bring them to bear against us with anything like the force I understand Avall called down on Ixti, we're all doomed and might as well throw down our swords now. The fact that they *haven't* brought the battle to us, either here or in Tir-Eron, tells me that they're afraid of what *we* can bring to bear. They know Avall can call down lightning on their citadel. That we don't do so will imply any number of things and keep them guessing. What we don't need for them to know at any cost is that we don't have the regalia. If we besiege them and fail, they'll know that—or suspect it strongly enough it'll mean the same thing. If, on the other hand, we pass them by, it'll imply that we don't consider their main hold worthy of notice and can clean it out anytime we choose."

"All of which supposes they know we're here," Avall observed. "Not that I have any doubt they aren't aware by now of who we are, where we are, and how many. They'd have this place ringed with spies, just like we would if we didn't want anyone to know we existed. And they've probably got multiple bolt-holes."

"Which may be their main weakness—if we can locate one."

"*If,*" Veen huffed. "A small word with a very big meaning."

"Well, then," Tryffon concluded, "this is what I'd suggest we do. Avall's right: They have to have been following our progress for days, but since the place we're camped is a logical place to camp anyway, there's reason for them to suppose we chose it by accident, since we're not supposed to know that's their citadel—if it is. With that in mind, we act like this is any other day—as if we plan to move on tomorrow. But tonight, we send out every good tracker we have to try to spy out entrances to that place. If we find any, we let their nature determine our action. If not—much as it pains me to shirk a fight—we probably should move on. Alternately, we leave a force here to keep these folks in check, just in case."

"Sounds reasonable," Avall acknowledged. "And I can't

think of anything better, though I don't like leaving an enemy at my back."

"We can leave watchers," Vorinn assured him. "They can get word to us if anything changes. Enough folks riding out of there to cause trouble would be impossible to hide."

"In any case, we should know more tomorrow," Tryffon sighed. "Not that I don't plan to spend the whole night thinking."

"Tomorrow," Avall echoed, as he rose. "Sometimes I think I spend my whole life waiting for tomorrow."

Rann flung an arm across his shoulders. "Considering some of the 'nows' we've had, that might be just as well."

"Nows?" from Bingg, who'd been serving as page.

Lykkon regarded him tolerantly and ruffed his hair. "You know: Avall and Rann being attacked out of the blue by the Ninth Face, Rann being clubbed in the head, Avall space-jumping to where Eddyn was, which resulted in Eddyn jumping away. That moment of panic at the Battle of Storms where we didn't know who Rrath was or what his intentions were."

"Speaking of Rrath," Avall murmured. "I suppose I ought to see how he's doing."

Riff was standing guard at the tapestry-covered flap that separated Avall's private room in the royal pavilion from the adjoining tent, which enclosed the caravans that ostensibly housed the royal regalia, but in fact housed that *and* Esshill, Rrath, and his official healer. The latter was Gynn's daughter, Aleeahn, to whom Avall had promised two years' exclusion from the Fateing in exchange for her cooperation on this venture. It was a fair trade, too: less than half a year of rigidly structured life in exchange for two of freedom such as few folk her age ever enjoyed. That she'd probably spend them healing anyway had nothing to do with the bargain. In any case, it was her choice, and she'd chosen. And if that meant feigning invisibility, so be it. If worse came to worst, it would be good to have another healer among their crew. He hoped it wouldn't come to that, but if it did—well, keeping her, Esshill, Rrath, or the regalia secret wouldn't matter.

Acknowledging Riff with a nod, he entered the gloom that surrounded two identical caravans. From the outside, they looked like any others, which fiction Avall had advocated by saying it would confuse anyone who might target them while in transit and single them out for attack. One housed the regalia—and Rrath. The other provided sleeping quarters for Esshill and Aleeahn, plus additional treasure and armor. The door to Rrath's was always locked, but Avall had one of the three keys, the other two belonging to the guard-of-record, and to Tryffon and Preedor, alternately.

Taking a deep breath, he mounted the three steps before it, rapped a courtesy cadence, waited for the requisite reply, then unlocked the door and entered. Aleeahn met him there, looking tired, but glad of the company—or weary of Esshill's. Her face fell, however, when he informed her he required some time alone with her patient. Almost she started to argue, but then her gaze seemed to catch the warning glint in his eye, and she acceded. What she'd do outside, he had no idea. Probably spend it pacing around the wagons, since she was forbidden to leave the tent that enclosed them.

He was sorry to do this to her, but this was *not* a casual visit, though even his closest friends didn't know that.

No, he was acting on a notion that had come to him halfway through the strategy session, when someone had mentioned the likelihood of the Ninth Face's citadel having multiple entrances. Rrath had actually been in the place, and locked inside Rrath's mind was more knowledge of its points of access than belonged to anyone else they knew of. More to the point, locked in the *gem* was, in theory, a way to reach that information. He should've told Rann and Lykkon, he knew, for what he was about to attempt was a mighty risk for a King to take on the eve of possible battle. But his friends would only try to talk him out of it, and he was fearful enough already, without additional nay-saying. Besides, logic said he should try now, while the madness—the passion—was upon him. Didn't the gem respond to strong desire? And if his desire for information was strong enough . . .

To no surprise, Esshill was sitting at Rrath's side on the narrow sleeping pad at the caravan's farther end, staring at him in the light of a single glow-globe. Two short paces took Avall to the chair beside the bed, where Aleeahn had set aside some embroidery. He claimed her place, noting absently that the seat was still warm.

"Out," he told Esshill finally, when the lad made no move to leave. "You need the air, and I need the privacy. No harm will come to him if I can prevent it—no harm that won't also come to me, at any rate. Now, scat!"

Esshill—almost—glared at him, then nodded and padded toward the door. Avall shot the bolt from within, then gazed at Rrath in earnest.

Poor Rrath. One more memorial to Eddyn's vanity. Once, in a different life, a thousand years ago, it seemed, but not even one in fact, Avall and Rrath had—almost—been friends. Certainly they'd gotten along well enough when they were roommates during their cycle at Weaver-Hold, though the boy had always been a little too fawning.

And here they were again, this time with the fate of a kingdom riding on what transpired next.

Steeling himself, Avall fished the master gem's pendant from inside his gambeson and quickly freed the stone, letting it roll onto the coverlet beside him. He was already fumbling for the knife he used to blood himself for important workings, when he had an idea. The last time he'd worked with the gem he'd made a small amount of progress at quelling its madness—enough that he thought he might be able to sidestep it sufficiently to interact with the part that was sane. But a great deal of that success had come from wanting something passionately enough to overrule his fears, while at the same time harnessing them to his own devices. Therefore, if he was worrying about Rrath's well-being, he'd be unable to worry about his own. Which, as Veen would say, was an awfully big if.

Yet still he hesitated. How should he go about this? More than once he'd considered blooding himself and Rrath, then setting the gem between, thereby linking the three of them. Maybe he could touch Rrath's mind that way, maybe not. In any case, it put Rrath's life at risk, and Avall owed him too much already. But perhaps there was another way—something he'd never tried. Perhaps he could link with Rrath without Rrath having to himself be linked to the gem. Maybe Avall's own blood could act as a buffer between the gem and Rrath. Maybe—

There was no more *maybe*. He simply had to do it. A deep breath, and he blooded his right hand, the one he'd use to bond with the gem. But instead of picking it up, he picked up Rrath's right hand and blooded it as well, then went on to blood his own left hand. "Eight go with me," he muttered, "and Nine, too, if you care." Whereupon he closed his eyes and grasped Rrath's bleeding hand with his gemless one. Nothing happened; then again, nothing was supposed to. Another, deeper breath to calm himself, and he found the gem by feel with his right.

The gem ravened at him—as expected—pulling at him as it always did, yet at the same time warning him away. But this time there was a place to which he could flee—into Rrath's mind, with the power of the gem pouring into him, yet dragging at him as well. He'd always had a desire for escape, but now he had somewhere to go that didn't risk his truest friends. He also had someone he wanted to protect, and those feelings proved a barely viable shield against the madness. It was as if he could still see Barrax's death, but through a glass window; as if he could feel the horror of that death, but through a layer of gauze. As if he could hear Barrax's unheard cries, but from underwater. They were present, but he could ignore them. Yet even so, the gem knew what he was doing and sensed another consciousness beyond Avall's, one it was desperate to share.

Already it was prodding the walls around Rrath's mind, the gem's desires lying beside Avall's own, so that he found himself in the odd position of holding them back, helping them forward, and shielding Rrath's mind at the same time he sought to join it.

If nothing else, they had a power Avall could perhaps bring to bear to finally break those walls Rrath had erected around his actual thoughts. And Rrath was weakening.

Harder, he pushed, even as he fought against the power of the gem that still wanted to snare him and drag him down to share its madness.

Harder again—then *through*. The power came with him like a phantom pack of geens trying to shoulder through a rift in the wall around a sheepfold, yet somehow he held it back.

And found himself in Rrath's mind. The power rumbled without, yet he could ignore it—for the moment. Which might be long enough.

He wanted one thing. That was the key: wanting one thing. The wanting was power itself, and what he wanted was some key to the Ninth Face's citadel.

An image swam before his eyes for the barest instant, clear yet unrecognizable, but with it came a series of impressions—or emotions—or memories. Enough to go on—maybe.

It didn't matter anyway, for the din beyond the barrier of their joining was become like the loudest thunder. And while he could face it, Rrath could not, nor could Avall defend him.

But Rrath had a power of his own, it seemed, or at least some sense of desire that his mind remain unscathed, and that alone propelled Avall past the madness that waited without. For a moment he felt nothing at all—absolutely *nothing,* as if he had briefly ceased to exist, in truth. And in the instant of panic that followed, he let go the gem—and found himself back in his own mind.

He must have fallen, for something hard smacked into his back, hip, and shoulder, knocking a number of boxes free to spill noisily on the floor amid the sound of splintering wood and clanging metal.

For a long moment he lay there panting, shivering, as chill after chill wracked his body. Still, he'd learned what he came for—he thought. But then he realized that he'd put Rrath through an ordeal he might not have survived. Those weren't *his* teeth chattering, they were Rrath's. And the gem had probably drawn on Aleeahn, Esshill, and Riff as well.

And—

He blinked, and looked around the gloom. The glow-globe had disappeared, so that the only light came from an unlikely direction: the doorway to his left.

Except, he realized, as every hair on his body stood erect, there *was* no doorway—any more than there was a caravan to contain one. There was the rug that should've been on the floor, covered with a number of fallen boxes, along with Avall's chair—and a vaulted, stone-paved, rock-walled corridor lit with tiny glow-globes leading off to the left.

He closed his eyes, counted three, and opened them again, saw exactly the same thing, then finally dared to check the right. Rrath still lay there, still atop the sleeping pad that had rested, in turn, atop the strongbox that held the regalia. But where the back wall should've been was only more corridor. Aside from a few bits and pieces, the caravan itself was gone.

No, Avall corrected himself, the caravan wasn't gone, *he* was. He had somehow space-jumped himself, Rrath, and their immediate environment somewhere else. The question was, where were they?

CHAPTER XXII:

MIDNIGHT EXCURSION

(NORTHWESTERN ERON—HIGH SUMMER: DAY LXII—EARLY EVENING)

Where was he indeed? As another chill shook Avall.

But then it came to him: a memory that was not his own, imposing itself on his consciousness like a veil of sylk on which someone had painted the requisite image. This was the route by which Rrath had left the Ninth Face's citadel. Which meant Avall had succeeded beyond his wildest dreams.

Except that he was trapped here with an unconscious man, and had no idea which way was out.

Another chill racked him. He was in *serious* trouble, a situation further complicated by the fact that he also had no idea whether this exit was guarded and when he could expect to be discovered. He'd completely bypassed any actual portal, which made him think that Rrath had not been allowed to see it, either; that *this* was the last thing the troublesome Priest had actually seen—a supposition reinforced by a feeling that was not quite a memory.

So, what did he do now?

Get out, if he was wise. In any case, he couldn't remain here, yet there wasn't much hope of moving Rrath. Which left one viable option, which was to explore a short distance either way and hope that presented more choices. If he knew Aleeahn and Esshill, they'd already figured out something was amiss and alerted Riff, who'd alert Rann, and so up the chain of command. A rescue attempt was surely in process at that very moment.

Of course they wouldn't know where to go, which put him back where he'd been: sitting in the near dark with an unconscious man and a strongbox full of functional but mundane armor.

Armor . . .

He was in the enemy's stronghold and that enemy was bound to discover him eventually, so he'd best be armed against that eventuality. And if the enemy also happened to think they faced the Lightning Sword—well, so much the better.

As for Rrath—he'd help him if he could, but if he had to be abandoned, this was as good a place as any, Esshill's probable protests notwithstanding.

And time was wasting.

Moving as quietly as he could, Avall eased Rrath far enough aside to reach the lock that sealed the strongbox. Fortunately, he had the key with him, and inserted it quickly. A panel in front clicked free, and Avall wasted no time reaching inside to retrieve the armor. Fortunately, too, he'd already been clad in a fair bit of war gear, including gambeson and light mail under a surcoat, so that he didn't feel unprotected or out of balance when he'd quickly donned the rest. For though the sword, helm, and shield were not the actual, magical ones, they were nevertheless fully functional in their purposes, and made of quality materials. Only the visible surfaces—cast from the originals, and to a very trained eye not so finely worked—were different, and that only when one had both sets to compare. Avall doubted even the smiths among the Ninth Face could tell this set from the originals. There were even gems fixed where they should be: clever fakes Avall had found among the Citadel's hoard of gems. He wished he'd been in a position to wheedle better ones from Gem or Glass, but that would've meant revealing his duplicity to other parties, and there were too many involved already.

Besides, he still had the real one—the master gem—which he restored to its case before returning it to its accustomed place around his neck. It occurred to him then that he could use it now, to attempt to jump himself back outside. But that might mean leaving Rrath, and—more to the point—he'd come this far; it would be a shame not to learn what he could while he had the opportunity.

A final check showed that Rrath was as safe as circumstances allowed, and Avall uttered a silent "sorry," followed by a brief prayer to that aspect of Fate known as the Lord of Fools, then set out in the direction that wasn't blocked by Rrath and the heavy iron strongbox.

The corridor was still deserted, which he found both encouraging and disconcerting, given that he was all but certain that the inhabitants of this fastness knew that Eron's army was camped on their doorsteps pretending their foe was nowhere about. On the other hand, any guard stationed here would have to endure long hours in near darkness or else betray his existence with light—which might also betray the entrance along with it.

Which didn't mean there wouldn't be guards farther on.

No, a memory that was not his own supplied. *This way is sacred. The locks are beyond the caverns.*

Caverns?

The Caverns of the Well, came that unheard reply. But when he sought more information, it was gone.

In any case, he had to hurry. As quietly as he could manage in war boots on hard stone, he trotted along the corridor, noting absently that it was too narrow to swing a sword in—which would hamper friend and foe alike. It also ran dead level, and the floor and walls were neatly squared, while the ceiling—half a span above his head—was a simple barrel vault.

It was hot, too, and clammy, like the air around a hot-bath. Unfortunately, it made him sweat, and perspiration was soon stinging his eyes in spite of the coif beneath his helm. Still, he moved on, increasingly aware of a subtle roar from somewhere ahead. The sound had a liquid quality, he noted, and he felt a jolt of genuine fear when he recalled how rife the area around the monolith had been with geysers and fumeroles. Being boiled alive by a sudden outrush of scalding water was not his idea of a glorious demise.

He continued for maybe two shots, alert at every moment for other passages or traps. He found none, or else he didn't trip them. And then the corridor turned a corner and the feeble light of the glow-globes revealed an open archway ahead, leading to a place lit by a marginally stronger light. He slowed abruptly, feeling his heart start to pound and his blood to race, letting his steps fall as lightly as possible while still maintaining a reasonable pace. The helm made hearing difficult, but he did catch the sounds of water far more clearly—water running, water rising and falling like fountains, water condensing and dripping from a roof. There was water underfoot, too— a little—courtesy of a trickle that issued from beyond the arch.

"Eight go with me," he murmured and stepped from the tunnel into what lay beyond.

A cavern, so it proved—or an immense low-ceilinged chamber that had been hewn from the stone so long ago it was indistinguishable from a natural hollowing. Steam filled the farther reaches so thickly it was like the densest winter fog, but in spite of that, it was possible to see pillars rising from the floor where drippings from the ceiling teased them into stubby stumps. The ceiling was prickly with stone spikes, some thinner than his smallest finger, some thicker than his body. Here and there spikes met pillars and made columns. Sheets of water glistened in low places, some puddles smaller than a footprint, some sheets the limits of which he couldn't see.

How *was* he seeing, anyway? But then he noticed that more glow-globes nested like clutches of eggs among those pillars: added proof he was near habitation.

But how did he go up? Anything worth the risk he was taking would be learned in the hold proper, not here.

Yet he lingered. He was getting sleepy, he realized, which surprised him, given that he'd drunk most of a pot of cauf during that last council session, never mind that fear—or anticipation—alone should sustain alertness.

Still, it wouldn't hurt to rest a moment, and with that in mind he slumped down on a convenient shelf thrust out from a particularly thick pillar. A yawn ambushed him, then another. He fought them off and stood again. Blinking, he saw something he'd missed before: a particularly large cluster of globes beside a pool three spans ahead and to the right. Curiosity got the better of him, and he remembered what Rrath had "said" about this being the Cavern of the Well. And since he *was* King, and part of his duty as King was to drink from the Wells on the Isle of The Eight, was it not therefore his duty to investigate other Wells when he came upon them?

Five breaths later, he stood beside it, looking down. Though no efforts had been made to change its shape, the area around this gleaming span of water had been smoothed flat, then strewn with soft white sand into which symbols had been incised, probably with a finger. Footprints showed there as well, most bare, but one set booted, and there was also a single handprint. Finally, there was a kind of chair, carved from one of the drip-stone pillars. A chalice sat beside it. Good work, by a smith who'd flourished two centuries back, if Avall wasn't mistaken. Impulsively, he sat down there. Perhaps that would give him some insight into the motivations of the masters of this place. Who were they, anyway, this Ninth Face? When had they splintered away from their master clan? How large were they? They seemed an elite brotherhood, rather like the Night Guard, save that there were more of them. And what were their motivations? Altruism or selfishness? Priest-Clan, though increasingly political, still did far more good than evil. Maybe he was wrong to confront them. Maybe he really should try to parley.

He just didn't know. He had no idea how they thought, these men—and women, he presumed. But if there was a Ninth Face, then that Face had to have a Well, and this was the logical place for that Well to be. And if there was a Well here, it stood to reason the Chief of this place drank from it for the same reason other Priests drank from theirs. As did Avall, when he was Avatar of The Eight. The presence of the goblet beside this Well all but confirmed that supposition. And the best way Avall could imagine to understand the Ninth Face was to drink what the Chief of the Ninth Face drank.

Steeling himself, and aware at some level that what he was about to undertake was foolish in the extreme, he filled the goblet and—after studying it a moment—raised it to where his lips were framed by openings in the helm.

The water—if that's what it was—tasted like cold metal, and it froze his throat, so that he had to fight to swallow—even to breathe, almost. It was unlike any previous sampling he'd experienced, yet exactly like them. It also invoked a euphoria not unlike that produced by working with the gems, as though time simultaneously slowed and expanded.

He *was* expanding, too; he could see everything in the cavern at once, from all angles—and *that* was more than his mind could encompass. Desperate, he clamped his eyelids shut, slapping a hand across them while the other dropped the goblet. He heard it hit the sand after an eternity of falling, and the sound was like a thousand tiny gongs being struck as one. Their ringing was at once immense enough to be deafening and too minute to be heard.

But he could still see, dammit! The only difference was that he now saw the landscape *behind* his eyes. And it *was* a landscape, too, for the thready lines of vessels had twisted into rivers, and the places where they met had become lakes, the tiny folds of his irises hills and mountain ranges. He was falling toward one of those lakes, he realized, falling faster and faster . . .

Then floating, as though he were a bird locked in a steady glide over some place his waking body had never seen.

He saw water—a lake, almost perfectly round, with an island in the center raising an equally perfect cone to heavens less
blue than that water. And he saw cliffs around it—of a height
so even that they resembled the top of a tower. Those walls were
pocked and fissured with caves, and ringed with concentric ter-
races, but little vegetation grew there. Beyond, if he banked
higher, he could just make out what he assumed was the sea.

Yet what truly impressed him—what made him want to
stop where he was and circle there forever—was the feeling of
warmth and peace that emanated from that place. A warmth
that was a balm to one born to rule a frigid land, a peace such
as he had never known.

Maybe he'd found it. Maybe he could stay there forever, cir-
cling, looking down on another series of circles: land around
water around land.

Like an eye in the earth. The World's Eye, he would call it,
if he ever found that place. For he had no doubt whatever that
somewhere in Eron it existed.

And then that eye blinked—and reality exploded.

The rattle of a lock somewhere behind him was like the
endless rattle of summer storms in the highest mountains: a
threat that demanded man and beast alike take shelter. The
scraping of the door against the jamb was like an earthquake.
He could feel the seat tremble beneath him, even where he sat.

The air that found him when it opened was like the gales of
winter, and the voices that rode with it were like bells and
lightning blasts amid a windstorm's thunder.

Yet somehow those words made sense.

"There . . . he . . . is . . ."

"I . . . told . . . you . . . there . . . was . . . an . . . invader."

Invader . . .

That word rang loudest in Avall's ears. And that part of
him that was not still seeking vainly after his vision of peace reminded him that the invader in question was probably him,
which meant he'd been discovered, and that what one normally did in such situations was run.

Slowly, as it seemed. As it seemed to take years to snare his shield and sword from beside the chair, where he didn't recall discarding them.

Somehow, he found his feet, and with every thunderous footfall he seemed to run more slowly, while every clap of thunder his boots produced made his head hurt worse, though with each pulse of pain, his vision—and mind—clarified.

Whether he had, in fact, been sought out and located, or had simply been chanced upon, he had no idea. All he knew was that he was in the enemy's citadel, being pursued by that same enemy.

They seemed to be holding back, however.

Probably because, among the many words he could hear his pursuers shouting, was the phrase "wearing the magic armor"— and, more troubling in its implications—"summon the others" and "can't let him escape."

So they thought he was wearing the magic armor? Good, that was his intent; perhaps he could turn it to his advantage. He had a head start already, had indeed reached the entrance to the tunnel by which he'd first come there. Which was the last place he could easily wield his sword. And so he stopped in front of the arch, drew his blade, whirled around in place, and yelled at the top of his lungs, "Stay where you are or face the lightning!"

And in that pause he got his first glimpse of his pursuers. Though their shapes were obscured by the pervasive steam, he could still make out that there were more of them than he'd thought, all in blue surcoats, but also with mail glittering here and there, some in helms, some without, as though they'd donned them quickly.

They were also slowing down, faces tense with uncertainty. Which was all the excuse he needed. "You are wise!" he shouted, then turned and fled into the tunnel. Only when he'd gone twenty strides did he realize that his eyes weren't adjusting well to the relative lack of light, and that darkness was, in fact, closing in. Yet still he ran, though he slipped and slid far too often and banged his shoulders painfully against the wall.

At first he heard no pursuit, but then ears still keen from the remnants of the Well's enhancement caught the sound of booted feet on stone, and another voice in the forefront yelling, "If he calls the lightning here, he will doom himself with us. Catch him before he reaches the shaft."

That was enough for Avall. Clutching his sword to his side, he ran as fast as he ever had in his life.

On and on and on, and finally he saw the clutter of objects that marked the place of his arrival. Which probably meant that the actual exit lay beyond. So did he stop here, defend Rrath, and risk everything he'd learned and planned? Or did he cut his losses and abandon Rrath to those who might be able to help him more than Avall could, and who would learn nothing more from him than they knew already?

Reflex decided, as much as intellect. He half scrambled, half leapt across Rrath, and continued on, even as his conscience nagged at him for twice abandoning Rrath to possible doom.

But maybe Rrath would slow those who pursued him enough to permit escape. If that was even possible.

In any case, the corridor continued on, and so did Avall, maintaining a steady trot past stonework that didn't change. And then he saw a different light ahead—the light of two moons filtering down what looked to be a shaft leading upward. Hope made him redouble his pace, and he sheathed his sword while he ran. Briefly, he considered abandoning the shield entirely, but his foes would have it then, and the entire masquerade would dissolve if they determined it wasn't magic. For they'd realize that there was no way he'd discard it if it was.

Which meant he'd have to wear it on his back, like a turtle's shell. He was already shrugging out of it when he reached the bottom of what proved to be a stone-walled well, with spikes driven into the walls at exactly the right intervals to serve as hand- and footholds. And while his pursuit had not ceased, neither had it grown closer. Desperate for haste, he fumbled with a shield strap that had caught on the wrist guard of a gauntlet. But then it was free and sliding off, and he slung it onto his back one-handed, praying that the catches would hold as he began to climb.

It was hard going, yet the spikes were spaced so that his legs did most of the work while his hands merely served for balance. In spite of his haste, his foes had reached the bottom before he reached the surface. A chill hit him abruptly—hard. *Maybe they had bows!* Lethal little crossbows, probably. Maybe any moment he'd feel a bolt lodge in his back, hips, or thighs. Or worse, given their angle of attack.

He pushed harder, breath loud within his helm, while sweat threatened to blind him.

But the opening above was growing larger, only to be obscured by two faces looking down. "He's coming," someone yelled. "And not alone."

Rann, he realized. *Rann.*

In spite of his situation, anger flared through him. Rann (and probably Lykkon) had somehow found him—and by so doing, placed themselves at risk. But hard on the heels of that emotion came a mix of relief and panic that almost made him physically ill.

Hands grabbed him as soon as he came in range, hauling him upward so quickly he nearly lost his grip and fell. A spike jabbed his thigh. Another raked his belly, ripping his surcoat and snagging on the mail beneath. He kicked outward, found surer purchase with his boots and half climbed, half dived the rest of the way over what proved to be the rim of one of the fumeroles that pocked the landscape thereabouts.

Abruptly, he was face-to-face with Rann and Lykkon—in full armor—with another twenty Royal Guardsmen—hastily assembled, to judge by their disheveled appearance, but likewise armed and armored—standing close at hand. Avall had never been so glad to see soldiers in his life.

For a moment he stood there swaying, then found his balance. "Pursued," he gasped. And was relieved to see a dozen swords and almost as many crossbows flash into the moonlight from the surrounding cover. It would be easy now; they could pick off his pursuers as they emerged.

But they did *not* emerge. More than enough time had elapsed, and Avall was on the verge of easing forward to look down the shaft again when disaster struck.

A crossbow quarrel took the man beside Lykkon in the belly, even as he started forward. Another swished past Avall's chin so close he felt the fletching against his flesh. "Attack!" someone yelled. "Behind us!"

"All *around* us!" someone else cried.

Avall had just time to unsheathe his sword and to note that their foes numbered twice their own number before the attack began in earnest. "Out of other holes," Rann spat beside him. "We should've looked. We should've known."

And then there was no more time for analysis. Someone in a blue surcoat was running straight toward him—no, *two* someones—rushing in from either side, past his confused Guard. They were unarmed, so he thought—until, too late, he realized that the dark mass they clutched before them was a net. The first cast merely tangled his sword arm; the next enclosed him neatly.

Avall struggled frantically, even as those men bore him back toward the shaft from which he'd just emerged. His helm slipped enough to block vision from one eye, but with the other he could see his Guard, one by one, cut down. "Rann!" he yelled desperately. "Lykkon!"

Maybe they heard. He didn't know. All he knew was that reality was spinning, his balance was out of kilter, and very large men were trying with all their strength to wrestle him down. More bolts swished. Men cried out and swore. Arrows thudded. Metal belled against metal, and at least one full-fledged sword duel was in progress, to judge by the sounds of combat.

He'd been a fool. He'd tried something stupid, and now he was caught and there was nothing he could do to alleviate the situation. And he desperately wanted out, away. And if he bloodied the gem, he might well manage that. Desperately, he fumbled at the chain around his throat. If he could crush the glass with the gauntlets, maybe he still had a chance. Maybe.

It was no use. His efforts only entangled him worse, and one of his captors saw—or suspected—what he was about and dragged his arm back with such force he feared it was dislocated. He gasped but did not cry out. He was still who he was, after all. King of all Eron. And more to the point, Avall syn Argen-a.

They'd ringed him now: a circle of tall men in blue surcoats— maybe fifteen, if he guessed correctly. More than enough right there to give his Guard a hard time. His only hope was that Rann and Lykkon had escaped. And that Riff, Myx, and Veen had not been involved.

And then it didn't matter, because someone clamped a cloth soaked in some kind of fluid over his face. It smelled like imphor, only a thousand times stronger. He fought it, but there was no way to pinch his nostrils closed, so he tried to take shallow breaths—until someone punched him smartly in the stomach, and he exhaled. The ensuing gasps were more than enough to take him away from himself into a place where there was neither dark nor light.

When reality returned, Avall found himself on horseback. Someone had bound him, blindhooded, into a saddle, with his feet firmly trussed into the stirrups and his hands tied around the saddle horn. As best he could tell through muddled senses and an aching head, he still wore mail—but the helm, shield, and sword were gone. Horses pounded along to either side at close to full gallop, which said a lot for their riders' horsemanship—and for whoever had trained the mount he rode, which seemed to match their moves precisely.

They were traversing woods—by the sound of hooves on leafy ground. But they seemed also to be on a path, else they'd not be able to make so much haste. Others rode around him, moving steadily onward. To where, he had no idea. He only hoped his army was intact enough to follow.

From what little he'd heard from his new companions, he wasn't certain. The force that had captured him had not been the only one; another had attacked the camp. Beyond that, he knew nothing. Nor wanted to know, just now. And so, tied there in the saddle, he slept. Or passed out. For him, at that moment, it didn't matter.

"I'll raze that place to the ground!" Rann raged, flinging his helm on the table in the royal strategy tent. He would, too, as soon as—well, as soon as he could get a counteroffensive mounted. He should be out there now, leading a force to take that pile of rock apart—grain by grain, if he had to.

"Maybe so," Lykkon murmured, laying an arm across Rann's shoulders and drawing him to his usual seat at the council table—the one to the right of Avall's empty one. "But not now," he continued. "Not until we can take stock—"

Rann flung the arm away. "Stock of what? My bond-brother's taken captive. Half his Guard are dead or wounded. I shouldn't be alive and neither should you. And"—he sniffed the air for emphasis—"the camp's on fire."

Only then did he pause in his rant to take true stock of who else joined him there. They seemed to have assembled of their own will, having seen to their various duties. Tryffon, Preedor, and Vorinn of War; Veen, Riff and Myx, himself, Lykkon and Bingg, and one or two others.

Veen shook her head. "The fires in camp have been put out. It wasn't much of a raid, actually. In fact, as best I can tell, it was mostly a feint to draw our attention from what I can only assume was a calculated attempt to capture Avall."

"Effort, my ass!" Rann spat. "They *did* capture him—and threw him on a horse and rode away with him before any of us managed so much as a shot."

"It was very well orchestrated," Tryffon agreed. "They have to have had us under close observation."

"Then why didn't they capture Avall when he wound up underground, if they knew he was down there?"

Tryffon stroked his beard. "I don't *know,* Rann. It was a rash—a crazy—thing to do. They can't have been expecting him to do anything quite like that. They also had good reason to think he was wearing the Lightning Sword, and I guess they assumed it was foolish to stand against that."

"The same way," Vorinn continued calmly, "that they knew it was foolish to attack our army with any real intent to defeat us."

"How so?"

"Because we almost certainly outnumber them." Vorinn paused and produced a sheet covered with tightly spaced but very neat figures. "I've been doing some ciphering. It's easy enough to guess the basic dimensions of their citadel. Based on analogy to other structures, we can make a rough guess as to how many rooms the place contains and how many of those are barracks. They'll have read the same manuals we have regarding such things, and I don't think they'll depart from them much, since men who are comfortable tend to be happier than those who aren't. Therefore, the place can't have been crammed to capacity, so that leaves us with a finite number it could actually hold. Subtract the number we think would be needed to subdue Gem, and we're left with a force maybe a tenth our size. And obviously not all of them took part in the attack."

"So you agree that the attack on the camp was a ploy?"

Vorinn nodded. "Put together on the spur of the moment

once they realized Avall had all but walked into their hands." He glanced sideways at Tryffon, whom he'd effectively contradicted.

Rann pounded the table—hard. "And I'll never forgive myself, either."

Preedor regarded him tolerantly. "It could've been worse," he observed. "If that link you lads share hadn't alerted you that something was wrong and given us a notion of where he was, which at least gave us time to make a stab at protecting him—"

"*What?*" Rann snapped. "He'd still be here? I don't think so! The first torches were already being thrown when Riff caught up with me. I couldn't find anyone—"

"Enough," Preedor said quietly, but the force of his personality silenced the assembly. "I was going to say that if you hadn't gone out there, we'd have even less idea how to proceed than we do now. They threw him on a horse and rode west, correct? They did *not* take him into the hold, that much is clear. That tells us two things. It tells us that whoever is in charge of this enterprise is probably at Gem-Hold; and it tells us that whatever stand they intend to make, they don't plan to make it here."

Tryffon nodded. "I think they've written this place off, frankly. Which implies that they have other bolt-holes. But I think that if we follow the route Avall took into that place, we'd find it all but deserted. We already know there are several ways out just in the field of fumeroles. There have to be others."

"At least one of which has to be large enough to accommodate horses," Riff noted. "We really should put a ring of scouts around the place."

"Several rings," Vorinn corrected, "if we're going to do that at all—which I think is like pouring drink from a broken bottle. In any case, we have no idea how far outside the hold itself such an exit might be. The one at War-Hold was almost a shot."

Rann glared at him, though he had no reason to. "So what

you're saying is that there's no sense staying here to besiege what may now be an empty citadel, when we now have two reasons to proceed to Gem?"

Vorinn fixed him with a calm, if compassionate, stare. "That's exactly what I'm saying. And another thing I'm going to say, though I may be out of line. They won't kill Avall as long as he's King and they have—or think they have—the armor. They'll want him to explain how it works, and he won't. He'll know we're out to rescue him, and that will give him strength to endure . . . whatever they do to him."

"They can do a lot!" Rann shot back. "Avall could still be alive and not have even one of his fingers. We've already seen their thinking about that. But if they really want to hurt him, they'll do it in a way that hurts forever."

"Oh, Eight!" Bingg groaned in the corner, then blushed furiously. Rann spared him a glance. The boy, though he fought very hard against it, was crying.

And that did it. Oblivious to the powerful men and women gathered round him, Rann likewise buried his face in his folded arms and wept. Lykkon was there in an instant, holding him, as was Myx, from the other side. The rest—he could feel their tolerant stares as though he actually saw them. Probably some of them were misty, too. For not one of them didn't have—or once have—a beloved bond-mate.

Finally, Preedor cleared his throat. "Rann," he began softly, "you were his second because he trusted you and you knew his mind and had actually met the Ninth Face. But I'm telling you nothing you don't know when I say, that for what may be coming up, you might not be the best commander."

"No," Rann managed. "I wouldn't be. I assumed Tryffon—"

Tryffon cleared his throat in turn. "It should be me in theory, but in fact there's someone better qualified to lead this army."

Rann looked up, blinking, startled and confused.

Tryffon smiled at him, then shifted his gaze to the right. "Vorinn has the best grasp of the minutiae of campaigns like this I've ever seen. He thinks well on his feet and he's charismatic. I know Avall was already talking of making him subcommander."

Rann shifted his gaze to the young man beside him. He was sitting there completely unself-consciously, neither beaming with pride nor denying the praise they'd already heaped upon him. Impervious: That was a good word for him. And thorough. He *would* make an excellent commander. And since he was from War-Hold already, as well as being brother-in-law to the King, he effectively united two potentially disparate factions: the royal party and Warcraft. Preedor was too old for actual battle, he freely admitted. And Tryffon was a better fighter than strategist—which deficiency he likewise acknowledged. But since they'd known Vorinn for years, they'd have no qualms about calling him down if need be. And Vorinn would know to a fine degree what they knew about this or that, and what they didn't.

"Well," Rann managed through a troubled grin, extending a hand to Vorinn, "it would seem that this army has a new commander."

"As you will," Vorinn replied calmly. "But only on one condition."

"What's that?"

"That in Avall's absence, you'll serve as Regent here in the camp."

"That's preposterous!"

"Is it?" Tryffon countered. "You're more a soldier than Avall was when we made him King, and he's done a fine job for one so young and indisposed to ruling. You know more about the gems than anyone here except maybe Lykkon, and half of what he knows is theoretical. You've been inside Gem-Hold more recently than the rest of us; you've actually met the Ninth Face, however briefly; and you represent a powerful clan and craft in your own right—and without Avall to lead it, the army will want proof that this is not simply a Warcraft venture. You're also—"

Rann silenced him with a raised hand. "Fine," he conceded. "You've convinced me—if for no other reason than because it'll put me in the best position to effect Avall's recovery." A pause, then: "Now: If I'm to be . . . Regent, I have a couple of orders to give. I have no idea what time it is, but I want a full report of damage and casualties delivered to me at sunrise. I intend to sleep until then, if I can. And I'd advise the rest of you to get some sleep as well. Because a hand *after* sunrise, we're riding out of here to rescue the King of Eron."

"Eron!" Tryffon cried, rising.

"Eron!" Preedor and Vorinn echoed as one, also on their feet.

"Eron!" the rest yelled in unison.

"Eron!" Rann shouted with them, at the top of his lungs. "And Avall!"

CHAPTER XXIII:

TREPIDATION

Zeff twisted the key in the lock and regarded Ahfinn sourly. "He didn't look much like a King, did he?" he said, after a moment. His gaze swept the empty corridor, noting the guards at either end and the additional barred archways beyond. Who— or what—Gem-Hold had expected this nice little suite of dungeons to restrain, he had no idea, but he was desperately grateful they were present. Save for the fact that they were windowless, they weren't much worse than some students' cells he'd seen. That and the fact that they were utterly devoid of anything that could be used to effect escape.

"What *does* a King look like, I wonder," Ahfinn replied amiably. "Put any High Clan man you know in a plain robe and house-hose and I defy you to tell the difference."

"Kings *should* be different, though," Zeff shot back, starting up the corridor toward the nearest guard station. "Not in face or figure, necessarily; or even age—we've had Sovereigns younger than Avall, though not in a while—but in bearing. In the look in their eyes."

"And how do Avall's eyes look?"

"Like yours or mine, except that he squints a little. That

could be the drugs, of course. Or all that complex metalwork he does."

"He could see well enough to defeat Barrax."

"Barrax's *surrogate*," Zeff corrected. "And he had help. He had that wretched regalia."

"Which we have now."

Zeff scowled and hissed Ahfinn to silence. What did his secretary mean, discussing such things where the guards could overhear? Equals, the fellows of the Ninth Face might be, but some were more equal than others; and the fewer who knew what lay locked in the table-safe in what had been Hold-Warden Crim's quarters, the better. Too many knew about the gem already—because too many had been there when Sian, who'd commanded the party that had captured the King, had fished it from inside the King's tunic.

It had been an afterthought, he conceded—and a potentially deadly mistake. They'd known to secure the regalia as soon as they'd set Avall's Guards to rout. And trapped as he was, it had been fairly easy to divest him of it. As to why Avall hadn't used it, Zeff wasn't certain, but had a pretty good idea, which centered around the fact that, from what he'd heard reported by certain spies at the Battle of Storms, the regalia worked as an ensemble, and all three pieces had to be activated. Avall hadn't had time to don the shield before he'd been overpowered. That was what Zeff was choosing to believe, in any case.

They'd reached the gate by then. "Out," he barked to the guard by the lock. He didn't recognize the . . . woman, this time, for she wore the same mouth-mask the rest of the Ninth Face did. But he did recognize quick and efficient execution of commands, which she summarily performed after looking at him keenly, as though she suspected Avall had taken his place and was even now escaping.

Ahfinn had been infected by her example, too, and was now proceeding in the silence appropriate to his station. And while

Zeff knew the lad was seething with questions, he also knew he'd let them wait until he had a more suitable time to voice them.

Too many of them, sometimes; for curiosity could be a dangerous virtue or an innocuous vice. Certainly Rrath had evinced both extremes. Zeff wondered what he should do with *that* troublesome little neophyte. The force that had first pursued Avall had retrieved him, of course, and brought him here as they cleared out that citadel. But beyond that—well, who knew what would become of the unfortunate lad. Death, if he was lucky, since he'd had the bad grace to betray both his clan and his King.

Far more troubling was how they'd found him: in bed in the middle of one of the exit tunnels, surrounded by a smattering of boxes, all atop a rug. It was completely irrational, is what it was. Nor was Avall saying anything.

Zeff was still pondering that conundrum, when he reached the stairs that led up to the level on which his suite lay. For a moment, he contemplated the beauty of the mosaics that lined this particular corridor. But only until he turned the last corner and saw the door to the suite ahead, and, beside it, a figure in distressingly dirty Ninth Face livery.

A messenger, it evolved. Straight from the Wild that moment with the latest intelligence on the progress of the Royal Army.

"They're still advancing," the youth told Zeff, once the ritual drink had been offered and accepted. "They're moving slowly because there are so many of them, and because they're taking extra care to scout every shot before they enter it—but they *are* still advancing. They apparently do very nicely without their King."

"He was a figurehead, anyway," Zeff spat. "He yea-said everything War told him."

"I'm not so sure about that," Ahfinn offered. "From what I've heard of this Vorinn—"

Zeff rounded on him. "And what *have* you heard?"

"That he's got the levelest head in his clan, and that he's also one of their best all-around . . . warriors, I guess."

"Then why haven't we heard more about him?"

"Because he's spent the last two years as War's subchief in North Gorge, except for a stint at Brewing. That's how he missed the war. I understand he was mightily peeved about that. It would also explain his thirst for battle."

"If he's the strategist that rumor suggests," Zeff snorted, "it would likewise explain why they didn't attack our citadel."

Ahfinn raised an eyebrow, looking confused.

"Because it would take more effort than it was worth," Zeff explained tolerantly. "And increase the odds that we'd either make good on our threat to destroy this place—which we probably still will—or that we'd contrive weapons even better than his."

Ahfinn nodded sagely, which looked rather silly and affected on someone his age. "Have you any other thoughts on that? The regalia, I mean. On why he didn't use it against us? Either as an aid to spying, or when he was attacked?"

"Because he hoped to negotiate, I suspect," Zeff sighed. "Avall's like most of us: He'd prefer to avoid confrontation if he can manage it. I wouldn't be at all surprised if he hadn't planned to arrive here at a carefully chosen time in full panoply and threaten to bring this place down around our ears if we didn't surrender. We won't, of course, but he'd have been counting on the effect the mere notion of confronting the sword would have on our troops. In other words, he'd have tried, first of all, to prompt defections if not actual rebellion."

"Is that what you think he'd have done? Or what you'd have done in his place?"

Zeff fixed Ahfinn with a glare that could've melted the goblet in his hand. "I will concede that Avall is the best goldsmith in generations. But I will not concede that he is, or is likely to be, anything more than an indifferent King. The problem is that he's young enough, smart enough, and reckless enough to question things. And questions are the enemy of equilibrium, therefore our enemy as well."

"As you say, Lord."

Zeff quaffed his wine, and only then remembered that the messenger was still present. "You heard none of this," he snapped. "*None* of it. You may think what you will, but your tongue, young sir, is mine."

The messenger nodded, wide-eyed. And looked mightily relieved when Zeff dismissed him with a wave of his hand.

Would that he could dismiss Ahfinn so easily. Yet for all his flaws, the lad had a good head for exactly the kind of minutiae that Zeff's position generated so copiously, but which were too dull or time-consuming to trouble a commander. The problem was, he never knew when he would need Ahfinn's services. Too, the lad did make a good sounding board, though Zeff was probably letting him see too many of his flaws.

"The regalia," Ahfinn asked boldly. "What about it?"

"What do you mean?"

"I assume you're going to try it on. You were imagining Avall wearing it to lead an attack against this place. I was imagining his army arriving to see *you* clad in it, threatening to call down lightning on them all!"

"It's an amusing image, I'll admit," Zeff chuckled. "And I will tell you this much. It isn't cowardice makes me delay donning it; it's circumspection. We know almost nothing of how the magic is triggered. And if we act from ignorance, we could undo everything we've accomplished."

"In other words—"

"In other words, if *Avall* risked capture rather than use it, *we* would be well served to be very cautious indeed."

"Indeed," Ahfinn echoed solemnly. "Indeed."

CHAPTER XXIV:

MEN AND HORSES

(SOUTHERN ERON—HIGH SUMMER: DAY LXV—AFTERNOON)

Merryn had discovered one of the disadvantages to having been a member-in-training of the Night Guard: that training, in effect, never left you. One of the Guard's stated goals had always been to subdue the enemy without harming him or her, which had included a fair bit of schooling in unarmed combat as well as instruction in securing a foe once he'd been defeated. Unfortunately, her tutor for all that had been Krynneth. The same Krynneth who, though clearly dancing close with madness, nevertheless had known enough to subdue her and keep her that way for the last five days.

Which was not to say he was inconsiderate or that she was uncomfortable—as much as she could be comfortable with her wrists bound before her by day, and behind her back at night—and with her ankles hobbled.

She walked because Krynneth did. *Why* Krynneth walked, she had no idea, save that riding might remind him too much of that mad ride he'd made back in the winter to report the fall of War-Hold to a startled King of Eron. He'd killed two mounts under him, then; perhaps that had been enough. Perhaps he now assumed he owed horsekind a favor. She was probably lucky he'd bothered to keep Boot, the packhorse. Then again, Boot carried the regalia, among other things. And Krynneth dared not let her touch it, nor would he wear it himself. She knew that much without asking.

"It calls fire," he kept saying, over and over. "I've had enough fire to last a lifetime." He'd sounded completely sane, too. Only his words were mad.

She stared at his back as they marched along. West, as it happened, following the spine of a mountain spur that ran just above the timberline, so that they navigated a sort of alpine meadow covered with knee-high gorse mingled with heather. They traveled below the ridge, however, once more in accordance with training. It didn't do to be visible against the sky if one was expecting enemies.

Krynneth was—though he wouldn't specify who. The burners, she supposed, which was to say the Ixtian army. But there was no cause to fear them here, and if he was sane enough to survive in the Wild, he ought also to be sane enough to understand that.

In any case, she was still fulfilling her quest—in a way. She'd planned to go west anyway, and that was where they were tending. And if swinging south to Ixti had ever truly been an option, it was becoming less so every hand. Sometimes, she reflected, it was good to have decisions made for one.

Eventually, too, Krynneth would drop his guard and she'd regain the upper hand. What she'd do then, with a crazy man in the Wild, she had no idea. And the trouble was, he was also a friend—someone she could've loved, frankly. Which meant she could neither abandon him nor kill him outright; her conscience wouldn't let her. And The Eight knew she had guilt enough already.

Meanwhile, and much to her chagrin, she was as content as a prisoner could be. But that didn't mean she didn't watch every move intently, or that she ever stopped plotting or waiting.

Still, it never hurt to do a little testing. "Where are we going?" she asked, when Krynneth showed signs of slowing.

That question, she'd discovered, was a good gauge of his sanity at any given moment. Sometimes it provoked fury—once so much he'd actually struck her. And been immediately contrite, like a boy who realized he'd broken something precious. More often he ignored her, which generally meant he was locked away inside himself somewhere—fighting battles, she had no doubt, but battles no one could see. And sometimes, if she was lucky, he talked to her as if they were friends on an all-day hike.

"You wanted to see the sea," he said finally, not stopping to turn. "The one to the west. I'm taking you there."

"You don't have to. I . . . can get there on my own."

"I owe it to you."

"Why?"

"Because I have to do a good thing to make up for the bad thing."

"What bad thing?"

"I failed in my duty."

"What duty?"

"My duty to protect the hold."

"You *were* protecting the hold. That's why you were trying to convince Lorvinn to take back the Wardenship."

He rounded on her, a dangerous glint in his eye. "Who told you that?"

"You did. Back in Tir-Eron."

"I was asleep then."

"You looked awake to me."

He shook his head. "The other me was riding."

A chill shook her at that. "Other me?"

"We've all got other selves. I simply know mine better."

Merryn shook her head in turn. Though not the first time she'd heard this notion propounded—at Lore-Hold, among other places—it was the first time she'd actually faced the reality of it herself. Things that intangible . . . bothered her. Even the gems bothered her, a little. Like the way Avall could speak to her across distance. Not only did that make reality a little too large; it was also reasonable proof that the soul was not bound to the body. Or the consciousness. More to the point, it was reasonable proof that consciousness truly was a thing apart from body and therefore worthy of separate consideration.

Maybe Priest-Clan had the right of it. Maybe it was better if people didn't know so much. Knowledge didn't always make one happy.

No! she told herself firmly. She would not think along those lines. Such notions were too close to what she'd heard espoused with distressing frequency among far too many Common Clan and clanless folk in South Bank taverns—which places she sometimes frequented in disguise, the better to gauge the public mind, and thus better advise her brother.

Still, there was a certain truth to it. Knowledge *didn't* always make one happy. The Eight knew she'd be much happier if Krynneth were not so knowledgeable about tying knots, for instance. She yanked at her wrists experimentally—and found exactly the same amount of slack as the last hundred times she'd tried.

She'd just started to ask another question, on the theory that Krynneth might ultimately talk his own way back to the road of sanity, when he stopped abruptly and flung himself forward in the heather. "Down!" he snapped, motioning her to ground.

Merryn did as requested, though the notion made little sense, given that the horse was in plain sight of whatever he was hiding from, and equally plainly laden. She scooted toward him, clumsy on elbows and knees. "What is it?" she hissed.

"Burners, down in the valley. I crested the ridge and saw them."

"Did they see you?"

"Maybe."

"Are you sure that's who they are? There are a lot more folks living in the Wild than you think."

"They had a flag. One I saw in the battle."

"Mounted?"

"They had horses."

"Cavalry, then."

He regarded her solemnly. "Which raises the odds of them being officers, which means they're more likely to be disaffected."

"Oh, Eight," Merryn groaned. What he'd said made far too much sense. If only he were that rational all the time. "Still," she whispered, mostly for his benefit, "that doesn't mean they're enemies. We're not at war, after all."

"Then why didn't they go straight home?" Krynneth shot back archly, sounding far *too* rational, of a sudden. "Because they respect neither our authority nor Ixti's," he answered himself.

She nodded back the way they'd come. "We need to retreat."

He nodded in turn, motioning her that way. She'd barely covered a span, however, when she heard a commotion behind her. Glancing around, she saw that which filled her with despair. Krynneth had not let go of the guide reins when he'd thrown himself to earth, and while Boot was usually placid—so much so Merryn suspected Krynneth of feeding her sugar laced with imphor—she was not that way now.

In fact, she was protesting—loudly. Whinnying and pawing while Krynneth growled curses at her through gritted teeth as he sought to get her subdued. And Merryn could do nothing to aid him, though she did manage to get back on her feet.

"Damned horse," Krynneth spat.

"She's scented the others," Merryn rasped, half-stumbling over to where he stood, "Give me the reins, I can hold them as well as you can. You try to get her calmed. Hood her if you can."

Fortunately, Krynneth saw the sense of her suggestion and thrust the reins into her hands. The ropes around her wrists actually helped strengthen her grip, but the longer one joining her ankles impeded her balance, so that she found herself yanked headlong into the heather, as the horse broke free of Krynneth and trotted down the hill. He followed, yelling, grabbing at the reins, even as she tried to release them. But the reins had somehow gotten tangled in the complex knot that bound her wrists, so that she could not free herself.

"Eight!" she cried, oblivious to who might hear. "Kryn! Cut me loose!"

To his credit, he grasped her situation in an instant and yanked out his belt knife, with which he slashed at the troublesome leather.

The blade flashed in the sunlight, which Boot evidently saw, which prompted her to run faster.

Still, Krynneth managed to sever the reins—so suddenly the shift in momentum caused Merryn, who'd already been dragged several spans, to flip head over heels, which in turn set her rolling.

She caught a glimpse of the Ixtian camp when she, very briefly, stopped tumbling. Enough to see that it did indeed include five—she thought—men, and as many horses. And, more to the point, to see that the men, who'd been sitting around a fire, were all afoot now, and running toward her.

And then she fetched up against a boulder and was summarily winded. The world spun. Blackness hovered near, alternating with a sky that seemed full of stars, even in the daytime.

And then blackness indeed. Which receded again, only to reveal stars of a different kind: three of them—embroidered in gold on the tattered black-velvet surcoat of a compact, square-faced Ixtian man who was looking down on her with a long, straight sword bright in his hand.

An Eronese sword, she noted. Which meant it was probably stolen. Which did not bode well.

Reality reeled again, as memories flooded back of her last captivity among Ixtians—memories so strong, she almost passed out again rather than confront them. And chief among them was herself, tied to chair on a mountaintop across from War-Hold, watching Kraxxi, with his father's hand guiding his own, slowly stab War-Hold's former Warden—who was also Strynn's aunt—through the heart, where she lay spread-eagled on the ground. And then, even worse, feeling the earth rock and heave, and looking up as an explosion lit the night, revealing all of War-Hold in flames, and half its walls blown down.

All her fault.

"Kill me," she gritted, only distantly aware that she'd spoken. "I don't deserve to live."

"Not for a while," the man replied, in accented Eronese, reaching down to haul her firmly, though not roughly, to her feet. She was taller than he, she realized. Not that it mattered. Still, he looked her in the face. "I know you," he continued. "You were the old king's prisoner."

Merryn didn't reply. The way she was standing, she could see over the man's shoulder—enough to note that two of his fellows had calmed poor Boot and were leading her to camp, and that two others were even now escorting a stoop-shouldered Krynneth down the hill, with his hands clasped before him in such a way as to imply that he, too, had been bound.

"Who are you?" the man repeated, first in Eronese, then in Ixtian.

Merryn tried to let her face go blank, as though she didn't understand the latter, though she did. They'd be more likely to betray themselves that way.

"Ivk," her captor called over his shoulder, "Come here."

The younger wrangler glanced up, then gave the mare a final, warning pat, and left her to the care of his fellow, as he waded across the scrub to where Merryn and her captor stood. He was little more than a boy, Merryn realized. Seventeen at most. And also in tattered, gold-starred livery.

"Inon? What?"

Inon, if that was his name, dipped his head toward Merryn. "Recognize her?"

Ivk studied her for a moment, then reached out to brush her hood off her face with a bravado that wasn't quite convincing— as if he were trying to impress the older men with an expertise he didn't possess. "She was . . . Barrax's prisoner, for a while."

Inon nodded. "More than that, too."

Ivk gnawed his lip, then nodded in turn. "Merryn, was it?" Then, incredulously, "The High King's sister!"

Inon smirked a challenge that yet held some affection, as though he were testing the boy. "And what do you think *she* would be doing here?"

Ivk shrugged in a way that made him seem even younger. "I have no idea."

"I do," said the other wrangler, joining them, with Boot still in tow. His eyes looked calm, Merryn thought, which might be good, or not. He, too, wore livery like Inon's.

"You have good ears," Inon chided him, with a grin.

"I also have good eyes," the horseman chuckled through a matching grin. "Good enough to recognize that the helmet these folk's packhorse was carrying is not just any helmet." He flicked his head to the right, where both helm and sword showed in plain view on the nearer side—another of Krynneth's unfathomable caprices.

Inon folded his arms and raised a brow. "I suppose you're going to tell us why?"

"Look at it!"

Inon did, though he didn't relax his grip on Merryn even slightly. "It's Eronese work. Very well made. *Very* well made," he repeated. "In fact, it's—" He broke off, mouth agape. "Gods forgive us, it's *that* helmet!"

A smug nod. "More to the point, it's *that* sword."

"How can you be certain?" Ivk dared, looking dubious.

Inon rounded on him, no longer indulgent comrade but imperious commander. "Because, fool of a boy, I was standing a span from the King of Eron when he was wearing it. I saw him call the lightning with it. Lightning that killed my brother—and your uncle."

"So what's it doing *here*?" Ivk challenged.

Inon looked sharply at Krynneth, then chuckled grimly. "For a moment there, I thought we might have more important prisoners than we know. But that one"—he indicated Krynneth—"has the wrong color eyes to be Eron's King, even in disguise.

Besides which, he's supposed to be this one's twin." He turned back around to stare at Merryn, and this time there was no gentleness in his gaze. "I would therefore say," he continued, "that she's either stolen it . . . or intends to hide it."

"Hide it?" Ivk looked incredulous.

"Think why she might, boy," Inon snapped. "Then, maybe, in a few days, I'll tell you."

"And what do we do with it—and her?" From the other man.

"Her? We do nothing with her until we know more. The man—maybe he's important, maybe he isn't. The armor—well, let's just say that whoever commands it can do whatever he damned well pleases."

"You don't know how to work it," Ivk protested.

"No," Inon told him calmly. "But if Avall of Eron can wield it, so can I."

"To attack Eron?"

"Maybe," Inon retorted. "Eventually. But that would be best done with a kingdom at my back."

It was all Merryn could do to keep from flinching.

PART III

CHAPTER XXV:

ARRIVALS

We should be there in the morning," Vorinn announced from the entrance of what had once been the Royal Pavilion, which Rann now shared with Lykkon.

"How *many* of us?" Rann replied, looking up from the map Vorinn had left him the night after Avall had been taken: the most detailed map they had of Gem-Hold and environs, along with a master plan of the hold itself. Not that the latter did much good, the various clans having designed and built their own quarters within their designated sections without recourse to any larger pattern. Not even the Hold-Warden knew all the ins and outs of that warren. Which could either aid a sneak attack, as had clearly been the case with the Ninth Face's seizure, or complicate one.

Not that there'd be much chance of room-to-room fighting. If it came to actual combat, this would be a siege, plain and simple. That was what had preoccupied Rann for the last five days. So much so he'd already forgotten he was engaged in nominal conversation.

"All of us," Vorinn said carefully, for emphasis.

Rann started, then recovered himself. "Even the baggage train?"

"They've been pushing to catch up."

"Even the portable trebuchets?"

Vorinn sighed tolerantly and gestured to a chair opposite Rann. "May I?"

"You're the commander," Rann replied. "I'm merely the acting Regent. We've equal status before Law."

"And before the men—the ones who'll actually fight?"

Rann shrugged and leaned back in his chair, fingers laced across his chest. Vorinn found a flask of cooling cider and poured himself a cup, not bothering to seek a clean one. "When you're sharing death," he chuckled softly, "why worry about what other things you might share?"

"Then why worry about who the men will follow?" Rann snapped. "No, don't answer that," he went on quickly. "I have no right to trivialize a serious matter. But the fact is, I think they'll follow *you*. They followed Avall because of what they thought he could do—what they were *afraid* he could do, more properly. You, they'll follow out of what they know you *can* do. Out of love, maybe. I wish we'd had you with us during the spring campaign."

"I wish I could've been there," Vorinn replied frankly. "Though I doubt anything would have turned out differently. I've looked over the accounts of the major battles. There wasn't much Gynn could've done that he didn't do. Or Barrax, either," he added. "One was fighting with impossible supply lines, but with the weather as his ally; the other with the fury of the invaded, but with his main point of defense gone, the pride of his traditional warriors wounded, a third of his army unable to reach the battlefields, and across terrain it was next to impossible to defend."

Rann prodded the map. "And this place?"

"A fortress-hold hollowed into a mountain, but itself situated in a hollow. We—"

He broke off, glancing at the entrance. Lykkon had returned, along with his brother, Bingg, bringing fresh meat rolls for dinner. They had company, too: Tryffon and Veen. Preedor wasn't feeling well, and not for the first time on this trip. Like Eellon, his vigor was deserting him all in a rush.

Rann made room for them around the map table, but let them find their own chairs, which they did. Bingg passed out napkins and distributed the rolls across a number of small camp tables, then went in search of clean mugs when Veen commented on the dirty ones. Tryffon called for ale.

"I guess this is a council of war," Rann sighed, leaning forward once again.

"More a precouncil," Tryffon offered. "It won't do for the most visible among us to seem less than fully informed—not that I'm impugning either the intellect or valor of anyone present." He was looking at Rann when he said that, but his gaze carried no condemnation. Which unnerved Rann a little. One never quite knew what Tryffon was thinking. Certainly no one would've guessed beforehand that he would be first to proclaim Avall King—though as coequal Chief of perhaps the most powerful clan, no one would have nay-said him, either. Still, he'd seemed a little distant then, perhaps at odds with King Gynn, or maybe with the fact that so much of their plan relied on untried weapons.

Now, however, he had his brother-son to hand, closer to him than Avall to Eellon or Tyrill to Eddyn. It was as if two parts of a machine had been reunited, which had finally set a larger mechanism working properly. Tryffon clearly loved to plot war with Vorinn.

"Mostly," Tryffon rumbled, "I thought I'd give you one final briefing on the basic layout of the place. I know you've been there recently, Rann," he went on, "but Veen somehow escaped being stationed there, so she's operating at a disadvantage. She'll see it for herself by midday tomorrow, if she chooses, but I'd rather she know what to expect when she arrives."

"I'm ready," Veen agreed through a mouthful of roll.

Rann scooted the map down so that she could see it, while

Tryffon stood behind her shoulder. "It's basically a D-shape," the older man explained. "The flat side is the mountain—Tar-Megon. The bottom two-thirds of the hold were actually carved out of a subsidiary peak that thrust out from it, and parts of the hold, including Priest-Clan's precincts, are back in Megon itself. The mines are below ground level, and can't be assailed—besides which, as we've heard, they were sealed with explosives. Maybe Zeff has cleared an access to them, maybe he hasn't, but we have to act on the assumption that he has, and therefore has access to gems beyond the one he presumably will have taken from Avall."

Vorinn cleared his throat. "You were talking about the layout of the place . . ."

Tryffon nodded. "The rest of it thrusts out maybe a quarter shot into a vale easily one shot wide and thrice that long, that being north and south. That area is kept open: grass in the summer, snow in winter. The Ri-Megon runs out of the mountains three shots north of it, then flows *under* the hold before issuing out the southern side. It's cased in rock for most of that distance—too far to hold one's breath, in case anyone was wondering—but part of it surfaces halfway through, which is how we happen to have Kylin. Megon Vale is surrounded by a ridge that's maybe a third as high as the hold. It's covered with trees, though there're signs that Zeff has considered establishing a third line of fortifications there—after the hold itself and that palisade he's built out from it." He looked at Vorinn, as though expecting him to take up some cue.

"I wouldn't have bothered," Vorinn responded at once. "Archers on the ridge could hit the hold, but the porches would block most of the arrows, just as the trees would block any arrows fired at them. He's cut some of them," Vorinn added, "to deny us shelter. But not as many as he ought. In other words, he may not have given himself enough room to play, if it comes to that. On the other hand, he's well sited to withstand a siege. If we come at the hold itself, he's got many levels of porches from which he can throw any number of obnoxious things down on us, and a long way in which to do it. The lower five spans of the hold are solid stone three spans thick, with very, very few apertures, and none of them is of a size to admit even a slender woman, never mind an average-sized man."

"What about the drains?" Veen ventured, eyeing Kylin, who'd slipped in silently a short time before.

Kylin looked up at that. "They're blocked with pierced-stone screens at the bottom, which are still two spans above the ground. The shafts inside are almost vertical part of the way and fully vertical the rest. You could climb them, but it would take forever."

"Not a viable option," Vorinn concluded. "At least not during a siege. So the bottom line is that we have to look at our strengths, which are numbers, resources, and maneuverability."

"Zeff, however, has blackmail on his side," Lykkon countered. "And hostages."

"He does," Vorinn conceded. "Be assured that I know that an actual attack is only one of many, many options."

Movement by the entrance caught Rann's eye. Bingg, who'd stationed himself there had looked up abruptly, then rose, cocked an ear, and pointed toward the canvas roof, where a steady patter was growing louder by the moment. Not for the first time did he wish they'd brought a weather-witch. But witches were sworn to Priest-Clan, and no one from that clan could, for the nonce, be trusted.

"Rain," Rann informed the company. "Which will complicate the assembly of the engines as well as their maneuverability, should the rain persist." He glanced at Tryffon anxiously. "I know some adepts from Weather claim to be able to call the rain, and folks say that's what Rrath did with the storm there at the last. But . . . *can* they? Is there any chance this is anything more than a natural occurrence?"

Tryffon shrugged. "I wouldn't put anything past Priest—not anymore."

Bingg was on his feet again, but this time he left the tent, only to return an instant later with his hair slicked against his skull. In spite of that, his bearing showed the subtle shift that indicated that, even without livery, he was functioning as royal herald. "Riders," he called clearly but politely. "By their tabards, I'd say they were messengers, but their colors mark them as from Argen."

Rann felt his blood run cold. "Confirm their business, then show them in," he called, in spite of the anxiety that, for no clear reason, suddenly washed over him.

The young woman who entered a moment later looked as though a strong breath could knock her over. She was soaked to the skin, for one thing, which added nothing to an already small stature, but her face was gaunt as well, in a way that reminded Rann of how Krynneth had looked when he'd come stumbling into the Citadel with word War-Hold had fallen. But surely her report couldn't be as bad as that.

The girl's words gave the lie to his optimism. "Priest-Clan has seized power in Tir-Eron," she panted. "And every Clan- or Craft-Chief in the city is either dead, missing, or in hiding."

Silence greeted her. Stunned silence.

Then, slowly, from Tryffon. "Not good news—but is anyone really surprised?"

If anyone was, they didn't affirm it. Nor did they all speak at once—save with eyes grown hard and grim as winter.

"When?" Vorinn asked eventually. "And any other details— but take your time. A hand's haste will make little difference in the long run."

"Tyrill?" Lykkon inserted cautiously.

"In hiding. It was she who sent me."

Rann nodded, feeling sick to his stomach. He didn't need this, not now, not with the present crisis about to enter another stage.

As if reading his mind, Vorinn spoke again. "Whatever's happened there," he said, "our work is here, where we have the smaller but ultimately more powerful force to face. If we go haring back to Tir-Eron, we'll waste time and give both factions a chance to strengthen their positions, to the point that we could get trapped between."

Rann nodded again, then motioned to the messenger. "Lady, at your leisure."

She wavered where she stood and would've fallen had Bingg and Vorinn not raced to catch her and lead her to a chair. Bingg stuffed a meat roll into one hand and a mug of hot cider into the other. She stared at them blankly, too tired even to eat or drink. But she told her story, clearly, and with surprising detail—but also with a certain flatness of voice that suggested she was merely repeating what had been long rehearsed.

"As for Tir-Eron itself," she said in conclusion, "it's theocracy on the one hand, anarchy on the other, and the people, as usual, caught between."

"They don't support Priest-Clan?"

"They support security over ideology, and tradition over revolution. That generally means Priest-Clan, but only from habit. I—I'm sorry. I can't think anymore. If you'll give me a moment—"

"You've told us enough for now," Rann assured her. "And Vorinn's right: There's nothing we can do about it anyway, from here. Nothing, that is, but worry."

"I'm more concerned about the rain," Vorinn remarked, gazing at the roof. "Anyone who's ever tried to move a siege tower or trebuchet through knee-deep mud can't help but be."

Rann lifted a brow in query. "And you have done these things?"

Vorinn nodded. "At War-Hold-Summer. The building and the moving were real. What wasn't real—that time—was the dying."

Rann regarded him solemnly for a long moment. Then: "Whatever legitimate government Eron has at present would seem to be in this tent."

Nor was there much to be done about it until a very tired girl awakened.

CHAPTER XXVI:

COMING TO A HEAD

(NORTHWESTERN ERON: GEM-HOLD-WINTER–
HIGH SUMMER: DAY LXVII–EVENING)

~~~~~~~~

Zeff was all but convinced that the helm was laughing at him. Perhaps it was the way the bronze browridges arched just so, or the way the cheek guards evoked laugh lines, there in the uncertain light of the single candle he'd brought with him here, to this most secure of strong rooms, to which he alone had the key.

Not that he didn't know that such speculation was preposterous—logically—if for no other reason than because, while the helm did, in fact, sport a chin strap, the area where mouth and chin should be was open; therefore, it was not equipped to laugh.

Yet still it called to him, haunting him in the night with dreams of possibilities. Why, with that helm—and the sword and shield that went with it—he could do almost anything. He could be King of Eron in an eighth. He could even be the first man to unite Eron and Ixti, and build a greater kingdom based on their complementary strengths. He could—

No! That way lay ambition—and power such as he conceived should not be confined to any one person's hands. The

Face needed the regalia for one reason alone: to control it, and—by implicit threat—reinstate the prewar equilibrium.

So why was he here now?

Because he couldn't sleep. Because he knew with absolute conviction that someone from Priest-Clan must eventually don all that fabulous workmanship and wrestle it for its secrets. Avall had said nothing initially—and damn him for it, too! Even under imphor he would say little. "It would be dangerous for you—or anyone not of the blood of him for which it was made." Or, after three days of imphor-augmented wheedling: "Blood is the trigger. It has to drink blood."

Which Zeff already knew. What he didn't know was how he would manage the other. Avall had worn it and hadn't gone any madder than most Kings turned out to be. On the other hand, Rrath had worn it and gone utterly insane, though there were extenuating circumstances. More than once Zeff wished he could pierce the shell of the young Priest's catatonia. There had to be *some* reason why Avall had spirited him out of Tir-Eron, then put him under lock and key at least as securely as he had the regalia. Another reason they'd both wound up in the tunnels below the Ninth Face's primary citadel.

Maybe he should act on a latent impulse, summon Ahfinn, and have *him* don the regalia. Except that would violate one of the Face's strongest tenets: All are equal before the Ninth Face. Advancement was based on merit, but conferred only additional duties, not additional indulgences. And no one but no one would ask someone to risk what they would not dare themselves.

Therefore, it had to be him, because he had taken all the other responsibility for this enterprise upon his shoulders. Besides, the fact that he would eventually *have* to confront what he was facing now would haunt him until he *did* confront it, robbing him of the sleep necessary to fulfill his duties properly. Such as preparing for what still looked very much like a siege.

And since he couldn't sleep anyway, there was no time like the present.

It wasn't as if he wasn't prepared. Once he'd reached the decision to confront the regalia tonight, he'd proceeded as he always did before combat. A half day's fasting, save for water and a tiny cup of very sweet wine. A ritual bath. Shaving. Waxing. The donning of one of two sets of never-worn livery he had brought with him, the other to wear when he next led his men to battle. A hand of meditation, and finally exactly at sunset, a cup of water from the Ninth Face's Well.

It should have spoken to him, should have shown him what was to come. In fact, all it had revealed was the same thing it had revealed the last four times he'd tasted it: the sword, shield, and helmet sitting on this selfsame steel-bound table-safe. Which he'd taken to mean that all futures depended on the fate of these three objects.

Nor could he wait any longer. Taking a deep breath, then another, and a third, which was part of the Rite of Calming, he advanced upon the regalia. Helm, shield, and sword in that order, so he assumed. Head, heart, and hand, if one chose to think in symbols.

A final breath, and he picked up the helm and, with considerable trepidation, set it on his head, careful not to trip the barb in the forehead that would feed his blood to the gem. Slowly, deliberately, he shifted it to an optimum fit—finding it a bit too small. Still, he took time to buckle the chin strap before retrieving the shield and likewise slipping it on. The sword came last, though he'd loosened the peace ties in the first mad moment after entering.

And so he stood there, three drops of blood away from being the most powerful man in two kingdoms. In all the world, so anyone reckoned. For no clear reason, he turned to face the door, though it was closed and locked in case of disaster.

"Eight go with me," he whispered, "and the Ninth speed our journey." And with that, he slapped his hand against the front of the helm, then squeezed the sword's hilt exactly as he squeezed the grip behind the shield.

Pain pricked him, and he could feel a trickle of blood running toward his eyes from the trigger in the helm.

And that was all.

No more power coursed through him than greeted the donning of his everyday war gear.

Which was impossible.

Logic reasserted, as training overruled baser reaction.

Either this was the regalia, or it wasn't. If it was, either he was working it correctly or he wasn't. If he wasn't, the fault either lay with him or the means of activation, namely the gems.

But this *was* the regalia; he was sure of it. There was no way it could be otherwise. He'd seen it with his own eyes, while in the guise of a common Ixtian soldier—first when worn by poor mad Rrath, then by brilliant, brave Avall. And while he was no smith, neither was he a tasteless fool who could not recognize incredible workmanship when he saw it.

So maybe Avall had *lied*. Maybe Zeff had triggered the elements incorrectly. Maybe he'd used the wrong sequence.

With that in mind, he tried again, in all six possible combinations—and only met more pain.

Furious, he slammed the sword back in its scabbard and shrugged out of the shield, then removed the helmet.

And only then—which he now acknowledged had been preposterously foolish of him—did he truly examine the gem that glittered balefully between the empty eyeholes.

It certainly *looked* real.

But real as what? The color definitely matched the gem he'd seen on the field, but he hadn't been close enough for a thorough inspection. Rumor said it contained inner fires like an opal, which this gem did. And the color and size were correct.

On the other hand, Avall's clan was allied with Stone, who still held some coercive power over Gem. Perhaps a bargain had been struck. He considered that, thinking what he would do himself if in Avall's place. Yes, it made a kind of sense. Helm, sword, and shield were the most dangerous and precious objects in Eron, but without the gems to wake them, they were only so much exquisitely fashioned metal. Too, the settings seemed to indicate that the stones were made for quick insertion and removal, which also made sense.

Had he therefore made a potentially disastrous mistake and captured the regalia without that which empowered it? If so, where were the proper gems? Avall hadn't mentioned any substitutions. Then again, Zeff might not have asked the right questions, and while one couldn't lie under imphor, one *could* finesse one's answers.

In any case, he still had the crucial elements of the equation: He had Avall, and he had the gem Avall had worn around his neck. And *that* one, he knew without doubt, was magic.

With that in mind, he acted.

Not bothering to store what might very well be useless regalia, Zeff unlocked the door in one rough motion and strode into the corridor beyond. "Open, now!" he yelled, well in advance of his arrival at the gate halfway up. The guard there looked startled, but that didn't keep him from obeying at once.

It was the same with the second gate, though that guard had clearly seen what transpired at the first and acted on his own initiative. Which might earn him a reprimand, when Zeff finished his present errand.

A quick detour by the table-safe in Zeff's private quarters produced what Avall had called in his mumblings the master gem. With it in hand, Zeff started for the dungeons. The few people he met in transit scattered before his gaze—which he found mildly amusing.

But Zeff was not in the least amused when two guards turned two keys in two locks and admitted him at last into Avall's cell.

Avall was exactly as Zeff had last seen him: lying on his back on his cot, with his legs crossed at his ankles and his arms folded across his chest. Overtly asleep, but Zeff knew better. He'd had enough stalling, wondering, and evading. He was going to have answers and he was going to have them now!

Without further deliberation, he covered the space between door and cot in two strides, grabbed Avall by the front of his sturdy woolen robe, and yanked him upright. Caught off guard, Avall struggled and flailed out, even as the fabric tore, tumbling him to the floor.

Zeff snatched him up again, this time with hands on his shoulders, and with the same motion slammed him against the wall. Abruptly they were face-to-face. Avall's eyes were wide-open now, and wavering between fear, anger, and confusion. His breath was strong in Zeff's nostrils. Evidently he'd been drinking wine. "You know what we did to Crim," Zeff rasped, shifting his grip to Avall's throat, and forcing his whole body against him, pinning him so that what small struggles he managed were ineffectual. Avall's hands clamped down on Zeff's wrists, trying to pull the priest's hands away from his throat, but Zeff knew more about combat than Avall, and only held on tighter. He was Ninth Face. The Ninth Face knew their strength to a fine degree. And Zeff knew with absolute conviction that not only was he older and larger than Avall, he was stronger.

"There are many things we could do and not kill you," Zeff went on. "Many things that would make you want to die every moment of your life. I could unKing you with a slice of my knife. A finger joint. An ear. Your manhood. Your balls."

"Do you think I care?" Avall snarled back. "I've done the most important thing I'll ever do. Nothing will ever be better. If I die now I'll always be remembered—and more to the point, remembered as being better than you."

Zeff wanted to ask what he meant by that, but this was no time for conversation. Instead he pushed himself away exactly long enough and far enough to slap Avall's face—hard.

Blood showed on Avall's lip, while more trickled from his mouth where teeth had cut the lining or his tongue.

"Blood," Zeff raged. "You said it took blood!"

"It *does* take blood. *My* blood."

"But there's more to it than that, isn't there?"

"Not for me! You put it on, you trigger the barbs so the gems can feast. And you wait until they feed you power. But the gems may not like you. And if they don't like you, they won't do anything."

"They worked for Rrath, and he hated you!"

"Did he?"

Zeff hit him again, this time on the other side. "I may be angry, but I'm no fool."

"What do you want of me? I've told you everything you've asked."

"Those aren't the right gems, are they?"

"They are for me!"

"Liar!"

"Put me in that regalia and I'll show you a liar."

Zeff slapped Avall a third time, then, for good measure, flung him to the floor. He lay there panting. Half his face was red with blood. Both cheeks were purpling. His breath was coming in gasps. Zeff was blooded, too, from where his hand had caught a freshly broken tooth.

"Blood," Zeff growled. "Blood."

And with that, he withdrew the gem from the pouch where he'd concealed it and thrust it into Avall's face. "Whether those others are real or not, I don't know. But I know this one is!"

Avall's eyes grew huge as he flinched away. Which was all the sign Zeff needed. He dropped down astride Avall's torso, pinning him to the floor while one hand fought off both Avall's arms, and the other drove the gem inexorably toward Avall's bleeding cheek.

Maybe Zeff screamed as it seemed his flesh caught fire. Maybe he screamed when his mind did, or when he felt the ravening of the madness that overlay Barrax's death. Perhaps it was the fascination—what he had wondered about so long made manifest. Or maybe Avall was actually holding him there, forcing him to confront what every instinct known to man shouted at him to flee.

And then he was falling into death. And not only Barrax's

death, it seemed, but also Avall's. His mind was tangled with Avall's mind, the two locked in combat as surely as their bodies had been. And Avall was dragging him farther and farther down a well down which he was already falling. *If I die here, you die, too,* Avall seemed to say. But all Zeff truly heard was *die, die, die, die, die.*

He *had* to escape, *had* to get away. But Avall wouldn't let him. Avall was there laughing at him, telling him that however much joy he'd have had cutting off Avall's fingers, Avall would get ten times as much watching Zeff's memories slowly wink out. *Death lives in here,* Avall whispered, in a voice loud as thunder. *Death would like company, and I think he likes you better.*

Yet Avall was frightened, too; Zeff could tell. Frightened out of his mind, to be so utterly out of control within that which he most feared. And Zeff turned that fear on Avall and showed him everything he'd considered doing to him the past few days. Everything that could be done to a body and have that body live.

No! Avall screamed. *No! No! No!*

He wanted out. No, *Zeff* wanted out. No, they both did.

And suddenly, somehow, they were elsewhere. And while there was no death there, neither was there anything else. Avall knew that place, and that recognition flashed across Zeff's mind as well.

The Overworld.

Avall grabbed at it—at something. At not-sand, or not-earth, or not-stones.

And somehow gained enough control to yank Zeff and himself back to their own place and time.

And to what was for all intents an explosion.

Power slammed through the room as though a lightning bolt had struck between their locked hands. Zeff felt himself picked up and flying. Avall simply lay where he'd been, but his robe was smoldering.

The gem lay between.

Somehow Zeff had sense enough to scoop it up in a wad of surcoat and stagger out the door. To the gaping guards he could only mumble, "If you ever speak of this, you are dead men. Now tend to what's in that room. And if he dies or is dead already, I will send you to the Nine myself!"

He didn't sleep that night, nor the next one. And when fatigue finally claimed him on the third day, all he dreamed about was falling, falling, falling . . .

And Death waiting at the bottom.

Rann stared out at the rain from the shelter of one of ten portable forges that had come up with the last of the baggage train. The first trebuchet was nearing completion out there, half a shot from the ridge that overlooked Megon Vale, though how they'd move it, he had no idea, so deeply were its wheels mired in mud. Could be worse, he supposed. Could be snow, and his hands turning blue, too numb to feel anything but cold pain.

He was due at a meeting in a moment. Another damned round of reports and discussions that all had the same resolution. As soon as they could, they would attack the hold. Maybe Zeff knew by now that the regalia he had was fake, and maybe he didn't, but the fact was, he was in defiance of Royal authority, and therefore a traitor, and the Law was clear on what must be done to such men.

That's what it had boiled down to. Not a matter of men, lives, clans, crafts, and alliances. But of Law.

Which, ironically enough, was the province of Priest-Clan.

Not that what passed for a government these days hadn't observed proper conventions.

They'd sent out heralds to parley, but after standing all day in the rain, unheeded, the heralds had been called back.

During one of the few lulls in the rain, they'd tested their archers to be certain the roofs and porches were actually within bowshot. They were. But the arrows had rattled harmlessly off stone.

Someone had suggested poisoning the river, but there was not a person in the army who did not have family or friends in the hold who would be at risk should they drink by accident. Besides which, there were cisterns.

And still Rann stared at the rain. He didn't see the two men who came up to join him on either side, but he knew them by their tread. Vorinn and Kylin. "This isn't good," he said to both without turning.

"No delay is good," Vorinn agreed calmly. "We maintain parity—barely—as far as those preparations we can actually see are concerned: our siege engines and their palisade in the Vale. And we're not that far off schedule. But they may be forging ahead in areas we can't see. I'd give a lot to know if they're still cut off from the mines."

Rann stared at the ground. Vorinn was a good man, a solid man, a smart and thoughtful man. But he was also a man who'd never been in love. He had no bond-brother, nor had he a wife. He'd sired two children on Lore-Hold women, but those had both been one-year bondings. He had no idea what it was like to have the person he loved best in the world locked away in the enemy's citadel, while that enemy (he had no doubt) employed every kind of ruthlessness to drain one's beloved of everything he knew, after which he would be of no more use save as a symbol, at which point he would be cast aside to die.

"Are you dreading the battle?" Vorinn wondered quietly. "Or are you dreading what the battle implies?"

Rann glared at him. "And what would that be?"

"That there are things of more import than your bond-brother's life."

"How about the life of a King?"

Vorinn caught Rann's gaze and held it. "Kings aren't that hard to come by. I'm sorry if that sounds harsh or cruel, but it's true. Kings need to know two things: how to decide and how to delegate."

"Then Avall is a fairly good King."

Vorinn nodded. "So far as I witnessed."

"But he wouldn't want to live if he knew he'd cost the death of that hold," Kylin said softly, causing them both to turn toward him.

"Which is why we're at least as concerned with taking the hold as simply keeping the Ninth Face imprisoned there," Vorinn replied. "Granted, they won't destroy the hold as long as they're trapped inside it. But we still have to get them out of there before they can find more gems."

"Assuming there are more," Rann snorted.

Vorinn regarded him solemnly. "There are bound to be. Logic demands it."

"Screw logic," Rann spat.

Vorinn reached over and laid an arm across his shoulder—as close as he ever got to affection. "You . . . you're very alone now, aren't you? Not only alone as Regent, because all decisions devolve to you, but because you're cut off from all those you're closest to. Worse, they're in danger and you can do nothing to change that. You can't even assess the degree of that danger. That's hard. Or so I'd think."

Rann shrugged numbly. "Avall . . . he and I have been separated before, but never like this. Even when I thought he was dead there was a certain peaceful finality to it. And when I found out he was alive, I never got a sense of him being actively threatened. Our only enemy then was the whole wide world, and that enemy was so huge it was the same as no enemy at all."

"But you didn't have Div, then," Kylin murmured. "Not like you had her later. And now that second anchor is far away—and oblivious to the added importance that rides, all unknown, on her mission."

Rann swallowed hard. "And Merryn's gone as well, and Strynn. I guess that leaves you, Kyl—of people with whom I have any real history. And Lykkon, of course, but he's so smart he scares me. Avall made me feel clumsy, but he never made me feel stupid."

"Lykkon's a loner, too," Vorinn advised. "Like me. The only difference is that he likes everyone too much and I . . . I guess I don't like anyone enough."

"Not even your sister?" Rann challenged.

"Not even her," Vorinn conceded sadly. "But I wish to Eight I was only having to rescue the King, not my sister's husband."

"You'll do the right thing—as logic dictates," Kylin said, turning his face to the rain he couldn't see.

"Yes," Vorinn agreed, "I will."

CHAPTER XXVII:

WISHING WELL

(ERON: TIR-ERON—HIGH SUMMER: DAY LXVIII—LATE AFTERNOON)

Olion shifted his grip on his spear and stared idly across the cobbled expanse of the River Walk. It was misting rain, which made him uncomfortable but not miserable; still, he'd just as soon it held off until his shift was over. Not that he expected to have trouble now that his clan—Priest-Clan—was in charge of Tir-Eron.

As much as anyone was in charge, anyway. In one sense, nothing had changed since the coup had effectively destroyed the Council of Chiefs, though he had no illusions that the few survivors weren't even now trying to contrive some way to revive it. Of course his clan was trying to revive it as well—on their terms—which mostly meant that the various Hold- and Hall-Priests were officiating, while the few surviving Chiefs of the Blood—who were also the ones most pliable—walked an uneasy line between the old order and the new.

As for himself—he was doing what he'd been told to do: guarding the Citadel where the new Priests of The Eight had moved, so they said, for their own safety.

But guarding was boring, and it was still two hands until

shift change, at sunset—though it might as well be sunset now, the way the clouds were glowering.

He shifted his spear again and tried to stand straighter, still feeling impossibly conspicuous in his new Ninth Face livery.

And that was a laugh, too. The newly visible Ninth Face claimed merely to be Priest-Clan's martial, enforcement arm. In fact, they controlled Priest-Clan. And when they'd come hunting recruits, Olion had known a good thing when he saw it. When a toss of the dice had come up Fate, why, that had confirmed his decision.

But still he wondered. Gynn, the old King, had been the King of Balance. Balance had always been important in Eron. And now, it seemed, things were badly out of balance. And while Olion's faction was ascendant right now, he wasn't entirely certain The Eight would approve of that—not if they'd wanted Balance a few years earlier.

He didn't know. He just didn't know. Which was why he was a guard: so he could simply obey orders and not have to think.

It was raining harder now, and the Walk was emptying of what few people dared use it these days. Scowling, he backed up half a pace, so that the parapet above would provide nominal shelter. People were scurrying for cover out there, too, but not as many as there should be.

That in itself was odd. Once Priest had restored order, which had all been done to benefit Common Clan and lower, he'd assumed they'd be out here in thankful droves.

They were not. People looked scared and uncertain and . . . furtive.

And there were suddenly many more poor people than he'd ever seen before, come to beg alms in the city when they'd grown tired of waiting for the Crown to rebuild their lives. He hoped his clan was up to it. Feeding the hungry, the displaced, the ruined: that was their job—but until recently there'd been very few such folk about. Now they were everywhere, all demanding that Priest-Clan help them, when before they'd have called on the King.

Olion wondered where His Majesty was, and what would befall him when word came that he no longer had any real control of his kingdom. And then the rain fell harder, and Olion's thoughts shifted to simpler questions of the weather.

If that was a guard, Tyrill thought, from where she crouched beneath the ragged awning of what had once been an ale vendor's booth set up for the Night of Masks, then she was a champion wrestler. The boy looked no more than eighteen, for Eight's sake, which wasn't legal age to exert any kind of authority. And he looked about as comfortable in that white cloak and blue surcoat as she would, never mind that they were too big for him. It was show, is what it was: Priest-Clan flexing authority they didn't legally possess, and wouldn't keep—if Tyrill had anything to do with it.

Which is why she was lurking in shadows and ruins a quarter shot down the River Walk from the Citadel's main gate—closed now, and guarded, as it had never been closed and guarded before. Which said a lot right there.

She shivered where she stood, for all it was summer, wondering grimly how she'd fare when winter came, especially with her rotten joints, which made movement agony even now. It was frustrating to know that a warm bed, a hot bath, and all the food she wanted lay out of reach a shot farther east, in Argen-Hall. But she dared not go there. The place was watched and most of the chiefs, sept-chiefs, and subchiefs were fled or dead—including the Clan-Chief-Elect, who hadn't lasted long enough to be installed in office. Anyone who remained there now was a traitor, as far as she was concerned. She only hoped the loyal ones—the apprentices, in particular—had been smart enough to flee to the clan's other holds.

It was the same everywhere.

The awning flapped briefly above her, distracting her with

the sound and scent of scorched leather. She stifled a sneeze, as the rain roused the scent of burned wood rather than quelled it. The River Walk looked terrible. After the Night of Masks had become the Night of Death, and the Royal Guard at the Citadel had, overnight, become the Ninth Face, no one had dared try to clean it. Or else they had other priorities. It was therefore still littered with masks, most soggy and trampled now, their beauty proved transitory indeed. There were straw daggers, too—many of them, and not a few stained with blood where they'd concealed daggers of another kind. Worst were the bodies. Most had been claimed, but more than once in the days since Tyrill had gone into hiding, she'd stumbled upon the bloated form of a man or woman who'd met death in an unlikely place. Or parts of bodies.

Fortunately, she had a strong stomach.

And a growling one, at the moment.

Not that she had time to pander to its demands, not when she had other business—business she could not dispatch as Tyrill san Argen-a.

The disguise had been Lynee's idea. The recent war in the south had inevitably displaced many people, the bulk of them, unfortunately, Common Clan or clanless, since most High Clanners had recourse to what was left of their holds in the gorges, or to one of the myriad lesser holds that dotted the landscape.

The lower clans, unfortunately, could claim far fewer options. Indeed, some had lost everything. It was therefore reasonable that many of them would have come north, seeking solace from Tir-Eron itself, since Eron Gorge was, for many refugees, the closest one that had emerged unscathed. Half Gorge and South Gorge were still rebuilding, and would be for a century yet.

So Tyrill had adopted the guise of a displaced clanless woman come from Half Gorge with a two-son and daughter who'd died on the way, leaving her stranded. She had some knife-sharpening skills, and those would keep her fed—until

she could somehow slip back into Argen-Hall in quest of resources more easily liquidated. High Clan dealt mostly in hard
goods, applied arts, and exchange of services among themselves, and drew servants mostly from the younger members of
their own class. They rarely used actual money. Now that she
needed it, however, money was proving to be both a novelty
and a nuisance. The latter because earning it kept her from her
principal goal: the destruction, once and for all, of the power of
Priest-Clan, and the restoration of the Eron she knew.

Then she could die happy. And if that death occurred in a
hovel, with her dressed in a dirty plaincloth gown and cast-off
woolen cloak and hood, so be it. The body, so Priest-Clan said
and Avall had effectively proven, was only a shell. And while
she certainly didn't approve of all the things Avall had done,
and could blame her current situation on him if she bothered
to try, he'd at least given her comfort in her old age. For it was
from him that she'd gained reasonable proof that part of her
was immortal.

Now, if she could just achieve her goal . . .

As for Priest-Clan—they were not as unassailable as they
thought, for they could not completely wall themselves away
from those who had depended on them for so long. And
among the places they could neither deny nor fortify were the
shrines of The Eightfold God that still rose, unmolested, on
the Isle of The Eight.

So it was that, shortly past sunset, with the rain pouring
down and the guard looking tired and miserable across the
River Walk, Tyrill set part of a newly hatched plan in motion.

One of the good things about being old, she reckoned, was
that one eventually became well connected. And one of the
most fruitful connections she'd made in many years had been
with the then-new Craft-Chief at Stone, one Firra san Eemon.
Firra was some kind of kin to Rann's two-father, who had first
brought her to Tyrill's notice. But soon enough, Tyrill and she
had struck up a friendship of their own. And since Firra had
come close to defecting to Lore in her early days, she'd had a

more eclectic education than most of her rather unimaginative kin.

Tyrill had been wrestling with a casting problem at the time, and had voiced that complaint in an abstract way to Firra. The situation, Tyrill vowed, was that sometimes casting in plaster took too long, and, worse, there was always a problem with bubbles. What she needed was some way to turn the water around an object solid—quickly. If one could immerse an object one wanted to mold to exactly the right depth, then add something that would turn its surroundings solid in a dozen breaths, it would simplify casting immensely.

Unbeknownst to her, Firra had turned her formidable intellect and skills fully to that project, and roughly half a year later—when Tyrill had completely forgotten the conversation—had presented her with a small bag of pinkish powder that did exactly what Tyrill desired. Tyrill had been overjoyed.

She'd also been jealous of her knowledge of the new technique. More to the point, she'd been in the throes of one of her periodic rivalries with Eellon, so she'd kept the existence of the powder to herself. As it was difficult to make, it would never see widespread use in any case. Still, Firra gave her what she could manage, out of friendship.

Then had come the plague. Firra had died. And with her, the secret of the powder had been lost. Tyrill had tried a few times to examine Firra's notebooks, but they were incomplete, and a crucial one had been lost during the contagion.

She'd guarded that small stash of powder ever since. More to the point, she'd guarded it in one of Argen-yr's private holds a dozen shots down the Ri-Eron. Which happened to be where the boat in which she and Lynee had fled Tir-Eron had deposited them.

She had that powder now: half of what remained. And while the use to which she intended to put it was not only wildly unethical, but bordered on vindictive, heretical, and blasphemous—well, she was far past caring.

It was raining damned hard, though. Maybe too hard to

risk showing herself in public. Old women weren't supposed to like being wet. Eight, *Tyrill* didn't like being wet. Worse, she feared she might attract too much attention if she visited the Isle of The Eight in this weather at this hour.

On the other hand, she had her dice insignia, token of devotion. She would simply say that a roll of the die had told her to visit the Isle at that time.

And if that ploy didn't work, there was always tomorrow.

Steeling herself, she flipped her hood as far forward as she could manage, snared the cane she certainly needed, and not for sympathy, and shuffled out into the rain. The cobbles were more a sea than a walkway now, and she headed toward an archipelago of raised stepping-stones set there to ensure dry feet.

And turned east, away from the Citadel and that unfortunate guard, who'd spared her a glance when she'd moved, then gone back to his misery. She was going away, and that was probably enough for him.

A quarter hand later, she'd reached the place where the bridge to the Isle pierced the wall beside the river. Another shivering guard stood there, but this one seemed more concerned with taunts from a trio of Common Clan boys than in one old woman, so he waved her past.

It was almost full dark when Tyrill reached the bridge's other terminus, where she made short work of disappearing into the woods. A short walk took her to the first forking, where the paths to Fate's fane split off. Fortunately, the Isle wasn't large, but the fanes had been placed and landscaped in such a way that each seemed utterly isolated. And if she was lucky, they would all be unoccupied.

Certainly Fate's fane was—and it was the most popular one. The Well looked the same as always, and Tyrill shuffled toward it and looked down. It was forbidden on pain of death for anyone save Priests and the King to drink of those Wells, but anyone could gaze into them for whatever the reflections there might deign to show, which was usually nothing.

Tyrill did exactly that, bending over to stare at what looked to her like a sheet of black glass. Trying to look as pious as she ever had in her life, she fumbled beneath her cloak until she found what she sought: a watertight leather bag. Hesitating but a moment, she reached into it and withdrew a handful of Firra's powder. Maybe this *was* blasphemy, maybe not, but Tyrill suspected she knew more about The Eight's will than Priest-Clan did, so she was only a little contrite when she reached out and— very calmly, but with great care and discretion—emptied the powder into the Well.

What happened next was extraordinary, and would've been more so had there been light enough to properly observe it. As it was, Tyrill saw the powder spread across the water like a slick of oil, and then saw that slick slowly solidify, like ice crystals forming on a window. But only for a moment before it went smooth again. Yet when she touched it, she knew, it would be hard as the glass it resembled—probably for half a span down.

Maybe farther.

She did the same at Craft's fane, and at Law's. Man's, too, she clogged, and Weather's. She was running low on powder by then, and hadn't reckoned on the moisture on her hands causing the stuff to cake upon them so that she felt as though she wore mittens of hot ice. She scraped off the worst of it, and finally, with three Wells to go, gave up, concluding her sabotage by simply dropping the nearly empty pouch in the Well of Strength and trusting the powder to act as it would.

It was near midnight when she left, and a different guard was on duty. She greeted him kindly, offered muttered thanks that Priest-Clan still respected the people's need to petition The Eight at any time, and that she hoped they'd seen the last of those who would deny the common folk the direct access they so desperately desired in these hard times.

The man finally ran her off to silence her.

Two days later, Tyrill, in another guise entirely, saw his head and one other, raised on pikes at the gates of the Citadel.

She didn't laugh, however. She could only feel sorry for those poor, poor boys.

As for her handiwork—Word had it that The Eight were displeased, and had turned the water in most of the Wells to mirrors, which were impossible to break. Some said this was a sign the future was fixed. Others that The Eight were withholding the future until things changed.

No one mentioned sabotage, because no one knew how the plugging of the Wells had been accomplished. Besides, hadn't Eron been rife with magic of late? And hadn't The Eight clearly shown that They had granted the King Their favor? If nothing else, Priest-Clan had some explaining to do.

There *was* rioting, of course—but not as much as might've been expected. Perhaps that was from fear of the Ninth Face guards that now prowled the island and elsewhere in ever-increasing numbers. Perhaps it was because it was typically the most powerless portion of the population who most often solicited the Wells, and then mostly for answers to fairly mundane questions, most of which could wait. Or perhaps it was simply because rumor had less force than fact, and most people were sufficiently concerned—as always—with their own lives to ponder greater problems.

In any case, Tyrill was more than pleased. Until she could think of something even more insidious.

(ERON: NEAR MEGON VALE—HIGH SUMMER: DAY LXVIII—NEAR MIDNIGHT)

"I can wait," Riff volunteered through a yawn.

Kylin shook his head. "I've learned it now. It's just a matter of counting steps, turns, and ups and downs. Besides which, I can see a little: anything bright. As long as none of the torches go out—"

Riff stretched hugely. "I'll trust you, then. I'm so tired my toenails are already snoring. So, if you don't mind . . ."

"Go! It's fine. And thanks, Riff. I appreciate this."

"Let just hope Esshill appreciates it as well."

Kylin stood where he was, waiting, listening to Riff's footsteps merge with the pervasive overnoise of the mostly sleeping camp. The latter was always the same, save that weather added things now and then: presently a squish to accompany steps that never lost their essential rhythm; and a steady drip, drip, drip. He felt bad about lying to Riff, too; but if he had any choice, he was unaware of it. Besides, the fewer that knew what he was about, the better. Even Esshill wouldn't know everything—if Kylin chose his words carefully.

He found the tent by feel—his fingertips, and a subtle warming that marked the juncture of warm canvas and cooler air. And the faintest blur of light from whatever lit the interior.

A deep breath, and he called out, "Esshill?"

Silence, save the soft heavy sounds of someone moving inside a camp bag, and the creak of the wooden frame.

"Esshill!"

A groan, then a grunt, then a groggy, "Who is it?"

"Kylin syn Omyrr. I would enter, if you permit."

"A moment." Which probably meant Esshill was dressing. People tended to forget that Kylin was blind—which was sometimes amusing.

An instant later Kylin felt a wash of warmth against his face, followed by a hand laid tentatively on his wrist. "Here."

He let himself be led into the tent, folding himself down close by the door, the better to hear without as well as within.

"What is it?" Esshill asked groggily. "You don't strike me as the sort for late-night visits to people you barely know."

Kylin shrugged. "Time is all the same to me, as far as night and day. As to knowing you—let us say that I knew your brother better."

"I have no brother."

"You did before you joined Priest-Clan. I tutored him when he was at Music, though he was older than I. He spoke of you."

A deep breath. "Why are you telling me this?"

"Because I need a favor," Kylin replied frankly. "But hear me out."

"I'm listening." Kylin caught the hard edge in Esshill's voice that hinted of danger or impatience.

Another breath. "He said you were very loyal. That you took a long time to bestow your trust and confidence, but once it was bestowed, you maintained it forever."

"Your point being?"

"That I'm the same way. And right now I need someone I can trust—so that I can maybe, possibly, achieve a greater good."

"Which would be?"

A third deep breath and Kylin said it: what, if Esshill failed him, would destroy the trust of many other folk who so far had kept faith with him, good intentions notwithstanding. "I may know a way to rescue the King. But I can't do it alone. I need you to help me."

"Why me?"

"Because you understand Rann's position, for one thing, and therefore understand why this battle may not fall out as it ought, which would be bad for all of us."

"I understand having a bond-brother at horrible risk," Esshill conceded harshly. "I hope you understand my anger at the way Avall used that bond-brother."

"Everyone's used him," Kylin retorted. "He's probably being used now—if Zeff can manage to wake him, which I doubt—but I promise you that he'd be better off out here."

A derisive chuckle. "And you think *you* can rescue him along with Avall?"

"I think there's a chance of that if you'll help me, where there's none if you don't. At worst, I fail; no one knows you're involved; and things stay as they are. At best, I rescue Avall and Rrath, and things are back to how they were eight days ago."

"You haven't told Rann about this, have you?"

Kylin shook his head. "Nor anybody—though Riff suspects, but he's another one who's careful where he confers his loyalty. In any case, Rann wouldn't let me do what I hope to do, for completely altruistic reasons. He'd be so appalled at the notion he wouldn't be able to look past that to the facts that underlie it. You, on the other hand—"

"You think I'm more reckless."

"I think you have less to lose and more to gain, and fewer folk expecting anything of you."

"That may be true."

"I hope for many people's sake that it is. Now, what I would ask of you is this: Is it true that you've been having trouble sleeping?"

Kylin could hear the distinctive swish of flesh against fabric that almost certainly meant Esshill was nodding.

"And I'm correct in assuming that you're taking a potion for it?"

"I . . . am."

"Very well, then. If you would be willing to part with some of that potion, here is how I think it might be used . . ."

It took Kylin most of a hand to explain his plan to Esshill's satisfaction, but long before then, he knew the Priest's cooperation was assured. And when he made his way back to his own tent, he indeed carried a phial of sleeping draught. Now all he had to do was find the right kind of wine.

CHAPTER XXVIII:

VISITOR

"I suppose we *could* continue on to War-Hold if you really want to," Strynn told Div, as she flung herself down on the bed pad she'd just stretched across the floor of the roofless foyer in what had once been an Argen-a summer hold, a dozen shots north of War-Hold-Winter. "It's not like we don't have plenty of time. It's just that I don't think it's wise."

Div paused where the main door had been, and turned, hands on hips, a currycomb in one hand. "I'm at least as tired as you are," she sighed. "And I agree that we can't afford to have you recognized. But *you* have to agree that the idea of sleeping in a real bed again does have a certain charm."

"As it does for me," Strynn assured her. "I truly thought Ixti would've missed this place. And, to be fair, there are so many people working down there, I suspect we *could* pass without notice. In the dark, anyway. But I still wouldn't advise it."

Div motioned toward something outside Strynn's line of sight. "At least the bathhouse is still intact."

Strynn flopped against a wall covered with flaking fresco. "This may be the last one, though."

Div's gaze shifted toward the horses barely visible in the forecourt beyond. The stables' stone walls were smoke-stained, but otherwise intact—as was the roof. "Maybe a roof would be good for the beasts," she murmured absently.

As if agreeing with her, one whinnied obligingly.

Div glanced around sharply, first at the animals, then at Strynn. A scowl creased her brow as she cocked her head.

Strynn straightened where she stood. Div looked alarmed, and it took a lot to alarm her friend. "Something wrong?" she demanded, even as her hand sought a dagger.

Div shrugged, but the scowl remained. "I don't know."

More whinnying. Div spun around and looked Strynn square in the eye. "Did you say something?"

Strynn shook her head. "What're you talking about? I—"

Another round of whinnying. Something had clearly spooked their mounts. Div vanished from the doorway. Strynn followed—with the dagger unsheathed now. More than once on their journey, and with increasing frequency as they got farther south, they'd heard tales of bands of renegade Ixtians terrorizing this small hold or that. Usually they preyed on Common Clan or clanless. But a few High Clan holds had also been hit—and one caravan. Word of their incursions had been sent to Avall, but no one knew how soon he'd respond. Would that they'd had the gem, Strynn thought. She hoped they weren't in for a fight now. Not that she couldn't take care of herself, being born to War-Hold, as she was. Div was no slouch either, and had been improving her skills steadily since joining the Royal Guard. But Strynn was also pregnant with the High King's child, and hated to put that child at risk.

Div had a hand on her horse now. The beast looked marginally more subdued, if wild-eyed, and the other seemed to be calming as well. "What's got into them, do you suppose?" Strynn asked, as she reached out to stroke a well-muscled neck.

Another shrug. "I don't know, but all of a sudden I'm hungry enough to eat—well"—Div eyed her mount wickedly—"let's just say I'm hungry. I tell you what: We'll do an early supper here, then trek down to the hold when it's dark and see what we can learn there, but not stay long or spend the night. A little dirt in the right place, and no one would recognize us."

"Or serve us, or pay attention to us," Strynn retorted.

"A dagger still speaks plenty loud," Div grinned.

Strynn started to speak, then shook her head, frowning. "That *would* be fun," she agreed. "But much as I hate to admit it, if anyone goes, it should probably be you—alone. I—" She broke off, eyeing the horses dubiously. They still seemed fractious, but not as much as heretofore. "I'll get some sugar. Maybe that'll soothe these fellows' nerves."

Div nodded, and Strynn ducked back inside. At first she started to retrieve sugar from the stash in her pack, but then she recalled that the hold's kitchen had looked reasonably intact, and that there might be a better supply there.

As soon as she pushed through the door, something growled.

She jumped back instantly, only to slam hard into Div, who'd come up behind her.

"Oh, Eight," Div breathed in her ear, in a mixture of awe, fear, and irritation. "It's a cold-cursed birkit."

And so it was. A very fine specimen, too: female and fairly young, to judge by its size, but still plenty large enough to make short work of either Strynn or Div—alone—never mind a pair of tethered horses. Yet this beast showed no sign of pressing either of those options, seeming content simply to sit atop the wood box beneath the shattered window by which it had probably entered. It regarded them briefly with calm green eyes, then bent down and began to groom itself with a length of gray-pink tongue.

"Friend of yours?" Strynn muttered to Div, between gritted teeth.

"Maybe—in theory," Div replied. "It could be one of those that shadowed Kylin and me to Tir-Eron. I never saw them after we reached the gorge. If they intended to maintain contact with me, it could easily have taken this long to locate our trail, what with having to cross the Ri, and all."

Strynn regarded the predator skeptically. "Then it knows about the pact?"

"Let's hope so."

Strynn eased forward experimentally. "I hunt," she said aloud, because it was all she could remember to say. That was the bond they shared. That which had kept this beast's kin from killing Avall, Rann, and Div back in the winter.

No reply formed in her mind, but she did feel a sort of . . . crowding, as though a second set of thoughts sought to lodge there. With it came an odd, unheard buzz, like a fly let loose inside her skull. At which point she had no doubt the beast was trying to communicate.

"Div?" she dared. "Is it . . . ? Are you . . . ?"

"Trying. But I'm not getting anything except that I think it's trying to talk to us. It'd be nice if we had a gem right now—or had used one recently. The residue seems to stay in the body for a while. That's what lets us talk to them."

Strynn indicated the birkit, which was looking at them again, front legs extended, but with its tail curled around its haunches. "Do you suppose it wants something?"

"Besides fresh horse?" Div snorted. "A year ago I'd have said no. Then again, a year ago I'd have an arrow in that nice pelt by now. Today, I'd say we have to consider the possibility. The question is, 'What does it want?' "

"I don't know," Strynn murmured. "But I'm pretty sure it's hungry. I was picking up that much."

Div rolled her eyes. "We've got some beef that's a little ripe," she sighed. "We can get more at the hold."

"I guess that decides it," Strynn agreed. "If we don't want to be dinner ourselves."

The birkit made the next move—which was the best approach with birkits. After seeing to the horses one last time and making sure they were sufficiently well hobbled that they wouldn't panic and bolt, Div and Strynn treated them with mouthfuls of sweets and reassuring pats, then left them where they were and returned to their nominal camp—where they discovered that the birkit had claimed a spot in the waning sunshine, which also happened to be atop Strynn's bed pad. She resisted an urge to tell it to move or prod it with a toe.

Yet to her surprise, she caught what might've been a reply. Certainly *something* that could've been an affirmation flashed through her consciousness. Coupled with that, the big predator did move. Exactly enough to make room for her.

"Bury me deep," she told Div, who was staring at her aghast. And with that, she—very slowly—sank down in the space provided.

A huge paw promptly flopped into her lap. And remained there, to all appearances content, while Div finished supper. "I haven't forgotten it was your turn tonight," Div warned as she sliced up tubers. "Still, I suppose birkits think they're High Clan, so I guess we'd best leave you to entertain."

Strynn chuckled at that, taking no offense from what had long since become a game.

Div promptly flung a chunk of smoked meat in her direction, which landed perilously near their pack. The odor of ripeness, if not true rottenness filled the air. Strynn wrinkled her nose.

The birkit didn't. A moment later, there was no sign of the meat but a greasy spot on the floor.

"You know," Strynn yawned, "I'm getting sleepy, and it's way too early for that. I wonder if I'm picking up this lady's desires."

Div tasted the stew again and puffed her cheeks. "Could be. We know strong desires are easier to pick up than otherwise. And birkits prefer to hunt at night. If this one's been following us—well, think how you'd feel if you'd had to walk all night for as long as we've been on the road."

Strynn didn't reply, because, quite suddenly, she was asleep.

* * *

She was at Weaver-Hold, Strynn discovered: the same room she'd occupied as a girl, facing the same loom, trying to learn the subtleties of tapestry. She had it threaded right, with the large warp threads running up and down. And she'd started to lay in the weft. She'd decided to do a map of the world—a common enough project for beginners, besides which it honed one's knowledge of geography. And she'd already completed the area south of Ixti, as much as was known—forest, mostly, but less every day, as the Ixtians burned their once-countless trees for fuel.

So she set her shuttle there and wove, back and forth, building a mountain of linen thread, following a stream of sylk, raising a city of fine-spun gold. And slowly, oh so slowly, Ixti grew before her. But this was boring work. It needed something, needed *life,* is what it needed. Perhaps, when it came time to weave the Flat, she would weave a portrait of someone into the sand. She'd be very subtle about it, so that no one would notice it if they weren't looking.

But whose face would she weave?

Merryn's of course. And so she began: chin, mouth, nose, finally eyes. But there was something wrong. She could see Merryn's face woven into the sands of the desert, but it wasn't the face she'd intended: the laughing, happy face of her bondsister. This face was frightened, ridged by the thick warp threads that were almost like prison bars. And then she *was* looking at Merryn's face through prison bars, and Merryn was screaming—"Help me! Help me! Help me!"

Strynn tried. She pushed at the fiber bars and discovered they were now bars of steel. She ripped at them, first with her fingers, then with her shears, until her fingers bled.

And still Merryn stared at her, no longer screaming, but crying—on and on and on. Endlessly.

And Merryn *never* cried.

That was what unnerved her, what startled Strynn back to consciousness only to find Div ladling stew into bowls.

"What?" Div asked, offhand.

"N-nothing," Strynn managed shakily. "I was . . . only dreaming."

"And I'm staying here tonight," Div replied pointedly.

"Nobody's seen her," Div announced the next morning, in reply to the scowl that Strynn tried to direct at her through a yawn. Strynn didn't know whether to be angry or relieved, since it was obvious that the "her" that her companion had referenced was Merryn. For all her well-considered arguments, she *had* wanted to go down to War-Hold; That was fact. *Why* she'd wanted to go, she didn't know. Perhaps because she was simply in need of more companionship than Div could provide— better that than admitting that she was human enough to want to gaze on disaster firsthand.

Well, she could do that anyway—from afar. And to judge by the way Div was staring at her, coupled with the way the birkit was starting to pace, she supposed that wouldn't be as long as she'd like, if rest and a leisurely breakfast were her priorities.

"She's not the only one no one's seen," Div continued quickly, by her relieved expression assuming she'd been forgiven her journey—though Strynn hadn't yet decided.

"Who?" Strynn asked absently, as she unwound herself from the blankets, which—perhaps at the birkit's urging— seem to have tried to swallow her in the night.

Div was poking through the breakfast supplies—which required she relinquish a small jug she was carrying. Strynn noted it for the first time, just as she caught a familiar aroma. "Is that what I think it is?"

Div nodded. "Fresh cauf, from a vendor in camp. I've got some hot sweet buns as well. Also some smoked fish for tonight. And many other things."

"All of which I appreciate," Strynn yawned, finally on her feet and starting to stretch. Her stomach growled and she patted it, remembering the child within. "Down, hellion," she murmured, stumbling over to where Div was filling her cauf mug without asking. *"Who?"* she repeated.

"Krynneth," Div said, passing her the mug without bothering to look up. "He disappeared from here shortly after Merryn left Tir-Eron. No one's seen him since, or had time to look for him, though the consensus is that he's gone west. He was apparently sane as he could be one day, and the next he was babbling about the 'burners' to anyone who would listen. Quite wild-eyed, they said. And then one day he simply wasn't there."

"Burners," Strynn mused. "I assume that means . . ."

"Ixtians was what the woman I talked to suggested," Div replied, sitting down on the hearth with a mug of her own. "We've noted ourselves that not all of them headed straight back home after the war—which makes sense, if you think of them as real people. Sure, Kraxxi made peace, but not everyone would've agreed to it. Many were promised booty they didn't get—especially after Kraxxi made them swear to return anything they'd stolen. And there are more poor people in Ixti than in Eron, and a *lot* more of them join the army . . ."

"So you're saying . . . ?"

"That this area has had a problem with raiders and renegades."

"Is there a difference?"

"Maybe," Div mumbled through a mouthful of tart. "Raiders want something specific; renegades just want to cause trouble—destruction, whatever."

Strynn stopped in mid-bite as the repercussions struck her—and not for herself. "Merryn," she choked. "I'll bet you anything those raiders are based in the Spine—and that's exactly where Merryn's heading."

"Think she can handle them?" Div inquired. Her voice was light, but her face was serious.

Strynn finally managed to swallow. "Depends on the number. A few . . . yes. But more, I don't know. The problem, Div, is that she's got the regalia. If one of them got hold of it . . ."

Div's jaw dropped open. "Oh, Eight!"

Strynn nodded grimly. "Another reason we need to find her quickly."

"And carefully," Div added. "The regalia's one thing, but the King of Eron's sister would make a damned fine hostage on her own."

Strynn rolled her eyes. "Oh, Eight, indeed! I hadn't thought of that."

"Think of it," Div said seriously. "All the time. And be wary." Already, though still savoring her breakfast, she was packing.

(NORTHWESTERN ERON: GEM-HOLD-WINTER— HIGH SUMMER: DAY LXXII—EARLY AFTERNOON)

Zeff stared at the phial in his hand.

Should he, or shouldn't he? he wondered.

The phial contained water from the Well of Knowledge— one of the septs of Strength, for it represented strength of mind.

But Knowledge never liked being consulted outright. Knowledge preferred that man seek information through his own initiative, simply because more knowing was involved that way, never mind that one often learned things on that journey that were more important than the knowledge initially sought.

But sometimes there wasn't time for such a journey.

Zeff sighed and leaned back in his Chieftain's Chair, closing his eyes, as though to shut out the need for decision. Unfortunately, the phial was still there: a hardness between his fingers, an afterimage beckoning his inner eye.

This was knowledge in the service of the Nine, he told himself. And Time, which the Ninth Face served, truly was at a premium. He could wait—until they wrested the secret of the gems from Avall. Or he could act now, perhaps precipitously, and save them both—and many other people—a wealth of trouble.

After all, even without the three gems that worked the Royal Regalia, he still possessed the master gem, which, from everything he knew, evinced the same powers they did—and perhaps evinced them more strongly. All one had to do was penetrate the veil of madness that cloaked all that power, at once lying over it and within it.

That was the trick, wasn't it?

And that was what the water in this phial *might* reveal.

In any case, he would change nothing by simply sitting there.

A deep breath, and he uncorked the phial.

Another breath, and he raised it to his lips and let one drop fall upon his tongue, then quickly restoppered it.

By which time, the first heady fumes were coiling through his mind.

He immediately felt more alive. And—more importantly—smarter. It was as though he could feel his brain coming awake, like a kennel's worth of hounds, first one rousing, then the next, so that soon the entire pack sat there attentively, waiting to see what he would have them do.

Almost he forgot to confront the problem—which was one of the risks of working with the Waters.

Almost, but not entirely.

Without him actively seeking it, the question put itself forward. Yet typical of such occasions, the question Knowledge answered was not the one he consciously planned to ask, but the one his deeper self truly wanted to know.

Not "How do I master the master gem?" but "How may I put the master gem to use?"

To the former, he suspected there was no answer. As for the latter—he now thought there might be.

The answer was simple, in fact. The gem was many things at many different times. But one thing it always was was hungry. So if one could feed it at the same time one distracted it from the other things that went with that feeding, not the least of them being—usually—some deep desire to master it . . .

Well, that was the secret then, wasn't it? Feed it, and then use it *without* trying to master it. Give it its own head, in other words—but point that head away from the wielder's *self*.

It was a frightening notion, Zeff acknowledged, but one he thought he could manage.

Once—if he used it properly.

And if he was lucky, once might be sufficient.

CHAPTER XXIX:

Musings in the Rain

(Northwestern Eron: Above Megon Vale— High Summer: Day LXXII—Afternoon)

~~~~~~~~

The only difference between the water pouring down outside the Royal bathing tent, and the water in which Rann, Lykkon, and Kylin were lolling, was the fact that their water had been heated to within a breath of intolerable. Which was how all three liked it. Otherwise, it was the same water that had been falling from the leaden sky for days, collected into barrels, then poured out and collected again, occasionally with a boiling in between. If there was one supply the army had in abundance it was water. It would be the cleanest army in history. Or the most mildewed.

In any case, Rann was grateful for the respite, for a chance to sprawl back in the enormous wooden tub that had taken up one whole wagon, and to lie there in the comfortable, herb-scented gloom inhaling potent vapors and sipping now and then on spiced wine. It wasn't decadence as much as practicality. Though they were long since ready to begin the siege, the weather wouldn't permit it. Therefore, anything that rendered Rann or his staff more comfortable or relaxed was to be encouraged. Besides, he was with several members of that staff, in case anyone dared challenge their situation.

That said, Rann was having a hard time keeping his eyes off Lykkon. Not because the youth was handsome, which he was; but because he looked a fair bit like Avall, especially in the gloom, amid the drifting vapors.

Lykkon caught him looking and smiled wanly, as though he'd read Rann's thought. Given the bond they'd shared through the gems on occasion, perhaps he had.

Not that they were there alone in the bathing tent. Besides Kylin—whom they assisted now and then, in spite of his protests—Riff and Myx had just availed themselves of this same luxury, and were sitting, towel-clad, in the shadows by the door. Bingg had recently gone off duty and was stripping on the other side, glad to share that small rite of equality with his elder friends and relatives.

He'd make it a tight squeeze, though—unless someone got out. But that was what this was for: a cultivation of trust and closeness.

Finally, there was Vorinn, undressing beside Bingg. They'd asked him to join them partly from courtesy, and partly because, while popular with the army at large, the people in this tent were the closest he had to friends. But he would never think to ask them to join him in something like this, any more than he'd ask to join them.

By unspoken consensus, all talk was of inconsequential things: the sound the rain made on the canvas, how long they could let themselves stay there until they needed to let someone else have a chance, what might be had for dinner.

Never the important things. Like the siege. Like their lovers—both Myx and Riff were betrothed to women involved in the rebuilding of War-Hold. Like the captive King and the lost regalia and where any of them would be a few days hence.

Not until voices sounded outside, prompting Riff to scamper off, clad only in a towel. A moment later, Tryffon poked his head in, squinting in the gloom, but with a wry smile on his face as though he wouldn't mind joining them.

"Good news," he told Vorinn. "All signs indicate that this rain may break by tomorrow noon. A day to dry, and—"

Vorinn coughed pointedly and nodded toward Rann.

Tryffon looked puzzled, then cleared his throat and strode over to address Rann. "Lord Regent," Tryffon began. "Apologies for my—"

"It's fine, Tryffon," Rann assured him. "I have few illusions about who should be in charge of this escapade, any more than the men have any about who they'd rather follow. Now, as you were saying . . ."

Tryffon nodded uncomfortably. "I was saying that another day for the land to dry, if the sun comes out and we get the heat we expect, and we can let the siege towers roll. If you feel like risking it, we could even heave a few fireballs at the place tonight."

Rann shook his head. "I thought we settled that. Too much risk to civilians. That said, if someone wanted to see about torching the lower doors or that Eight-damned palisade, that would both prevent our enemies escaping that way initially and, when they burned through, give us one more means of entrance."

Vorinn nodded vigorously, utterly in command of the situation for all that he was also stark naked. "Of course our foes will have figured that out as well and planted surprises for us. Which is why, for all the trouble it'll cause, we need the siege towers. They'll give us far better access to the lower porches, which will be much harder to defend. As for the palisade— well, they'll hold us back—for a while—but they'll also give us a chance to drop something down on them!"

Tryffon nodded in return. "That was really all I needed to tell you, and I guess it could've waited." He eyed the water speculatively. "Though if that's still hot when you lads finish, it'd be a shame to pour it out."

"Give us half a hand," Rann chuckled, "and it's yours. The wine as well. And Bingg would probably be glad to—"

"I've my own squires," Tryffon huffed gruffly. "And now . . . good evening. Let's hope we get to breakfast in the sunshine."

"And two days after that in Gem-Hold," Vorinn chuckled. "We can even invite Zeff—his head, anyway."

Tryffon chuckled as well, as did Myx and Bingg. Kylin, however, looked very troubled indeed.

Rann tried to ignore him, though something was clearly bothering the harper he wouldn't talk about, and not simply missing Strynn. Which was one reason they'd invited him to join them. He was another misfit, he supposed—as Bingg and Lykkon were too young, himself too inexperienced, and Vorinn too self-contained.

"I'm sorry," Vorinn murmured unexpectedly, helping himself to a seat on the side of the tub.

Rann peered up at him through a veil of sodden hair. "For what?"

"For the fact that"—he looked down, mouth a thin, grim line—"for the fact that people treat me like the Regent, instead of you."

"They should," Rann told him flatly. "I'm doing this for my friend and that's all. I can fake soldiering because I'm reasonably smart, have the same minimal training we all get, understand human nature decently well, and survived actual combat in the recent war. But you love it like I love lying here with my friends. That's all I really care about, Vorinn. I can do my craft, but if I never carved another stone, laid out another wall, or engineered another archway, I wouldn't miss it. My idea of paradise is a bed with me in the middle, Avall on one side, and Div on the other. And good food, good drink, and once in a while a bath."

"Do *you* want to be King?" Lykkon asked Vorinn, as he climbed out to make room for the other man. "Nobody's ever asked you, to my knowledge."

Vorinn shot him a piercing look in passing. "I'd be lying if I said I hadn't seen them wishing with their eyes . . . and the fact is, I can think of worse things. I doubt it would be a drudgery for me and—forgive me, everyone—I think I could see my way clearer. I think there'd be fewer ways for people to get at me."

"And the soldiers would still love you," Lykkon added. "And will love you more after the battle."

"If I survive."

"Rann's still Regent, though," Myx said from the door flap, where he was now donning livery, aided by an open flap that helped disperse the steam.

"Only until I get to Tir-Eron. After that . . . Tyrill's Regent there—if she still lives. If for some reason we're actually able to restore the old order, I'd promise to rule until Sundeath. Period. After that, it's whatever Div wants to do."

"And Avall?" Lykkon challenged.

"I'm assuming the worst. I won't *be* Regent if we rescue him."

"We will," Bingg said with conviction, easing into the tub beside the man who might be his future King, as Rann stood to leave. Kylin rose as well; Rann passed him a towel.

"Two days," Rann said. "Two days and then we'll know."

It wouldn't be two days if Kylin had anything to do with it. Not even two hands.

He'd had the plan in place for a good while now. Ever since word had come from Tir-Eron of how desperate things were there. It was simple enough, really. He was a common sight around the camp, he reckoned, and neither Rann, Tryffon, nor Vorinn had ever tried to deny him access to any part of it. Not even to the edge of the forest, where the trebuchets and siege towers were a-building. And since he was blind, he'd asked them—or whoever they'd assigned to him—to describe what they saw there, and what images went with the sounds. The upshot of all such lurking about was that no one would think twice about seeing him at the front. And since he was known to be a member of the "Royal Party," no one would question him turning up in *odd* places, either, even blind as he was.

And it wasn't as if he were *totally* blind anyway. He could tell dark from light. He could gaze at a daytime sky and say if anything was cut out before it—anything close enough to register as dark, anyway.

In any case, he knew where the hold was.

It would only take a few moments, if he worked it right.

It was twilight and still raining, which would also help. Most of the workmen would have left, and most of the guards would be more concerned with stuffing down their bread and cheese than doing their jobs. After all, it would be easy enough to see anyone leaving Gem-Hold. And they'd have to cross a quarter shot of short grass and mud before they could even reach the palisade. There was no way a sneak attack could be mounted from that quarter.

So it was that Kylin dressed himself in the dullest clothes Esshill could find for him without drawing attention to his change in wardrobe, and began a careful amble toward what he assumed would be the most thinly manned part of the front. He passed soldiers going the other way: toward the mess tent, one of the other baths, or their own tents and caravans. A few hailed him. He called them back by name often as not. When one woman asked him why he was going away from dinner, he told her he was also going away from noise. That satisfied her.

And sure enough, the noises of the camp fell away, as he made his way toward the edge of the ridge. Once, granted, he almost tripped over a pine stump, and more than once he had to fumble his way past construction debris that had a tendency to poke out at unexpected angles. But it wasn't long until he found his goal: the guard station closest to the southern end of the ridge, where the camp butted up against the road. Someone hailed him there: a young guardswoman who was distant kin to him. He hailed her back and turned his face unerringly in her direction.

"What are you doing here, cousin?" she asked, rising by reflex to assist him back to her station: a waxed canvas shelter between two trees, from which she could watch without being completely soaked to the skin. She even had a small fire, which Kylin could both feel through his own damp clothes, and—barely—see.

"I need quiet," Kylin told her. "I knew I could tell you to be quiet without insulting you."

"You think so?" she challenged through a chuckle. "It gets lonely out here, and I'm not due for relief for another hand."

"I brought you a friend," Kylin laughed back, patting a pair of wineskins at his waist. "Two, actually: one for you, one for me."

"The best kind of friend," the guard retorted. "The kind that warms you on the inside."

Kylin laughed again, as he lowered himself onto the bench in the watch-tent.

"I can't have any, though. Not until I'm off duty."

"It's still warm from Rann's own fire—and it's Royal vintage. You won't get better. Besides which, I want some, and I don't want to drink alone. And if you drank it slowly, it wouldn't affect you until you were off duty."

"I don't know . . ."

Kylin sighed dramatically. "Two sips, then—one for friendship, one for kinship—and I'll say no more."

A pause, then: "I suppose I could manage that much."

Kylin grinned and reached to the frontmost flask—suede leather in lieu of plain—then unscrewed the nozzle and passed it to her. He heard her hesitate, then sniff it, sighing approval at the heady odor. And he heard the eager splat of the first squirt against the back of her mouth.

An odd gasp followed, then the sound of her slowly slipping to the ground, as the very potent sleeping drug Kylin had acquired from Esshill, and with which the draught was mingled, set her dreaming.

Kylin acted quickly. It was already twilight, waxing into true night, and with the ever-present rain, the world would be all one color.

Against which he was simply another shape. This part of the slope was pocked with boulders, he'd been told. For one of which, if he moved slowly, he might be mistaken.

Not that he would have that option for very long. Steeling himself, and uttering a prayer to Luck to go with him, and another to the Lord of Fools not to let him be noted too soon, he began to steer a course into the no-man's-land between the ridge and the palisade beyond the hold. The first dozen breaths were the worst, because he'd have been in clear sight of at least one other guard tent, but then the rain—as if by blessing—came harder, and he went on. He fell once—in the mud, which actually helped—and once back on his feet, began to stagger as though he were drunk.

He was miserable. He was also almost invisible, for Esshill had chosen a gray tunic patterned with thin vertical stripes of a lighter gray that from a distance merged with the rain.

He fell again, rose once more, continuing on with an exaggerated stagger. Somewhere along the way, he contrived to drop the drugged flask still in his hand, but retrieved the other from his belt and drank from it. If anyone saw him, they'd see a poor drunk gone awry. But if someone saw him now, they'd be from Gem-Hold: from one of the patrols that constantly ranged the arcades far above, or the wooden palisade that loomed ever nearer.

He was near that palisade now; he could smell the freshly cut wood, even if he couldn't see the head-high, shaved wood tree trunks that comprised it. And now that he was closer to his foes than his comrades, and had the rain between him and the Eronese camp, he started singing—loudly, with the slurred tones of a drunk. He tried to dance, too, and staggered, and then managed to trip himself on purpose and sprawled backward in the mud, arms outstretched, singing at the top of his lungs, when he wasn't filling his mouth with wine he surreptitiously spat out again.

And then he lay still, as though he'd passed out.

And felt, rather than saw, the light from the shielded torches of the men who gathered around him a quarter hand later, and without pause or comment, hoisted him roughly up by arms and legs and carried him inside. He heard oak slam, and a lock click, followed by the scrape of heavy timber, which was followed in turn by the rusty screech of a portcullis descending. And then he was being carried up many stairs, muttering snatches of songs all the while, with the scent of spilled wine so strong in his nostrils it almost made him drunk in fact.

"I don't know who he is," Ahfinn told Zeff frankly, peering through the iron-barred vision-hatch at the slim, unconscious form now sprawling drunkenly in a clean robe on a clean cot in one of Gem-Hold's dungeon cells. "It's exactly as you were told: He came staggering out of the woods just south of the enemy camp right around sunset. He was obviously drunk and seemed to have been in the Wild for a while, based on how dirty he was. He hasn't said anything, because as best we can tell he's passed out. He's also blind. Or at least he had a band of sylk around his neck that might've slipped down from his eyes."

Zeff rubbed his chin suspiciously. "Any clan tattoo?"

"Omyrr."

"Music. That tells me some things right there."

"Such as?"

"Crim had a pet blind harper for a while. I'm not sure what became of him, except that he showed up at Avall's court after the war."

"Do you think that's him?"

"There's a good chance it might be. If so, that raises the question of what he was doing with the army, why he was drunk, and how he managed to get here without his own folk noticing and bringing him back."

Ahfinn scowled. "The drunk part makes sense enough—if he's blind."

"It might, but Crim's harper was supposed to have made peace with his deficiency."

"So you don't think it's him?"

"I don't know. A blind man in the wilderness—that can't be chance. He'd have to be attached to somebody; he couldn't survive out there alone."

"We know there were several hunting parties out of the hold when we took over. He could've been attached to one of them."

"That's true. But now that I think of it, wasn't Crim visiting Omyrr when we attacked?"

"She was. And someone arrived under Royal escort a few days before . . ."

"This fellow?"

"Makes as much sense as anything else Avall does."

"And he hasn't been seen since . . ."

"No, and that's what bothers me. He can't have been wandering around on his own; therefore, he'd have had to be attached to the army. But then why . . . ?"

"He could be a spy."

"He's blind."

"He still has ears."

Ahfinn gnawed his lip. "Well, we're unlikely to learn anything until he regains consciousness. I'd say let him sleep it off, and then we start at him with imphor."

Zeff scowled. "That could take a while unless we want to risk breaking his mind. We may not have a while. It's obvious the army is only waiting for the weather to change before they act."

A matching scowl. "And us no closer to either mastering the armor or finding gems of our own."

"Not the situation I would've chosen, no. But we still have many, many options, Ahfinn."

"So, what do we do with this lad?"

"As you said. Let him sleep it off, then bring him to me. I'll try to win him with sugar, first—I'll ask him to play for me. Then we'll try imphor. Then . . . well, he has very pretty fingers, don't you agree?"

"It always seems to come 'round to that, doesn't it?"

A sly nod. "In a nation of artisans, that's always an option. The problem lies in the fact that the rest of us are trained from birth either to revere them, or to be artisans of another kind. I once had a craft, too, you know."

Ahfinn lifted a brow ever so slightly.

"You didn't know, did you? Never asked?"

"Once we vow to the Face, we have no clans. Isn't that the rule? That's why we have their signs erased."

"And for other reasons. But having no clans doesn't mean we never had them. We're fools to make ourselves slaves to the past, but we're also fools to forget it."

"And you . . . ?" Ahfinn dared.

Zeff grinned a conspiratorial grin. "Omyrr."

A brow shot up again. "So you think—? Oh, Eight, Chief; you're not saying you and this one are kin?"

"No longer. But maybe once. I'd need to know his sept. He'd have been born after I joined the Face, to look at him."

"So you think to appeal to kinship in order to break him?"

"I hope I don't have to. What I hope, Ahfinn, if nothing else, is—just once more before all this comes to whatever conclusion Fate wills—to hear some truly accomplished harping."

"And then?"

"We shall see. And I hope our blind friend here sees as well."

With that they departed.

And Kylin, who had very sharp ears indeed, could only continue to feign unconsciousness while his mind raced like a diving falcon to consider the ramifications of these new facts he'd just been given to ponder.

Not quite two days after passing War-Hold, Div and Strynn found the campsite.

It wasn't hard, really; Strynn had a reasonably strong grasp of how Merryn would think when it came to determining a route west. She'd have been unable to resist looking in on War-Hold, Strynn knew, but after that, she'd have hugged the tree line for as long as possible so as not to draw attention to herself by appearing as a silhouette atop the ridges. She'd have done that for at least a day, since it would take that long to clear man-made structures indicated on the newest maps. After that, she'd have been in virgin country, so she'd have hurried, which meant taking the ridges where she could, simply because the vegetation was lower there and the views more impressive.

Magnificent, in fact: a vast, breathtaking jumble of angles, at least a third of which were raw rocks, or raw rocks covered in snow. Smoke drifted from some of them—or steam—and one, far off, belched fire.

Merryn would've loved that, besides which, Div had found a much more prosaic, if surer, sign, in a set of tracks: two horses, one more laden than the other. And around sunset the second day out, they found human prints as well, of a size that could easily have been Merryn's. After that, it was easy to follow her trail downhill into the woods where she'd made camp. The pole holes and fire pit were still present. There was also a pool nearby, fed by a handsome waterfall, which Strynn knew Merryn would've found impossible to resist—in more ways than one.

So they were on the right route at last—and not as far behind as they'd feared, to judge by the fact that the tracks had certainly been made after the last rainstorm, which had come three days back.

Indeed, Strynn was elated by that fact, so much so that she almost walked away when she saw Div's troubled expression as she returned from a more thorough examination of the campsite. One hand was fisted, she noted, as though to confine something.

"Two of 'em," she volunteered. "One male—I can't tell more, except that he was either Eronese or had stolen boots from someone who was. But both of them were barefoot for a while, and that tells me they bedded down here—along with more obvious signs, of course." She paused, gnawing her lip, then extended her clinched hand and unfolded it.

Gold and red glittered there: garnet set in precious metal. Strynn didn't have to look twice to recognize one of a set of earrings she'd given her bond-sister four years back. She held out her hand impassively as Div deposited the bauble with equal solemnity.

Strynn examined it carefully in the waning light. It was as she feared; the catch hadn't been opened to free the wire for removal. Which meant it hadn't fallen out by accident. A closer inspection showed what looked like bloodstains on the mounting.

"This isn't good," Strynn breathed, trying to remain calm. "Were there other—?" She broke off, as something occurred to her. "Oh, Eight, Div, you don't suppose it could've been *Krynneth,* do you? He disappeared from War-Hold, and you said they thought he might've gone west . . ."

Div scowled thoughtfully. "There'd be no point in him going north, since he'd just come from there. East is the sea and not much between the hold and there, but south is Ixti, and we already know he was afraid of the so-called burners. Also, for what it's worth, those tracks *were* about his size."

Strynn shook her head, not liking what the evidence implied. "But that earring . . . he *couldn't* have! He liked her. They were almost lovers."

"Liked her once, perhaps," Div countered. "But if he's gone mad, there's no telling how he might think of her—if he even recognized her. If he's obsessed with the burning, he might well have remembered who caused it."

Strynn's eyes were huge, and her heart was beating at twice its normal rate. "Oh, Div, we really do have to hurry!"

"And hope," Div added quietly. "After all, we're only assuming it's him—not that the alternative is any better. In any case, we know one of them is Merryn, and I can track her while the ground's fairly springy. But over rocks . . ."

As if in reply, the birkit nudged her now-empty hand, then padded the half pace to where Strynn stood dumbfounded. It nuzzled her hand as well, and she had to resist an urge to snatch it away. Something buzzed in her head—a sign that the beast was thinking at her. She had no idea what it said or what it wanted, but it seemed interested in the earring. Casting Div a dubious glance, she opened her hand and took the bauble in the fingers of the other so it could dangle while permitting her a modicum of control.

The beast sniffed it, then sniffed the ground. It paused, looked at them, then ran a short way back up the bank. They had little choice but to follow. It was sitting when they arrived, and between its enormous front paws was another set of tracks. It sniffed them as well, then trotted off.

Div and Strynn followed.

"Well," Div sighed, after they'd followed the beast half a shot, a good part of it across an expanse of bare rock, "I guess we know how to find them. How they'll *be* when we find them—well, I hate to be negative, but I'd say that was anybody's guess right now."

CHAPTER XXX:

A Gift in the Night

~~~~~~~~

Eddyn's shrine, in the water court behind Smith-Hold-Main, was as close as Tyrill dared come to her former seat of power, and she ran considerable risk even going that far. Which was why she only dared visit it at night, when she could navigate as much by feel and memory as by eyesight—which wasn't what it had been, anyway. She'd become a moonshadow, she decided: something that only appeared after sunset. Days she spent in Lynee's house on South Bank or in one of the caves in the cliffs behind Smith-Hold, depending on whether dawn or fatigue found her first.

Why she continued to come here, she had no idea. Perhaps because it was one of the few remaining links to her previous life. Perhaps because it was just close enough to both Argen-Hall and Smith-Hold that she could observe something of what transpired there. She had Avall to thank for that, for it was he who had gifted her with the pair of distance lenses she'd accidentally left here the afternoon before the Night of Masks. She'd been amazed to find them still present eight days later, when she'd finally returned. Fate—or someone—was clearly looking out for her.

As to what she'd seen through them—not much, in Argen-Hall. Little more in Smith, save day before yesterday, when she'd observed a phalanx of Priest-Clan soldiers marching most of the apprentices out, along with what had to be the hold's supply of sword blanks. The captives were probably at work now: pounding out blades in the forges beneath the Citadel—blades to use against their own kind. And plotting escape, if she knew her kin.

She was plotting escape, too, but escape of a different kind. Escape of the souls of Priest-Clan's Chiefs from the traitorous bodies that confined them.

How she would accomplish that, she had no idea. All she had at the moment was strength of conviction.

But that wasn't uppermost in her mind, as she waited with increasing impatience for the night to advance to a time—generally two hands after sunset—when she felt safe to dare Eddyn's shrine. There were still lights on in the hall—a few. Mostly, by the colors, second-rate candles, which meant someone was either economizing or being stingy. Meanwhile, she crouched beneath the arch of a hedge arbor, into which she could melt if required.

And continued waiting.

She had just started to creep out to begin the routine of dash-and-hide that would take her to her goal when she saw other movement in the garden. Another person, it appeared, lurking in the shadows directly across the shrine from her, so that she could make out almost nothing save that whoever it was moved furtively and fast. Which logic told her meant that figure was young, and instinct that he or she might not have the best interest of her foes in mind.

If only she could be certain. Maybe that figure was seeking *her*. Maybe her tracks had been discovered and she was moments away from facing death in truth. It was what she deserved, she supposed, for maintaining even this small degree of predictability. After all, it was the predictability of her fellow

Chiefs that had got most of them killed. Only the fact that she had not behaved as predicted had saved her.

Or Fate.

In any case, she was at once very frightened and very curious—so much so that she let the latter rule long enough to peer around the hedge's close-clipped corner. She saw no one at first. But then there was another flurry of motion, this time somewhat closer, and by squinting into the gloom she saw a black-cloaked figure edge around the shrine on the side away from the hall, crouch into the denser shadows there, and slowly crawl toward the open archway that was the shrine's only entrance. Tyrill snorted. Not even she was that furtive, though perhaps she might've been, had scooting along on hands and knees been an option for someone her age.

But what was he—she?—whoever?—doing? Whoever it was had reached the steps and flowed up them like an incarnate shadow, to disappear inside.

But only for a moment. The figure reappeared no more than three breaths later, and this time stood full upright, a blot of shadowed moonlight against twilight. Female, Tyrill guessed, by the height, though that was a guess indeed.

To her amazement, the figure seemed to look straight at her, made a series of quick hand motions that were almost certainly meant to evoke the hammer-strokes of forging, then raised one hand to her mouth and drew it outward in the sign that generally meant "wait so many breaths"—and followed with five raised fingers.

Then, with a swirl of graceful movement, the figure melted back in the shadows on the shrine's other side. Which put her in sight of the hold if anyone was looking, and out of Tyrill's sight as well.

Well, this was a pretty situation! She'd almost certainly been found out, though how she could've been seen, she had no idea. Still, whoever that had been had obviously known her habits, and more to the point, who she was. Which could be good, or not. This could well be a trick, a ruse designed to lure her into the open.

But that was ridiculous. Everything she'd seen of Priest-Clan since the coup indicated that they moved by the straightest route to their objectives. If they knew she was here, they'd simply have taken her where she stood. There was no need for this game of feint and deception.

Besides which, Eddyn's shrine was legally consecrated. No blood could be shed there, nor anyone be removed from it against their will.

Maybe they intended to starve her out. In any case, she wasn't even certain she knew what the stranger had meant. Had she meant to wait five breaths and follow, to some clandestine meeting? Or five breaths and enter the shrine itself?

"Eight go with me," she murmured—and before she realized that she had, in fact, decided, she eased into the open.

Nothing moved in response, but she hadn't really wanted it to. She'd made her decision, now she had to stick with it. All that remained was plotting the proper path through the shadows—for the multiple moons changed that every night.

She was breathing hard and cursing her aged joints as vehemently as she ever had in her life when she finally found herself beside the shrine's steps, in the same place that other figure had stood.

It was now or never, she realized. Ignorance or knowledge—or death, which was itself a kind of knowledge. And she'd never know which unless she went inside.

A deep breath, and she managed to make it up the stairs. Another, at the top, and she slipped inside. In the slight, steady light of the votive flame, Eddyn's statue almost looked alive. Indeed, his cast bronze eyes seemed to gaze down on her with compassion—so much so that she felt tears start in her eyes. She rubbed them away ruthlessly. Whatever she'd first come for, she had another agenda now. Another mystery to solve.

So intent was she in gazing upward as she slowly made her way, that she forgot to watch her steps—until her foot came down atop something cylindrical, which sent her stumbling forward, arms flailing. Somehow she kept her feet, if not her balance, but she still fell heavily against the pedestal on which the statue stood. Her arms went around the bronze knees, and she leaned there desperately, catching her breath, as frightened as she'd ever been for so little reason.

Or maybe not. She could've broken something, and then where would she be? Captive, is where. Or dead. Perhaps very visible and dramatically dead, so as to leave no doubt who was in charge of Eron Gorge, and why there was no reason to expect that to change.

On the other hand, she'd been here two nights ago and whatever she'd slipped on hadn't been here then. And there was that figure . . .

Steeling herself, while trying not to think about a new pain across her lower ribs, and a matched set on her shins, she turned, still bracing the pedestal with one hand.

Something gleamed in the moonlight. No, *two* somethings. One was, as expected, cylindrical: as long as her forearm, but no bigger around than her largest finger, and apparently made of something pale, most likely wood or bone. The other was a leather bag no longer than her hand, and irregular in a way that said it wasn't empty.

Cautiously, she crouched down where she stood, and only when her knees were on the floor did she begin to creep toward where they lay a span away. She reached the larger cylinder first, and flicked it toward her. It rolled smoothly across the marble.

The votive light behind her cast it into shadow, so that she had to twist around to see it properly. It was hollow, perfectly cylindrical, and there was writing—or etching—on it. By squinting in the light and moving it closer yet, she saw that it was in Ixtian. A name, it appeared, which told her nothing. Probably the person who'd made it. But what was it? She studied it curiously, then shrugged and retrieved the leather bag. A flap covered one end, tied with laces, which she undid, wondering even as her fingers worked at them, why she was doing this here, when she should be seeking some place of greater safety. That fatal curiosity, she supposed. A final tug, and she got the flap open, to reveal at least three dozen tiny glass darts, carefully packed in cork and cotton. A finger proved how sharply they were pointed. Abruptly she knew what she had. A blowgun. An Ixtian weapon little practiced in Eron.

Someone had deliberately left her a blowgun—so she could only assume. But who? And why?

Well, there were still a fair number of Ixtians around, though none that she knew well, or who knew her, as far as she was aware.

But why a blowgun? That was the real mystery.

And then it came to her, like a moon from behind a cloud. A blowgun was a distance weapon. It didn't demand much strength, was easily hidden or disguised, and was an Ixtian weapon. Any use of one would therefore be difficult to trace, and that trail would lead, at first, in a false direction.

Of course a blowgun dart was of itself not very dangerous unless one happened to strike one of a very few particularly vulnerable places. But with proper ... augmentation ...

She examined the dart case again, and this time located a separate pocket at the opposite end from where the darts were housed. A double clasp closed this one, and she had to work to free it.

She gasped at what rolled into her hand. A tiny brass jar, no larger than her eye. And graven on the lid, which seemed to screw on, was a symbol that made her skin crawl.

A scorpion.

Which didn't exist in Eron. But which she knew, from talking to both Eddyn and Merryn, was the source of Ixti's most virulent poison.

One mystery solved, she acknowledged, as she tucked it away with a shudder. And one created. She had a means to do some damage, that was a fact.

But who was that nameless person who had given her such an outlandish weapon? And was it worth her trouble to try to find out?

One thing was certain, she concluded, as she collected her newfound treasures, and—with extravagant care, and a fair bit of pain besides—made her way back to the hedge arcade: She had a new ally. And a new way to exact revenge.

She had only to learn how to use it.

But *that,* so far as she could tell, was not much harder than breathing.

CHAPTER XXXI:

FACE-OFF

(NORTHWESTERN ERON: GEM-HOLD-WINTER– HIGH SUMMER: DAY LXXIV–DAWN)

When the first rays of morning sunlight struck the golden ball above the Gemcraft standard waving from the topmost tower of that captive hold, Eron moved.

Ahfinn saw it first, having been unable to sleep the entire night before. Not been *allowed* to sleep, rather. Zeff had kept him awake with one demand or another, initially to midnight, which had proven the first of three false alarms, and finally right up until a hand before dawn. Some of it was legitimate work, granted, for word had come of a potential breakthrough in the diggings, which Ahfinn had been dispatched to investigate. But most was simply fetch-and-run, bringing this or that supply or diversion to his Chief. Which was fine, in moderation; it was what he'd expected when Zeff had taken him on as secretary. But not when the main function of those errands seemed to be placating a Chief's personal anxieties. Something had happened to Zeff a few nights ago, of that Ahfinn was certain. He didn't know what, exactly, save that it had involved Avall, the armor, and the gem. But things had been different thereafter.

Or maybe it was simply the presence of Kylin, whose music

Zeff was requesting with increasing frequency. Whether that was good, in that it served to soothe his Chief's ever more volatile temper; or bad, as a potential reminder of a life Zeff was supposed to have left behind, Ahfinn had no idea.

In any case, Zeff was proving increasingly difficult—which was why Ahfinn was strolling the third arcade from the top so very, very early in the morning. Trying to work off the frustration that was preventing him from getting much-needed sleep, now that he was finally off duty.

He saw it first as a line of darkness a fair way back in the woods. Initially he thought it was simply morning light on shadows—until those shadows moved. And as they moved, they solidified, slowly joining into a fragmentary line just behind the nearer trees. Larger shapes moved behind them, indistinguishable from trees at first, then growing clearer as they approached the ridge that topped the slope above Megon Vale. He paused there, entranced, though he knew that even now he should be spreading the alarm. And he would—in just a moment. The longer he waited, the more he would have to report. It would take only a breath.

And that was exactly how long it took for those fragments of darkness to advance another half dozen paces, which put them full into the light at the top of the ridge, where, in one smooth movement that filled Ahfinn with awe, they joined abruptly into what looked to him like a continuous line of black metal rolling like an impossibly enormous serpent out of the forest. *Shields,* logic told him. Tall as a man and half as wide, and linked at the edges by some type of quick-release joints he couldn't make out in the dim light. Their wielder's feet were invisible in the thin mist that still hugged the heights.

And then they moved again, and Ahfinn saw and was amazed. The vanguard of Eron's army stretched as far as he could see to north and south. Easily far enough to encircle the entire accessible side of the hold with an unbroken line of man-high metal. Easily a thousand men, he reckoned. And that was only the beginning.

"Attack!" he yelled—finally.

As a dozen other throats yelled the same from high above him.

From his place behind the center of the line, Rann watched the shield wall advance. Though armed with swords and crossbows to a man, and followed a pace back by archers only slightly less well-shielded, the vanguard of their force was mostly for effect. It was a symbol, if one would call it by its true name: a physical manifestation of the fact that Eron intended to keep the whole of the Ninth Face exactly where it was. The Priests might destroy the hold. But they'd do it with themselves inside.

There was no movement within either hold or palisade that he could see, save an odd bit of excited dashing about on the arcades, as lookouts began to earn their keep and alert the force within.

And still the shield wall advanced. Slowly, oh so slowly. A pace every dozen breaths. Walk and rest, walk and rest. Only when they'd traversed a dozen paces did the first siege weapons show. There was a staggered line of them, but Zeff wouldn't know that at first. No, what the Ninth Face Chief would see initially would be a dozen siege towers advance, alternating with the same number of trebuchets. That many more waited half a shot back in the woods, sheathed, like those to the forefront, in thin sheets of metal to ward off fire.

As to their purpose—the towers gave them height, but even so they came nowhere near even the lower arcades. Still, they'd allow the archers who manned them from platforms at various levels to shoot farther into the arcades than otherwise, and farther into the roofs as well. Frankly, as Vorinn had told him, the towers were for intimidation, along with the shield wall—a way of saying to Zeff, "We know you're there. Get out if you can. We can circle you as deeply as we like. Endlessly."

Meanwhile the trebuchets would bring the hold down on

their heads a little at a time. Rann hoped it wouldn't come to that. He hadn't forgotten, nor could he forget for even a moment, that close to a thousand innocent Eronese citizens, most of them High Clan, were prisoners within. How many Ninth Face accompanied them, he wasn't certain, though Vorinn was laying odds it was at least half that many. In this regard, the coup back in Tir-Eron was an advantage, because later reports had indicated that the Ninth Face was also active there. And battle on two fronts, even if it was not yet physical combat, was never easy.

In any case, Rann had more concerns than the civilians within. Avall was in there, too, along—apparently—with Rrath and Kylin. And damn the little harper for a thrice-cursed fool! What had possessed him to pull the trick he had, Rann had no idea. He probably had a good reason—likely, it was part of some stupid plot to rescue Avall. But Rann was tired of well-intentioned heroes.

As for battle, he was armed for it and primed for it, but he did not truly expect it to come. At least not today.

Zeff watched impassively from behind a shield wall of his own, though he doubted they were necessary, there on the arcade. An archer could target him, perhaps, but there was plenty of time to see the arrow in flight, plenty of time to raise shields to meet it. Plenty of time, in fact, to duck behind the rail of this, the highest arcade, and let them pass harmlessly above him. However high those siege towers were, even Gem-Hold's lowest arcades were over two times higher.

Not that they weren't marvels of engineering. Nine spans high, more or less, and a third that square at the base, for stability; they were in effect mobile houses, elegantly built, braced for lightness, and faced with metal to ward off fire. There were five fighting platforms within them, but only the bottom two would likely be needed, and that only to engage the soldiers out at the palisade. Even the top one was mostly for show.

And it was, Zeff conceded, an impressive display, especially with all that Warcraft crimson mingled with Argen maroon contrasting so nicely with the black-painted shields and the incredible green of the midsummer grass. A hand after they'd begun easing over the surrounding ridgeline, the first of what had proven to be three shield walls stopped moving. It had covered half the distance between the ridge and the palisade, and just enough more that the siege engines sat on level ground, their man-high wheels gleaming in the sun. And behind that first shield wall, there was not a span of ground that was not defended by a well-armed man or woman. They had him ten to one, he suspected. But he had some things they didn't.

For maybe half a hand, they simply stood there, unmoving. Playing for an effect Zeff acknowledged they'd probably be having—if they faced any force but his own. His men, however, had long since been warned. And only a few were even being allowed out here. The rest were manning the palisade or securing the hold, putting everyone not under his direct command under lock and key.

And still he waited, still and silent, aware at some level that the entire hold and vale seemed to be holding its breath, fearing perhaps that the next breath either took would be rank with the stench of war.

A hand after the shield wall halted, something changed.

Not much, but Zeff noticed it. There was movement at the center of the ridgeline, directly behind the central tower—which bore the Royal Standard of Eron. By squinting, he could make out roughly a dozen figures on identical white horses riding toward that tower. Closer they came, with one in the front, two behind, three more behind them, then four more, in a wedge. The ranks made way for them, then melted back in place.

Soon enough, they reached the tower, where they dismounted one by one and disappeared within. Zeff lost sight of them briefly, then caught a flurry of movement on the platform immediately below the top. An adjustment of the distance lens Ahfinn had finally found and passed him clarified the motion into the same group he'd seen earlier: one man standing in the forefront, with two flanking him behind. The one on the left he identified easily enough, by his bulk, his age, his blood-red cloak and surcoat, and his beard, as Tryffon, Craft-Chief of War. The man to the right looked like a younger, leaner, clean-shaven version of the other—and not unlike Avall's consort, Strynn, from which Zeff divined that he was Tryffon's brother's-son, Vorinn, though Zeff had never met him. He carried a distance lens, Zeff noted—which did not surprise him.

The man in the middle wore a surcoat of Eemon midnight-blue quartered with Stonecraft black and gray, beneath a cloak of Warcraft crimson slashed with Argen maroon. Mail showed on his arms and legs, and one of those men two ranks behind him carried a helm. Black hair flowed close upon his shoulders, and gold rings flashed at his ears. He was a handsome young man, and neatly built.

But he was *not* King of the Eronese.

"Rann syn Eemon-arr," Ahfinn informed him quietly. "It would appear they've made him Regent."

"They'd have done better to elect Tryffon," Zeff snorted. "Such as he is, I'd assume he's a figurehead."

"A well-defended one," Istahnn mused from Zeff's other side. "I—"

"Shush," Zeff hissed. "He's getting ready to speak."

And so he was. Rann had raised a gold-foiled speaking-horn to his lips, and even at half a shot's remove, his voice carried clear across Megon Vale.

"Zeff of no known clan, who calls himself Chief-Commander of the traitorous heretics named by his own tongue the Ninth Face, hear the words of Rann syn Eemon-arr, appointed Viceroy of the North and Regent by acclamation of the Kingdom of Eron and High Commander of the most true and loyal army of Eron, in the name of Avall syn Argen-a, High King of that same land." A pause to let the echoes settle, then: "Be it known that you have been declared by your actions guilty of an act of treason, and guilty by your words of performing that same act in clear premeditation, for which you have been duly proclaimed by the Council of Chiefs acting in concert to be a traitor, subject to you making your own defense before His Majesty and His Majesty's Throne in Tir-Eron. Be it known that we hold those under your command guiltless until their acts prove otherwise, and that any who throw down their weapons and leave that hold of their own free choice will be taken into our ranks and treated like our own.

"But know you that if you do not yourself surrender yourself and your force to us, and this hold to its rightful Warden, we will bring it down around you. Destroy it yourself, you may—as you have threatened. But destruction means very little to the dead."

There was no mention of Avall, Zeff noted. Which he thought strange. But perhaps that meant that this Rann, though he was in fact Avall's bond-brother, was more pragmatic than he thought. For now, anyway. In any case, Rann had raised the speaking-horn again.

"I will give you until noon to consider," he said. "In the meantime, five thousand loyal warriors of Eron will sit and wait. And be warned, Zeff of the Ninth Face, not all the warriors at our command have yet come to this field."

Which was probably true, Zeff conceded. But possibly also a feint. Two men left in camp would support Rann's claim. But he doubted Rann was that subtle.

In the meantime, Zeff had raised his own speaking-horn. "I will provide an answer at noon, if that be amenable to you," Zeff called smoothly. "In the meantime, enjoy your rest. It may be the last you have for quite a while."

And with that, he withdrew. But only far enough to hand Ahfinn a certain key, and to whisper in his ear, "You know what to do."

• • •

Time had slowed to a crawl. So it seemed to Rann, who'd never been patient at the best of times. How it must be to those further down the chain of command—many of whom probably had little idea what was going on, or why they weren't even now shooting bows, climbing ladders, swinging swords, and killing men—he didn't want to ponder.

It was enough simply pondering what Zeff was doing. He had at least one gem. That was a fact. A *mad* gem—which Rann assumed he knew by now, to his caution if not his detriment. But he might have others as well, though why he wouldn't have used them heretofore, Rann had no idea. There was also some chance he might also have known, or found, some means of curing Avall's gem of its madness.

Finally, he had Avall, and that was not an advantage to be dismissed. Not when the nominal commander of the opposing force was Avall's bond-brother, and the commander-in-fact his brother-in-law.

Time passed. Rann remained where he was, watching, trying not to appear nervous. Talking occasionally to Lykkon, Riff, or Veen. Sharing a midmorning drink with them, and another at a hand before noon.

As the sun neared the center of the sky, he put on his helm, squared his shoulders, and stepped as close to the rail of the platform as its construction allowed. As an afterthought, he unsheathed the sword he'd brought with him. The Sword of Air, as it happened. Not that he would ever use it in anger as Gynn, unfortunately, had—to his shame and possible doom. Still, it was a symbol, and this was a day for symbols. By his command Veen carried the Crown of Oak, and Lykkon the Cloak of Colors. Tryffon bore the Sword of War, which was his alone to display before battle, in token that the King acted by the consent of the Council of Chiefs.

Half a finger.

A quarter.

A dozen breaths before noon, Rann motioned to Bingg to bring him the speaking-horn. He had just raised it to his lips, when a commotion erupted on the lowest arcade. He paused, waiting. An instant later, Zeff appeared, clad now in the captured regalia.

Rann felt a chill at that. It was fake; he *knew* it was. But it was still set with bloodwire to join the replica gems to the wielder's blood. Suppose Zeff had found new gems. Now would be the time for him to try them.

Or perhaps it was simply that the man likewise knew the power of display, and was appearing in the best he had. Even the replica regalia surpassed all equivalents in Argen in terms of beauty.

Zeff said nothing, merely marched to a point directly opposite where Rann stood, then reached to his side and unsheathed the sword that hung there. It glittered in the noonday light. And even as Rann steeled himself to address that far more impressive figure, Zeff raised that sword on high and drew it down, as though he would cleave the sky all the way to the land.

Rann's heart double-beat, for that was exactly the gesture Avall used to call the lightning. Beside him, he heard Lykkon gasp and Bingg gulp, even as a rush of alarm swept through the assembled host. They'd been at the Battle of Storms, many of them. How many of them, Rann wondered, could feel their deaths upon them now? How many *would* be dead a breath from now?

If the gem in that sword was real.

Nothing happened.

Not in the sky, at any rate.

What occurred on the arcade was another matter entirely.

Zeff's display had clearly been some sort of signal. For barely had he raised the sword again when a host of warriors appeared to his right, bearing what Rann first thought was the circular top of a gaming table, which they proceeded to heave over the side of the rail so that it hung there, fixed by hooks on its upper rim.

A white cloth covered it—one of the Ninth Face cloaks by the look of it. But as soon as the object was set in place, a pair of warriors slowly raised that fabric to reveal—

Avall.

Crucified.

So it looked at first to a speechless Rann, until inspection through Vorinn's distance lens showed that they'd clamped his arms in steel rings at his wrists, elbows, and armpits, his legs the same at ankles and knees. And contrived a platform he could stand on, so as not to suffer the slow suffocation that most commonly brought death to those thus displayed.

It was an Ixtian torture, Rann knew. And wished he had never heard of it, for he knew far too well how it could be manipulated to many unpleasant ends.

Avall was naked, too; they'd not granted him even that much dignity. But his face, when Rann saw it, was composed, if very, very grim. He wished he could see his bond-brother's eyes, but Avall had closed them.

And even as Rann stood there gaping, Zeff raised his own speaking-horn. "Here is my answer," Zeff cried. "He is whole— for now. I will give *you* until dawn tomorrow to withdraw."

In spite of himself, Rann knew he had to give some reply or appear a coward before the assembled army. Raising the horn to his mouth, he called out in turn, "And if we do not?"

Zeff's reply was to raise the sword again—and slash it down in the direction of the trebuchet six spans to the right of the tower in which Rann's party stood.

A blinding flash of light and fire enclosed the trebuchet. Wood splintered, metal squealed. Men screamed and shouted. The tower in which Rann stood rocked but remained up-right. Blood splattered his face and arms from a source he didn't want to contemplate. And when his eyes blinked back to normal, the machine was a shattered mass of wood and twisted metal. A dozen bodies surrounded it, not one of them moving, and only three of them even remotely intact.

As for Zeff, there was no sign of him.

Rann looked first at Vorinn, then at Tryffon. "Well, lads," he breathed at last, still half in shock. "I guess it's time we did some talking."

Tryffon merely nodded, though it was Vorinn who laid an arm across Rann's shoulders as they started toward the stairs. No one looked back at Gem-Hold-Winter.

No one dared.

CHAPTER XXXII:

SCHISM

(NORTHWESTERN ERON: NEAR MEGON VALE– HIGH SUMMER: DAY LXXIV–JUST PAST NOON)

~~~~~~~~~~

The two-shot trek back to the Royal Pavilion was the longest ride Rann had ever taken. He could feel eyes on him every step of the way: eyes seeking him as he approached and boring down on his back as he departed. Already he was cursing himself. He was Regent, for Eight's sake—and that was what he should've let the army see. Not him turning tail as soon as he was faced with a decision of any consequence. A moment it would have taken—a dozen words to shout Zeff back to confront them, so that they, not he, would have last say. The proper words at the proper time, and it would be Zeff pondering ultimatums.

But Rann didn't have the proper words—and never would.

He was fooling himself, he knew, as he dismounted beside the Royal Pavilion and let an unknown squire take his horse. There *was* no counterthreat he could level at Zeff. They had the army and siege machines, aye, but Zeff had called his bluff. Zeff had the King and the gem, and he had a sword that was close enough to being the *real* sword that a gem that was close to being the real gem was able to activate it. The rest—He didn't want to think about it.

Ignoring those who'd followed him inside, Rann doffed his helm and flopped down in his chair, then snared a bottle of wine from the table beside it and indulged himself in a long, reckless draught. He was no King, anyway, and certainly no commander. Let people see what he really was and to Cold with them, anyway!

He'd raised the wine for a second swig when Tryffon stopped him by the simple expedient of clamping an iron-strong hand around his wrist. Rann started to glare at him, then thought better of it. The only enemy here was himself. That was clear enough.

A pause to collect himself showed Vorinn, Lykkon, Veen, Tryffon, and Preedor with him—and that was all. The rest of his entourage waited without. This looked less like a council of war than personal confrontation. Disappointment, sympathy, toleration, and anger: All that was in their eyes, though no single emotion fixed in any one face for more than an instant.

Vorinn cleared his throat. "Two things, Lord Regent," he said formally. "Two things you should know before you say anything."

Rann lifted a brow and slowly disengaged Tryffon's hand, then set the bottle down. He folded his arms across his chest. "I'm listening."

"First," Vorinn began, "there was no way you could've prevailed back there, for the simple reason that what just happened was a pissing contest between two men—and Zeff left before you could reply. That implies arrogance. It also implies confidence—too much of the latter, I suspect."

"You also did right not to order an attack then and there," Tryffon added. "Zeff was trying to goad you into that—which shows how much he's underrated you. An attack would've cost you your army—maybe—if he was profligate with the use of that sword. But it would've cost Zeff as well: first, because such blatant disregard for life from someone who's supposed to respect it would dispel any notion about who the real aggressor is here, which could have very bad consequences in the long term, if word got back to the populace at large—which it would. Never mind the simple fact that we could still have got off most of the trebuchets before he could blast them, which would've given him problems of his own, both with damage control and increased potential for uprising inside the hold."

"Which ties back into what I was about to say," Vorinn retorted, somewhat irritably. "About Zeff, I mean. You may have noticed and you may not, but I certainly did because I was watching Zeff through my distance lens every instant he was out there—his face, more than anything—what I could see under that helm, which wasn't much. But it wasn't hard to tell that he was almost as scared as you were. I have no way to prove it, but . . . I think he was scared of the sword. That tells me several things. First, we know that the sword he has isn't the real sword, and the gem he has—which has to be Avall's mad gem—isn't the gem that's designed to activate it. Still, it worked, which tells me in turn that he's tried the regalia at least once, so he now knows it's fake, and that he's had sufficient contact with Avall's gem that he knows what it can do. Given that he was facing an army larger than his, with Law on its side while he only had blackmail on his, he didn't have much to lose by trying what he did. But I don't think he had any idea what was going to happen until it occurred. I think he was playing for an effect he didn't expect, and then, when he got one, it scared him enough that he left, rather than tip his hand."

Veen shook her head. "I don't quite understand."

Vorinn shifted his gaze in her direction. "It's complicated, and I'll admit I'm making a lot of guesses and working in part from report, not things I've witnessed myself. But think: Everything I've heard about when Avall first tried the sword indicates that its effects aren't things one can easily hide. He tested it in the Citadel's war court, as I recall. And there were reports all over of strange flashes in the sky. We've seen nothing like that, and there's not been a moment since we got here when that place hasn't been watched by a dozen pairs of eyes."

"What about *before* we got here?" Veen shot back. "Zeff had plenty of time to master it before we arrived."

"Not as much as you'd think," Vorinn countered. "Don't forget, he'd have had to find out how the sword and the gem work, and his best source for that would've been Avall, who wouldn't tell him. They'd surely have used imphor, but it would take a while for that to do any good. So yes, you're right in that an interval existed in which, under optimum circumstances, Zeff could've figured everything out. But if he knew that much about it, why not just call the lightning down on us to start with?"

"It did rain for days," Rann countered.

"It did—but I don't think that was him. Rrath once managed to call a storm, but Rrath was a weather-witch. Zeff, so far as we know, isn't."

Rann cleared his throat. "So what I'm getting from this is that Zeff has a dangerous weapon that he may not know how to control as well as he would like us to think."

Vorinn grinned. "That's exactly what I'm getting at. He's probably somewhere this very minute trying to figure out if he dares use the thing again—which would have the same heartening effect on his armies as it did on ours—or if he should try some other tactic, in case the thing turns on him like it did on Barrax; or if he simply loses control of it entirely, like almost happened to Merryn."

"True," Tryffon agreed. "Don't anyone forget that he's only got the one gem, so far as we know, and that the real ensemble needs three to maintain proper balance, never mind what this replica set might need. Also, I can't stress enough that the parts he's put together weren't made to work together, and that the last we knew anything about it, Avall's gem was mad. Say what you will about Avall, he's strong-willed; and if he couldn't regain control of the gem, I seriously doubt Zeff could. We could well have been looking at desperation in the guise of bravado."

Rann shook his head again. "I hate not knowing," he said

simply. "And that's what this has boiled down to. We don't know what he can do; he doesn't really know what we can do, and the whole thing reduces to who steps into the air first."

"And you say you're not a strategist!" Vorinn chuckled. "In any case, we still need to come up with a reply."

"One possibility comes to mind at once," Tryffon rumbled.

"What's that?"

"The fact that he gave us until dawn doesn't mean we have to wait that long. He's only seen half the trebuchets, and those were the ones we wanted him to see. An order from you, Rann, and the two dozen more we've got hidden in the trees could do a fair job on the roof of that hold. At minimum, it would scare some people—and rest assured, whatever face the Ninth Face puts forth, it's made of men like us, and not all of them signed up to put their lives at risk. There's also the fact that any impact damage would have to be addressed if not repaired. There could be fires. And there'd also be the people— the prisoners. An attack would make them fearful, but it might also stir their blood enough to goad them into action. At the very least, Zeff would suddenly have many more problems to address."

"One of which," Vorinn took up, "would be whether to use the sword again, since I'm sure beyond doubt that he's almost as scared of it as we are."

Rann scowled. "So you're saying that we should force him to use it? That seems a dangerous game."

Veen nodded. "It does. It's a fact that he can wield it, after a fashion. It's only a supposition that he can't control it and would therefore hesitate to use it again. Excuse me if I sound impertinent here, but everyone I know who's worked with weapons always got better the more they used them, not worse."

Rann stood abruptly. "There's something you're all leaving out of this," he said stiffly.

"What's that?" From Vorinn.

"Avall," Lykkon replied, locking glances with Rann before exiting without apology, excuse, or explanation.

Rann didn't know if he was grateful that the boy had voiced what he dared not speak himself, or angry with him for bringing up the subject, then leaving him to confront it alone. But he was right.

"You're forgetting that Avall is hanging out there right now, stark naked and probably scared out of his mind," Rann began. "And yes, I know that displaying him like that is a very calculated and deliberate ploy on Zeff's part both to taunt us and to dispirit us. And you know what? It's working. One attack, and Avall is dead. Simple as that. The wrong kind of attack, and Avall is dead by our hands. I can't even imagine that!"

He sat down again, staring at the table, breathing heavily.

"If they kill him," Vorinn said calmly, "they provide a massive reason for full retaliation. At minimum, he'll keep us from turning arrows or trebuchet missiles toward the center of the hold. But there's only one of Avall, and the hold is almost a span long. That's a lot of target."

"It is," Tryffon conceded.

"How long can he live that way?" Rann asked, swallowing hard, still not looking up.

"He's on display, not being tortured," Vorinn replied. "They may feed him; they may not. It would be a way to get at us more than at him. He could live a long time there, as long as he got water. That would play on our nerves, too, because no one likes to see another person hurt. No right-thinking person, anyway, and certainly not if they think there's something they could do about it."

"Not an answer," Rann spat.

"Days," Vorinn replied, glaring at him. "How many depends on Avall. I doubt they'll take him down at night, frankly, because that gives us that much more advantage, and we're playing with fragments of advantage here. Nor do we know what effect the gems have had on him. You've said yourself that they work to sustain you. They heal you faster than you'd heal naturally, and—"

"Avall has no gem," Rann snapped.

"He has the residue in him, I'd assume. That has to count for something. That's all I'm saying."

"You're not saying enough," Rann growled, all his anger come to a boil at once. He rose again, glaring at Vorinn. "What I've heard here is facts and cold logic, and that's not enough. I've heard a tally of weaknesses, but I've not heard anything that tells me how to win this—and not one *word* that tells me how to do this without killing Avall. I've heard no speculation about even making an attempt at rescuing him, which tells me that you've written him off."

"Sometimes you have to," Vorinn said coldly.

"*You* can say that!" Rann raged. "You've never been close to anybody! I've known Avall as long as I've been alive. There have been times he's almost been my other self, we were so close. And after what we went through with the gems, there's no way I can explain that unless you've been inside it."

"No," Vorinn agreed softly, "there isn't. But nobody's written him off yet, Rann. This situation isn't even a hand old; we're still throwing out ideas, and I've no doubt that with the intellect we can bring to bear on this we can come up with some solution—martial, diplomatic—magical—I have no idea. The fact is, we have to wait. That's not hard."

"It's the hardest thing in the world!" Rann shouted. "Maybe *you* can wait—you who spent the entire war sitting up there in North Gorge. I've been in this thing four times longer than you have. I waited to find out what was making my bond-brother act so oddly when he first found the gem, and then I waited to see what he was going to do about the Eight-cursed thing, and then I waited to see if we were going to get to Tir-Eron alive, and then I waited to hear if Avall was alive—I've already lost him once, Vorinn, I will *never* do that again—and then I waited through the war. You can ask me to do a lot, Vorinn, but you'd better be very careful of asking me to wait more than a very little while longer!"

"You may have to, Rann. It's part of soldiering."

"I'm a stonemason," Rann shot back.

"And we're talking of throwing stones at stones. It was you who identified where the weak places in the hold's stonework might be."

Rann glared at him. "And right now I'm identifying where the weak places in me are. I've had enough of this! I have no idea why I'm even doing this. Nothing I say will make a dust mote's difference in what happens. I'm holding you all back. You know what has to happen, and the only thing that's stopping you is me. So . . ." he paused, breathless. "So I'm giving you that. Once and for all." He flung his Regent's circlet on the table. "It's yours, Vorinn. Maybe you want it, maybe you don't, but you're now the most powerful man in the Kingdom—under Law. I won't hold you back anymore, and if you need anything from me about something I actually know about, ask me, and I'll do my best to tell you. But do not ever, ever, *ever* ask me to pronounce death sentence on my best friend. Zeff's already asked me to do that, and Zeff's the enemy!"

He stopped speaking then, and stared around the chamber. He was shaking, he realized, and his pulse was racing like someone who'd just fought a daylong battle. He'd said it now, and done it. He hadn't said it like a man, either, but like a boy. But he *was* a boy—almost. He wasn't cut out for this, and he'd just done the best thing he could. He'd given the choices to those best equipped to make them.

"If you need me," he told Vorinn, "I'll be in Lykkon's quarters." And with that, he stomped out of the tent into sunshine so bright and guileless that it shocked him.

Lykkon looked as tired as Rann had ever seen him, when Rann stormed into the younger man's shelter. But at least he looked glad to see him. Rann hadn't wanted to see how anyone else looked at him—after that last fiasco. If the army's gaze had been difficult to endure when fixed on his back, Vorinn's gaze—and Tryffon's, Veen's, and Preedor's—had been ten times worse. The army only suspected. The others knew. Lykkon would know soon enough, and Rann was only grateful that Lyk had slipped out after making that one-word pronouncement, for whatever reason.

Nor was Lykkon alone, Rann realized. Bingg was present as well, along with Riff, but not Myx. Which meant Myx was probably checking on Esshill, which duty he'd taken upon himself.

"It's over," Rann announced.

"What's over?"

"*Not* the war," Rann growled, helping himself to the only spare stool in the tent. "My involvement in it. I've quit. The only reason to stay in it is for Avall, and I can't help Avall. All I can do is buy him time, and that's time in which he'll only wish himself dead every instant. I know *that* much. Every route I take brings me back to that. Avall won't survive this. He can't survive this. The choice is who kills him and when. I can control one or the other, but I refuse to control either."

"What are you going to do, then?" Lykkon asked softly. "If you stay here?"

Rann looked up at him shyly, vastly relieved at having to present no facade of competence before someone who certainly knew better. "That assumes I *do* stay here."

"Merryn could still arrive," Bingg ventured, from the corner. "We tend to forget that we've still got that whole other variable to consider. She could be priming those gems to jump even as we speak."

Lykkon nodded. "And if she does, she's more likely to jump to where Avall is than anywhere. Don't forget, they have no way of knowing where we are. They'll assume that we've reached this place, but the only reliable target is Avall. It could be happening even now."

"A nice story," Rann told him, though he made an effort to smile, for Lykkon and Bingg were certainly not his enemies. "I wish I could believe it."

"Don't underestimate belief," Lykkon retorted. "Now, if it won't drive you mad to repeat it, do you think you could tell me what happened after I left? I had to piss," he added sheepishly.

Rann shook his head. "I suppose you should know, given that you're still part of the army."

"I'm legally too young to soldier," Lykkon reminded him. "I'm here because Avall's my—I don't know *what* he is, but he's my friend and my hero and a lot of other things. And to tell you what I wouldn't tell many other people, I don't know if I could stand watching Avall suffer, knowing it was my fault and that I couldn't do anything to stop it that wouldn't kill him."

"Which means," Bingg added a little too smugly, "that if Lyk and I refuse to fight, we're not traitors."

"Which only leaves one of us," Rann growled.

"Two," Riff put in. "I've thought this was stupid from the first. I thought we should've made Priest-Clan come to us. But Avall was in an impossible situation—and now we're in one. I'd support my country if I thought it was right—or if I thought it was wrong and doing that wrong thing for a right reason—but this is far too complex. Nobody's talking to each other. It's just feint and parry and acting like brainless bullies, except we've got really big swords and really loud voices."

Rann gaped at him. It was as much as he'd ever heard Myx's bond-brother say.

"I'll fight if Vorinn or Tryffon or Preedor specifically ask me to," Riff went on fiercely. "I've got that much honor. And I'll fight for Myx or my lady if the war comes here. I'll fight for you lads because you're my friends. And I'll fight for Avall if there's any chance of saving him. But I won't do it in Megon Vale. I don't believe in futility, and that's all I can see out there."

Rann nodded sadly, then looked up at Lykkon again. "You're the smartest person I know," he murmured. "Do you see *any* way out of this situation? Any way at all to save Avall? Any way we haven't thought of? Even if it uses magic."

"No," Lykkon sighed. "But this might be a good time to start searching."

CHAPTER XXXIII:

WATCHING THROUGH BARS

(SOUTHWESTERN ERON—HIGH SUMMER: DAY LXXIV—MIDAFTERNOON)

Well, I wanted to go west, Merryn thought grimly, *and this is west.*

Southwest, actually; angling, as far as she could tell, toward a finger of the Flat that probed among Eron's southern mountains as though it would tickle them. She could see it distantly: a yellowish blur amid darker, bluish peaks. She'd also seen it on a map, which was comforting because she now knew where she was, which meant she knew where the nearest refuge lay, should she ever escape to seek it.

That wouldn't be soon, she reckoned. Not with her wrists cuffed *and* chained together, her arms lashed to her sides, and her legs tied to the saddle of the Ixtian man named Orkeen who presently rode behind her. At least it wasn't Shaul-the-wrangler, who'd been her saddle partner the day before. He had frisky hands, and in the course of the ride they'd frisked over every part of her they could reach, which was most of her. He was doubling with Krynneth now, and from what she could tell, subjecting her comrade to much the same inspection.

Which, lest it be with permission, was, by Eronese Law,

assault without permanent injury. If they ever got him in Eronese custody, she'd see he met the full force of the Law, too! If she let him live that long.

In the meantime, she endured and tried to plot ways to escape these fellows, and—much more frequently—worried about the regalia.

Not only had she failed in her mission, she'd also failed in the worst way possible: by delivering the whole crux of the balance of power between Eron and Ixti into radical Ixtian hands. Inon, who'd evidently been fairly high-ranking in Barrax's army, had made no secret of the fact that he intended to rally every renegade band he could find and, when he had enough, contest Kraxxi's right to Ixti's throne.

Which, she supposed, made her thrice-cursed now, since she'd betrayed her hold, her brother, and—apparently—her former lover. If she kept on, she'd probably betray everyone she knew. Which would surely get her listed in the Histories, but not in a way she wanted to ponder.

To distract herself from such dark imaginings, she studied the landscape more closely; then, when that grew boring, gave herself over to practicing some of the meditation routines Warcraft taught as a means of distancing oneself from one's body while under torture. Often, too, they served as aids to sleep, or simply as ways to make time pass when time proved intolerable—as, for instance, when one was awaiting battle.

Still, she was surprised to be lost in tranquillity one moment, then jostled from it the next, to find herself staring down from a final low ridge to that very same finger of the Flat that had seemed so distant earlier.

"Down," Orkeen snapped in bad Eronese, then remembered she couldn't get down without assistance, whereupon he swore and roughly untied the ropes that bound her wrists to the saddle horn. Honor made her try to club him with her fists, but he laughed and dodged, whereupon that same honor made her kick at him as he unbound her feet from the stirrups. He gave her a casual shove on her second trial, knocking her to the ground. Breath huffed out of her where she lay sprawling, half-stunned.

Orkeen's shadow fell atop her, and he yanked her up, only to draw back his fist and knock her down again, this time with a blow to the jaw that made her see stars and taste blood. She was trying to struggle back to her feet, with instinct alone in control, when Inon grabbed her assailant from behind, spun him around, and gave him a taste of what he'd given her. "She's the King of Eron's sister," Inon spat. "I've no illusions about either of them ever being allies, but I'd as soon give them no more cause to hate me than they already have. An injured hostage is worth less than a hale hostage, however slight the injury, and that's a fact."

Orkeen had risen by then, with more than a glint of challenge in his eyes. He started to charge Inon again, but Inon moved aside with a speed and grace that would've done one of the Night Guard proud, adding a kick in the rump as he passed, which sent the other man headlong into the mixture of scrubby weeds and sand that marked the start of the Flat. As if an afterthought, Inon strolled casually over and kicked Orkeen smartly in the groin, which doubled him up immediately. "That's in case you might be tempted to try what Shaul thought I didn't see." With that he turned back to Merryn. "Are you all right?" he asked in the best Eronese of the five.

"Considering," she muttered.

"We'll camp near here tonight," Inon told the group in general. Merryn tried not to betray the fact that she understood him.

A cloud of dust from the north proved to be young Ivk arriving, with more dust in his wake. "We missed it," he announced, pointing back the way he'd come. "It's around that next ridge, maybe a shot."

"Close enough to walk when you've been riding all day," Inon sighed. "Orkeen, you can untie the prisoners' legs, but keep them hobbled."

"Aye," Orkeen managed from the ground, where he was still clutching his crotch.

"Now."

Orkeen staggered to his feet, shooting Inon an evil glare when he thought his commander wasn't looking. Merryn merely watched in bland amusement as Orkeen—with Ivk and the remaining man, Tahlone, observing—placed hobble-cuffs on Merryn's ankles. Tahlone, who seemed older and more world-weary than the rest, stared impassively while Krynneth was also unhorsed and freed.

A moment later, they were walking north, where a line of trees showed beside what Merryn reckoned might be a river. The land underfoot was more sand than anything else, for the summer winds blew from the south and carried grit that way, but this finger of the Flat was not as bare as most of that no-man's-land.

In fact—as she discovered to her surprise when Orkeen, who walked ahead of her, moved aside so she could actually see—there was, or had been, a small hold here.

The architecture proclaimed it Eronese, as—once they'd forced the locked gate in the high outer wall—did the artifacts ranged around the forecourt, including what had been a caravan of the sort used on treks. Everything looked abandoned, however, and any paint the caravan had sported that could have given some clue to its origin had long since been washed, scoured, or sun-bleached away. No carved clan sigils were visible, either, which said a lot right there—notably that the hold had probably belonged to clanless folk, a fair number of whom had gone west in the years before the plague, or else fled it.

In any case, the buildings looked solid, if hastily built, though the caravan had already been old when the plague began. Too bad there was no way to discover more without being free, and she didn't see that as an option anytime soon.

She wondered if Krynneth had drawn the same conclusions. More to the point, she wondered if he'd drawn any conclusions at all. Ever since their capture, he'd been silent, like a man who had endured one thing too many and retreated inside himself. Perhaps he had. As it was, she'd heard him speak exactly four words since they'd fallen in with these folks: "Piss," "shit," "yes," and "no." Those kept him from soiling himself, which was apparently all their captors required. That she was the prize was obvious.

Wordlessly, almost cautiously, they pushed through a second gate into a walled side court, of which the hold itself made one side, while another consisted of a row of stables so solidly built they seemed an outlandish extravagance.

Inon studied the area appraisingly, nodded satisfaction, and tossed his reins to Shaul. "Geen country," he said tersely. "That's why the stone and the bars on the windows."

Merryn blinked at that: She hadn't noted those things and probably should have. Especially the windows. Geens were pack hunters and as likely to hunt at night as by day. They were also smart enough to raise wooden door latches and open shutters. Thick walls and steel bars were the only sure defense where they were common. And since they liked to eat horses, and stabled horses were easy meat—well, that explained the sturdy construction.

"I need a bath," Inon announced abruptly.

"So do I," Ivk—whom Merryn had decided was Inon's nephew—agreed. Orkeen snorted.

Inon glared at him. "We all do, actually, but we can't leave the prisoners unguarded, and I don't want to bring them with us." He stroked his chin thoughtfully, eyeing the stables. "Ivk, see if there's somewhere we can lock them away unsupervised in there. A tack room or feed room, maybe."

Ivk nodded, and he and Tahlone half led, half dragged Merryn and Krynneth to the long, low, stone-walled building. Typical of such places, a single main door gave on an enclosed exercise area that fronted the standard eight stalls, all of which sported sturdy oak doors, with two more rooms flanking that area at either end. One of those doors had stripped its hinges, however, while another opened onto a room that had lost its roof, which only left two options unless they used the stalls. "Together or separate?" Ivk wondered aloud.

Tahlone patted his pouch. "Only got one lock, so I guess it'll have to be together."

Leaving Merryn and Krynneth in Tahlone's care, Ivk tried both doors and decided on the right-hand one. "In," he said in Eronese, motioning them forward. Merryn thought about balking, but Tahlone's sword suddenly pressed against her back. Oh well, if she was lucky, she'd get a chance to talk to Krynneth alone for the first time since their capture.

A final shove sent her sprawling into old hay atop cobblestones, and she was just starting to rise when Krynneth piled in atop her. The door slammed. The key grated in the lock.

"Could be worse," she said aloud, not so much to Krynneth as to convince herself. At least it wasn't as dark as she'd feared, for the room sported a pair of narrow, barred windows that looked into the side court. Shaul was leading the horses there now, prior to stabling them. Inon was nowhere to be seen. Likely he'd made good on his vow to bathe in the river. Which struck her as odd. Even the poorest Eronese hold had a bathhouse.

But probably not running water, at least not here.

"Piss," Krynneth said abruptly, sounding distinctly embarrassed. Merryn rolled her eyes, thinking he was asking for aid. She glanced around at him, but he was facing the wall by then, and the sound of liquid splattering against the stone was loud in the dusty gloom. At least they'd given him that much dignity: tying his hands so he could reach himself. Which set her to wondering exactly where the limits of their consideration lay.

Inon wasn't a bad sort, if one remembered that he was a soldier from a defeated army. Ivk was also a decent lad, if naive and given to worship of his kinsman. The other three had the feel of men who were used to being commanded—and hated it, but weren't smart enough to function well in an alien land on their own. Which perhaps explained their brutality. It was sublimated frustration given an outlet in the most obvious symbols they had to hand. At home—if they had homes—they were probably decent men as well.

Krynneth had finished by then and turned around, looking sheepish. Giving the little puddle in the corner a glare of contempt, he shuffled over to stand beside her, then slowly let himself slide down the wall. She sank down beside him. "Damn," he said. A fifth word.

"Yes," she replied sadly. "I agree."

To Merryn's surprise, she dozed—though not for long, for the light was much the same as it had been when they'd been imprisoned. The shadows were a *little* longer, she reckoned, but not enough to account for more than half a hand.

Still, much had changed in the courtyard that their captors were evidently making their base in lieu of the house. Tahlone had a fire going, and Shaul was making constant trips into what must've been the pantry, for he kept emerging with food.

And drink.

Drink they all approved, judging by the howls of joy that greeted its arrival. *Eight,* Merryn thought, when she saw one distinctive barrel. *That's walnut brandy!* Which was as potent a beverage as existed. They'd best go easy with that, she reckoned, then chuckled to herself. Knowing soldiers, they wouldn't. She'd enjoy their headaches the next day— if those headaches didn't translate into violence toward prisoners.

Inon was back from his bath now, and wandering around in just his breeches, revealing a fine, compact physique. Ivk had evidently fallen in fully clothed and returned in a blanket, which Orkeen had promptly grabbed, leaving the naked youth to chase him around the yard while Inon watched, his expression a mix of amusement and disgust.

It was nearing sunset, and Tahlone was making dinner over a fire, which told Merryn that the kitchen itself had collapsed. Still, the food smelled heavenly—for camp fare. She caught the scent of onions and garlic, which had probably been hung dried inside, preserved by the arid climate thereabouts.

In any case, her captors seemed more interested in the drink than the food, and more again when three bottles of wine and one of beer were found and opened. The latter spewed half its contents before Orkeen stuffed it into his mouth, to the applause and laughter of the others. Ivk found a small cask of mead and filled a mug. And nursed it, Merryn noted with approval, for by so doing, he was showing himself the wisest of the lot. She had her eye on him: As youngest, he might also be the most susceptible to bribery—or guile—of whatever kind she could contrive.

It being summer, darkness came late, so the men were still full awake by the time they'd finished their meal, which meant they still had plenty of time for drinking—which seemed to be their intent. Merryn tried to hear what they were discussing, but only caught snatches. Inon, however, was far enough into his cups to be espousing details of his ever-evolving scheme to use the regalia to assemble a band of followers with whom to contest the crown. Orkeen—the drunkest of the lot—was claiming first one high-ranking title, then another.

"Won't matter," Shaul grumbled, "if we don't know for absolute fact that we've captured the real thing."

"I saw it at the battle," Inon snapped back. "Close up."

Orkeen shrugged. "I saw a bloody lot of armor, and all of it well made."

"Yeah," Shaul chimed in again, cheerfully drunk, "but how come you had time to look at armor, anyway?"

"I didn't—until the last. Not until Avall and Lynnz were

preparing to fight. I was in the third circle out from them. I saw."

"One way t' prove it," Shaul said.

Ivk looked up sharply. "Not smart," he muttered.

Already drunk, Shaul turned nasty all in a moment's time. He turned in a flash and stomped over to where Ivk sat quietly. Ivk had barely time to raise his arm before Shaul backhanded him across the face, catching his mug of mead in the process.

Orkeen howled with laughter, but Inon and Tahlone were on Shaul in an instant, hauling him off Ivk, who was bleeding from the nose. "You're drunk," Inon growled. "Now leave the boy alone. If you want to do us all a favor, take a bath. You stink."

Shaul stiffened, then managed to jerk free of Tahlone long enough to swing at Inon. Inon fended him off well enough, but Shaul was persistent—and larger. A final jerk freed his other hand, and he hurled himself full into Inon. Both crashed to the ground close enough to the fire to knock one log free. Ivk hopped back, then started to dive into the fray on Inon's side, but Tahlone reined him back with a curt, "This has been coming for a while, might as well let them finish it."

Merryn could only watch with a certain grim satisfaction as the two men struggled on the ground. Eventually Inon got Shaul beneath him, striding his hips and pinning his arms to his sides, while the larger man wriggled, twisted, and swore.

"Enough!" Inon kept yelling, sounding more than a little drunk himself. Which made sense if he'd been into the walnut liquor, as it tended to do its damage all at once.

"Enough! Enough! Enough!"

"Enough indeed!" another voice roared from the direction of the house. The voice had a hollow sound, but Merryn recognized it exactly as Inon did.

"Orkeen, stay out of this," Inon shouted.

"By the Gods, I will not!" Orkeen yelled back, and stepped into the light.

Merryn's blood froze.

The helm gleamed on Orkeen's head. His right hand held the sword; his left, the shield.

He hadn't activated them, as far as she could tell, but that was surely sheer blind luck.

"Take that off!" Inon roared without relaxing his grip on Shaul.

"Mine now," Orkeen laughed roughly. "If you're good, I might still let you have, oh, say, a province. As long as I get to be king."

"Idiot!" Inon yelled again. "Ivk, Tahlone, tend to him."

Tahlone was on his feet at once, but Ivk hung back, clearly reluctant to engage in violence with someone he knew—who was also drunk and wearing magic armor.

"Stay back!" Orkeen warned, leveling the sword at the both of them as Tahlone dodged past Inon and Shaul.

And in that leveling, he shifted his grip, which finally triggered the blood barb in the hilt. At least that's what Merryn assumed afterward. What she saw was a sudden jerk in Orkeen's sword arm. With it came another from his shield side, by which she assumed one shift had prompted another.

He still hadn't activated the helm-gem, however, which meant the other two were both feeding him power, while also, in a sense, contending for attention.

And Orkeen was an enemy to everyone the gems knew. They wouldn't like what was happening.

"Eight," Merryn gasped, clutching at Krynneth's arm. "Oh, Eight, Kryn—"

Lightning masked the rest.

An explosion of light, rather, followed by a clap of thunder and a roar of flame that raked out from the sword's tip to blast the tree nearest the campfire.

"Orkeen!" Inon yelled, and finally released his hold on Shaul.

Too late, because the power had hold of Orkeen but Orkeen could not control it. And as reflex sent Inon rushing toward him, Orkeen's reflexes set the shield before him. Inon hit it—and bounced back, screaming, his entire torso a mass of red where the shield had ripped the top few fingers of skin, muscle, and bone away, and sent them to the Overworld.

It was his own momentum that did it, Merryn knew. The sword called matter from there and manifested it here as force; the shield took force from here and manifested it there as matter. But if that force was attached to something solid, that substance went with it.

"Dead," Krynneth breathed beside her. A sixth word.

"No, but he'll wish he was and probably soon will be. I—"

"Bastard!" Ivk screamed, as he likewise threw himself at Orkeen.

Orkeen turned toward him and brought the sword around. Lightning flashed again. Merryn saw Ivk's body as a blot of darkness against that light, and then he crumpled. But even as his body collapsed into the fire, Shaul finally made it to his feet. "Hey, 'Keen," he called drunkenly. "Le' me try tha'."

But Orkeen was mad by then—or frightened. It didn't matter. Faster than Merryn could see, he spun around again, and a third time lightning spoke. Shaul died where he stood.

"Ork . . ." Tahlone dared from where he was backing away. He was trying to sound reasonable, but Merryn had carried that sword when first it had been made and knew better than anyone how it liked to have its way.

"No!" Orkeen shouted. "Mine!"

The bolt that killed Tahlone rode the sweep of the sword down from the sky. But it killed him as effectively.

"I'm king!" Orkeen roared. "Now rise and acknowledge me."

No one did, because everyone was dead.

He took a step forward and froze. Abruptly he dropped the sword, then the shield. Both hands reached for the helm and wrenched it off. It made a dull thump as it hit the sand.

Not the pavement, a part of Merryn that never slept entirely was glad to note. The helm had suffered too much abuse already.

As for Orkeen—He was simply standing there, eyes glittering in the firelight, while the stench of scorched leather, burning fabric, and cooking meat filled the air. Something wet glistened between his eyes where the helm-gem had pricked him. To no avail or too late.

And then, he was moving again—slowly, oh so slowly, as though he had to consider each moment, or was prisoner of some vast unseen hand that propelled him along. One step, two steps, and Merryn saw his features more clearly as he approached the fire.

And most clearly of all right before he stepped into it.

For a moment she didn't believe what she was witnessing. A man—even a madman—would not do that. Instinct would prevent it.

If instinct lived.

In any case, it wouldn't live long, because the fire had ignited Orkeen's breeches, and a flame from them had found one baggy sleeve, which in turn set fire to his braid.

In an instant he was burning all over.

At some point pain—or something—regained sufficient control to tell him what was happening, and he began to scream, long and loud and helplessly. But his body didn't move.

The good thing about screaming, Merryn thought dully, was that it let the fire into the lungs, and that hastened death.

What actually killed him, however, she never knew, because she was still throwing up her last meager meal when the screaming ended.

Only when she was on her feet again and fumbling for the water pitcher Ivk had left, so as to rinse out her mouth, did Krynneth block her hand. She looked at him blankly. He stared back, and added a seventh word to his vocabulary.

"Key."

It took Merryn a moment to realize what he meant. And then fear filled her in truth. *The only key to this place was somewhere on a dead man outside!*

And the tack room—as she discovered over the next several hands—had been built very well indeed.

CHAPTER XXXIV:

DESPERATION

(NORTHWESTERN ERON: GEM-HOLD-WINTER – HIGH SUMMER: DAY LXXIV–SHORTLY BEFORE SUNSET)

It made no sense. Then again, nothing Kylin had experienced since he'd hatched his ill-considered scheme to get himself captured made much sense.

And hadn't *that* turned into a fiasco? Instead of being left alone in the dungeons—from which Kylin had assumed he might possibly find some way into the ventilation system that had served him so admirably before—he had, after that first day, been installed in Zeff's quarters. In a windowless closet adjacent to them, more properly, from which he could hear not a word, but into which food appeared at intervals sufficient to keep him healthy, and from which he was fetched from time to time and asked to play.

Not that they didn't ply him with questions, but not one had been anything to which they didn't already have the answer, as far as he could tell. Besides which, he was proving to have a decent natural immunity to imphor, so *that* interrogation was progressing very slowly indeed.

Which was all well and good, except that he was no closer to rescuing Avall than he'd been when he'd arrived there with some notion of accessing his friend through the vent system and smuggling him out that way. He'd hoped they'd leave his hands unbound, counting on his blindness to preclude any major subterfuge. Which would have left him free to proceed as planned. Barring that, he was reasonably certain he'd have been able to pick any lock they'd put on him, using a pick he'd sewn into the hem of his sylk eye mask.

He hadn't counted on becoming Zeff's pet.

Of course, he'd taken what advantage of that situation he could, but had mostly learned that Zeff knew the armor he'd captured was not the armor he'd expected. More to the point, he knew that Zeff had had some kind of bad experience with the insane master gem—but that he had, perhaps recklessly, decided to mount it in the sword anyway, using information (so Ahfinn had let slip) that had come to him when he'd drunk from a Well.

In any case, what mattered now was keeping his feet as he was hustled along by two burly Ninth Face guards, neither of whom seemed to recall that he was blind and *couldn't* maintain the pace they set without an occasional foray into clumsiness. A third person had his harp, but what their destination was, he had no idea. Something had changed—he knew that much from the scraps of conversation he'd picked up since awakening. But it was impossible to tell more than that Eron had finally made some sort of move.

He wasn't even certain where they were, save that they had gone down several levels and might've been tending outward. Fortunately, that situation clarified when Kylin heard one guard jog ahead, followed by the distinctive squeak that characterized the hinges of the arcade doors. He smelled wood polish, too, which no one else would even have noticed. A moment later, his location was confirmed when he felt a breath of wind that could only have originated outside. The footing changed as well, from solid stone to pebble-stone.

It was an arcade, then.

But not—to his surprise, if Eron was about to attack—a full one.

Indeed, as best he could tell, the place was almost deserted, though he wasn't in a position to assess the minutiae of his situation until they'd steered him to a seat. By comparing paces they'd covered to the known width of the arcade, he suspected he was within a span of the balustrade—a supposition borne out by the increased strength of the breezes thereabouts, which he'd felt more than once in happier times.

Someone set his harp down close by his side and backed away. He waited for a request to play, but no such request was forthcoming. Which freed him to do what he'd become very good at of late: assessing his surroundings. So it was that he determined several things fairly quickly. One was that the men who'd brought him there, along with what he thought were three others already present, were all dressed in war gear. It was their boots that revealed as much: Ninth Face soldiers had studs in their boot soles that gave their tread a distinctive metallic quality, especially when they trod on stone. And of course there was also the rustly jingle of mail and the occasional clink of metal on metal that marked heavier armor, all softened by thick, ribbed fabric. More telling was the breathing: short, impatient bursts that hinted of haste and worry.

But there were more subtle sounds as well, for by tuning his hearing toward the Vale at large, he caught the creak of siege machines and the susurration of voices from the battlefield: impossible to hear singly, but a gentle rush of language when multiplied several thousandfold.

Finally, there was a sound that simply didn't fit, though it most resembled a large tavern sign blowing against the wall of a stone building. More to the point, it came from very close by, to the right, and carried with it the raspy, gritty growl of iron grinding against granite. Even more puzzling was the fact that every time it impacted, Kylin caught a soft grunt or groan, which he didn't understand at all.

He glanced that way reflexively, but saw nothing through his mask but a slight brightening that represented all the vast, intricate detail of the world beyond the railing.

By the quality of the air and light, he reckoned it was late afternoon. From far off, he caught the scent of woodsmoke. Closer in came the sharper tang of metal oil and leather. Soldier smells.

His fingers sought his harp for comfort, flailing a little before someone moved it into range. "Should I play . . . ?" he asked carefully.

"Wait," someone replied. Young. Female. That was all he knew.

"Zeff will be back anon," someone else added. "He would not like it if you anticipated him."

Kylin sat. And waited.

Before long, he caught the slap of Ninth Face boots approaching. Zeff, by the stride and heaviness of the step. He wondered, suddenly, what Zeff looked like. If he had the gem—if someone sighted had the gem, rather, and would share it with him—he *would* know. As he would know many things. But with sight such a rare and precious thing, why waste it on the face of an enemy when he'd not even seen the faces of all those he considered friends?

By the sound of leather sliding onto cloth, displacing mail in transit, Kylin determined that Zeff had sat down across from him and crossed his legs. Someone poured wine. He caught the splash and the heady odor, and heard leather gloves touch metal as Zeff accepted a gobletful.

"Play for me," Zeff murmured. "I need—" He broke off. "It doesn't matter what I need. Play something soft to help me wait."

Wait for what? Kylin wondered. *Battle, probably,* he answered himself. Except that didn't make sense, given that Kylin was all but certain that the day was waning. An ultimatum, then? Or an answer? But given by whom to whom?

"Play!" Zeff snapped. "Now! Or I'll pitch you over the rail."

Kylin did. Or rather his fingers did. They found strings

where they expected, touched them just so, and brought forth melody—soft music, as requested, and traditional tunes at first, since there was comfort in familiarity: "Sunrise Song," and "All the Leaves," and "Dancer Fast Asleep." He paused after the latter, awaiting some indication he should continue, then shrugged and began "Stone of Shadows."

"That's too morbid," Zeff growled. "Play 'Winterqueen's Lament.'"

"It's morbid, too," Kylin replied, before he could stop himself.

"Play it anyway."

"I'd rather not. It has . . . sentimental value."

"Play it!"

"No."

"No," came another voice, weak and tentative, from Kylin's right. He started at that. It had sounded like—

"Avall," Kylin whispered, before he could stop himself.

"Silence!" Zeff spat. "Or Eron will watch both of you die."

Kylin almost cried out, not so much from the threat and what it implied, as for what he'd just learned about Avall. Suddenly he felt better. Stronger. As though his life were moving again, if only because he was no longer alone among hostile strangers.

As for Avall—He wasn't sure what had befallen his friend, but it didn't sound encouraging. He hoped there was no connection between those tavern-sign sounds and Avall, but his heart told him otherwise. The sounds were one with each other.

To mask his confusion, Kylin played. And in spite of himself, he played "Winterqueen's Lament"—but only because it was something he could play without thinking, while his mind worked furiously.

What he *wanted* more than anything was to talk to Avall. To find out how he was and what he knew, and to assure him that—

What?

There was nothing he could do! And certainly not now. Not with Zeff sitting half a span away, waiting . . .

But suppose there *was* something?

He and Avall had never bonded formally, but both of them *had* engaged in mental traffic through the master gem. And longer and more frequent bondings had certainly left a link between Avall and Rann that was sufficiently strong for the two of them sometimes to feel what the other was feeling, or think what the other was thinking, without gems being actively involved. Too, if the gems indeed left residue, both he and Avall should still contain some of whatever it was that allowed that linkage to occur.

Not daring to ponder his impulse further, lest contemplation lead to dangerous doubts, Kylin tried to extend his thought toward Avall. The gems worked on desire, so perhaps whatever was in them that empowered human will would awaken to desire as well.

And by wishing that at all, it made the wishing stronger.

Reality shifted ever so slightly—and he was suddenly aware of other wishing reaching toward him from somewhere else. A wishing that seemed familiar. A wishing he dared not hope was—

He was *out* of himself, he realized with a start, even as his fingers went right on playing. It was scary, too, for before he'd always had the comfort of human touch when in that situation.

Fear—or shock—dragged him back to himself, where he found wonder and determination to try again. It wasn't much of a chance, but it might be all the chance he was given. And that other wishing was still there, but weak, oh so very weak. He sought for it desperately.

—And was out of himself again, but this time he remained there long enough to determine three things. One was that Avall was clamped spread-eagled against a round tabletop, with one hand less than a span from Kylin's right shoulder. Another was that Zeff sat roughly the same distance from

Kylin's feet, more or less behind the tabletop, forming an equilateral triangle with Kylin and Avall.

More importantly, however, Zeff had the replica sword into which he had indeed inserted the very real, if presumably mad, master gem.

It is *real,* came a voice in his head. Faintly, as though heard at a great distance, the voice of that other wishing: *You think loudly,* it added. *It takes little effort to hear you, but much to speak.*

Avall?

The sword. The gem. A wish.

And that was all.

That and the image he'd had before: Zeff sitting across from him, eyes half-closed. Listening. Waiting. With the sword loose in its sheath beside him, where he'd unbelted it upon sitting down.

Maybe it was the image itself, maybe it was the fact that Kylin suddenly realized that part of him was still discorporate and that the nonphysical part of him could see.

In any case, it was sufficiently alarming that he snapped back into himself.

And missed a note.

Kylin heard Zeff's breath catch.

"I don't blame you," Zeff yawned, which surprised him even more. "This isn't a good situation for any of us."

"No," Kylin agreed, daring candor.

"Wine?"

It took Kylin a moment to realize that had been an offer, not a request. "If you would," he agreed. A brush of fingers stilled the harp. He leaned back, letting his back and shoulders relax in what was a deep-seated harper's reflex.

"Here." Zeff's voice—close by, as though he were reaching. Kylin smelled thick wine and soldier's soap. He reached for the cup he was imagining between the two of them.

Then, fast as he'd ever moved, reached past the cup and seized the hilt of Zeff's sword. And with it, triggered the gem. Madness raged there, but with it came a welcoming that fought down that more aggressive sensation. Along with both came that slowing of time that had been the first gem magic Avall had ever observed.

Time enough to move, to act, to think. Time enough for relief and joy to briefly overpower fear, hate, and madness. Time enough for him to yank that sword free and move with all possible speed toward the table on the other side of which Avall was fixed.

Time enough to reach around and grab Avall's hand.

Strength roared into him with the first touch. And with it came an enormous tide of relief that was yet tinged with a dreadful fear that this was all too quickly and rashly done and would ultimately come to naught. Certainly Zeff was moving, as were the other guards. But they moved like men in dreams. Slowly, oh so slowly.

Which proved too much distraction and let the madness come ravening into Kylin's brain from the gem in the sword hilt. Worse, it flowed through him into Avall, so that he felt like thread coated with quick-fire, to which someone had set a spark.

Which was too much. He had to escape. *Had to.* Had to get away from all this: from Zeff and his own fear and Avall's impossible situation.

With that he wished, and found another wishing in turn.

Reality jerked and spun.

Kylin *wasn't*.

And then he was on fire, with that fire spreading outward from his hand.

While his other hand held Avall's.

And still Kylin *wasn't*.

And then, very suddenly, he *was*.

And with him, like a pack of hounds that had finally caught the quarry, came the madness.

And this time he had no strength left for anything but running.

CHAPTER XXXV:

(NORTHWESTERN ERON: MEGON VALE— HIGH SUMMER: DAY LXXIV—NEAR SUNSET)

Rann took another long draught from the bottle he'd not released for the last half hand and slammed the thick green glass down on the table before him so hard, Lykkon had to snare his own bottle lest it topple. Bingg yipped, and grabbed for his brother's drink as well. Riff looked startled. Myx merely looked drunkenly grim.

But not as grim as Rann felt.

It was sunset, with all that implied. Light fading into darkness, but a darkness from which Rann knew he would never emerge, because it marked what was effectively a sentence of death for Avall. It only remained to determine what form that death would take. Zeff might be merciful, he might not. It would depend on how he wanted to manipulate affairs. If he was smart, he wouldn't do anything at all, merely let Avall's own army work his doom. Which they wouldn't do deliberately, but which would inevitably occur, if the siege continued long enough.

"They won't kill him outright," Lykkon murmured, staring at the bottle he now gripped between his two hands. "He's the only thing that's holding us back, and they know that. If they kill him—"

"The blood will be on their head," Bingg finished for him.

But all Rann heard was "blood." It was as if time spoke of blood, too, for the day was dying outside, spilling its life force in ruddy light that lanced like crimson spears through the door slit of Lykkon's tent.

Too much red, he thought: maroon canvas, crimson carpet, and the maroon and crimson surcoats and tabards he and his comrades wore—now wakened to glowing brightness by the day's last rays. It washed their faces with red, too: red for blood, revenge, and anger and the shame he also felt, which emotions he suspected his companions in rebellion shared.

He spoke that word without knowing.

"Rebel."

"Depends," Lykkon murmured.

Rann glared at him, drink having made him surly, even as part of him tried to keep a clear head, to remind himself that Lykkon was as rational a mind as they had to hand at the moment, for all he'd been drinking, too.

"On what?" Rann managed at last.

"On whether you count Kingdom and King as one thing or separate. If one takes the traditional tack: that what's good for the King is good for the Kingdom—"

"Then we're on th' right side 'cause we're acting for the good of the King," Myx slurred.

"But if the good of the Kingdom supersedes that of the King—" Riff broke in, scowling.

"We're not rebels while Avall's alive," Lykkon snapped. "That's a legal fact. While he lives, they don't dare touch us, because we're sworn to him. And while we live, Vorinn has tacit support for anything he does, in that we're not actually trying to stop him."

Rann glared at him—again. "Do you ever stop being logical? Do you ever do anything from just your gut?"

Lykkon regarded him levelly. "I'm here, aren't I?"

Riff shook his head and rose, starting to pace. "At least no one's saying that other word—yet."

"What other word?" from Myx.

"Traitor," Bingg hissed at him.

Lykkon shook his head. "I don't think anyone *will* say that word. They know the circumstances too well. If worse comes to worst, they'll simply assume whatever authority they have to and act from that position. There's no advantage to them calling members of their own clans traitor, besides which, we've done nothing to stop them. All we've done is abdicate responsibility."

Rann glared at him. "That's easy for you to say. You're from Avall's clan. Mine's just seen their best chance at true power in a century slip through their fingers."

He fell silent at that. They all did. Against his will Rann's thoughts moved past the trauma of the present to the time when, for good or ill, this would all be over, he would still be alive, and Avall wouldn't.

Which would leave him only Div.

If she could fill that vacuum.

If anyone could.

If she survived this herself.

All at once the awfulness of it all crashed down upon him. He'd known Avall all his life, along with Merryn and Lykkon. Even Eddyn. He'd always felt more a part of their clan than his own. But his life had always been one of adding things—mostly good things—to an established base. Even last winter when he'd thought Avall was dead he'd had the comfort of his growing attachment to Div and the wonder of the gems. But now . . .

Life was contracting, it seemed, with things falling out of it everywhere he looked. And for the first time in his life he found himself confronting that most awful of words.

Loneliness.

Even if Lyk and Bingg and Riff and Myx and the others kept him company for as long as he lived, there would still be a void in him that neither they—nor Div—could ever fill.

Ever.

Riff rose to look outside. "Sun's sitting on the mountain."

"Close that, and come back in," Rann growled. "Dark thoughts thrive best in darkness." He took another draught—which emptied the bottle. Purely for dramatic effect, he extended his arm straight out and let the bottle fall. It thumped to the floor but did not shatter. A pity, that: One could do so much with broken glass. "Another," he snapped to his companions in general.

Bingg exchanged glances with Lykkon, even as Myx and Riff—more accustomed to obeying orders unquestioned—obligingly began searching for more wine—or beer—or ale. Anything that would quell the pain they all felt.

Rann—who was still coherent enough to recall where Lykkon kept his private stash—had just started to rise in quest of it, when the air between him and Bingg ripped asunder.

Not so loud as a lightning strike, but loud enough. Not as bright as noonday glare, either—but bright aplenty in the ruddy gloom. Mostly, it was a wavering in the space between the two, like heavy fabric rippling in a gentle wind.

And then that space was empty no longer.

Rann flinched away from reflex, so much so that he unbalanced his camp chair and toppled backward in an untidy heap. He picked himself up clumsily, squinting into the gloom through eyes addled by that sudden brief flare of light. And saw—

—Saw a slight youth in a simple white robe clutching another young man by the hand. Saw that the second man was naked, and then saw him crumple to the floor.

But only long enough to shake himself and rise on all fours, blinking wide eyes beneath a tangled mop of uncombed black hair.

"Avall!" That was Bingg.

"—and Kylin." From Riff.

Avall indeed.

"Rann," the rising figure mumbled. And joy filled Rann so fast he couldn't breathe—could do nothing but remain where he was: kneeling on the floor with one hand frozen on the table where he'd begun to lever himself up, staring at his bond-brother across no more than a span.

And then the span closed through no effort he recalled making, and his arms were clamped around Avall, their faces were pressed into each other's shoulders, and they were, for all intents and purposes, one being.

That joy—that relief and release—lasted for an eternal instant before it was ruthlessly shattered.

"No! No! Nonononononononononononono!" someone howled, in what took Rann a moment to realize was Kylin's voice. Or maybe he *didn't* realize it. Maybe it was the fact that *Avall* knew it was Kylin's voice, and he and Avall were one. Or maybe it was Lykkon who called Kylin's name.

In any case, he released his friend and looked around—to see Kylin standing where he'd first arrived, one hand still frozen in air as if it still clutched Avall's hand, while the fingers of the other curled around an all-too-familiar sword. He looked stiff enough to shatter if he moved.

Except his eyes. He'd lost his blindfold, and for all that he was blind in truth, his eyes were darting about as though they saw things no one else present could see. Worse, the pupils were dilating and expanding at a fearful rate without reference to each other.

His lips were working, too, but the litany of "nos" had ended.

For maybe a dozen breaths.

Then, like a rising tide of terror, Kylin found language again.

"Death" was the first word Rann heard clearly, and that alone sent chills over him. But fast upon it came others, mixed with a slur of syllables that might make sense to Kylin and might not. "Death and the dark, and the dark hides death, and death hides in the dark, and reaches through it, and there are dead things in the dying dark that want to drink me down, and the dead drink the dying daily, in the dark, in the dark that I dare not enter, but that drinks me, and it's drinking me and drawing me down to death, and death desires to drink me, too, too many deaths drinking there in the dark, the dark, the dark, the dying dark of death, the dark the dark—"

On and on, in a kind of singsong chant, until Riff had sense enough to ease behind him and clamp a hand gently but firmly across Kylin's mouth. He tensed—if it was possible for him to tense more—but the babbling ceased.

"The sword," Lykkon cried. "Get it away from him—now!"

Myx did—by accident. Drunker than the rest, yet ever the good soldier, he turned to respond, lost his balance, and fell, which took him into Riff and Kylin together, sprawling them across the floor. Riff grunted, but kept his hold on Kylin. The sword tumbled free and went sliding across the rug until stopped by a table leg, where it lay against the dark wood, gleaming. There was blood on the hilt, Rann saw. He dared not think whose it might be.

"He's mad," Riff dared, even as he sought to extricate his bond-brother from Kylin's supine form. As for the harper—he was no longer simply lying flat on his back where he'd fallen, but had shifted onto his side and was curling up around himself, like an unborn child. The litany had resumed, too, but more softly. All Rann could hear was an occasional "death" or "dark" or "doom."

"Mad," Lykkon echoed dully. "Poor Kylin."

"Mad indeed." And *that* had been Avall. The first words he'd spoken. "I . . . could . . . feel it clamp around him when he wasn't looking," he went on, sounding as tired as a man could sound. "I have to—That is, I need to—I can't," he finished heavily. Rann felt him go limp. "It got him," Avall murmured into his shoulder. "He sacrificed himself for me."

Lykkon cleared his throat, leaving Riff to tend to Kylin, since Bingg was simply standing where he'd been, slack-jawed. "Has anybody besides me realized what's just occurred?"

"Avall's back," Rann replied. "That's enough for now."

"Not on the eve of battle," Lykkon countered. "This changes everything."

"It does indeed," Avall agreed harshly, pushing Rann away. He blinked into the gloom. "Give me that," he demanded, pointing to the sword.

Rann hesitated, then started toward it. But Avall was faster. Indeed, he moved as fast as he ever had in his life, so that he reached the sword before Rann did and closed his fist around the blade. He stood then, all in one fluid rush of movement. His eyes were wild, Rann realized, too late: wild and feverish. Almost as wild as Kylin's had been.

Yet he was powerless to stop his oldest, closest friend as he swung around to face the jeweler's anvil Lykkon kept in the tent, mostly—he said—to help repair mail.

"Avall!" Bingg yelped—but Avall paid him no mind whatsoever as, still possessed of that preternatural speed, he set the sword's hilt atop the anvil, snared a planishing hammer with his other hand—and slammed the hammer down atop the gem.

Rann wasn't certain he heard the words that accompanied that sickening crunch, or merely felt them in his mind. Whichever way they reached him, he knew what consumed Avall's thoughts at the moment he destroyed the gem. *You have hurt Kylin. You will never hurt anyone I love again!*

And for the second time since the sun had touched the horizon, the air inside the tent was ripped asunder. But this time the few beams of light that still made their way through the slit of the tent flap shone on nothing but naked ground.

"Empty," Tryffon spat incredulously, less than a finger later. He drew the flap aside for Vorinn to see as well. "Everything is gone."

"Let me see!" Vorinn cried, pushing his way into what, indeed, looked like an empty tent—though not completely. A confusion of items, from stools to armor, lay strewn about the bare earth in a disarray that made no sense.

Tryffon drew him back with a sturdy hand upon his shoulder. "Avall's vanished as well," he rumbled. "There's no possible way the two aren't connected."

"Will Zeff still attack at dawn?" Veen wondered beside Vorinn.

Vorinn—almost—grinned at her. "The question is," he chuckled, "will we?"

Rann awoke gradually, from his innermost brain out.

The first thing he had to do was breathe—which was not a given, since his lungs seemed paralyzed—or perhaps frozen in ice would have been a more apt description. In any case, they were empty for an endless moment, as though his breath had been knocked out of him. Perhaps he was dead, in which case it wouldn't matter. But air was prodding the gates of his nose and mouth, demanding to be admitted. He sucked it greedily, and felt life return.

And then instinct took over—enough to inform him that he was warm and safe—but that all other givens of reality had undergone some fundamental alteration, and not just in the way he was perceiving it.

He hid from it, glad for the nonce simply to breathe and feel his heart beat. But that feeling made him aware of others. Most particularly, it made him aware of the air around him, which was very warm indeed and quite dry, where it should've been moderately warm, somewhat stuffy, and musty-damp. Yet the rug was still beneath him, which didn't make sense, though someone had tilted the earth on which it rested and replaced the woodland loam with what felt suspiciously like solid rock.

At which point he realized he was lying flat on his back, as if he'd been hurled away from something, and that his left hand lay atop what felt like firm young human flesh. Maybe alive, maybe not; it was too cold to tell.

Another breath, and his awareness leaped up a level. He could taste nothing but the residue of wine, but that was to be expected. *Smell,* however . . . again, the familiar overlapped the utterly strange. Wine, beer, ale, and liquors, both poured and spilled, were strongest. But more subtly he caught the odors of fresh-tanned leather, well-oiled mail, and the general tang of naked metal. He smelled soldier's soap, too, but also sweat, with an overall cast of mildew. Yet threading through it all was a cleaner suite of scents: hot, bare rocks; conifers; flowers; and water.

And while part of him knew he should not be able to smell water, another part of himself suggested that this was no normal state of awareness, and that when he became slightly more cognizant, he would recall why that was so.

But he felt no sense of urgency, still content to let himself drift up to consciousness—and to observe that journey.

Which had now reached hearing.

He heard wind soughing through treetops. He heard the breathing of what he was pleased to discover were six other people besides himself; punctuated now and then by what sounded like teeth chattering. He also heard a bird cry. What he did *not* hear was the steady murmuring rumble of the camp. No voices. No clang of weapons. No urgent footsteps. No creak of tent ropes or flap of canvas.

And then—at last—Rann dared open his eyes.

Raw stone arched at least three spans above his head and vanishing out of sight to either side, though more brightly lit to his left. A deep breath, and he leaned up on his elbow—and saw an arc of light cast upon the distant wall, by a sun invisible beyond—

Beyond what?

He didn't know, and so he let his gaze slide down.

Lykkon sprawled on his side next to him, lying athwart the

carpet from the tent. A smaller shape beyond was Bingg, shivering in what might be either sleep or unconsciousness. Two more shapes lay across Lykkon's feet: Myx and Riff, he assumed by their livery and Riff's fair hair. He almost didn't see the shape between them, for it had drawn in upon itself like a child asleep and remembering the womb.

Kylin.

Reality spun, returned, spun again.

Rann closed his eyes. But then he remembered.

Avall.

He twisted around, as a hand's worth of preposterous memories returned.

And saw, indeed, that Avall was there.

He lay on his back, much as Rann had lain, but with his arms outstretched. One arm held a hammer. The other . . .

Most recently it had held a sword, which in turn had held the master gem.

Now—

Nothing.

Avall's eyes were wide and staring like a dead man's. And had he not been naked, so that Rann could see the slightest rise and fall of his chest and the tiny twitch of pulse at his throat, he would've assumed him dead.

Instead, he called his name. Once. Softly.

Nothing.

Rann glanced around frantically, only then realizing that along with his companions some of the other contents of the tent were present: the table they'd been sitting around, for instance. A few stools and chairs. A couple of cases of wine. The rug on which they'd stood.

The sword. And more to the point, the gem.

The gem . . .

He sought the latter desperately, not believing that Avall had possessed the temerity to smash it. The table on which the anvil had stood was missing, but the anvil itself was present, a span beyond Avall's feet. And lying between, like ruby stars upon a sky of maroon figured with blue and white, lay a number of glittering shards, each one of which was faintly glowing.

A groan.

Avall, he reminded himself. *He had to awaken Avall.* Maybe with wine—if there was wine.

Somehow he made it to his knees, and saw, miraculously, Bingg's half-full cup still upright in the boy's hand. He snatched it, and held it to Avall's lips while he worked his arm beneath his bond-brother's head.

And was unprepared when Lykkon spoke behind him. "Where are we?"

And with that, the impossibility of the situation crashed down on Rann in truth. "I don't know," he replied finally. "But wherever we are, it's a long way from the war."

"Why do you say that?" Lykkon replied, through a bout of shivers.

Rann nodded toward the open space behind them. "Because it was sunset where we were. Here—it's only approaching."

"You mean we've traveled in time?" Lykkon gasped, incredulously.

"No," came another voice: a groggy one so close to Rann he started. "In space."

"Avall!" Rann gasped. "You're alive."

"Yes," Avall slurred sleepily. "I wonder if that's good or not."

"I don't know," Rann told him wearily. "I fear we may have traded one war for another."

He stared at the wall again, but this time let his gaze continue past the arc of light—which seemed to have shifted in shape and intensity—to where he'd dared not look before.

To where unworked stone surrounded a vista of cloudless, sunset sky; the tops of a file of cliffs; and, below them all, a glimmer of pure blue water.

He shuddered again, and had no way of telling whether those chills were born of cold, of fear, or of joy.

ABOUT THE AUTHOR

TOM DEITZ grew up in Young Harris, Georgia, a tiny college town in the north Georgia mountains that—by heritage or landscape—have inspired the setting for the majority of his novels. He holds BA and MA degrees in English from the University of Georgia, where he also worked as a library assistant in the Hargrett Rare Books and Manuscript Library until quitting in 1988 to become a full-time writer. His interest in medieval literature, castles, and Celtic art led him to co-found the Athens, Georgia, chapter of the Society for Creative Anachronism, of which he is still sort-of a member. A "fair-to-middlin" artist, Tom is also a frustrated architect and an automobile enthusiast (he has two non-running '62 Lincolns, every *Road & Track* since 1959 but two, and over 900 unbuilt model cars). He also hunts every now and then, dabbles in theater at the local junior college, and plays *toli* (a Southeastern Indian game related to lacrosse) when his pain threshold is especially high.

After twenty-five years in Athens, he has recently moved back to his hometown, the wisdom of which move remains to be seen. *Summerblood* is his seventeenth novel.

COMING IN AUGUST 2002

THE STUNNING CONCLUSION TO THE SERIES . . .

WARAUTUMN

"Now or never," Rann whispered in his ear. And before Avall could stop himself, he set heels to Boot's sides and rode into the river. The middle channel was deepest, but still not deep enough to reach higher than Boot's breast, which was a problem they had not considered.

"Fate help us now," Avall muttered. "I can't."

And with that, he slammed his sword hand into his forehead, tripping the blood trigger there, then clamped down with both hands as hard as he could on sword and shield alike, letting go the reins, and—relying on balance alone—thrusting both hands into the water, one to either side.

Willpower did the rest.

Wanting this done and over was enough, and "done and over" meant returning to Tir-Eron.

Avall tried to drag his hands back above the water, but the water knew him, sang to him, seized him and pulled him apart like waves eating up a sand sculpture at the seashore.

The last thing he saw was mountains above woodland above river. The last thing he heard was Vorinn splashing through the water behind them yelling, "Not without me! Not yet! No!"

Enter the fantastic world of

⟞⟝ TOM DEITZ ⟞⟝

BLOODWINTER

___57646-1 $6.50/$9.99 in Canada

⟞⟝◉⟞⟝

SPRINGWAR

___57647-X $6.50/$9.99

⟞⟝◉⟞⟝

SUMMERBLOOD

___58206-2 $6.50/$9.99

Bantam Dell Publishing Group, Inc.	TOTAL AMT	$_____
Attn: Customer Service	SHIPPING & HANDLING	$_____
400 Hahn Road	SALES TAX (NY, TN)	$_____
Westminster, MD 21157	TOTAL ENCLOSED	$_____

Name _____

Address _____

City/State/Zip _____

Daytime Phone (_____)_____